Samuel Richardson

The Works of Samuel Richardson

With a Prefatory Chapter of Biographical Criticism by Leslei Stephen: Vol. I.

Samuel Richardson

The Works of Samuel Richardson
With a Prefatory Chapter of Biographical Criticism by Leslei Stephen: Vol. I.

ISBN/EAN: 9783337098681

Printed in Europe, USA, Canada, Australia, Japan

Cover: Foto ©Andreas Hilbeck / pixelio.de

More available books at **www.hansebooks.com**

THE WORKS

OF

SAMUEL RICHARDSON.

WITH A

PREFATORY CHAPTER OF BIOGRAPHICAL CRITICISM

BY

LESLIE STEPHEN.

IN TWELVE VOLUMES.

VOL. I.

HENRY SOTHERAN & CO.,

LONDON: 136 STRAND—36 PICCADILLY.

MANCHESTER: 49 CROSS STREET.

MDCCCLXXXIII.

PAMELA;

OR,

VIRTUE REWARDED.

𝔍𝔫 𝔞 𝔖𝔢𝔯𝔦𝔢𝔰 𝔬𝔣 𝔉𝔞𝔪𝔦𝔩𝔦𝔞𝔯 𝔏𝔢𝔱𝔱𝔢𝔯𝔰.

IN THREE VOLUMES.

VOL. I.

HENRY SOTHERAN & CO.,
LONDON: 136 STRAND—36 PICCADILLY.
MANCHESTER: 49 CROSS STREET.
MDCCCLXXXIII.

RICHARDSON'S NOVELS.*

INTRODUCTION.

... literary artifice, so often patronised by Lord Macaulay,
... ibing a character by a series of paradoxes, is of course,
... sense, a mere artifice. It is easy enough to make a
... grey black and light grey white, and to bring the
... o unnatural proximity. But it rests also upon the
... le, which is more of a platitude than a paradox, that
... of faults often lie close to our chief merits. The
... man is perhaps one who is so equably developed
... has the strongest faculties in the most perfect
... ium, and is apt to be somewhat uninteresting to the
mankind. The man of lower eminence has some one
faculties developed out of all proportion to the rest,
o natural result of occasionally overbalancing him. A
e gymnast with enormous muscular power in his arms
... st, and comparatively feeble lower limbs, can some-
... erform the strangest feats in consequence of his con-
... on, but owes his awkwardness to the same singularity.
... onishes us for the time more than the well-propor-
... man who can do fewer wonders and more useful
... In the intellectual world the contrasts in one man
... ten greater. Extraordinary memories with weak
... faculties, wonderful imaginative sensibility with a
... to absence of self-control, and other defective confor-
... s of mind, supply the raw materials for a luminary of

... rinted (with additions and alterations), by the kind permission of the
... rs, Messrs Smith, Elder, & Co., from "Hours in a Library" (first
... by Leslie Stephen.

b

the second order, and imply a predisposition to certain faul'
which are natural complements to the conspicuous merits.

Such reflections naturally occur in speaking of one of o
greatest literary reputations. whose popularity is far fro
being in proportion to his celebrity. Every one knows t.
names of Sir Charles Grandison and Clarissa Harlowe. The
are amongst the established types which serve to point
paragraph; but the volumes in which they are describe.
remain too often in undisturbed repose, sleeping peaceful
amongst Charles Lamb's *biblia a-biblia*, books which are
books, or, as he explains, those books 'which no gentlema:
library should be without.' The modern reader shud
at a novel in eight volumes, and declines to dig for am
ment in so profound a mine; when some bold inquirer
into their pages he generally fancies that the sleep of
has been somehow absorbed into the paper; a cer
soporific aroma exhales from the endless files of fictit
correspondence. A bare contrast between popularity
celebrity is not so rare as to deserve special notice. Richar
son is only one of many authors whose fame seldom rouses
very lively curiosity. Richardson's slumber may be deepe
than that of most men of equal fame, but it is not quit
unprecedented. The string of paradoxes, which it would
easy to apply to Richardson, would turn upon a differe
point. The odd thing is, not that so many people sho
have forgotten him, but that he should have been remembe
by people at first sight so unlike him. Here is a man,
might say, whose special characteristic it was to be a mil
sop—who provoked Fielding to a coarse hearty burst
ridicule—who was steeped in the incense of ceaseless adula.
tion from a throng of middle-aged lady worshippers—wl
wrote his novels expressly to recommend little unimpeac'
able moral maxims, as that evil courses lead to unhap
deaths, that ladies ought to observe the laws of propriet
and generally that it is an excellent thing to be thoroug'
respectable; who lived an obscure life in a petty coterie
fourth-rate London society, and was in no respect at a po'
of view more exalted than that of his companions. W
greater contrast can be imagined in its way than th

between Richardson, with his second-rate eighteenth-century priggishness and his twopenny-tract morality, and some of those modern French novelists, who are certainly not prigs, and whose morality is by no means that of tracts? We might have expected *à priori* that they would have summarily put him down, as, indeed, M. Taine seems inclined to put him down, as a hopeless Philistine. Yet Richardson has been idolised by some of their best writers; Balzac, for example, and George Sand, speak of him with reverence; and a writer who is singularly unlike Richardson—Alfred de Musset—calls ' Clarissa ' *le premier roman du monde.* What is the secret which enables the steady old printer, with his singular limitation to his own corner of time and space, to impose upon the emancipated Parisian of the next century? Amongst his contemporaries, Diderot expresses an almost fanatical admiration of Richardson for his purity and power, and declares characteristically that he will place Richardson's works on the same shelf with those of Moses, Homer, Euripides, and other favourite writers; he even goes so far as to excuse Clarissa's belief in Christianity on the ground of her youthful innocence. To continue in the paradoxical vein, we might ask how the quiet tradesman could create the character which has stood ever since for a type of the fine gentleman of the period; or how from the most prosaic of centuries should spring one of the most poetical of feminine ideals? We can hardly fancy a genuine hero with a pigtail, or a heroine in a hoop and high-heeled shoes, nor believe that persons who wore those articles of costume could possess any very exalted virtues. Perhaps our grandchildren may have the same difficulty about the race which wears crinolines and chimney-pot hats.

It is a fact, however, that our grandfathers, in spite of their belief in pigtails and in Pope's poetry, and other matters that have gone out of fashion, had some very excellent qualities, and even some genuine sentiment, in their compositions. Indeed, now that their peculiarities have been finally packed away in various lumber-rooms, and the revolt against the old-fashioned school of thought and manners has become triumphant instead of militant, we are beginning to see the picturesque side of their character. They have gathered something of the halo that comes with the lapse of years; and social habits that looked prosaic enough to contemporaries, and to the generation which had to fight against them, have gained a touch of romance. Richardson's characters wear a costume and speak a language which are indeed queer and old-fashioned, but are now far enough removed from the present to have a certain piquancy; and it is becoming easier to recognise the real genius which created them, as the active aversion to the forms in which it was necessarily clothed tends to disappear. The wigs and the high-heeled shoes are not without a certain pleasing quaintness; and when we have surmounted this cause of disgust, we can see more plainly what was the real power which men of the most opposite schools in art have recognised.

Richardson's qualifications for representing one aspect of contemporary thought may be inferred from his life. Little is known of him beyond the facts given in Mrs. Barbauld's biography, prefixed to the curious collection of letters published in 1804. We can, however, learn enough to form a tolerably distinct picture of the worthy printer. He was a thoroughly typical specimen of the industrious apprentice of Hogarth's period. His father was a joiner in London, a business, as Richardson says, more distinct then than now— 'now' is the middle of the eighteenth century, and 'then' the last half of the seventeenth—from that of carpenter. It seems from his account that the joiner of the earlier period approached more nearly to the rank of builder and decorator. The elder Richardson had some knowledge of architecture and drawing. His talents commended him to Monmouth and the first Lord Shaftesbury. He must also, it would seem, have shared their principles, and been one of the London tradesmen who upheld the Whig and Protestant cause in the dark days of James II. After the 'decollation,' as Richardson calls it, of Monmouth, he found it expedient, though a 'quiet and inoffensive' man, to retire into Derbyshire. There Samuel Richardson was born in 1689. He was thus a year younger than Pope, and twenty years older than Johnson. The father intended him for the Church, but was unable, through losses in business, to give him the necessary education. The lad loved reading, but never learnt any language except his own. He was apprenticed to a printer, choosing that business because he hoped that it would give him opportunities for reading; and after serving his time, and then acting for some years as compositor and corrector of the press, he set up in business for himself, first in Fleet Street, and afterwards in Salisbury Court. He married his master's daughter, according to precedent, and prospered in his affairs. He became known as a deserving person to various people in power, and was employed by Speaker Onslow to print the Journals of the House of Commons. The business was not very profitable, as it appears that at one time a sum of £3000 was due to him, which, in spite of pressure, he had been unable to obtain. He was also employed to print various periodicals, and by one means or other he reached a modest prosperity. He was able to afford himself the true citizen's luxury of a country-house at North End in Hammersmith. The region is now being rapidly swallowed up in brick and mortar, though Richardson's house and garden still remain, and are still sacred to art. In 1754 he moved to Parson's Green, and, so far as we can perceive from his letters, his journeys rarely extended beyond these modest limits. In 1754 he also attained his highest civic honour. He was elected Master of the Stationers' Company, a position, we are told, profitable as well as honourable. His prosperity is also proved by the fact that in 1755 he rebuilt his premises in Salisbury Court, and in 1760 bought a moiety of the patent of law-printer. The next year, on the 4th of July 1761, he died of apoplexy, and was buried in St. Bride's Church.

Behind these prosaic facts there lies an inner history, of which we have only occasional glimpses. We hear that in his childhood he, like Scott and many other novelists, was famous amongst his schoolfellows for his powers of story-telling. He composed a history 'on the model of Tommy Pots'—a work unknown to me even by report—which must have been an odd anticipation of 'Pamela.' It recorded

the preference of a fine young lady for a virtuous servant-
man above a libertine lord. Even at this period, he says,
his stories always had a useful moral. He showed both his
didactic tendency and his passion for letter-writing at the
early age of eleven, when the precocious child addressed a
remonstrance full of Scripture texts to a widow of fifty,
entreating her to give up the practice of spreading scandal.
Young women in the neighbourhood used to make him read
to them whilst they were at work, and three of them, each
without the knowledge of the others, employed him in the
composition of love-letters. Whilst an apprentice he carried
on a correspondence upon things in general with a gentleman
'greatly his superior in degree and of ample fortune,' and in
later years he turned the experience thus gained to good
account. Two booksellers (Rivington and Osborne) asked him
to write a volume of letters to suit the taste of country readers.
In pursuance of this plan, he wrote some letters intended
to suggest proper sentiments to handsome servant-girls, who
might be exposed to temptation in service. The plan
developed under his hands, and became his first novel,
'Pamela.' The two first volumes were written in three
months in the winter of 1739–40, Richardson being already,
it may be noted, fifty years old. 'Clarissa Harlowe' was
essentially a further development of the same scheme; the
first four volumes appeared at the close of 1747, and the
remainder about a year later. 'Sir Charles Grandison,'
which is a pendant to 'Clarissa Harlowe,' appeared in
1753. Thus one may say that Richardson's later master-
pieces were a working out of the vein already opened in his
childhood, though he did not come before the world as an
author until the ripe age of fifty, and then by a kind of
accident.

He had gone through domestic trials, of which we know
little. By his first wife he had five sons and one daughter;
some of them lived to be 'delightful prattlers,' and the
death of one accelerated the death of the mother. By his
second wife, sister of a bookseller, he had five daughters and
one son, but only four daughters grew to maturity. Whilst
mentioning these losses, he speaks also of the death of his

father, of two brothers, and a friend 'more valuable than
most brothers,' and counts 'eleven affecting deaths in two
years.' His nerves, he says, were greatly affected by his
losses, and for the last seven years (in the end of 1748) he
has 'forborne wine and flesh and fish.' Throughout life,
indeed, he seems to have been a nervous and sensitive little
man. He was never able to ride, and kept, we are told, a
'chamber horse' at each of his houses—an animal, we presume, of the rocking-horse variety, capable of affording
moderate exercise. For years before his death he was
unable to raise a glass to his lips without help. His dread
of possible altercations prevented him from often going
amongst his workmen. He preferred to give his directions
by notes, that he might not have the trouble of bawling
into the ears of a deaf foreman. He gives a portrait of himself in a letter to a female correspondent, the fidelity of which
enabled her, as she afterwards tells him, to recognise him
'above three hundred yards off.' The description is, therefore, worth quoting :—' Short ; rather plump than emaciated,
notwithstanding his complaints ; about 5 foot 5 inches ;
fair wig, lightish cloth coat, all black besides ; one hand
generally in his bosom, the other a cane in it, which he
leans upon under the skirts of his coat usually that it may
imperceptibly serve him as a support when attacked by
sudden tremors or startings and dizziness, which too
frequently attack him, but, thank God, not so often as
formerly ; looking directly fore-right, as passers-by would
imagine, but observing all that stirs on either hand of him
without moving his short neck ; hardly ever turning back ;
of a light-brown complexion ; teeth not yet failing him ;
smoothish faced and ruddy cheeked ; at some times looking to
be about sixty-five, at other times much younger' [his true
age sixty] ; 'a regular, even pace, stealing away ground
rather than seeming to rid it ; a grey eye, too often over-
clouded by mistinesses from the head ; by chance lively ;
very lively it will be if he have hopes of seeing a lady whom
he loves and honours ; his eye always on the ladies ; if they
have very large hoops, he looks down and supercilious, and
as if he would be thought wise, but perhaps the sillier for

that; as he approaches a lady his eye is never fixed first
upon her face, but upon her feet, and thence he raises it up
pretty quickly for a dull eye; and one would think (if we
thought him at all worthy of observation) that from her air
and (the last beheld) her face, he sets her down in his mind
as *so* and *so*, and then passes on to the next object he meets;
only then looking back, if he greatly likes or dislikes, as if he
would see if the lady appear to be all of a piece, in the one
light or the other.' The portraits tally with this bit of
characteristic self-portraiture. He looks like a plump white
mouse in a wig, with an air at once vivacious and timid; a
quick, excitable nature taking refuge in the outside of a
snug, portly tradesman. Two coloured engravings in Mrs.
Barbauld's volumes give us Richardson amidst his surround-
ings. One shows him toddling along at the pantiles at
Tunbridge Wells, amidst groups of ladies with huge hoops,
including the bigamous Duchess of Kingston. Amongst
the company are the great Mr. Pitt and Speaker Onslow,
and Dr. Johnson deferentially attending a bishop, and Colley
Cibber following a lord in a splendid blue coat, and 'the
Baron (a German gamester)' and shrivelled-up Dr. Whiston
(a harmless heretic with a slight crack in his understanding)
stealing away in one corner. Richardson, we can see, is
making mental notes for 'Clarissa;' and though Lady Mary
assures us, as is indeed clear enough, that he was never
admitted to fashionable circles, he could catch some rapid
glimpses with his keen little eyes in such gatherings at the
old resorts of the gay world. One might walk the pantiles
a long time now before meeting such a mixed collection of
celebrities. The other picture introduces us to Richardson
at home. Half-a-dozen ladies and gentlemen are sitting by
the open window in his bare parlour looking out into the
garden. There is only one spindle-legged table and a set of
uncompromising wooden chairs, just enough to accommodate
the party. There is the admirable Miss Mulso, afterwards
Mrs. Chapone, whose very name has a fine flavour of
eighteenth - century proprieties, and two or three other
Mulsos; whilst Miss Highmore, whose hoop can scarcely
be squeezed into her strait-backed chair, is quietly sketch-

ing the memorable scene. We are truly grateful to her;
for there sits the little idol of the party 'in his usual
morning dress,' a nondescript brown dressing-gown, with a
cap on his head of the same materials. His plump little
frame fills the chair, and he is apparently raising one foot
for an emphatic stamp (or is it only that the artist has found
it difficult to plant both feet fairly on the ground?) as he
reads a passage of 'Sir Charles Grandison.' We can see
that as he concludes he will be applauded with deferential
gasps of heartfelt admiration.

The relation of Richardson to his little circle of admirers
is amusingly indicated in his correspondence. He had the
good sense to be thoroughly satisfied with his position in
life. He recognised that as a fact Temple Bar corresponded
to a social as well as a geographical line of distinction, and
declares himself to be 'very shy of obtruding himself on
persons of condition.' He was not servile nor ashamed of
his shop; but he took it for granted, as a part of the provi-
dential order of society, that men in his own rank should be
deferential towards their social superiors. The upper classes
naturally took the same view, and nobody seems to have
wished to elevate the respectable printer into a higher sphere.
His literary talents, indeed, were unknown till he was past
fifty, and was too independent to desire or permit himself to
be petted and lionised by the aristocracy. His connection
with literature procured for him the acquaintance of various
authors. He respected them profoundly, and even gave
pecuniary proofs of his esteem. He did not, like Pope, who
had sprung from a similar rank in society, become the asso-
ciate of great men and ministers. 'Pamela' brought him
into communication with that literary phœnix, but at a very
respectful distance. Pope's lieutenant, the great Warburton,
wrote a letter to Richardson. 'Good sir' is the form of
address, representing the two fingers of dignified condescension. Warburton acknowledges a present of 'Pamela,' and
makes a suggestion from Pope and himself. Richardson would
do well, thought these great men, to continue 'Pamela' as
a satire upon the follies of high life, 'Pamela' being ex-
cellently qualified to act as an *ingénue,* astonished, like an

Indian amongst Europeans, by the absurdities of civilisation. Richardson had the good sense not to adopt a scheme for which he had not the necessary experience. Warburton condescended in 1747 to write a preface to 'Clarissa Harlowe,' pointing out very superfluously the nature of the intended moral; but he afterwards took offence—he was the most easily offended of men—at a supposed reference in the same book to one of Pope's satirical remarks upon women. Richardson was on more familiar terms with more than one of the minor luminaries, whose relations to the pair of literary autocrats were anything but friendly. He was intimate with Edwards, whose 'Canons of Criticism' is a very amusing attack upon the great Warburton's audacious maltreatment of Shakespeare; and with Aaron Hill, a writer now remembered chiefly, if he can be properly said to be remembered at all, for a controversy in which Pope, according to his lamentable custom, first assailed his antagonist and then tried to back out of the assault at the cost of elaborate lying. Hill's letters to Richardson are worth reading. They contain as good a moral for literary vanity as could have been desired by Richardson himself. He writes to Richardson upon Pope's death, explaining (with Richardson's sympathy, it seems) that the popularity of the great man was already waning, and had been due to 'meditated little personal assiduities and a certain bladdery swell of management.' 'Rest his memory in peace!' he exclaims. 'It will very rarely be disturbed by the time he is himself ashes.' And then, by way of showing that his attack upon Pope does not spring from jealousy, he remarks upon his own indifference to fame. 'Never mortal courted her,' he says, 'with less solicitude than I.' Under existing circumstances, he would rather not be famous. Unluckily Richardson is forced to explain to him, from the publisher's point of view, that this modest wish is granted. As a matter of fact, the world does not care for his writings, though the world, as Richardson is careful to add, is entirely to blame in the matter. Poor Hill has to accept this view with a very wry face. He always knew and expected that his writings would be unpopular, 'nor shall I see them in another light;

but there will rise a time in which they *will* be seen in a far different one: I know it, on a surer hope than that of vanity.' He proceeds to revile the taste of the times, and to add that he has a piece in his desk which may have some charms, in spite of 'the supercilious narrowness in vogue,' and so forth. Richardson, whose ' Clarissa ' was just at this time carrying all before it, probably had a better opinion of the judgment of his contemporaries, but he could afford to be kindly to the unpopular Hill, and indeed seems to have helped him not only with praise but with more solid accommodation.

Richardson was familiar with other and more famous men. His letters show that he exchanged compliments and criticism with Young of the ' Night Thoughts,' whose peculiar vein of religious sentimentalism was congenial to the author of ' Clarissa.' Some phrases in Young's letters seem to point to more tangible assistance. Johnson was another of Richardson's friends. The only number of the ' Rambler ' which had a large sale came from Richardson's pen. Johnson was released by Richardson from an arrest for debt, and he always spoke of Richardson, in turn, in a strain of eulogy which certainly does not err from want of warmth. All the critics repeat the Johnsonian statement that Richardson taught the passions to move at the command of virtue ; and we may remember the rather unlucky statement that Fielding only saw the hands of the clock, whereas Richardson knew the working of the wheels. The same comparison, one may remark in passing, is made by Richardson himself to Fielding's sister, in order to illustrate the superiority of her own knowledge of human nature to her brother's. The quaintest of all these friendships was that with Colley Cibber, a man who in real life would have been an admirer of Lovelace much more than of Sir Charles Grandison — a graceless, frivolous, conceited old fop, who had abundant sprightliness and good temper, but who is a queer contrast to the reputable Richardson. It is odd that the man whom Fielding most heartily despised as a representative, both on and off the stage, of the frivolous rake of the old comedy, should have been taken up by Fielding's didactic censor. A hearty admiration for 'Clarissa' covered a good many faults. Mrs. Pilkington, a disreputable adventuress, known chiefly for her acquaintance with Swift, writes to Richardson, whose charity supported her in her worst distress, to describe Cibber's raptures over the unpublished 'Clarissa.' 'The dear gentleman,' she says, 'did almost rave. When I told him that she (Clarissa) must die, he said G— d—n him if she should, and that he should no longer believe Providence or Eternal Wisdom or Goodness governed the world if merit and innocence and beauty were to be so destroyed. "Nay," added he, "my mind is so hurt with the thought of her being violated, that were I to see her in heaven, sitting on the knees of the Blessed Virgin and crowned with glory, her sufferings would still make me feel horror, horror distilled." These were his strongly emphatical expressions.' As a delicate return for this praise, we may notice that Clarissa finds amongst the books which have been put by Lovelace in her lodgings, in order to convince her of the respectable character of the house, 'that genteel comedy of Mr. Cibber's,' the 'Careless Husband,' a comedy which has its merits, but which would scarcely even then have served as a credential of respectability along with the 'Spectator,' Steele's virtuous comedies, and other edifying literature. Cibber, when he comes to write himself, is hardly so emphatic, but is quite as lively, as in Mrs. Pilkington's version. 'The delicious meal I made off Miss Byron on Sunday last,' he writes, 'has given me an appetite for another slice of her, off from the spit, before she is served up to the public table; if about five o'clock to-morrow afternoon will not be inconvenient, Mrs. Brown and I will come and nibble upon a bit more of her.' And we have grace after meat as well as before. 'The devil take the insolent goodness of your imagination!' exclaims the lively old buck, who had now passed his eightieth year, and was as brisk and well preserved as if he had never been exposed to Pope's 'scathing' satire (does satire ever 'scathe'?) or Fielding's rough ridicule. One of Richardson's lady admirers sees Cibber still flirting with fine ladies at Tunbridge Wells in 1754 (he was born in 1671), and miserable when he found himself neglected for a moment by the greatest *belle*

in the society. He professed to be only seventy-seven!
This may bring us back to the inner circle of admirers whom
Richardson really preferred, in passing, to poets and moralists
with little vanities of their own requiring attention. A whole
congregation of enthusiastic young ladies gathered round the
old gentleman, whose writings had touched their hearts.
They called him their dear papa. They passed long days
at his feet at North End and Parson's Green. He was
allowed to escape for a time to a little summer-house in the
garden, to add a charming letter to the correspondence of
Clarissa or Miss Byron. After an early dinner all the ladies
called for a reading, though the poor man complains with
amusing *naïveté* that they were sometimes inclined to take
a walk when he was ready to read. Generally they got out
their embroidery or their drawing-boards, and he sat down
to give them the promised treat. Then followed a delightful
consultation. They considered the fates of the characters,
or discussed the little points of morality which arose. When
they were absent, he wrote letters which are obviously con-
tinuations of the verbal utterances. They are full of little
friendly quarrels, picked in order to be made up ; reproaches
and caresses, and small confidences ; and keen discussions of
the burning questions of the day. Is Lovelace's soul to be
saved ? Is Sir Charles to be allowed to fight a duel ? Does
a reformed rake make the best husband ? Should a lady
be allowed to learn Latin ? What are the proper limits
of parental authority ? Should a young woman indulge
herself in a correspondence, and if so, should she venture to write to persons of another sex ? Richardson in
his childhood had been a confidant, and now he became a
kind of confessor. The relation was natural and harmless
enough, though the style is gossippy and twaddling ; and it
must be admitted that the incessant steam of incense was
hardly calculated to strengthen his moral fibre. But at the
time of the novel-reading Richardson was old enough to be
beyond much risk of spoiling. That had been done already,
so far as it could be done. Perhaps the biggest compliment
that he ever received was the assertion that if some of the
'Clarissa' letters had been found in the Bible, they would

be regarded as manifest proofs of divine inspiration. This, indeed, came from a 'minister of the gospel.' But Richardson's recognised position was that which is assigned to him by Miss Collier. She regards him as the 'only champion and protector' of her sex. Women thought that he understood the feminine heart, as their descendants afterwards thought of Balzac. They ought to be the best judges; and at any rate, he knew how to make them adore him. Amongst the various feminine worshippers, Miss Mulso, and Miss Fielding, and Miss Highmore, and Miss Westcomb, and others who play more or less conspicuous parts in the correspondence, two are specially remarkable. The letters of Mrs. Klopstock, the wife of the 'very German Milton,' are admirably touching in their pretty broken English. Her account of her little love-story is perfect in its way, but I have only space to quote her own introduction of herself to Richardson, as an indication of the power which he was exerting beyond the limits of his own country. 'Honoured sir,' she writes, 'will you permit me to take this opportunity, in sending a letter to Dr. Young, to address myself to you? It is very long ago that I wished to do it. Having finished your "Clarissa" (oh, the heavenly book!), I would have prayed you to write the history of a *manly* Clarissa, but I had not courage enough at that time. I should have it no more to-day, as this is only my first English letter; but I have it! It may be because I am now Klopstock's wife (I believe you know my husband by Mr. Hohorst), and then I was only the single young girl. You have since written the manly Clarissa without my prayer; oh, you have done it to the great joy and thanks of all your happy readers! Now you can write no more, you must write the history of an angel!'

Poor Mrs. Klopstock died shortly afterwards; but she had the pleasure of learning by experience that Richardson was not so rare an exception to the race of authors as to resent such a charming intrusion. His correspondence with Lady Bradshaigh is much longer, and indeed, though only a selection is given, is nearly a quarter of the whole. She was the wife of a Lancashire country gentleman, a sensible, wholesome, fresh-coloured lady, who discharged her domestic

duties energetically, but having no family, was able to devote
much time to reading. She had all the horror of a respectable person of the day for the strange, anomalous creatures
who wrote books. She felt so strongly upon this point, that
having obtained Richardson's portrait, she altered the name
on the frame to Dickenson, in order that no one might suspect her of corresponding with an author. After reading
the first four volumes of 'Clarissa,' she at last wrote under a
feigned name to entreat him to alter the impending catastrophe. She spoke as the mouthpiece of a 'multitude of
admirers,' who were anxious to see Lovelace reformed and
married to Clarissa. 'Sure you will think it worth your
while to save his soul, sir!' she exclaims. Richardson,
whatever his failings, was far too good an artist not to see
the objections to this plan, though in 'Pamela' he had fallen
into an error of the same kind. He was rewarded by her
account of her emotions upon reading the last volumes. She
laid down the book in agonies, took it up again, let fall a
flood of tears, and threw herself upon her couch to compose
her mind. Her husband, who was plodding along after her,
begged her to read no more. But she had promised Richardson to go through with it. She nerved herself for the task
again : her sleep was disturbed, she awoke up crying in the
night, and burst into tears at her meals. In short, she
enjoyed her misery with a heartiness not to be exceeded, and
became Richardson's friend for the rest of her life, though it
was a long time before she could get courage to reveal her
name and meet a real live author face to face.

Lady Bradshaigh, in spite of this little extravagance,
seems to have been a really sensible woman, and could
discuss various small social problems with plenty of vivacity
and common sense. The only thing, in fact, which is rather
painful in Richardson's letters is the spirit in which he regarded contemporaries. He had some of the spitefulness of
the true lover of gossip, and a large share of an author's
jealousy. He is on the look-out for discreditable anecdotes
against Pope and Swift, and his tone about Fielding is
offensive. Fielding had provoked him by ridiculing 'Pamela'
(not more, perhaps, than it deserved) in 'Joseph Andrews.'

Very few readers of 'Joseph Andrews' will think that Fielding's offence was very grave, as, indeed, 'Pamela' is now remembered chiefly as having served in some degree to suggest Fielding's admirable performance. The only reference to Richardson to be found in Fielding's later works is a generous compliment. But Richardson is never tired of abusing his famous contemporary, whilst his correspondents evidently make their court to him by adopting the same strain. He claims to have been himself the cause of Fielding's success. 'The "Pamela,"' he says, 'which he abused in his "Shamela" taught him how to write to please, though his manners are so different. Before his "Joseph Andrews" (hints and names taken from that story with a lewd and ungenerous engraftment) the poor man wrote without being read, except when his "Pasquins," &c., roused party attention.' 'I *could not help telling his sister*,' he says elsewhere, a sister whose merits Fielding had acknowledged with his usual warmth of generosity, 'that I was equally surprised at and concerned for his continued lowness. Had your brother, said I, been born in a stable, or been a runner at a spunging-house, we should have thought him a genius, and wished he had had the advantage of a liberal education, and of being admitted into good company, but now——' It is painful to read this kind of stuff, and yet it shows only too plainly what we might have anticipated, that Richardson, cockered and courted by his female senate, had acquired a morbid sensitiveness, which was outraged beyond bearing at a touch of ridicule.

Another great writer came just in time to receive Richardson's judgment. 'Who is this Yorick?' asks a bishop, who hears that 'Tristram Shandy' has been countenanced—dreadful to relate!—by some 'ingenious Dutchess.' Richardson briefly replies that the bishop cannot have looked into the books, 'execrable I cannot but call them.' There is, indeed, one extenuating circumstance about them: they are 'too gross to be inflaming.'

Richardson may be excused, indeed, for some protest against the moral tone of Sterne's writings. He would have been astonished if he had been told that he was not altogether free from responsibility in the matter. Yet it is undeniable that Richardson gave one of the first impulses to that kind of morbid sentimentalism which Sterne turned to account with greater artistic power than his own. The use of the phrase in its modern acceptation is noticed in a letter of Lady Bradshaigh's, written apparently in 1749. 'What is the meaning,' she asks, 'of the word *sentimental,* so much in vogue amongst the polite, both in town and country? Everything clever and agreeable is comprehended in that word; but I am convinced a wrong interpretation is given, because it is impossible everything clever and agreeable can be so common as that word.' She has heard of a *sentimental* man, a *sentimental* party, or a *sentimental* walk, and has been applauded for applying the same phrase to a letter. In 1752 the word is still used in an older sense in the title to a pamphlet 'on *sentimental* differences in point of faith'— meaning, differences of sentiment. When, a few years later, Sterne published his '*Sentimental* Journey,' Wesley asked what was the meaning of the new phrase, and remarked that you might as well say *continental.* The growth of the new epithet implies the growth of a peculiar vein of feeling, the analysis of which may be left to philosophical historians. For our purpose, it is enough to note Richardson's position in the matter. He had become, as I have said, a kind of Protestant confessor. He was more skilled than any of his contemporaries in the mysteries of the feminine heart. He knew what his worshippers liked, and was prepared to supply it in any quantities. Now we may say roughly that at this period there was a vast amount of vague feeling longing for some effective channels of utterance. The theology of the time was cold and too exclusively logical, according to modern writers, and is too faithfully reflected in such frigid performances as Pope's 'Essay on Man.' A vague desire for something warmer and more emotional was showing itself in various directions. It may be observed, for example, in Young's 'Night Thoughts,' in Hervey's 'Meditations,' and in much of the religious writings of the school which sympathised with Wesley and Whitfield. In literature proper, the tendency is equally marked. The contagion of Richardson's sentimentalism spread rapidly on the Continent, as is indicated by poor Mrs. Klopstock's enthusiasm.

The influence of his novels in Germany is noticed in
the 'Warheit und Dichtung,' and was amongst the causes
predisposing to the Wertherism of the succeeding generation. 'Clarissa' doubtless transmigrated into the heroine
of the 'Nouvelle Heloïse,' dropping some of her insular
prejudices on the way. And though his countrymen
generally sympathised with Fielding's masculine contempt
for this sickly sentimentalism, the readers of Richardson
were prepared to receive 'Ossian' with enthusiasm, and
to weep over 'Tristram Shandy.' Richardson's creed was
doubtless as different as can well be conceived from
that of Rousseau, and he regarded Sterne as unmistakably one of the wicked; but the creed to which a man
may swear allegiance gives but a very vague indication of
the sentiment which he encourages. There are many worshippers, and even sincere and genuine worshippers, of
respectability, who are stimulating the very revolt which
would most shock their prejudices. The time was favourable. Richardson in fact, though the good orthodox little
man had no suspicion of his own tendencies, was encouraging
a tone of thought ominous of many things. The temporary
eclipse of the priest, the natural spiritual guide of feminine
natures, gave a chance to such lay preachers to enjoy a
homage not altogether healthy to those who rendered or to
those who received it. Nothing, however, can be imagined
less revolutionary in intention than Richardson's writings.
He is a sentimentalist pure and simple, who means nothing
less than to direct the feelings which he evokes against
either kings or priests. He is a Tory by principle, though
he may be a corrupter by temperament. He describes
passion sympathetically, but he holds that it should be confined within the strictest limits of decorum and morality.
He is not the only writer who has helped to evoke a spirit
which he would be the last to sanction.

Meanwhile his sympathy with women gives a remarkable
power to his works. Nothing is more rare than to find a
great novelist who can satisfactorily describe the opposite

been astonished it

sex. Women's heroes are women in disguise, or mere lay-figures, walking gentlemen who parade tolerably through their parts, but have no real vitality. Miss Brontë, for example, showed extraordinary power in 'Jane Eyre;' but Jane Eyre's lovers, Rockingham and St. John, are painted from the outside; they are, perhaps, what some women think men ought to be, but not what any man of power at all comparable to Miss Brontë's could ever have imagined. Her most successful men—such as M. Paul, in 'Villette'—are those who have the strongest feminine element in their composition. On the other hand, the heroines of male writers are for the most part unnaturally strained or quite colourless; male hands are too heavy for the delicate work required. Milton could draw a majestic Satan, but his Eve is no better than a good managing housekeeper who knows her place. It is, therefore, remarkable that Richardson's greatest triumph should be in describing a woman, and that most of his feminine characters are more life-like and more delicately discriminated than his men. Unluckily, his conspicuous faults result from the same cause. His moral prosings savour of the endless gossip over a dish of chocolate in which his heroines delight; we can imagine the applause with which his admiring feminine circle would receive his demonstration of the fact, that adversity is harder to bear than prosperity, or the sentiment that 'a man of principle, whose love is founded in reason, and whose object is mind rather than person, must make a worthy woman happy.' These are admirable sentiments, but they savour of the serious tea-party. If 'Tom Jones' has about it an occasional suspicion of beer and pipes at the bar, 'Sir Charles Grandison' recalls an indefinite consumption of tea and small-talk. In short, the feminine part of Richardson's character has a little too much affinity to Mrs. Gamp—not that he would ever be guilty of putting gin in his cup, but that he would have the same capacity for spinning out indefinite twaddle of a superior kind. And, of course, he fell into the faults which beset the members of mutual admiration societies in general, but especially those which consist chiefly of women. Men who meet for purposes of mutual flattery become unnaturally solemn and priggish ; they never free themselves from the suspicion that the older members of the coterie may be laughing at them behind their backs. But the flattery of women is so much more delicate, and so much more sincere, that it is far more dangerous. It is a poultice which in time softens the hardest outside. Richardson yielded as entirely as any curate exposed to a shower of slippers. He evidently wrote under the impression that he was not merely an imaginative writer of the highest order, but also a great moralist. Richardson thought that, in Johnson's phrase, he was placing the passions under the command of virtue. He was reforming the world, putting down vice, sending duelling out of fashion, and inculcating the lessons of the pulpit in a far more attractive form. A modern novelist is half-ashamed of his art ; he disclaims earnestly any serious purpose ; his highest aim is to amuse his readers, and his greatest boast that he amuses them by honourable or at least by harmless means. There are, indeed, novelists with a purpose, who write to inculcate High-Church or Low-Church principles, or to prove that society at large is out of joint ; but a direct intention to prove that men ought not to steal or get drunk, or commit any other atrocities, is generally considered to be beside the novelist's function, and its introduction to be a fault of art. Indeed, there is much to be said against it. In our youth we used to read a poem about a cruel little boy who went out to fish and was punished by somehow becoming suspended by his chin from a hook in the larder. It never produced much effect upon us, because we felt that the accident was, to say the least, rather exceptional ; at most, we fished on, and were careful about the larder. The same principle applies to the poetic justice distributed by most novelists. When Richardson kills off his villains by violent deaths, we know too well that many villains live to a good old age, leave handsome fortunes, and are buried under the handsomest of tombstones, with the most elegant of epitaphs. This very rough device for inculcating morality is of course ineffectual, and produces some artistic blemishes. The direct exhortations to his readers to

be good are still more annoying; no human being can long
endure such a mixture of preaching and story-telling. For
Heaven's sake, we exclaim, tell us what happens to Clarissa,
and don't stop to prove that honesty is the best policy! In
a wider sense, however, the seriousness of Richardson's purpose is of the highest value. He is so keenly in earnest, so
profoundly interested about his characters, so determined to
make us enter into their motives, that we cannot help being
carried away; if he never spares an opportunity of giving
us a lecture, at least his zeal in setting forth an example
never flags for an instant. The effort to give us an ideally
perfect character seems to stimulate his imagination, and
leads to a certain intensity of realisation which we are apt
to miss in the purposeless school of novelists. He is always,
as it were, writing at high-pressure and under a sense of
responsibility.

The method which he adopts lends itself very conveniently to heighten this effect. Richardson's feminine delight
in letter-writing was, as we have seen, the immediate cause
of his plunge into authorship. Richardson's novels, indeed,
are not so much novels put for convenience under the form
of letters, as letters expanded till they become novels. A
genuine novelist who should put his work into the unnatural
shape of a correspondence would probably find it a very
awkward expedient; but Richardson gradually worked up to
the novel from the conception of a collection of letters; and his
method, therefore, came spontaneously to him. He started
from the plan of writing letters to illustrate a certain point
of morality, and to make them more effective attributed them
to a fictitious character. The result was the gigantic tract
called 'Pamela'—beyond all comparison the worst of his
works—of which it is enough to say at present that it succeeds neither in being moral nor amusing. It shows, however,
a truly amazing fertility in a specially feminine art. We
have all suffered from the propensity of some female minds
(the causes of which we will not attempt to analyse) for pouring forth indefinite floods of correspondence. We know the
heartless fashion in which some ladies, even in these days of
penny postage, will fill a sheet of note-paper and proceed to

cross their writing till the page becomes a chequer-work of
unintelligible hieroglyphics. But we may feel gratitude in
looking back to the days when time hung heavier, and
letter-writing was a more serious business. The letters of
those times may recall the fearful and wonderful labours
of tapestry in which ladies employed their needles by way of
killing time. The monuments of both kinds are a fearful
indication of the *ennui* from which the perpetrators must
have suffered. We pity those who endured the toil as we
pity the prisoners whose patient ingenuity has carved a
passage through a stone wall with a rusty nail. Richardson's
heroines, and his heroes too, for that matter, would have been
portents at any time. We will take an example at hazard.
Miss Byron, on March 22, writes a letter of fourteen pages
(in the old edition of collected works). The same day she
follows it up by two of six and of twelve pages respectively.
On the 23rd she leads off with a letter of eighteen pages, and
another of ten. On the 24th she gives us two, filling
together thirty pages, at the end of which she remarks that
she is *forced* to lay down her pen, and then adds a post-
script of six more; on the 25th she confines herself to two
pages; but after a Sunday's rest she makes another start of
equal vigour. In three days, therefore, she covers ninety-
six pages. Two of the pages are about equal to three in
this volume. Consequently, in three days' correspondence,
referring to the events of the day, she would fill something
like a hundred and forty-four of these pages—a task the
magnitude of which may be appreciated by any one who
will try the experiment. We should say that she must
have written for nearly eight hours a day, and are not
surprised at her remark, that she has on one occasion only
managed two hours' sleep.

It would, of course, be the height of pedantry to dwell
upon this, as though a fictitious personage were to be in all
respects bounded by the narrow limits of human capacity.
It is not the object of a really good novelist, nor does it
come within the legitimate means of high art in any
department, to produce an actual illusion. Showmen in
certain mansions call upon us to admire paintings which

we cannot distinguish from bas-reliefs; the deception is, of course, a mere trick, and the paintings are simply childish. On the stage we do not require to believe that the scenery is really what it imitates, and the attempt to introduce scraps of real life is a clear proof of a low artistic aim. Similarly a novelist is not only justified in writing so as to prove that his work is fictitious, but he almost necessarily hampers himself, to the prejudice of his work, if he imposes upon himself the condition that his book shall be capable of being mistaken for a genuine narrative.   Every good novelist lets us into secrets about the private thoughts of his characters which it would be impossible to obtain in real life.   When Mr. Pendennis relates the history of the Newcomes, he very excusably gives us long conversations, and even soliloquies and meditations, of which a real Mr. Pendennis must have been necessarily ignorant.   We do not, therefore, blame Richardson because his characters have a power of writing which no mortal could ever attain.   His fault, indeed, is exactly the contrary.   He very erroneously fancies that he is bound to convince us of the possibility of all his machinery, and often produces the very shock to our belief which he seeks to avoid.   He is constantly trying to account by elaborate devices for the fertile correspondence of his characters, when it is perfectly plain that they are simply writing for purposes of the fiction.   We should never have asked a question as to the authenticity of the letters, if he did not force the question upon us; and no art can induce us for a moment to accept the proffered illusion.   For example, Miss Byron gives us a long account of conversations between persons whom she did not know, which took place ten years before.   It is much better that the impossibility should be frankly accepted, on the clear ground that authors of novels, and consequently their creatures, have the prerogative of omniscience.   At least, the slightest account of the way in which she came by the knowledge would be enough to satisfy us for all purposes of fiction.   Richardson is not content with this, and elaborately demonstrates that she might have known a number of minute details which it is perfectly plain that a real Miss

Byron could never have known, and thus dashes into our
faces an improbability which we should have been quite
content to pass unnoticed.

. The method, however, of telling the story by the correspondence of the actors produces more important effects.
The hundred and forty-four pages we have noticed are all
devoted to the proceedings of three days. They are filled,
for the most part, with interminable conversations. The
story advances by a very few steps; but we know all that
every one of the persons concerned has to say about the
matter. We discover what was Sir Charles Grandison's
relation at a particular time to a certain Italian lady, Clementina. We are told exactly what view he took of his
own position; what view Clementina took of it; what Miss
Byron had to say to Sir Charles on the subject, and what
advice her relations bestowed upon Miss Byron. Then we
have all the sentiments of Sir Charles Grandison's sisters,
and of his brothers-in-law, and of his reverend old tutor;
and the sentiments of all the Lady Clementina's family,
and the incidental remarks of a number of subordinate
actors. In short, we see the characters all round in all
their relations to each other, in every possible variation
and permutation; we are present at all the discussions
which take place before every step, and watch the gradual
variation of all the phases of the positions. We get the
same sort of elaborate familiarity with every aspect of affairs
that we should receive from reading a blue-book full of some
prolix diplomatic correspondence; indeed, 'Sir Charles
Grandison' closely resembles such a blue-book, for the plot
is carried on mainly by elaborate negotiations between three
different families, with proposals, and counter-proposals, and
amended proposals, and a final settlement of the very complicated business by a deliberate signing of two different
sets of articles. One of them, we need hardly say, is a
marriage settlement; the other is a definite treaty between
the lady who is not married and her family, the discussion
of which occupies many pages. The extent to which we
are drawn into the minutest details may be inferred from the
fact that nearly a volume is given to marrying Sir Charles

Grandison to Miss Byron, after all difficulties have been surmounted. We have at full length all the discussions by which the day is fixed, and all the remarks of the unfortunate lovers of both parties, and all the criticisms of both families, and finally an elaborate account of the ceremony, with the names of the persons who went in the separate coaches, the dresses of the bride and bridesmaids, and the sums which Sir Charles gave away to the village girls who strewed flowers on the pathway. Surely the feminine element in Richardson's character was a little in excess.

The result of all this is a sort of Dutch painting of extraordinary minuteness. The art reminds us of the patient labour of a line-engraver, who works for days at making out one little bit of minute stippling and cross-hatching. The characters are displayed to us step by step and line by line. We are gradually forced into familiarity with them by a process resembling that by which we learn to know people in real life. We are treated to few set analyses or summary descriptions, but by constantly reading their letters and listening to their talk we gradually form an opinion of the actors. We see them, too, all round; instead of regarding them steadily, as is usual in modern novels, from one point of view; we know what each person thinks of every one else, and what every one else thinks of him; they are brought into a stereoscopic distinctness by combining the different aspects of their character. Of course, a method of this kind involves much labour on the part both of writer and reader. It is evident that Richardson did not think of amusing a stray half-hour in a railway-carriage or in a club smoking-room; he counted upon readers who would apply themselves seriously to a task, in the hope of improving their morals as much as of gaining some harmless amusement. This theory is explicitly announced in the preface to 'Clarissa,' contributed by Warburton. Warburton was one of the worst of critics, and his approbation is anything but a recommendation. But it must also be said that, considering the cumbrous nature of the process, the spirit with which it is applied is wonderful. Richardson's own interest in his actors never flags. The distinct style of every correspondent is faithfully preserved with singular vivacity. When we have read a few letters we are never at a loss to tell, from the style alone of any short passage, who is the imaginary author. Consequently, readers who can bear to have their amusement diluted, who are content with an imperceptibly slow development of plot, and can watch without impatience the approach of a foreseen incident through a couple of volumes, may find the prolixity less intolerable than might be expected. If they will be content to skip two letters out of every three, they may be entertained with a series of pictures of character and manners skilfully contrasted and brilliantly coloured, though with a limited allowance of incident. Within his own sphere, no writer exceeds him in clearness and delicacy of conception.

In another way, the machinery of a fictitious correspondence is rather troublesome. As the author never appears in his own person, he is often obliged to trust his characters with trumpeting their own virtues. Sir Charles Grandison has to tell us himself of his own virtuous deeds; how he disarms ruffians who attack him in overwhelming numbers, and converts evil-doers by impressive advice; and, still more awkwardly, he has to repeat the amazing compliments which everybody is always paying him. Richardson does his best to evade the necessity; he couples all his virtuous heroes with friendly confidants, who relieve the virtuous heroes of the tiresome task of self-adulation: he supplies the heroes themselves with elaborate reasons for overcoming their modesty, and makes them apologise profusely for the unwelcome task. Still, ingenious as his expedients may be, and willing as we are to make allowance for the necessities of his task, we cannot quite free ourselves from an unpleasant suspicion as to the simplicity of his characters. 'Clarissa' is comparatively free from this fault, though Clarissa takes a questionable pleasure in uttering the finest sentiments and posing herself as a model of virtue. But in 'Sir Charles Grandison' the fulsome interchange of flattery becomes offensive even for fiction. The virtuous characters give and receive an amount of eulogy enough to turn the strongest stomachs. How amiable is A.! says B.; how virtuous is

C., and how marvellously witty is D. ! And then A., C., and D. go through the same performance, adding a proper compliment to B. in place of the exclamation appropriate to themselves. The only parallel in modern times is to be found at some of the public dinners, where every man proposes his neighbour's health with a tacit understanding that he is himself to furnish the text for a similar oration. But then at dinners people have the excuse of a state of modified sobriety.

This fault is, as we have said, aggravated by the epistolary method. That method makes it necessary that each person should display his or her own virtues, as in an exhibition of gymnastics the performers walk round and show their muscles. But the fault lies a good deal deeper. Every writer, consciously or unconsciously, puts himself into his novels, and exhibits his own character even more distinctly than that of his heroes. And Richardson, the head of a little circle of conscientious admirers of each other's virtues, could not but reproduce on a different scale the tone of his own society. The Grandisons, and the families of Miss Byron and Clementina, merely repeat a practice with which he was tolerably familiar at home; whilst his characters represent to some extent the idealised Richardson himself; —and this leads us to the most essential characteristic of his novels. The greatest woman in France, according to Napoleon's brutal remark, was the woman who had the most children. In a different sense, the saying may pass for truth. The greatest writer is the one who has produced the largest family of immortal children. Those of whom it can be said that they have really added a new type to the fictitious world are indeed few in number. Cervantes is in the front rank of all imaginative creators, because he has given birth to Don Quixote and Sancho Panza. Richardson's literary representatives are far indeed below these, but Richardson too may boast that, in his narrower sphere of thought, he has invented two characters that have still a strong vitality. They show all the weaknesses inseparable from the age and country of their origin. They are far inferior to the highest ideals of the great poets of the world ;

they are cramped and deformed by the frigid convention-
alities of their century and the narrow society in which
they move and live. But for all that they stir the emotions
of a distant generation with power enough to show that
their author must have pierced below the surface into the
deeper and more perennial springs of human passions.
These two characters are, of course, Clarissa and Sir Charles
Grandison; and I may endeavour shortly to analyse the
sources of their enduring interest.

Sir Charles Grandison has passed into a proverb. When
Carlyle calls Lafayette a Grandison-Cromwell, he hits off
one of those admirable nicknames which paint a character
for us at once. Sir Charles Grandison is the model fine
gentleman of the eighteenth century—the master of correct
deportment, the unimpeachable representative of the old
school. Richardson tells us with a certain *naïveté* that he
has been accused of describing an impossible character;
that Sir Charles is a man absolutely without a fault, or at
least with faults visible only on a most microscopic observation. In fact, the only fault to which Sir Charles himself
pleads guilty, in seven volumes, is that he once rather loses
his temper. Two ruffians try to bully him in his own
house, and even draw their swords upon him. Sir Charles
so far forgets himself as to draw his own sword, disarm both
of his opponents, and turn them out of doors. He cannot
forgive himself, he says, that he has been 'provoked by two
such men to violate the sanctity of his own house.' His
only excuse is, 'that there were two of them; and that tho'
I drew, yet I had the command of myself so far as only to
defend myself, when I might have done with them what I
pleased.' According to Richardson, this venial offence is
the worst blot on Sir Charles's character. We certainly do
not blame him for the attempt to draw an ideally perfect
hero. It is a perfectly legitimate aim in fiction, and the
only question can be whether he has succeeded: for Richardson's own commendation cannot be taken as quite sufficient,
nor can we quite accept the ingenious artifice by which
all the secondary characters perform as decoy-birds to attract
our admiration. They do their very best to induce us to

join in their hymns of praise. 'Grandison,' says a Roman Catholic bishop, 'were he one of us, might expect canonisation.' 'How,' exclaims his uncle, after a conversation with his paragon of a nephew, 'how shall I bear my own littleness?' A party of reprobates about town have a long dispute with him, endeavouring to force him into a duel. At the end of it one of them exclaims admiringly, 'Curse me, if I believe there is such another man in the world!' 'I never saw a hero till now,' says another. 'I had rather have Sir C. Grandison for my friend than the greatest prince on earth,' says a third. 'I had rather,' replies his friend, 'be Sir C. Grandison for this one past hour than the Great Mogul all my life.' And the general conclusion is, 'what poor toads are we!' 'This man shows us,' as a lady declares, 'that goodness and greatness are synonymous words;' and when his sister marries, she complains that her brother 'has long made all other men indifferent to her. Such an infinite difference!' In the evening, according to custom, she dances a minuet with her bridegroom, but whispers a friend that she would have performed better had she danced with her brother.

The structure, however, of the story itself is the best illustration of Sir Charles's admirable qualities. The plot is very simple. He rescues Miss Byron from an attempt at a forcible abduction. Miss Byron, according to her friends, is the queen of her sex, and is amongst women what Sir Charles is amongst men. Of course, they straightway fall in love. Sir Charles, however, shows symptoms of a singular reserve, which is at last explained by the fact that he is already half-engaged to a noble Italian lady, Clementina. He has promised, in fact, to marry her if certain objections on the score of his country and religion can be surmounted. The interest lies chiefly in the varying inclinations of the balance, at one moment favourable to Miss Byron, and at another to the 'saint and angel' Clementina. When Miss Byron thinks that Sir Charles will be bound in honour to marry Clementina, she begins to pine; 'she visibly falls away; and her fine complexion fades;' her friends 'watch in silent love every turn of her mild and patient eye, every change of her charming countenance; for they know too well to what to impute the malady which has approached the best of hearts; they know that the cure cannot be within the art of the physician.' When Clementina fears that the scruples of her relatives will separate her from Sir Charles, she takes the still more decided step of going mad; and some of her madness would be very touching, if it did not remind us a trifle too much of the conventional pattern of feminine madness in Sheridan's 'Critic.' Whilst these two ladies are breaking their hearts about Sir Charles they do justice to each other's merits. Harriet will never be happy unless she knows that the admirable Clementina has reconciled herself to the loss of her adored; when Clementina finds herself finally separated from her lover, she sincerely implores Sir Charles to marry her more fortunate rival. Never was there such a display of fine feeling and utter absence of jealousy. Meanwhile a lovely ward of Sir Charles finds it necessary to her peace of mind to be separated from her guardian; and another beautiful, but rather less admirable, Italian actually follows him to England to persuade him to accept her hand. Four ladies—all of them patterns of all physical, moral, and intellectual excellence—are breaking their hearts; and though they are so excellent that they overcome their natural jealousy, they can scarcely look upon any other man after having known this model of all his sex. Indeed, every woman who approaches him falls desperately in love with him, unless she is his sister or old enough to be his grandmother. The plot of the novel depends upon an attraction for the fair sex which is apparently irresistible; and the men, if they are virtuous, rejoice to sit admiringly at his feet, and if they are vicious retire abashed from his presence, to entreat his good advice when they are upon their deathbeds.

All this is simple enough. A novelist can make his women fall in love with his hero as easily as, with a stroke of the pen, he can endow him with fifty thousand a year, or bestow upon him every virtue under heaven. Neither has he any difficulty in making him the finest dancer in England, or giving him such marvellous skill with the small-sword that

he can avoid the sin of duelling by instantaneously disarming his most formidable opponents. The real question is,
whether he can animate this conglomerate of all conceivable
virtues with a real human soul, set him before us as a living
and breathing reality, and make us feel that if we had
known him, we too should have been ready to swell the full
chorus of admiration. It is rather more difficult to convey
the impression which a perusal of his correspondence and
conversation leaves upon an unprejudiced mind. Does Sir
Charles, when we come to know him intimately—for, with
the ample materials provided, we really seem to know him—
fairly support the amazing burden thrown upon him? Do
we feel a certain disappointment when we meet the man
whom all ladies love, and in whom every gentleman confesses
a superior nature?

A couple of characteristic anecdotes about Sir Charles
may be enough to suggest some answer. Voltaire, we
know, ridiculed the proud English, who with the same
scissors cut off the heads of their kings and the tails
of their horses. To this last weakness Sir Charles was
superior. His horses, says Miss Byron, 'are not docked;
their tails are only tied up when they are on the road.'
She would wish to find some fault with him, but as she
forcibly says, 'if he be of opinion that the tails of these
noble animals are not only a natural ornament, but of real
use to defend them from the vexatious insects that in
summer are so apt to annoy them, how far from a dispraise
is this humane consideration!' Here is another instance
of exquisite propriety. When Sir Charles goes to church he
does not, like some other gentlemen, bow low to the ladies of
his acquaintance, and then to others of the gentry. No! 'Sir
Charles had first other devoirs to pay. He paid us his
second compliments.' From these two exemplary actions
we might infer his whole character. The most trifling details
of his conduct are regulated on the most serious considerations.
He is one of those solemn beings who can't shave themselves without implicitly asserting a great moral principle.
He finds sermons in his horses' tails; he could give an
excellent reason for the quantity of lace on his coat, which

was due, it seems, to a sentiment of filial reverence; and
he could not fix his hour for dinner without an eye to the
reformation of society. In short, he was a prig of the
first water; self-conscious to the last degree; and so
crammed with little moral aphorisms that they drop out of
his mouth whenever he opens his lips. And then his
religion is in admirable keeping. It is intimately connected
with the excellence of his deportment; and is, in fact,
merely the application of the laws of good society to the
loftiest sphere of human duty. He pays his second compliments to his lady, and his first to the object of his adora-
tion. He very properly gives the precedence to the being
he professes to adore—but it is only a precedence. As he
carries his solemnity into the pettiest trifles of life, so he
considers religious duties to be simply the most important
part of social etiquette. He would shrink from blasphemy
even more than from keeping on his hat in the presence of
ladies; but the respect which he owes in one case is of the
same order with that due in the other : it is only a degree
more important.

We feel, indeed, a certain affection for Sir Charles
Grandison. He is pompous and ceremonious to an insufferable degree; but there is really some truth in his sister's
assertion, that his is the most delicate of human minds;
through the cumbrous formalities of his century there shines
a certain quickness and sensibility; he even condescends to
be lively after a stately fashion, and to indulge in a little
'raillying,' only guarding himself rather too carefully
against unbecoming levity. Indeed, though a man of the
world at the present day would be as much astonished at
his elaborate manners as at his laced coat and sword, he
would admit that Sir Charles was by no means wanting in
tact; his talk is weighted with more elaborate formulæ than
we care to employ, but it is good vigorous conversation in
the main, and, if rather overlaid with sermonising, can at
times be really amusing. His religion is not of a very exalted character; he rises to no sublime heights of emotion,
and would simply be puzzled by the fervours or the doubts
of a more modern generation. In short, it seems to be

compounded of common sense, and a regard for decorum—
and those are not bad things in their way, though not the
highest. He is not a very ardent reformer; he doubts
whether the poor should be taught to read, and is very
clear that every one should be made to know his station;
but still he talks with sense and moderation, and even gets
so far as to suggest the necessity of reformatories. He is
not very romantic, and displays an amount of self-command
in judicially settling the claims of the various ladies who
are anxious to marry him, which is almost comic; he is
perfectly ready to marry the Italian lady, if she can sur-
mount her religious scruples, though he is in love with Miss
Byron; and his mind is evidently in a pleasing state of
equilibrium, secure, in all events, of the happiness which he
deserves. Indeed, for so chivalric a gentleman, his view of
love and marriage is far less enthusiastic than we should
now require. One of his benevolent actions, which throws
all his admirers into fits of eulogy, is to provide one of his
uncles with a wife. The gentleman is a peer, but has
hitherto been of disreputable life. The lady, though of
good family and education, is above thirty, and her family
have lost their estate. The match of convenience which
Sir Charles patches up between them has obvious prudential
recommendations; and of course it turns out admirably.
But one is rather puzzled to know what special merits Sir
Charles can claim for bringing it to pass.

Such a hero as this may be worthy and respectable,
but is not a very exalted ideal. Neither do his circumstances increase our interest. It would be rather a curious
subject of inquiry why it should be so impossible to make
a virtuous hero interesting in fiction. In real life, the
men who do heroic actions are certainly more attractive
than the villains. Domestic affection, patriotism, piety,
and other good qualities, are pleasant to contemplate in the
world; why should they be so often an unspeakable bore
in novels? Principally, no doubt, because our conception
of a perfect man is apt to bring the negative qualities into
too great prominence; we are asked to admire men because
they have not passions—not because they overcome them.

But there are further difficulties; for example, in a novel it is generally so easy to see what is wrong and what is right—the right-hand path branches off so decidedly from the left,—that we give a man little credit for making the proper choice. Still more is it difficult to let us sufficiently into a man's interior, to let us see the struggle and the self-sacrifice which ought to stir our sympathies. We witness the victories, but it is hard to make us feel the cost at which they are won. Now, Richardson has, as we shall directly remark, overcome this difficulty to a great extent in 'Clarissa;' but in 'Sir Charles Grandison' he has entirely shirked it; he has made everything too plain and easy for his hero. Becky Sharp's famous reflection upon the moral effect of five thousand a year might have been suggested by Sir Charles's history. To be young, handsome, healthy, active, with a fine estate and a grand old house; to be able, by your eloquence, to send a sinner into a fit (as Sir Charles does once); to be the object of a devoted passion from three or four amiable, accomplished, and beautiful women—each of whom has a fine fortune, and only begs you to throw your handkerchief towards her, whilst she promises to bear no grudge if you throw it to her neighbour—all these are favourable conditions for virtue—especially if you mean the virtues of being hospitable, generous, a good landlord and husband, and in every walk of life thoroughly gentlemanlike in your behaviour. But the whole design is rather too much in accordance with the device of enabling Sir Charles to avoid duels by having a marvellous trick of disarming his adversaries. 'What on earth is the use of my fighting with you,' says King Padella to Prince Giglio, 'if you have got a fairy sword and a fairy horse?' And what merit is there in winning the battle of life, when you have every single circumstance in your favour? It is to be hoped that we are not moved by jealousy; but we begin to resent the superlative good luck of this prosperous young Sir Charles, rich with every gift the gods can give him, and of whom the most we can say is, that the possession of all those gifts, if it has made him rather pompous and self-conscious, has not made him close-fisted or hard-

hearted. Sir Charles, then, represents a rather carnal ideal ;
he suggests to us those well-fed, almost beefy and cor-
pulent angels, whom the contemporary school of painters
sometimes portray. No doubt they are angels, for they
have wings and are seated in the clouds; but there is
nothing ethereal in their whole nature. We have no love
for asceticism ; but a few hours on the column of St. Simon
Stylites, or a temporary diet of locusts and wild honey,
might have purified Sir Charles's exuberant self-satisfaction.
For all this, he is not without a certain solid merit, and the
persons by whom he is surrounded—on whom we have not
space to dwell—have a large share of the vivacity which
amuses us in the real men and women of their time. Their
talk may not be equal to that in Boswell's ' Johnson ;' but
it is animated and amusing, and they compose a gallery
of portraits which would look well in a solid red-brick
mansion of the Georgian era.

We must, however, leave Sir Charles, to say a few words
upon that which is Richardson's real masterpiece, and
which, in spite of a full share of the defects we have
noticed in Grandison, will always command the admiration
of persons who have courage enough to get through eight
volumes of correspondence. The characters of the little
world in which the reader will pass his time are in some
cases the same who reappear in Grandison. The lively
Lady G. in the last, is merely a new version of Miss Howe
in the former. Clarissa herself is Miss Byron under altered
circumstances, and receives from her friends the same
shower of superlatives whenever they have occasion to touch
upon her merits. Richardson's ideal lady is not at first
sight more prepossessing than his gentleman. After Clarissa's
death, her friend Miss Howe writes a glowing panegyric on
her character. It will be enough to give the distribution
of her time. To rest it seems she allotted six hours only.
Her first three morning hours were devoted to study and
to writing those terribly voluminous letters which, as one
would have thought, must have consumed a still longer
period. Two hours more were given to domestic management, for, as Miss Howe explains, ' she was a perfect

mistress of the four principal rules of arithmetic.' Five
hours were spent in music, drawing, and needlework, this
last especially, and in conversation with the venerable
parson of the parish. Two hours she devoted to breakfast
and dinner; and as it was hard to restrict herself to this
allowance, she occasionally gave one hour more to dinner-
time conversation. One hour more was spent in visiting
the neighbouring poor, and the remaining four hours to
supper and conversation. These periods, it seems, were not
fixed for every day; for she kept a kind of running account,
and permitted herself to have an occasional holiday by
drawing upon the reserved fund of the four hours for
supper.

Setting aside the fearfully systematic nature of this
arrangement—the stern determination to live by rule and
system—it must be admitted that Miss Harlowe was what
used, in outworn phrase, to be called a very 'superior' person.
She would have made an excellent housekeeper, or even a
respectable governess. We feel a certain gratitude to her for
devoting four hours to supper; and, indeed, Richardson's
characters are always well cared for in the victualling department. They always take their solid three meals, with a liberal
intercalation of dishes of tea and chocolate. Miss Harlowe,
we must add, knew Latin, although her quotations of
classical authors are generally taken from translations.
Her successor, Miss Byron, was not allowed this accomplishment, Richardson's doubts of its suitability to ladies having
apparently gathered strength in the interval. Notwithstanding this one audacious excursion into the regions of
manly knowledge, Miss Harlowe appears to us as. in the
main, a healthy, sensible country girl, with sound sense,
the highest respect for decorum, and an exaggerated regard
for constituted, especially paternal, authority. We cannot
expect, from her, any of the outbreaks against the laws of
society customary with George Sand's heroines. If she had
changed places with Maggie Tulliver, she would have
accepted the society of the 'Mill on the Floss' with perfect
contentment. respected all the family of aunts and uncles,
and never repined against the tyranny of her brother Tom.

She would have been conscious of no vague imaginative
yearnings, nor have beaten herself against the narrow bars
of stolid custom. She would have laid up a vast store of
linen, and walked thankfully in the path chalked out for
her. Certainly she would never have run away with Mr.
Stephen Guest without tyranny of a much more tangible
kind than that which acts only through the finer spiritual
tissues. When Clarissa went off with Lovelace, it was not
because she had unsatisfied aspirations after a higher order
of life, but because she had been locked up in her room, as
a solitary prisoner, and her family had tried to force her
into marriage with a man whom she had excellent reasons
for hating and despising. The worst point in Clarissa's
character is perhaps that which is indicated in a very shrewd
remark of Johnson's. There is always something, he said,
which Clarissa prefers to truth. I do not know that this
charge could be justified in detail; but it is a fact that
Clarissa's love of respectability involves some insincerity.
We feel that she is a little over-anxious to keep up appearances, or, as a stern censor might say, too tolerant of shams.
A juster sense of the relation between true morality and
conventional propriety would raise her in our esteem.

Yet the long tragedy in which Clarissa is the victim is
not the less affecting because the torments are of an in-
telligible kind, and require no highly-strung sensibility to
give them keenness. The heroine is first bullied and then
deserted by her family, cut off from the friends who have a
desire to help her, and handed over to the power of an un-
scrupulous libertine. When she dies of a broken heart, the
most callous and prosaic of readers must feel that it is the
only release possible for her. And in the gradual development of his plot, the slow accumulation of horrors upon the
head of a virtuous victim, Richardson shows the power which
places him in the front rank of novelists, and finds pre-
cisely the field in which his method is most effective and
its drawbacks least annoying. In the first place, in spite of
his enormous prolixity, the interest is throughout con-
centrated upon one figure. In 'Sir Charles Grandison'
there are episodes meant to illustrate the virtues of the

' next-to-divine man' which have nothing to do with the
main narrative. In ' Clarissa ' every subordinate plot—and
they abound—bears immediately upon the central action of
the story, and produces a constant alternation of hope and
foreboding. The last volumes, indeed, are dragged out in a
way which is injurious in several respects. Clarissa, to use
Charles II.'s expression about himself, takes an unconscion-
able time about dying. But until the climax is reached, we
see the clouds steadily gathering, and yet cherish an increas-
ing hope that they may be suddenly cleared up. The only
English novel which produces a similar effect, and impresses
us with the sense of an inexorable fate, slowly but steadily
approaching, is the ' Bride of Lammermoor '—in some
respects the best and most artistic of Scott's novels. Superior
as is Scott's art in certain directions, we scarcely take the
same interest in his chief characters, though there is the
same unity of construction. We cannot feel for the Master
of Ravenswood the sympathy which Clarissa extorts. For in
Clarissa's profound distress we lose sight of the narrow
round of respectabilities in which her earlier life is passed ;
the petty pompousness, the intense propriety which annoy
us in ' Sir Charles Grandison ' disappear or become pathetic.
When people are dying of broken hearts we forget their
little absurdities of costume. A more powerful note is
sounded, and the little superficial absurdities are forgotten.
We laugh at the first feminine description of her dress—
a Brussels-lace cap, with sky-blue ribbon, pale crimson-
coloured paduasoy, with cuffs embroidered in a running
pattern of violets and their leaves ; but we are more disposed to cry (if many novels have not exhausted all our
powers of weeping) when we come to the final scene. ' One
faded cheek rested upon the good woman's bosom, the kindly
warmth of which had overspread it with a faint but charming
flush ; the other paler and hollow, as if already iced over by
death. Her hands, white as the lily, with her meandering
veins more transparently blue than ever I had seen even
hers, hanging lifelessly, one before her, the other grasped by
the right hand of the kindly widow, whose tears bedewed
the sweet face which her motherly bosom supported, though

unfelt by the fair sleeper; and either insensibly to the good woman, or what she would not disturb her to wipe off or to change her posture. Her aspect was sweetly calm and serene; and though she started now and then, yet her sleep seemed easy; her breath indeed short and quick, but tolerably free, and not like that of a dying person.' Allowing for the queer grammar, this is surely a touching and simple picture. The epistolary method, though it has its dangers, lends itself well to heighten our interest. Where the object is rather to appeal to our sympathies than to give elaborate analyses of character, or complicated narratives of incident, it is as well to let the persons speak for themselves. A hero cannot conveniently say, like Sir Charles Grandison, 'See how virtuous and brave and modest I am;' nor is it easy to make a story clear when it has to be broken up and distributed amongst people speaking from different points of view; it is hard to make the testimonies of the different witnesses fit into each other neatly. But a cry of agony can come from no other quarter so effectively as from the sufferer's own mouth. 'Clarissa Harlowe' is in fact one long lamentation, passing gradually from a tone of indignant complaint to one of despair, and rising at the end to Christian resignation. So prolonged a performance in every key of human misery is indeed painful from its monotony; and we may admit that a limited selection from the correspondence, passing through more rapid gradations, would be more effective. We might be spared some of the elaborate speculations upon various phases of the affair which pass away without any permanent effect. Richardson seems to be scarcely content even with drawing his characters as large as life; he wishes to apply a magnifying-glass. Yet, even in this incessant repetition there is a certain element of power. We are forced to drain every drop in the cup, and to appreciate every ingredient which adds bitterness to its flavour. We are annoyed and wearied at times; but as we read we not only wonder at the number of variations performed upon one tune, but feel that he has succeeded in thoroughly forcing upon our minds, by incessant hammering, the impression which he desires to produce. If the blows are not all very powerful, each blow tells. There is something impressive in the intensity of purpose which keeps one end in view through so elaborate a process, and the skill which forms such a multitudinous variety of parts into one artistic whole. The proportions of this gigantic growth are preserved with a skill which would be singular even in the normal scale; a respect in which most giants, whether human or literary, are apt to break down.

To make the story complete, the plot should have been as effectively conceived as Clarissa herself, and the other characters should be equally worthy of their position. Here there are certain drawbacks. The plot, it might easily be shown, is utterly incredible. Richardson has the greatest difficulty in preventing his heroine from escaping, and at times we must not look too closely for fear of detecting the flimsy nature of her imaginary chains. There is, indeed, no reason for looking closely; so long as the situations bring out the desired sentiment, we may accept them for the nonce, without asking whether they could possibly have occurred. It is of more importance to judge of the consistency of the chief agent in the persecution. Lovelace is by far the most ambitious character that Richardson has attempted. To heap together a mass of virtues, and christen the result Clarissa Harlowe or Charles Grandison, is comparatively easy; but it is a harder task to compose a villain, who shall be by nature a devil, and yet capable of imposing upon an angel. Some of Richardson's judicious critics declared that he must have been himself a man of vicious life, or he could never have described a libertine so vividly. This is one of the smart sayings which are obviously the proper thing to say, but which, notwithstanding, are little better than silly. Lovelace is evidently a fancy character—if we may use the expression. He bears not a single mark of being painted from life, and is formed by the simple process of putting together the most brilliant qualities which his creator could devise to meet the occasion. We do not say that the result is psychologically impossible; for it would be very rash to dogmatise on any such question. No one can say what strange amalgams of virtue and vice may have sufficient stability to hold together during a journey through this world. But it is plain that Lovelace is not a result of observation, but an almost fantastic mixture of qualities intended to fit him for the difficult part he has to play. To exalt Clarissa, for example, Lovelace's family are represented as all along earnestly desirous of a marriage between them; and Lovelace has every conceivable motive, including the desire to avoid hanging, for agreeing to the match. His refusal is unintelligible, and Richardson has to supply him with a reason so absurd and so diabolical that we cannot believe in it. It reminds us of Hamlet's objecting to killing his uncle whilst at prayers, on the ground that it would be sending him straight to heaven. But we may, if we please, consider Hamlet's conceit as a mere pretext invented to excuse his irresolution to himself; whereas Lovelace speculates so long and so seriously upon the marriage, that we are bound to consider his far-fetched arguments as sincere. And the supposition makes his wickedness gratuitous, if we believe in his sanity. Lovelace suffers, again, from the same necessity which injures Sir Charles Grandison; as the virtuous hero has to be always expatiating on his own virtues, the vicious hero has to boast of his own vices. It is true that this is, in an artistic sense, the least repulsive habit of the two; for it gives reason for hating not a hero but a villain. Unluckily it is also a reason for refusing to believe in his existence. The improbability of a thorough-paced scoundrel writing daily elaborate confessions of his criminality to a friend, even when the friend condemns him, expatiating upon atrocities that deserved hanging, and justifying his vices on principle, is rather too glaring to be admissible. And by another odd inconsistency, Lovelace is described as being all the time a steady believer in eternal punishment and a rebuker of sceptics—Richardson being apparently of opinion that infidelity would be too bad to be introduced upon the stage, though a vice might be described in detail. A man who has broken through all moral laws might be allowed a little free-thinking. We might add that Lovelace, in spite of the cleverness attributed to him, is really a most imbecile schemer. The first principle of a villain should be to tell as few lies as will serve his purpose; but Lovelace invents such elaborate and complicated plots, presenting so many chances of detection and introducing so many persons into his secrets, that it is evident that in real life he would have broken down in a week.

Granting the high improbability of Lovelace as a real living human being, it must be admitted that he has every merit but that of existence. The letters which he writes are the most animated in the voluminous correspondence. The respectable domestic old printer, who boasted of the perfect purity of his own life, seems to have thrown himself with special gusto into the character of a heartless reprobate. He must have felt that there was a certain piquancy in writing down the most atrocious sentiments in his own respectable parlour. He would show that the quiet humdrum old tradesman could be on paper as sprightly and audacious as the most profligate man about town. As quiet people are apt to do, he probably exaggerated the enormities which such men would openly avow; he fancied that the world beyond his little circle was a wilderness of wild beasts who could gnash their teeth and show their claws after a terribly ostentatious fashion in their own dens; they doubtless gloated upon all the innocent sheep whom they had devoured without any shadow of repentance. And he had a fancy that, in their way, they were amusing monsters too; Lovelace is a lady's villain, as Grandison is a lady's hero; he is designed by a person inexperienced even in the observation of vice; and inclined perhaps to exaggerate the charm a good deal more than the atrocity. We must also admit that when the old printer was put upon his mettle he could be very lively indeed. Lovelace, like everybody else, is at times unmercifully prolix; he never leaves us to guess any detail for ourselves; but he is spirited, eloquent, and a thoroughly fine gentleman after the Chesterfield type. An admirer of Clarissa, indeed, has complained of the application of such a title to a villain. 'The devil take such fine gentlemen!'

he exclaims; and indeed, if the devil does not, I see little use
(to quote the proverbial old lady) in having a devil. But as
Johnson adduces Lovelace to prove that a very wicked man
may be also 'very genteel,' I shall venture to use the phrase.
Richardson lectures us very seriously on the evil results which
are sure to follow bad courses; but he evidently holds in his
heart that, till the Nemesis descends, the libertines are far the
most amusing part of the world. In Sir Charles Grandison's company, we should be treated to an intolerable deal
of sermonising, with an occasional descent into the regions
of humour—but the humour is always admitted under
protest. With Lovelace we might hear some very questionable morality, but there would be a never-ceasing flow of
sparkling witticisms. The devil's advocate has the laugh
distinctly on his side, whatever may be said of the argument.
Finally, we may say that Lovelace, if too obviously con-
structed to work the plot, certainly works it well. When
we coolly dissect him and ask whether he could ever have
existed, we may be forced to reply in the negative. But
whilst we read we forget to criticise; he seems to possess
more vitality than most living men; he is so full of
eloquent brag, and audacious sophistry, and unblushing
impudence, that he fascinates us as he is supposed to have
bewildered Clarissa. The dragon who is to devour the
maiden comes with all the flash and glitter and overpowering
whirl of wings that can be desired. He seems to be
irresistible—we admire him and hate him, and some time
elapses before we begin to suspect that he is merely a
stage dragon, and not one of those who really walk this
earth.

Richardson's defects and limitations are of course obvious
enough. It would be waste of time to insist upon the defects
of his style, or to point out his want of certain qualities
which we, perhaps, are inclined to over-estimate. Nobody,
for example, could care less than Richardson for what we
now call the beauties of nature. He was quite content with
the views to be obtained in a walk from Hyde Park Corner to
North End, Hammersmith. There is scarcely throughout his
books one description showing the power of appealing to emo-

tions through scenery claimed by every modern scribbler. In passing the Alps, the only remark which one of his characters has to make, beyond describing the horrible dangers of the Mont Cenis, is that 'every object which here presents itself is excessively miserable.' His ideal scenery is a 'large and convenient country-house, situated in a spacious park,' with plenty of 'fine prospects,' which you are expected to view from a 'neat but plain villa, built in the rustic taste.' And his views of morality are as contracted as his taste in landscapes. The most distinctive article of his creed is that children should have a reverence for their parents which would be exaggerated in the slave of an Eastern despot. We can pardon Clarissa for refusing to die happy until her stupid and ill-tempered old father has revoked a curse which he bestowed upon her. But we cannot quite excuse Sir Charles Grandison for writing in this fashion to his disreputable old parent, who has asked his consent to a certain family arrangement in which he had a legal right to be consulted :—

'As for myself,' he says, 'I cannot have one objection; but what am I in this case? My sister is wholly my father's; I also am his. The consideration he gives me in this instance confounds me. It binds me to him in double duty. It would look like taking advantage of it, were I so much as to offer my humble opinion, unless he were pleased to command it from me.'

Even one of Richardson's abject lady correspondents was revolted by this exaggerated servility. But narrow as his vision might be in some directions, his genius is not the less real. He is a curious example of the power which a real artistic insight may exhibit under the most disadvantageous forms. To realise his characteristic power, we should take one of the great French novelists whom we admire for the exquisite proportions of his story, the unity of the interest and the skill—so unlike our common English clumsiness—with which all details are duly subordinated. It is remarkable, indeed, that Richardson describes himself as writing without a plan. He compares himself to a poor woman laying herself down upon the hearth to blow up a wretched little fire of green sticks. He had, it seems, to live from hand to mouth. But the want of a plan, in the sense of an elaborate plot, is not fatal to the unity of design. He seems rather to be watching the development of the situation than devising it. He has so lively a faith in his characters that he does not lay down a course of action, but is a spectator asking how they will act. This gives at turns an air of rather too much deliberation to his actors. They do not move by impulses, but by careful reflection on all the circumstances of the case. Yet, on the other hand, it implies an evolution of the story from the very necessities of the characters, under a given situation, which involves a certain unity, and gives an air of necessary scientific deduction to the whole scheme of his stories. Our imaginary artist should have, too, the comparative weakness of French novelists, a defective perception of character, a certain unwillingness in art as in politics to allow individual peculiarities to interfere with the main flow of events; for, admitting the great excellence of his minor performers, Richardson's most elaborately designed characters have a certain stamp of artificiality, due to the careful adaptation *N B* to the leading purpose of the story. Then we must cause our imaginary Frenchman to transmigrate into the body of a small, plump, weekly printer of the eighteenth century. We may leave him a fair share of his vivacity, though considerably narrowing his views of life and morality; but we must surround him with a court of silly women whose incessant flatteries must generate in him an unnatural propensity to twaddle. All the gossiping propensities of his nature will grow to unhealthy luxuriance under this unnatural stimulant, and the fine edge of his wit will be somewhat dulled in the process. He will thus become capable of being a bore—a thing which is impossible to any unsophisticated Frenchman. In this way we might obtain a literary product so anomalous in appearance as 'Clarissa'—a story in which a most affecting situation is drawn with extreme power, and yet so overlaid with twaddle, so unmercifully protracted and spun out, as to be almost unreadable to the present generation. But to complete Richardson, we must inoculate him with the propensities of another school: we must give him a liberal share of the feminine sensitiveness and closeness of observation of which Miss Austen is the great example. And perhaps, to fill in the last details, he ought, in addition, to have a dash of the more unctuous and offensive variety of the dissenting preacher—for we know not where else to look for the astonishing and often ungrammatical fluency by which he is possessed, and which makes his best passages remind us of the marvellous malleability of some precious metals.

Any one who will get through the initial difficulties and read himself fairly into the story—a condition which must also be fulfilled by the reader of Balzac's most powerful novels —will end by acknowledging the author's power. Thackeray records an anecdote which he heard from Macaulay, for the truth of which we have also Mr. Trevelyan's authority. ' Not read " Clarissa!"' cried out the historian. ' If you have once thoroughly entered on " Clarissa," and are infected by it, you can't leave it. When I was in India I passed one hot season at the Hills, and there were the Governor-General and the Secretary of Government and the Commander-in-Chief, and their wives. I had " Clarissa" with me; and as soon as they began to read, the whole station was in a passion of excitement about Miss Harlowe and her misfortunes and her scoundrelly Lovelace. The Governor's wife seized the book, and the Secretary waited for it, and the Chief-Justice could not read it for tears!' The fact was no doubt that in the remote Indian station the little society was for the time in the state of the original society which wept over ' Clarissa ' at her first appearance. They had leisure, and at that date probably had not circulating libraries. As soon as they gave Richardson a fair chance, his power became manifest; and any one who will go, say, to the seaside for a month with no other volumes than Richardson, will probably be able to appreciate the old enthusiasm. And this may suggest one concluding moral, for in writing about Richardson one ought to end with a moral. It is that the ordinary condemnation of novels ' with a purpose' involves a misstatement. A

' purpose ' is a very dangerous thing when it implies that the writer is interested about some proposition really extraneous to his book, when therefore he is not really believing in his characters, but using them to illustrate some abstract principle. But when, as in Richardson's case, the purpose is compatible with or even conducive to a vivid interest in the ideal world, it may be occasionally vexatious, but it may also be a condition of success. The intensity of Richardson's belief in the creatures of his own imagination is one main secret of the fascination which can still exist, and the fascination is not the less powerful because Richardson's interest was primarily due to considerations strictly alien to the direct artistic purpose.

PAMELA.

CONTENTS OF VOL. I.

—o—

LETTER VII.

LETTER VIII.

LETTER IX.

LETTER X.

LETTER XI.

LETTER XII.

LETTER XIII.

LETTER XIV.

LETTER XXXII.

HER JOURNAL,

THE JOURNAL CONTINUED.

CONTENTS.

PAGE

NAMES OF THE PRINCIPAL PERSONS.

—— o ——

MEN.

Mr. B——.
Mr. Andrews, father to Pamela.
Lord Davers, brother-in-law to Mr. B——.
Mr. H——, nephew to Lord Davers.
Sir Jacob Swynford, uncle to Mr. B——.
Sir Simon Darnford.
Rev. Mr. Peters.
Rev. Mr. Williams.
Rev. Mr. Adams.
Earl of D——.
Mr. Martin.
Mr. Dormer.
Sir Thomas Atkyns.
Mr. Brooks.
Mr. Arthur.
Mr. Chapman.
The Dean of ——.
Mr. Turner.
Mr. Longman, steward to Mr. B——.
Mr. Jonathan, butler to Mr. B——.
Mr. Colbrand, a Swiss, valet to Mr. B——.

WOMEN.

PAMELA.
Mrs. Andrews, mother to Pamela.
Lady Davers, sister to Mr. B——.
Miss Sally Godfrey, a young lady seduced by Mr. B——.
Miss Goodwin, the fictitious name of Mr. B——'s natural daughter.
Lady Darnford.
Miss Darnford.
Miss Nancy Darnford.
Mrs. Peters.
Countess of C——.
Mrs. Arthur.
Mrs. Brooks.
Lady Towers.
Miss L——, daughter to the Dean of L——.
Countess of D——.
Mrs. Chapman.
The Dowager Countess of ——.
The Viscountess ——.
Mrs. Jervis, housekeeper of Mr. B——'s Bedfordshire house.
Mrs. Jewkes, housekeeper of Mr. B——'s Lincolnshire house.
Mrs. Worden, waiting-woman to Lady Davers.

PAMELA;

OR,

VIRTUE REWARDED.

—o—

LETTER I.

DEAR FATHER AND MOTHER,—I have great trouble, and some comfort, to acquaint you with. The trouble is, that my good lady died of the illness I mentioned to you, and left us all much grieved for the loss of her; for she was a dear good lady, and kind to all us her servants. Much I feared, that as I was taken by her ladyship to wait upon her person, I should be quite destitute again, and forced to return to you and my poor mother, who have enough to do to maintain yourselves; and, as my lady's goodness had put me to write and cast accounts, and made me a little expert at my needle, and otherwise qualified above my degree, it was not every family that could have found a place that your poor Pamela was fit for: but God, whose graciousness to us we have so often experienced at a pinch, put it into my good lady's heart, on her death-bed, just an hour before she expired, to recommend to my young master all her servants, one by one; and when it came to my turn to be recommended (for I was sobbing and crying at her pillow), she could only say, My dear son!—and so broke off a little; and then recovering—Remember my poor Pamela —And these were some of her last words! Oh how my eyes run—don't wonder to see the paper so blotted.

Well, but God's will must be done!—And so comes the comfort, that I shall not be obliged to return back to be a clog upon my dear parents! For my master said, I will take care of you all, my good maidens; and for you, Pamela (and took me by the hand; yes, he took my hand before them all), for my dear mother's sake, I will be a friend to you, and you shall take care of my linen. God bless him! and pray with me, my dear father and mother, for a blessing upon him, for he has given mourning and a year's wages to all my lady's servants; and I having no wages as yet, my lady having said she should do for me as I deserved, ordered the housekeeper to give me mourning with the rest; and gave me with his own hand four golden guineas, and some silver, which were in my old lady's pocket when she died; and said, if I was a good girl, and faithful and diligent, he would be a friend to me, for his mother's sake. And so I send you these four guineas for your comfort; for Providence will not let me want: And so you may pay some old debt with part, and keep the other part to comfort you both. If I get more, I am sure it is my duty, and it shall be my care, to love and cherish you both; for you have loved and cherished me, when I could do nothing for myself. I send them by John, our footman, who goes your way: but he does not know what he carries; because I seal them up in one of the little pill-boxes, which my lady had, wrapt close in paper, that they mayn't clink; and be sure don't open it before him.

I know, dear father and mother, I must give you both grief and pleasure; and so I will only say, Pray for your Pamela; who will ever be

Your most dutiful DAUGHTER.

I have been scared out of my senses; for just now, as I was folding up this letter in my late lady's dressing-room, in comes my young master! Good sirs! how was I frightened! I went to hide the letter in my bosom; and he, seeing me tremble, said, smiling, To whom have you been writing, Pamela?—I said, in my confusion, Pray your honour forgive me!—Only to my father and mother. He said, Well then, let me see how you are come on in your writing! Oh how ashamed I was!—He took it, without saying more, and read it quite through, and then gave it me again;—and I said, Pray your honour forgive me!—Yet I know not for what: for he was always dutiful to *his* parents; and why should he be angry that I was so to *mine?* And indeed he was not angry; for he took me by the hand, and said, You are a good girl, Pamela, to be kind to your aged father and mother. I am not angry with you for writing such innocent matters as these: though you ought to be wary what tales you send out of a family.—Be faithful and diligent; and do as you should do, and I like you the better for this. And then he said, Why, Pamela, you write a very pretty hand, and spell tolerably too. I see my good mother's care in your learning has not been thrown away upon you. She used to say you loved reading; you may look into any of her books to improve yourself, so you take care of them. To be sure I did nothing but courtesy and cry, and was all in confusion, at his goodness. Indeed he is the best of gentlemen, I think! But I am making another long letter: So will only add to it, that I shall ever be

Your dutiful daughter,
PAMELA ANDREWS.

—*o*—

LETTER II.

[In answer to the preceding.]

DEAR PAMELA,—Your letter was indeed a great trouble, and some comfort, to me and your poor mother. We are troubled, to be sure, for your good lady's death, who took such care of you, and gave you learning, and, for three or four years past, has always been giving you clothes and linen, and everything that a gentlewoman need not be ashamed to appear in. But our chief trouble is, and indeed a very great one, for fear you should be brought to anything dishonest or wicked, by being set so above yourself. Everybody talks how you have come on, and what a genteel girl you are; and some say you are very pretty; and, indeed, six months since, when I saw you last, I should have thought so myself, if you was not our child. But what avails all this, if you are to be ruined and undone!—Indeed, my dear Pamela, we begin to be in great fear for you; for what signify all the riches in the world, with a bad conscience, and to be dishonest! We are, 'tis true, very poor, and find it hard enough to live; though once, as you know, it was better with us. But we would sooner live upon the water, and, if possible, the clay of the ditches I contentedly dig, than live better at the price of our child's ruin.

I hope the good 'squire has no design: but when he has given you so much money, and speaks so kindly to you, and praises your coming on; and, oh, that fatal word! that he would be kind to you, if you would do *as you should do*, almost kills us with fears.

I have spoken to good old widow Mumford about it, who, you know, has formerly lived in good families; and she puts us in some comfort; for she says, it is not unusual, when a lady dies, to give what she has about her person to her waiting-maid, and to such as sit up with her in her illness. But, then, why should he smile so kindly upon you? Why should he take such a poor girl as you by the hand, as your letter says he has done twice? Why should he stoop to read your letter to us, and commend your writing and spelling? And why should he give you leave to read his mother's books?—Indeed, indeed, my dearest child, our hearts ache for you; and then you seem so full of *joy* at his goodness, so *taken* with his kind expressions (which, truly, are very great favours, if he means well), that we *fear*—yes, my dear child, we *fear*—you should be *too* grateful,—and reward him with that jewel, your virtue, which no riches, nor favour, nor anything in this life, can make up to you.

I, too, have written a long letter, but will say one thing more; and that is, that, in the midst of our poverty and misfortunes, we have trusted in God's goodness, and been honest, and doubt not to be happy hereafter, if we continue to be good, though our lot is hard here; but the loss of our dear child's virtue would be a grief that we could not bear, and would bring our grey hairs to the grave at once.

If, then, you love us, if you wish for God's blessing, and your own future happiness, we both charge you to stand upon your guard: and, if you find the least attempt made upon your virtue, be sure you leave everything behind you, and come away to us; for we had rather see you all covered with rags, and even follow you to the churchyard, than have it said, a child of ours preferred any worldly conveniences to her virtue.

We accept kindly of your dutiful present; but, till we are out of pain, cannot make use of it, for fear we should partake of the price of our poor daughter's shame: so have laid it up in a rag among the thatch, over the window, for a while, lest we should be robbed. With our blessings, and our hearty prayers for you, we remain,

Your careful, but loving Father and Mother,
JOHN AND ELIZABETH ANDREWS.

——o——

LETTER III.

DEAR FATHER,—I must needs say, your letter has filled me with trouble, for it has made my heart, which was overflowing with gratitude for my master's goodness, suspicious and fearful; and yet I hope I shall never find him to act unworthy of his character; for what could he get by ruining such a poor young creature as me? But that which gives me most trouble is, that you seem to mistrust the honesty of your child. No, my dear father and mother, be assured that, by God's grace, I never will do anything that shall bring your grey hairs with sorrow to the grave. I will die a thousand deaths, rather than be dishonest any way. Of that be assured, and set your hearts at rest; for although I have lived above myself for some time past, yet I can be content with rags and poverty, and bread and water, and will embrace them, rather than forfeit my good name, let who will be the tempter. And of this pray rest satisfied, and think better of

> Your dutiful DAUGHTER till death.

My master continues to be very affable to me. As yet I see no cause to fear anything. Mrs. Jervis, the housekeeper, too, is very civil to me, and I have the love of everybody. Sure they can't *all* have designs against me, because they are civil! I hope I shall always behave so as to be respected by every one; and that nobody would do me more hurt than I am sure I would do them. Our John so often goes your way, that I will always get him to call, that you may hear from me, either by writing (for it brings my hand in), or by word of mouth.

—o—

LETTER IV.

DEAR MOTHER,—For the last was to my father, in answer to his letter; and so I will now write to you; though I have nothing to say, but what will make me look more like a vain hussy, than anything else: However, I hope I shan't be so proud as to forget myself. Yet there is a secret pleasure one has to hear one's self praised. You must know, then, that my Lady Davers, who, I need not tell you, is my master's sister, has been a month at our house, and has taken great notice of me, and given me good advice to keep myself to myself. She told me I was a pretty wench, and that everybody gave me a very good character, and loved me; and bid me take care to keep the fellows at a distance;

and said, *that* I might do, and be more valued for it, even by themselves.

But what pleased me much, was what I am going to tell you; for at table, as Mrs. Jervis says, my master and her ladyship talking of me, she told him, she thought me the prettiest wench she ever saw in her life; and that I was too pretty to live in a bachelor's house; since no lady he might marry would care to continue me with her. He said, I was vastly improved, and had a good share of prudence, and sense above my years; and that it would be pity, that what was my merit should be my misfortune.—No, says my good lady, Pamela shall come and live with me, I think. He said, with all his heart; he should be glad to have me so well provided for. Well, said she, I'll consult my lord about it. She asked how old I was; and Mrs. Jervis said, I was fifteen last February. Oh! says she, if the wench (for so she calls all us maiden servants) takes care of herself, she'll improve yet more and more, as well in her person as mind.

Now, my dear father and mother, though this may look too vain to be repeated by me; yet are you not rejoiced, as well as I, to see my master so willing to part with me? —This shews that he has nothing bad in his heart. But John is just going away; and so I have only to say, that I am, and will always be,

> Your honest as well as dutiful DAUGHTER.

Pray make use of the money. You may now do it safely.

———*o*———

LETTER V.

MY DEAR FATHER AND MOTHER,—John being to go your way, I am willing to write, because he is so willing to carry anything for me. He says it does him good at his heart to see you both, and to hear you talk. He says you are both so sensible, and so honest, that he always learns something from you to the purpose. It is a thousand pities, he says, that such worthy hearts should not have better luck in the world! and wonders that you, my father, who are so well able to teach, and write so good a hand, succeeded no better in the school you attempted to set up; but was forced to go to such hard labour. But this is more pride to me, that I am come of such honest parents, than if I had been born a lady.

I hear nothing yet of going to Lady Davers; and I am very easy at present here: for Mrs. Jervis uses me as if I were her own daughter, and is a very good woman, and makes my master's interest her own. She is always giving me good counsel, and I love her next to you two, I think, best of anybody. She keeps so good rule and order, she is mightily respected by us all; and takes delight to hear me read to her; and all she loves to hear read is good books, which we read whenever we are alone; so that I think I am at home with you. She heard one of our men, Harry, who is no better than he should be, speak freely to me; I think he called me his pretty Pamela, and took hold of me, as if he would have kissed me; for which, you may be sure, I was very angry: and she took him to task, and was as angry at him as could be; and told me she was very well pleased to see my prudence and modesty, and that I kept all the fellows at a distance. And indeed I am sure I am not proud, and carry it civilly to everybody; but yet, methinks, I cannot bear to be looked upon by these men-servants; for they seem as if they would look one through; and, as I. generally breakfast, dine, and sup with Mrs. Jervis (so good she is to me), I am very easy that I have so little to say to them. Not but they are very civil to me in the main, for Mrs. Jervis's sake, who they see loves me; and they stand in awe of her, knowing her to be a gentlewoman born, though she has had misfortunes.

I am going on again with a long letter; for I love writing, and shall tire you. But, when I began, I only intended to say, that I am quite fearless of any danger now: and, indeed, cannot but wonder at myself (though your caution to me was your watchful love), that I should be so foolish

as to be so uneasy as I have been: for I am sure my master
would not demean himself, so as to think upon such a poor
girl as I, for my harm. For such a thing would ruin his
credit, as well as mine, you know: who, to be sure, may
expect one of the best ladies in the land. So no more at
present, but that I am

Your ever dutiful DAUGHTER.

—o—

LETTER VI.

DEAR FATHER AND MOTHER,—My master has been very
kind since my last; for he has given me a suit of my late
lady's clothes, and half a dozen of her shifts, and six fine
handkerchiefs, and three of her cambric aprons, and four
holland ones. The clothes are fine silk, and too rich and
too good for me, to be sure. I wish it was no affront to him
to make money of them, and send it to you: it would do
me more good.

You will be full of fears, I warrant now, of some design
upon me, till I tell you, that he was with Mrs. Jervis when
he gave them me; and he gave her a mort of good things,
at the same time, and bid her wear them in remembrance
of her good friend, my lady, his mother. And when he
gave me these fine things, he said, These, Pamela, are for
you; have them made fit for you, when your mourning is
laid by, and wear them for your good mistress's sake. Mrs.
Jervis gives you a very good word; and I would have you
continue to behave as prudently as you have done hitherto,
and everybody will be your friend.

I was so surprised at his goodness, that I could not tell
what to say. I courtesied to him, and to Mrs. Jervis for
her good word; and said, I wished I might be deserving of
his favour and her kindness: and nothing should be wanting in me, to the best of my knowledge.

Oh how amiable a thing is doing good!—It is all I envy
great folks for.

I always thought my young master a fine gentleman, as everybody says he is: but he gave these good things to us both with such a graciousness, as I thought he looked like an angel.

Mrs. Jervis says, he asked her, if I kept the men at a distance? for, he said, I was very pretty; and to be drawn in to have any of them, might be my ruin, and make me poor and miserable betimes. She never is wanting to give me a good word, and took occasion to lanch out in my praise, she says. But I hope she has said no more than I shall try to deserve, though I mayn't at present. I am sure I will always love her, next to you and my dear mother. So I rest

Your ever dutiful DAUGHTER.

—o—

LETTER VII.

DEAR FATHER,—Since my last, my master gave me more fine things. He called me up to my late lady's closet, and, pulling out her drawers, he gave me two suits of fine Flanders laced head-clothes, three pair of fine silk shoes, two hardly the worse, and just fit for me (for my lady had a very little foot), and the other with wrought silver buckles in them; and several ribands and top-knots of all colours; four pair of white fine cotton stockings, and three pair of fine silk ones; and two pair of rich stays. I was quite astonished, and unable to speak for a while; but yet I was inwardly ashamed to take the stockings; for Mrs. Jervis was not there: If she had, it would have been nothing. I believe I received them very awkwardly; for he smiled at my awkwardness, and said, Don't blush, Pamela: dost think I don't know pretty maids should wear shoes and stockings?

I was so confounded at these words, you might have beat me down with a feather. For you must think, there was no answer to be made to this: So, like a fool, I was ready to cry; and went away courtesying and blushing, I am sure, up to the ears; for, though there was no harm in what he said, yet I did not know how to take it. But I went and told all to Mrs. Jervis, who said, God put it into his heart to be good to me; and I must double my diligence. It looked to her, she said, as if he would fit me in dress for a waiting-maid's place on Lady Daver's own person.

But still your kind fatherly cautions came into my head, and made all these gifts nothing near to me what they would have been. But yet, I hope, there is no reason; for what good could it do to him to harm such a simple maiden as me? Besides, to be sure no lady would look upon him, if he should so disgrace himself. So I will make myself easy; and, indeed, I should never have been otherwise, if you had not put it into my head; for my good, I know very well. But, may be, without these uneasinesses to mingle with these benefits, I might be too much puffed up: So I will conclude, all that happens is for our good; and God bless you, my dear father and mother; and I know you constantly pray for a blessing upon me; who am, and shall always be,

Your dutiful DAUGHTER.

—o—

LETTER VIII.

DEAR PAMELA,—I cannot but renew my cautions on your master's kindness, and his free expression to you about the stockings. Yet there may not be, and I hope there is not, anything in it. But when I reflect, that there *possibly* may, and that if there should, no less depends upon it than my child's everlasting happiness in this world and the next; it is enough to make one fearful for you. Arm yourself, my dear child, for the worst; and resolve to lose your life sooner than your virtue. What though the doubts I filled you with, lessen the pleasure you would have had in your master's kindness; yet what signify the delights that arise from a few paltry fine clothes, in comparison with a good conscience?

These are, indeed, very great favours that he heaps upon you, but so much the more to be suspected; and when you say he looked so amiably, and like an angel, how afraid I am, that they should make too great an impression upon you! For, though you are blessed with sense and prudence above your years, yet I tremble to think, what a sad hazard a poor maiden of little more than fifteen years of age stands against the temptations of this world, and a designing young gentleman, if he should prove so, who has so much *power* to oblige, and has a kind of *authority* to command, as your master.

"I charge you, my dear child, on both our blessings, poor as we are, to be on your guard; there can be no harm in that. And since Mrs. Jervis is so good a gentlewoman, and so kind to you, I am the easier a great deal, and so is your mother; and we hope you will hide nothing from her, and take her counsel in everything. So, with our blessings, and assured prayers for you, more than for ourselves, we remain

Your loving FATHER and MOTHER.

Be sure don't let people's telling you, you are pretty, puff you up; for you did not make yourself, and so can have no praise due to you for it. It is virtue and goodness only that make the true beauty. Remember that, Pamela.

——o——

LETTER IX.

DEAR FATHER AND MOTHER,—I am sorry to write you word, that the hopes I had of going to wait on Lady Davers are quite over. My lady would have had me; but my master, as I heard by the by, would not consent to it. He said her nephew might be taken with me, and I might draw him in, or be drawn in by him; and he thought, as his mother loved me, and committed me to his care, he ought to continue me with him; and Mrs. Jervis would be a mother to me. Mrs. Jervis tells me the lady shook her head, and said, *Ah! brother!* and that was all. And as you have made me fearful by your cautions, my heart at times misgives me. But I say nothing yet of your caution, or my own uneasiness, to Mrs. Jervis; not that I mistrust her, but for fear she should think me presumptuous, and vain and conceited, to have any fears about the matter, from the great distance between such a gentleman and so poor a girl. But yet Mrs. Jervis seemed to build something upon Lady Davers's shaking her head, and saying, *Ah! brother!* and no more. God, I hope, will give me His grace; and so I will not, if I can help it, make myself too uneasy; for I hope there is no occasion. But every little matter that happens, I will acquaint you with, that you may continue to me your good advice, and pray for

Your sad-hearted

Pamela.

———o———

LETTER X.

Dear Mother,—You and my good father may wonder you have not had a letter from me in so many weeks; but a sad, sad scene, has been the occasion of it. For to be sure, now it is too plain, that all your cautions were well grounded. Oh my dear mother! I am miserable, truly miserable!—But yet, don't be frightened, I am honest!—God, of His goodness, keep me so!

Oh this angel of a master! this fine gentleman! this gracious benefactor to your poor Pamela! who was to take care of me at the prayer of his good dying mother; who was so apprehensive for me, lest I should be drawn in by Lord Davers's nephew, that he would not let me go to Lady Davers's: This very gentleman (yes, I *must* call him gentleman, though he has fallen from the merit of that title) has degraded himself to offer freedoms to his poor servant! He has now showed himself in his true colours; and, to *me*, nothing appear so black, and so frightful.

I have not been idle; but had writ from time to time,
how he, by sly mean degrees, exposed his wicked views;
but somebody stole my letter, and I know not what has
become of it. It was a very long one. I fear, he that was
mean enough to do bad things, in one respect, did not stick
at *this*. But be it as it will, all the use he can make of it
will be, that he may be ashamed of *his* part; I not of *mine:*
for he will see I was resolved to be virtuous, and gloried in
the honesty of my poor parents.

I will tell you all, the next opportunity, for I am watched
very narrowly; and he says to Mrs. Jervis, This girl is
always scribbling; I think she may be better employed.
And yet I work all hours with my needle, upon his linen,
and the fine linen of the family; and am, besides, about
flowering him a waistcoat.—But, oh! my heart's broke
almost; for what am I likely to have for my reward, but
shame and disgrace, or else ill words, and hard treatment!
I'll tell you all soon, and hope I shall find my long letter.

Your most afflicted DAUGHTER.

May-be, I *he* and *him* too much: but it is his own fault
if I do. For why did he lose all his dignity with me?

———o———

LETTER XI.

DEAR MOTHER,—Well, I can't find my letter, and so I'll
try to recollect it all, and be as brief as I can. All went
well enough in the main for some time after my letter but
one. At last, I saw some reason to *suspect;* for he would
look upon me, whenever he saw me, in such a manner as
showed not well; and one day he came to me, as I was in
the summer-house in the little garden, at work with my
needle, and Mrs. Jervis was just gone from me; and I
would have gone out, but he said, No, don't go, Pamela;
I have something to say to you; and you always fly me
when I come near you, as if you were afraid of me.

I was much out of countenance, you may well think; but said, at last, It does not become your poor servant to stay in your presence, sir, without your business required it; and I hope I shall always know my place.

Well, says he, my business does require it sometimes; and I have a mind you should stay to hear what I have to say to you.

I stood still confounded, and began to tremble, and the more when he took me by the hand; for now no soul was near us.

My sister Davers, said he (and seemed, I thought, to be as much at a loss for words as I), would have had you live with *her;* but she would not do for you what I am resolved to do, if you continue faithful and obliging. What say'st thou, my girl? said he with some eagerness; had'st thou not rather stay with me, than go to my sister Davers? He looked so, as filled me with affrightment; I don't know how; wildly, I thought.

I said, when I could speak, Your honour will forgive me; but as you have no lady for me to wait upon, and my good lady has been now dead this twelvemonth, I had rather, if it would not displease you, wait upon Lady Davers, *because*——

I was proceeding, and he said, a little hastily—*Because* you are a little fool, and know not what's good for yourself. I tell you I will make a gentlewoman of you, if you be obliging, and don't stand in your own light; and so saying, he put his arm about me, and kissed me!

Now, you will say, all his wickedness appeared plainly. I struggled and trembled, and was so benumbed with terror, that I sunk down, not in a fit, and yet not myself; and I found myself in his arms, quite void of strength; and he kissed me two or three times, with frightful eagerness.—At last I burst from him, and was getting out of the summer-house; but he held me back, and shut the door.

I would have given my life for a farthing. And he said, I'll do you no harm, Pamela; don't be afraid of me. I said, I won't stay. You won't, hussy! said he: do you

know whom you speak to? I lost all fear, and all respect,
and said, Yes, I do, sir, too well!—Well may I forget that
I am your servant, when you forget what belongs to a
master.

I sobbed and cried most sadly. What a foolish hussy
you are! said he: have I done you any harm?—Yes, sir,
said I, the greatest harm in the world: You have taught
me to forget myself and what belongs to me, and have
lessened the distance that fortune has made between us, by
demeaning yourself to be so free to a poor servant. Yet,
sir, I will be bold to say, I am honest, though poor: and if
you was a prince, I would not be otherwise.

He was angry, and said, Who would have you otherwise,
you foolish slut! Cease your blubbering. I own I have
demeaned myself; but it was only to try you: If you can
keep this matter secret, you'll give me the better opinion of
your prudence; and here's something, said he, putting some
gold in my hand, to make you amends for the fright I put
you in. Go, take a walk in the garden, and don't go in till
your blubbering is over: and I charge you say nothing of
what is past, and all shall be well, and I'll forgive you.

I won't take the money, indeed, sir, said I, poor as I am:
I won't take it. For, to say truth, I thought it looked like
taking earnest, and so I put it upon the bench; and as he
seemed vexed and confused at what he had done, I took the
opportunity to open the door, and went out of the summer-
house.

He called to me, and said, Be secret, I charge you,
Pamela; and don't go in yet, as I told you.

Oh how poor and mean must those actions be, and how
little must they make the best of gentlemen look, when they
offer such things as are unworthy of themselves, and put it
into the power of their inferiors to be greater than they!

I took a turn or two in the garden, but in sight of the
house, for fear of the worst; and breathed upon my hand
to dry my eyes, because I would not be too disobedient.
My next shall tell you more.

Pray for me, my dear father and mother; and don't be

angry I have not yet run away from this house, so late my
comfort and delight, but now my terror and anguish. I
am forced to break off hastily.

Your dutiful and honest DAUGHTER.

—*o*—

LETTER XII.

DEAR MOTHER,—Well, I will now proceed with my sad
story. And so, after I had dried my eyes, I went in, and
began to ruminate with myself what I had best to do.
Sometimes I thought I would leave the house and go to the
next town, and wait an opportunity to get to you; but then
I was at a loss to resolve whether to take away the things
he had given me or no, and how to take them away:
Sometimes I thought to leave them behind me, and only go
with the clothes on my back, but then I had two miles and
a half, and a by-way, to the town; and being pretty well
dressed, I might come to some harm, almost as bad as what
I would run away from; and then may-be, thought I, it
will be reported, I have stolen something, and so was forced
to run away; and to carry a bad name back with me to my
dear parents, would be a sad thing indeed!—Oh how I wished
for my grey russet again, and my poor honest dress, with
which you fitted me out (and hard enough too it was for
you to do it!) for going to this place, when I was not twelve
years old, in my good lady's days! Sometimes I thought
of telling Mrs. Jervis, and taking her advice, and only
feared his command to be secret; for, thought I, he may
be ashamed of his actions, and never attempt the like
again: And as poor Mrs. Jervis depended upon him,
through misfortunes, that had attended her, I thought it
would be a sad thing to bring his displeasure upon her for
my sake.

In this quandary, now considering, now crying, and not
knowing what to do, I passed the time in my chamber till
evening; when desiring to be excused going to supper, Mrs.

Jervis came up to me, and said, Why must I sup without
you, Pamela? Come, I see you are troubled at something;
tell me what is the matter.

I begged I might be permitted to lie with her on nights;
for I was afraid of spirits, and they would not hurt such a
good person as she. That was a silly excuse, she said; for
why was not you afraid of spirits before?—(Indeed I did
not think of that.) But you shall be my bed-fellow with
all my heart, added she, let your reason be what it will;
only come down to supper. I begged to be excused; for,
said I, I have been crying so, that it will be taken notice of
by my fellow-servants; and I will hide nothing from you,
Mrs. Jervis, when we are alone.

She was so good to indulge me; but made haste to come
up to bed; and told the servants, that I should lie with her,
because she could not rest well, and would get me to read
her to sleep; for she knew I loved reading, she said.

When we were alone, I told her all that had passed; for
I thought, though he had bid me not, yet if he should come
to know I had told, it would be no worse; for to keep a
secret of such a nature, would be, as I apprehended, to deprive myself of the good advice which I never wanted more;
and might encourage him to think I did not resent it as I
ought, and would keep worse secrets, and so make him do
worse by me. Was I right, my dear mother?

Mrs. Jervis could not help mingling tears with my tears;
for I cried all the time I was telling her the story, and
begged her to advise me what to do; and I showed her my
dear father's two letters, and she praised the honesty and
inditing of them, and said pleasing things to me of you
both. But she begged I would not think of leaving my
service; for, said she, in all likelihood, you behaved so
virtuously, that he will be ashamed of what he has done,
and never offer the like to you again: though, my dear
Pamela, said she, I feel more for your prettiness than for
anything else; because the best man in the land might
love you: so she was pleased to say. She wished it was in
her power to live independent; then she would take a

little private house, and I should live with her like her daughter.

And so, as you ordered me to take her advice, I resolved to tarry to see how things went, except he was to turn me away; although, in your first letter, you ordered me to come away the moment I had any reason to be apprehensive. So, dear father and mother, it is not disobedience, I hope, that I stay; for I could not expect a blessing, or the good fruits of your prayers for me, if I was disobedient.

All the next day I was very sad, and began my long letter. He saw me writing, and said (as I mentioned) to Mrs. Jervis, That girl is always scribbling; methinks she might find something else to do, or to that purpose. And when I had finished my letter, I put it under the toilet in my late lady's dressing-room, whither nobody comes but myself and Mrs. Jervis, besides my master; but when I came up again to seal it, to my great concern, it was gone; and Mrs. Jervis knew nothing of it; and nobody knew of my master's having been near the place in the time; so I have been sadly troubled about it: But Mrs. Jervis, as well as I, thinks he has it, somehow or other; and he appears cross and angry, and seems to shun me, as much as he said I did him. It had better be so than worse!

But he has ordered Mrs. Jervis to bid me not pass so much time in writing; which is a poor matter for such a gentleman as he to take notice of, as I am not idle other ways, if he did not resent what he thought I wrote upon. And this has no very good look.

But I am a good deal easier since I lie with Mrs. Jervis; though, after all, the fears I live in on one side, and his frowning and displeasure at what I do on the other, make me more miserable than enough.

Oh that I had never left my little bed in the loft, to be thus exposed to temptations on one hand, or disgusts on the other! How happy was I awhile ago! How contrary now!—Pity and pray for

Your afflicted

PAMELA.

LETTER XIII.

MY DEAREST CHILD,—Our hearts bleed for your distress, and the temptations you are exposed to. You have our hourly prayers; and we would have you flee this evil great house and man, if you find he renews his attempts. You ought to have done it at first, had you not had Mrs. Jervis to advise with. We can find no fault in your conduct hitherto: But it makes our hearts ache for fear of the worst. Oh my child! temptations are sore things; but yet, without them, we know not ourselves, nor what we are able to do.

Your danger is very great; for you have riches, youth, and a fine gentleman, as the world reckons him, to withstand; but how great will be your honour to withstand them! And when we consider your past conduct, and your virtuous education, and that you have been bred to be more ashamed of dishonesty than poverty, we trust in God, that He will enable you to overcome. Yet, as we can't see but your life must be a burthen to you, through the great apprehensions always upon you; and that it may be presumptuous to trust too much to your own strength; and that you are but very young; and the devil may put it into his heart to use some stratagem, of which great men are full, to decoy you; I think you had better come home to share our poverty with safety, than live with so much discontent in a plenty, that itself may be dangerous. God direct you for the best! While you have Mrs. Jervis for an adviser, and bed-fellow (and oh, my dear child! that was prudently done of you), we are easier than we should be; and so committing you to the Divine protection, remain

Your truly loving, but careful,

FATHER AND MOTHER.

—o—

LETTER XIV.

DEAR FATHER AND MOTHER,—Mrs. Jervis and I have lived very comfortably together for this fortnight past; for my master was all that time at his Lincolnshire estate, and at his sister's, the Lady Davers. But he came home yesterday. He had some talk with Mrs. Jervis soon after, and mostly about me. He said to her, it seems, Well, Mrs. Jervis, I know Pamela has your good word; but do you think her of any use in the family? She told me she was surprised at the question, but said, That I was one of the most virtuous and industrious young creatures that ever she knew. Why that word *virtuous*, said he, I pray you? Was there any reason to suppose her otherwise? Or has anybody taken it into his head to *try* her?—I wonder, sir, says she, you ask such a question! Who dare offer anything to her in such an orderly and well-governed house as yours, and under a master of so good a character for virtue and honour? Your servant, Mrs. Jervis, says he, for your good opinion; but pray, if anybody *did*, do you think Pamela would let *you* know it? Why, sir, said she, she is a poor innocent young creature, and I believe has so much confidence in me, that she would take my advice as soon as she would her mother's. *Innocent!* again, and *virtuous*, I warrant! Well, Mrs. Jervis, you abound with your epithets; but I take her to be an artful young baggage; and had I a young handsome butler or steward, she'd soon make her market of one of them, if she thought it worth while to snap at him for a husband. Alack-a-day, sir, said she, it is early days with Pamela; and she does not yet think of a husband, I daresay: and your steward and butler are both men in years, and think nothing of the matter. No, said he, if they were younger, they'd have more wit than to think of such a girl; I'll tell you my mind of her, Mrs. Jervis: I don't think this same favourite of yours so very artless a girl as you imagine. I am not to dispute with your honour, said Mrs. Jervis; but I daresay, if the men will let her alone, she'll never trouble herself about them. Why, Mrs. Jervis, said he, are there any men that will not let her alone, that you know of? No, indeed, sir, said she; she keeps herself so much to herself, and yet behaves so prudently, that they all esteem her, and show her as great a respect as if she was a gentlewoman born.

Ay, says he, that's her art, that I was speaking of: but, let me tell you, the girl has vanity and conceit, and pride too, or I am mistaken; and, perhaps, I could give you an instance of it. Sir, said she, you can see farther than such a poor silly woman as I am; but I never saw anything but innocence in her.—And *virtue* too, I'll warrant ye! said he. But suppose I could give you an instance, where she has talked a little too freely of the kindnesses that have been shown her from a *certain quarter*; and has had the vanity to impute a few kind words, uttered in mere compassion to her youth and circumstances, into a design upon her, and even dared to make free with names that she ought never to mention but with reverence and gratitude; what would you say to that?—Say, sir! said she, I cannot tell what to say. But I hope Pamela incapable of such ingratitude.

Well, no more of this silly girl, says he; you may only advise her, as you are her friend, not to give herself too much licence upon the favours she meets with; and if she stays here, that she will not write the affairs of my family purely for an exercise to her pen, and her invention. I tell you she is a subtle, artful gipsy, and time will show it you.

Was ever the like heard, my dear father and mother? It is plain he did not expect to meet with such a repulse, and mistrusts that I have told Mrs. Jervis, and has my long letter too, that I intended for you; and so is vexed to the heart. But I can't help it. I had better be thought artful and subtle, than be so, in *his* sense; and, as light as he makes of the words *virtue* and *innocence* in me, he would have made a less angry construction, had I less deserved that he should do so; for then, may be, my *crime* should

have been my *virtue* with him; naughty gentleman as
he is!

' I will soon write again; but must now end with saying,
that I am, and shall always be,

Your honest DAUGHTER.

———o———

LETTER XV.

DEAR MOTHER,—I broke off abruptly my last letter; for
I feared he was coming; and so it happened. I put the
letter in my bosom, and took up my work, which lay by me;
but I had so little of the *artful*, as he called it, that I looked
as confused as if I had been doing some great harm.

Sit still, Pamela, said he, mind your work, for all me.
You don't tell me·I am welcome home, after my journey to
Lincolnshire.—It would be hard, sir, said I, if you was not
always welcome to your honour's own house.

I would have gone; but he said, Don't run away, I tell
you. I have a word or two to say to you. Good sirs, how
my heart went pit-a-pat! When I was a *little kind* to you,
said he, in the summer-house, and you carried yourself so
foolishly upon it, as if I had intended to do you great harm,
did I not tell you you should take no notice of what passed
to any creature? and yet you have made a common talk of
the matter, not considering either my reputation, or your
own.—I made a common talk of it, sir! said I: I have
nobody to talk to, hardly.

He interrupted me, and said, *Hardly!* you little equivocator! what do you mean by *hardly?* Let me ask you,
have not you told Mrs. Jervis for one? Pray your honour,
said I, all in agitation, let me go down; for it is not for
me to hold an argument with your honour. Equivocator,
again! said he, and took my hand, what do you talk of an
argument? Is it holding an argument with me to answer
a plain question? Answer me what I asked. Oh, good sir,

said I, let me beg you will not urge me farther, for fear I forget myself again, and be saucy.

Answer me then, I bid you, says he, have you not told Mrs. Jervis? It will be saucy in you if you don't answer me directly to what I ask. Sir, said I, and fain would have pulled my hand away, perhaps I should be for answering you by another question, and that would not become me. What is it you would say? replies he; speak out.

Then, sir, said I, why should your honour be so angry I should tell Mrs. Jervis, or anybody else, what passed, if you intended no harm?

Well said, pretty *innocent* and *artless!* as Mrs. Jervis calls you, said he; and is it thus you taunt and retort upon me, insolent as you are! But still I will be answered directly to my question. Why then, sir, said I, I will not tell a lie for the world: I *did* tell Mrs. Jervis; for my heart was almost broken; but I opened not my mouth to any other. Very well, bold-face, said he, and equivocator again! You did not open your *mouth* to any other; but did not you write to some other? Why now, and please your honour, said I (for I was quite courageous just then), you could not have asked me this question, if you had not taken from me my letter to my father and mother, in which I own I had broken my mind freely to them, and asked their advice, and poured forth my griefs!

And so I am to be exposed, am I, said he, *in* my own house, and *out* of my house, to the whole world, by such a saucebox as you? No, good sir, said I, and I hope your honour won't be angry with me; it is not I that expose you, if I say nothing but the truth. So, taunting again! Assurance as you are! said he: I will not be thus talked to!

Pray, sir, said I, of whom can a poor girl take advice, if it must not be of her father and mother, and such a good woman as Mrs. Jervis, who, for her sex-sake, should give it me when asked? Insolence! said he, and stamped with his foot, am I to be questioned thus by such a one as you? I fell down on my knees, and said, For Heaven's sake, your honour, pity a poor creature, that knows nothing of her duty, but how to cherish her virtue and good name: I have nothing else to trust to; and, though poor and friendless here, yet I have always been taught to value honesty above my life. Here's ado with your honesty, said he, foolish girl! Is it not one part of honesty to be dutiful and grateful to your master, do you think? Indeed, sir, said I, it is impossible I should be ungrateful to your honour, or disobedient, or deserve the names of bold-face and insolent, which you call me, but when your commands are contrary to that first duty which shall ever be the principle of my life!

He seemed to be moved, and rose up, and walked into the great chamber two or three turns, leaving me on my knees; and I threw my apron over my face, and laid my head on a chair, and cried as if my heart would break, having no power to stir.

At last he came in again, but, alas! with mischief in his heart! and raising me up, he said, Rise, Pamela, rise; you are your own enemy. Your perverse folly will be your ruin: I tell you this, that I am very much displeased with the freedoms you have taken with my name to my housekeeper, as also to your father and mother; and you may as well have *real* cause to take these freedoms with me, as to make my name suffer for *imaginary* ones. And saying so, he offered to take me on his knee, with some force. Oh how I was terrified! I said, like as I had read in a book a night or two before, Angels and saints, and all the host of heaven, defend me! And may I never survive, one moment, that fatal one in which I shall forfeit my innocence! Pretty fool! said he, how will you forfeit your innocence, if you are obliged to yield to a force you cannot withstand? Be easy, said he; for let the worst happen that can, *you* will have the merit, and *I* the blame; and it will be a good subject for letters to your father and mother, and a tale into the bargain for Mrs. Jervis.

He by force kissed my neck and lips; and said, Whoever blamed *Lucretia?* All the shame lay on the ravisher only: and I am content to take all the blame upon me, as I have already borne too great a share for what I have not deserved. May I, said I, *Lucretia* like, justify myself with my death, if I am used barbarously! Oh, my good girl, said he tauntingly, you are well read, I see; and we shall make out between us, before we have done, a pretty story in romance, I warrant ye.

He then put his hand in my bosom, and indignation gave me double strength, and I got loose from him by a sudden spring, and ran out of the room! and the next chamber being open, I made shift to get into it, and threw to the door, and it locked after me; but he followed me so close, he got hold of my gown, and tore a piece off, which hung without the door; for the key was on the inside.

I just remember I got into the room; for I knew nothing further of the matter till afterwards; for I fell into a fit with my terror, and there I lay, till he, as I suppose, looking through the key-hole, 'spyed me upon the floor, stretched out at length, on my face; and then he called Mrs. Jervis to me, who, by his assistance, bursting open the door, he went away, seeing me coming to myself; and bid her say nothing of the matter, if she was wise.

Poor Mrs. Jervis thought it was worse, and cried over me like as if she was my mother; and I was two hours before I came to myself; and just as I got a little up on my feet, he coming in, I fainted away again with the terror; and so he withdrew: but he stayed in the next room to let nobody come near us, that his foul proceedings might not be known.

Mrs. Jervis gave me her smelling-bottle, and had cut my laces, and set me in a great chair, and he called her to him: How is the girl? said he: I never saw such a fool in my life. I did nothing at all to her. Mrs. Jervis could not speak for crying. So he said, She has told you, it seems, that I was kind to her in the summer-house, though, I'll assure you, I was quite innocent then as well as now; and I desire you to keep this matter to yourself, and let *me* not be named in it.

Oh, sir, said she, for your honour's sake, and for Christ's sake!—But he would not hear her, and said—For *your own* sake, I tell you, Mrs. Jervis, say not a word more. I have done her no harm. And I won't have her stay in my house; prating, perverse fool, as she is! But since she is so apt to fall into fits, or at least pretend to do so, prepare her to see me to-morrow after dinner, in my mother's closet, and do you be with her, and you shall hear what passes between us.

And so he went out in a pet, and ordered his chariot and four to be got ready, and went a visiting somewhere.

Mrs. Jervis then came to me, and I told her all that had happened, and said, I was resolved not to stay in the house: And she replying, He seemed to threaten as much; I said, I am glad of that; then I shall be easy. So she told me all he had said to her, as above.

Mrs. Jervis is very loath I should go; and yet, poor woman! she begins to be afraid for herself; but would not have me ruined for the world. She says to be sure he means no good; but may be, now he sees me so resolute, he will give over all attempts: and that I shall better know what to do after to-morrow, when I am to appear before a very bad judge, I doubt.

Oh how I dread this to-morrow's appearance! But be as assured, my dear parents, of the honesty of your poor child, as I am of your prayers for

Your dutiful DAUGHTER.

Oh this frightful to-morrow; how I dread it!

—*o*—

LETTER XVI.

MY DEAR PARENTS,—I know you longed to hear from me soon; and I send you as soon as I could.

Well, you may believe how uneasily I passed the time, till his appointed hour came. Every minute, as it grew nearer, my terrors increased; and sometimes I had great courage, and sometimes none at all; and I thought I should faint when it came to the time my master had dined. I

could neither eat nor drink, for my part; and do what I
could, my eyes were swelled with crying.

At last he went up to the closet, which was my good
lady's dressing-room; a room I once loved, but then as
much hated.

Don't your heart ache for me?—I am sure mine fluttered
about like a new-caught bird in a cage. O Pamela! said I
to myself, why art thou so foolish and fearful? Thou hast
done no harm! What, if thou fearest an unjust judge,
when thou art innocent, would'st thou do before a just one,
if thou wert guilty? Have courage, Pamela, thou knowest
the worst! And how easy a choice poverty and honesty is,
rather than plenty and wickedness.

So I cheered myself; but yet my poor heart sunk, and
my spirits were quite broken. Everything that stirred, I
thought was to call me to my account. I dreaded it, and
yet I wished it to come.

Well, at last he rung the bell: Oh, thought I, that it was
my passing-bell! Mrs. Jervis went up, with a full heart
enough, poor good woman! He said, Where's Pamela?
Let her come up, and do you come with her. She came
to me: I was ready to go with my feet; but my heart was
with my dear father and mother, wishing to share your
poverty and happiness. I went up, however.

Oh how can wicked men seem so steady and untouched
with such black hearts, while poor innocents stand like
malefactors before them!

He looked so stern, that my heart failed me, and I wished
myself anywhere but there, though I had before been sum-
moning up all my courage. Good Heaven, said I to myself,
give me courage to stand before this naughty master! Oh
soften him, or harden me!

Come in, fool, said he angrily, as soon as he saw me
(and snatched my hand with a pull); you may well be
ashamed to see me, after your noise and nonsense, and
exposing me as you have done. I ashamed to see *you!*
thought I: Very pretty indeed!—But I said nothing.

Mrs. Jervis, said he, here you are both together. Do

you sit down; but let her stand, if she will. Ay, thought
I, if I *can ;* for my knees beat one against the other. Did
you not think, when you saw the girl in the way you found
her in, that I had given her the greatest occasion for complaint, that could possibly be given to a woman? And that
I had actually ruined her, as she calls it? Tell me, *could*
you think anything less? Indeed, said she, I feared so at
first. Has she told you what I did to her, and *all* I did to
her, to occasion all this folly, by which my reputation
might have suffered in your opinion, and in that of all the
family.—Inform me, what she has told you?

She was a little too much frightened, as she owned afterwards, at his sternness, and said, Indeed she told me you
only pulled her on your knee, and kissed her.

Then I plucked up my spirits a little. *Only !* Mrs.
Jervis? said I; and was not that enough to show me what
I had to fear? When a master of his honour's degree demeans himself to be so free as *that* to such a poor servant
as me, what is the next to be expected?—But your honour
went further, so you did; and threatened me what you
would do, and talked of *Lucretia,* and her hard fate.—
Your honour knows you went too far for a master to a
servant, or even to his equal; and I cannot bear it. So I
fell a crying most sadly.

Mrs. Jervis began to excuse me, and to beg he would pity a
poor maiden, that had such a value for her reputation. He
said, I speak it to her face, I think her very pretty, and
I thought her humble, and one that would not grow upon
my favours, or the notice I took of her; but I abhor the
thoughts of forcing her to anything. I know myself better,
said he, and what belongs to me: And to be sure I have
enough demeaned myself to take notice of such a one as she;
but I was bewitched by her, I think, to be freer than became
me; though I had no intention to carry the jest farther.

What poor stuff was all this, my dear mother, from a
man of his sense! But see how a bad cause and bad actions
confound the greatest wits!—It gave me a little more courage then; for innocence, I find, in a low fortune, and

weak mind, has many advantages over guilt, with all its
riches and wisdom.

So I said, Your honour may call this jest or sport, or
what you please; but indeed, sir, it is not a jest that becomes the distance between a master and a servant. Do
you hear, Mrs. Jervis? said he: do you hear the pertness
of the creature? I had a good deal of this sort before in
the summer-house, and yesterday too, which made me
rougher with her than perhaps I had otherwise been.

Says Mrs. Jervis, Pamela, don't be so pert to his honour:
you should know your distance; you see his honour was
only in jest.—Oh dear Mrs. Jervis, said I, don't *you* blame
me too. It is very difficult to keep one's distance to the
greatest of men, when they won't keep it themselves to
their meanest servants.

See again! said he; could you believe this of the young
baggage, if you had not heard it? Good your honour,
said the well-meaning gentlewoman, pity and forgive the
poor girl; she is but a girl, and her virtue is very dear to
her; and I will pawn my life for her, she will never be
pert to your honour, if you'll be so good as to molest her
no more, nor frighten her again. You saw, sir, by her fit,
she was in terror; she could not help it; and though your
honour intended her no harm, yet the apprehension was
almost death to her: and I had much ado to bring her to
herself again. Oh the little hypocrite! said he; she has
all the arts of her sex; they were *born* with her; and I
told you awhile ago you did not know her. But this was
not the reason principally of my calling you before me
together. I find I am likely to suffer in my reputation by
the perverseness and folly of this girl. She has told you
all, and perhaps more than all; nay, I make no doubt of
it; and she has written letters (for I find she is a mighty
letter-writer!) to her father and mother, and others, as far
as I know, in which representing herself as an angel of
light, she makes her kind master and benefactor, a devil
incarnate—(Oh how people will sometimes, thought I, call
themselves by their right names!)—And all this, added he,

I won't bear; and so I am resolved she shall return to the
distresses and poverty she was taken from; and let her be
careful how she uses my name with freedom, when she is
gone from me.

I was brightened up at once with these welcome words,
and I threw myself upon my knees at his feet, with a most
sincere glad heart; and I said, May your honour be for
ever blessed for your resolution! Now I shall be happy.
And permit me, on my bended knees, to thank you for all
the benefits and favours you have heaped upon me; for the
opportunities I have had of improvement and learning,
through my good lady's means, and yours. I will now forget all your honour has offered me: and I promise you, that
I will never let your name pass my lips, but with reverence
and gratitude: and so God Almighty bless your honour, for
ever and ever! Amen.

Then rising from my knees, I went away with another-
guise sort of heart than I came into his presence with: and
so I fell to writing this letter. And thus all is happily over.

And now, my dearest father and mother, expect to see
soon your poor daughter, with an humble and dutiful mind,
returned to you: and don't fear but I know how to be as
happy with you as ever: for I will lie in the loft, as I used
to do; and pray let my little bed be got ready; and I have
a small matter of money, which will buy me a suit of clothes,
fitter for my condition than what I have; and I will get
Mrs. Mumford to help me to some needlework; and fear
not that I shall be a burden to you, if my health continues.
I know I shall be blessed, if not for my own sake, for both
your sakes, who have, in all your trials and misfortunes, preserved so much integrity as makes everybody speak well of
you both. But I hope he will let good Mrs. Jervis give me
a character, for fear it should be thought that I was turned
away for dishonesty.

And so, my dear parents, may you be blest for me, and
I for you! And I will always pray for my master and Mrs.
Jervis. So good-night; for it is late, and I shall be soon
called to bed.

I hope Mrs. Jervis is not angry with me. She has not
called me to supper: though I could eat nothing if she had.
But I make no doubt I shall sleep purely to-night, and
dream that I am with you, in my dear, dear, happy loft
once more.

So good-night again, my dear father and mother, says

Your poor honest DAUGHTER.

Perhaps I mayn't come this week, because I must get up
the linen, and leave in order everything belonging to
my place. So send me a line, if you can, to let me
know if I shall be welcome, by John, who will call for
it as he returns. But say nothing of my coming away
to him, as yet: for it will be said I blab everything.

——o——

LETTER XVII.

MY DEAREST DAUGHTER,—Welcome, welcome, ten times
welcome shall you be to us; for you come to us innocent,
and happy, and honest; and you are the staff of our old
age, and our comfort. And though we cannot do for you
as we would, yet, fear not, we shall live happily together;
and what with my diligent labour, and your poor mother's
spinning, and your needlework, I make no doubt we shall
do better and better. Only your poor mother's eyes begin
to fail her; though, I bless God, I am as strong and able,
and willing to labour as ever; and oh, my dear child! your
virtue has made me, I think, stronger and better than I
was before. What blessed things are trials and temptations,
when we have the strength to resist and subdue them!

But I am uneasy about those same four guineas: I think
you should give them back again to your master; and yet
I have broken them. Alas! I have only three left; but I
will borrow the fourth, if I can, part upon my wages, and
part of Mrs. Mumford, and send the whole sum back to
you, that you may return it, against John comes next, if he
comes again before you.

I want to know how you come. I fancy honest John will be glad to bear you company part of the way, if your master is not so cross as to forbid him. And if I know time enough, your mother will go one five miles, and I will go ten on the way, or till I meet you, as far as one holiday will go; for that I can get leave to make on such an occasion.

And we shall receive you with more pleasure than we had at your birth, when all the worst was over; or than we ever had in our lives.

And so God bless you till the happy time comes! say both your mother and I, which is all at present, from

Your truly loving PARENTS.

——o——

LETTER XVIII.

DEAR FATHER AND MOTHER,—I thank you a thousand times for your goodness to me, expressed in your last letter. I now long to get my business done, and come to my new old lot again, as I may call it. I have been quite another thing since my master has turned me off: and as I shall come to you an honest daughter, what pleasure it is to what I should have had, if I could not have seen you but as a guilty one. Well, my writing-time will soon be over, and so I will make use of it now, and tell you all that has happened since my last letter.

I wondered Mrs. Jervis did not call me to sup with her, and feared she was angry; and when I had finished my letter, I longed for her coming to bed. At last she came up, but seemed shy and reserved; and I said, My dear Mrs. Jervis, I am glad to see you: you are not angry with me, I hope? She said she was sorry things had gone so far; and that she had a great deal of talk with my master, after I was gone; that he seemed moved at what I said, and at my falling on my knees to him, and my prayer for him, at my going away. He said I was a strange girl; he

C

knew not what to make of me. And is she gone? said he:
I intended to say something else to her; but she behaved
so oddly, that I had not power to stop her. She asked, if
she should call me again? He said, Yes; and then, No, let
her go; it is best for her and me too; and she shall go,
now I have given her warning. Where she had it, I can't
tell; but I never met with the fellow of her in my life, at
any age. She said, he had ordered her not to tell me all:
but she believed he would never offer anything to me
again; and I might stay, she fancied, if I would beg it as a
favour; though she was not *sure* neither.

I stay! dear Mrs. Jervis, said I; why it is the best news
that could have come to me, that he will let me go. I do
nothing but long to go back again to my *poverty* and *distress*, as he threatened I should; for though I am sure of
the poverty, I shall not have the distress I have had for
some months past, I'll assure you.

Mrs. Jervis, dear good soul! wept over me, and said,
Well, well, Pamela, I did not think I had shown so little
love to you, as that you should express so much joy upon
leaving me. I am sure I never had a child half so dear to
me as you are.

I wept to hear her so good to me, as indeed she has
always been, and said, What would you have me *to do*,
dear Mrs. Jervis? I love you next to my own father and
mother, and to leave you is the chief concern I have at
quitting this place; but I am sure it is certain ruin if I
stay. After such offers, and such threatenings, and his
comparing himself to a wicked ravisher in the very time
of his last offer; and turning it into a jest, that we should
make a pretty story in romance; can I stay and be safe?
Has he not demeaned himself twice? And it behoves me
to beware of the third time, for fear he should lay his
snares surer; for perhaps he did not expect a poor servant
would resist her master so much. And must it not be
looked upon as a sort of warrant for such actions, if I stay
after this? For, I think, when one of our sex finds she is
attempted, it is an encouragement to the attempter to pro-

ceed, if one puts one's self in the way of it, when one can help it : 'Tis neither more nor less than inviting him to think that one forgives, what, in short, ought *not* to be forgiven : Which is no small countenance to foul actions, I'll assure you.

She hugged me to her, and said, *I'll assure you!* Pretty-face, where gottest thou all thy knowledge, and thy good notions, at these years? Thou art a miracle for thy age, and I shall always love thee.—But, do you resolve to leave us, Pamela?

Yes, my dear Mrs. Jervis, said I; for, as matters stand, how can I do otherwise?—But I'll finish the duties of my place first, if I may; and hope you'll give me a character, as to my honesty, that it may not be thought I was turned away for any harm. Ay, that I will, said she; I will give thee such a character as never girl at thy years deserved. And I am sure, said I, I will always love and honour you, as my third-best friend, wherever I go, or whatever becomes of me.

And so we went to bed; and I never waked till 'twas time to rise; which I did as blithe as a bird, and went about my business with great pleasure.

But I believe my master is fearfully angry with me; for he passed by me two or three times, and would not speak to me; and towards evening, he met me in the passage, going into the garden, and said such a word to me as I never heard in my life from him to man, woman, or child ; for he first said, This creature's always in the way, I think. I said, standing up as close as I could (and the entry was wide enough for a coach too), I hope I shan't be long in your honour's way. D—mn you! said he (that was the hard word), for a little witch; I have no patience with you.

I profess I trembled to hear him say so; but I *saw* he was vexed; and, as I am going away, I minded it the less. Well! I see, my dear parents, that when a person will do wicked things, it is no wonder he will speak wicked words. May God keep me out of the way of them both!

Your dutiful DAUGHTER.

LETTER XIX.

DEAR FATHER AND MOTHER,—Our John having an opportunity to go your way, I write again, and send both letters at once. I can't say, yet, when I shall get away, nor how I shall come, because Mrs. Jervis showed my master the waistcoat I am flowering for him, and he said, It looks well enough: I think the creature had best stay till she has finished it.

There is some private talk carried on betwixt him and Mrs. Jervis, that she don't tell me of; but yet she is very kind to me, and I don't mistrust her at all. I should be very base if I did. But to be sure she must oblige him, and keep all his lawful commands; and other, I daresay, she won't keep: She is too good; and loves me too well; but *she* must stay when *I* am gone, and so must get no ill will.

She has been at me again to ask to stay, and humble myself. But what have I done, Mrs. Jervis? said I: if I have been a sauce-box, and a bold-face, and a pert, and a creature, as he calls me, have I not had reason? Do you think I should ever have forgot *myself*, if he had not forgot to act as my *master?* Tell me from your own heart, dear Mrs. Jervis, said I, if you think I could stay and be safe: What would *you* think, or how would *you* act, in *my* case?

My dear Pamela, said she, and kissed me, I don't know how I should act, or what I should think. I hope I should act as *you* do. But I know nobody else that would. My master is a fine gentleman; he has a great deal of wit and sense, and is admired, as I know, by half a dozen ladies, who would think themselves happy in his addresses. He has a noble estate; and yet I believe he loves my good maiden, though his servant, better than all the ladies in the land; and he has tried to overcome it, because you are so much his inferior; and 'tis my opinion he finds he can't; and that vexes his proud heart, and makes him resolve you shan't stay; and so he speaks so cross to you, when he sees you by accident.

Well, but, Mrs. Jervis, said I, let me ask you, if he can stoop to like such a poor girl as me, as perhaps he may (for I have read of things almost as strange, from great men to poor damsels), what can it be *for?*—He may condescend, perhaps, to think I may be good enough for his harlot; and those things don't disgrace men that ruin poor women, as the world goes. And so if I was wicked enough, he would keep me till I was undone, and till his mind changed; for even wicked men, I have read, soon grow weary of wickedness with the same person, and love variety. Well, then, poor Pamela must be turned off, and looked upon as a vile abandoned creature, and everybody would despise her; ay, and *justly* too, Mrs. Jervis; for she that can't keep her virtue, ought to live in disgrace.

But, Mrs. Jervis, continued I, let me tell you, that I hope, if I was sure he would always be kind to me, and never turn me off at all, that I shall have so much grace, as to hate and withstand his temptations, were he not only my master, but my king; and that for the *sin's* sake. This my poor dear parents have always taught me; and I should be a sad wicked creature indeed, if, for the sake of riches or favour, I should forfeit my good name; yea, and worse than any other young body of my sex; because I can so contentedly return to my poverty again, and think it a less disgrace to be obliged to wear rags, and live upon rye-bread and water, as I used to do, than to be a harlot to the greatest man in the world.

Mrs. Jervis lifted up her hands, and had her eyes full of tears. God bless you, my dear love! said she; you are my admiration and delight.—How shall I do to part with you!

Well, good Mrs. Jervis, said I, let me ask you now:—You and he have had some talk, and you *mayn't* be suffered to tell me all. But, do you think, if I was to ask to stay, that he is sorry for what he has done? Ay, and *ashamed* of it too? For I am sure he ought, considering his high

degree, and my low degree, and how I have nothing in the
world to trust to but my honesty: Do you think in *your*
own conscience now (pray answer me truly), that he would
never offer anything to me again, and that I could be safe?

Alas! my dear child, said she, don't put thy home
questions to me, with that pretty becoming earnestness in
thy look. I know this, that he is vexed at what he has
done; he was vexed the *first* time, more vexed the *second*
time.

Yes, said I, and so he will be vexed, I suppose, the *third,*
and the *fourth* time too, till he has quite ruined your poor
maiden; and who will have cause to be vexed then?

Nay, Pamela, said she, don't imagine that I would be
accessory to your ruin for the world. I only can say, that
he has, yet, done you no hurt; and it is no wonder he
should love you, you are so pretty; though so much beneath
him: but, I dare swear for him, he never will offer you
any force.

You say, said I, that he was sorry for his *first* offer in
the summer-house. Well, and how long did his sorrow
last?—Only till he found me by myself; and then he was
worse than before: and so became sorry *again.* And if he
has deigned to love me, and you say can't *help* it, why, he
can't *help* it neither, if he should have an opportunity, a
third time to distress me. And I have read that many a
man has been ashamed of his wicked attempts, when he
has been repulsed, that would never have been ashamed of
them, had he succeeded. Besides, Mrs. Jervis, if he really
intends to offer no *force,* what does *that* mean?—While
you say he can't *help* liking me, for *love* it cannot be—
does it not imply that he hopes to ruin me by my own
consent? I *think,* said I (and I hope I should have grace
to *do* so), that I should not give way to his temptations on
any account; but it would be very presumptuous in me to
rely upon my own strength against a gentleman of his
qualifications and estate, and who is my *master;* and thinks
himself entitled to call me bold-face, and what not! only
for standing on my necessary defence: and that, too, where

the good of my soul and body, and my duty to God and my parents, are all concerned. How then, Mrs. Jervis, said I, can I *ask* or *wish* to stay ?

Well, well, says she, as he seems very desirous you should *not* stay, I hope it is from a good motive ; for fear he should be tempted to disgrace himself as well as you. No, no, Mrs. Jervis, said I; I have thought of that too; for I would be glad to consider him with that duty that becomes me : but then he would have let me go to Lady Davers, and not have hindered my preferment : and he would not have said, I should return to my *poverty* and *distress,* when, by his mother's goodness, I had been lifted out of it; but that he intended to fright me, and *punish* me, as he thought, for not complying with his wickedness : And this shows me well enough what I have to expect from his future goodness, except I will deserve it at his own dear price.

She was silent ; and I added, Well, there's no more to be said ; I must go, that's certain : All my concern will be how to part with *you :* and, indeed, after you, with *every-body ;* for all my fellow-servants have loved me, and you and they will cost me a sigh, and a tear too, now and then, I am sure. And so I fell a crying: I could not help it. For it is a pleasant thing to one to be in a house among a great many fellow-servants, and be beloved by them all.

Nay, I should have told you before now, how kind and civil Mr. Longman our steward is ; vastly courteous, indeed, on all occasions ! And he said once to Mrs. Jervis, he wished he was a young man for my sake ; I should be his wife, and he would settle all he had upon me on marriage : and, you must know, he is reckoned worth a power of money.

I take no pride in this; but bless God, and your good examples, my dear parents, that I have been enabled so to carry myself, as to have everybody's good word : Not but our cook one day, who is a little snappish and cross some-times, said once to me, Why this Pamela of *ours* goes as fine as a lady. See what it is to have a fine face !—I wonder what the girl will come to at last !

She was hot with her work; and I sneaked away; for I seldom go down into the kitchen; and I heard the butler say, Why, Jane, nobody has your good word: What has Mrs. Pamela done to you? I am sure *she* offends nobody. And what, said the peevish wench, have I said to her, *fool-atum;* but that she was pretty? They quarrelled afterwards, I heard: I was sorry for it, but troubled myself no more about it. Forgive this silly prattle, from

Your dutiful Daughter.

Oh! I forgot to say, that I would stay to finish the waistcoat, if I might with safety. Mrs. Jervis tells me I certainly may. I never did a prettier piece of work; and I am up early and late to get it over; for I long to be with you.

——o——

LETTER XX.

Dear Father and Mother,—I did not send my last letters so soon as I hoped, because John (whether my master mistrusts or no, I can't say) had been sent to Lady Davers', instead of Isaac, who used to go; and I could not be so free with, nor so well trust Isaac; though he is very civil to me too. So I was forced to stay till John returned.

As I may not have opportunity to send again soon, and yet, as I know you keep my letters, and read them over and over (so John told me), when you have done work (so much does your kindness make you love all that comes from your poor daughter), and as it may be some little pleasure to me, perhaps, to read them myself, when I am come to you, to remind me of what I have gone through, and how great God's goodness has been to me (which I hope, will further strengthen my good resolutions, that I may not hereafter, from my bad conduct, have reason to condemn myself from my own hand as it were): For all these reasons, I say, I will write as I have time, and as matters happen, and send the scribble to you as I have opportunity; and if I don't every time, in form, subscribe as I ought, I am sure you will always believe, that it is not for want of duty. So I will begin where I left off, about the.talk between Mrs. Jervis and me, for me to ask to stay.

Unknown to Mrs. Jervis, I put a project, as I may call it, in practice. I thought with myself some days ago, Here I shall go home to my poor father and mother, and have nothing on my back, that will be fit for my condition; for how should your poor daughter look with a silk nightgown, silken petticoats, cambric head-clothes, fine holland linen, laced shoes, that were my lady's; and fine stockings! And how in a little while must these have looked, like old cast-offs, indeed, and I looked so for wearing them! And people would have said (for poor folks· are envious as well as rich), See there Goody Andrews' daughter, turned home from her fine place! What a tawdry figure she makes! And how well that garb becomes her poor parents' circum-stances!—And how would they look upon me, thought I to myself, when they should come to be threadbare and worn out? And how should I look, even if I could pur-chase homespun clothes, to dwindle into them one by one, as I got them?—Maybe, an old silk gown, and a linsey-woolsey petticoat, and the like. So, thought I, I had better get myself at once equipped in the dress that will become my condition; and though it may look but poor to what I have been used to wear of late days, yet it will serve me, when I am with you, for a good holiday and *Sunday* suit; and what, by a blessing on my industry, I may, perhaps, make shift to keep up to.

So, as I was saying, unknown to anybody, I bought of farmer Nichols's wife and daughters a good sad-coloured stuff, of their own spinning, enough to make me a gown and two petticoats; and I made robings and facings of a pretty bit of printed calico I had by me.

I had a pretty good camblet quilted coat, that I thought might do tolerably well; and I bought two flannel under-coats; not so good as my swanskin and fine linen ones, but what will keep me warm, if any neighbour should get me to go out to help 'em to milk, now and then, as sometimes I used to do formerly; for I am resolved to do all your good neighbours what kindness I can; and hope to make myself as much beloved about you, as I am here.

I got some pretty good Scotch cloth, and made me, of mornings and nights, when nobody saw me, two shifts; and I have enough left for two shirts, and two shifts, for you my dear father and mother. When I come home, I'll make them for you, and desire your acceptance.

Then I bought of a pedlar two pretty enough round-eared caps, a little straw-hat, and a pair of knit mittens, turned up with white calico; and two pair of ordinary blue worsted hose, that make a smartish appearance, with white clocks, I'll assure you; and two yards of black riband for my shift sleeves, and to serve as a necklace; and when I had 'em all come home, I went and looked upon them once in two hours, for two days together: For, you must know, though I lie with Mrs. Jervis, I keep my own little apartment still for my clothes, and nobody goes thither but myself. You'll say I was no bad housewife to have saved so much money; but my dear good lady was always giving me something.

I believed myself the more obliged to do this, because, as I was turned away for what my good master thought want of duty; and as he expected other returns for his presents than I intended to make him, so I thought it was but just to leave his presents behind me when I went away; for, you know, if I would not earn his wages, why should I have them?

Don't trouble yourself about the four guineas, nor borrow to make them up; for they were given me, with some silver, as I told you, as a perquisite, being what my lady had about her when she died; and, as I hope for no wages, I am so vain as to think I have deserved all that money in the fourteen months, since my lady's death: for she, good soul, overpaid me before, in learning and other kindnesses. Had *she* lived, none of these things might have happened!—But

I ought to be thankful 'tis no worse. Everything will turn about for the best; that's my confidence.

So, as I was saying, I have provided a new and more suitable dress, and I long to appear in it, more than ever I did in any new clothes in my life; for then I shall be soon after with you, and at ease in my mind—But, mum! Here he comes, I believe.—I am, &c.

—o—

LETTER XXI.

My dear Father and Mother,—I was forced to break off; for I feared my master was coming; but it proved to be only Mrs. Jervis. She said, I can't endure you should be so much by yourself, Pamela. And I, said I, dread nothing so much as company; for my heart was up at my mouth now, for fear my master was coming. But I always rejoice to see dear Mrs. Jervis.

Said she, I have had a world of talk with my master about you. I am sorry for it, said I, that I am made of so much consequence as to be talked of by him. Oh, said she, I must not tell you all; but you are of more consequence to him than you think for——

Or *wish* for, said I; for the fruits of being of consequence to him, would make me of none to myself, or anybody else.

Said she, Thou art as witty as any lady in the land: I wonder where thou gottest it. But they must be poor ladies, with such great opportunities, I am sure, if they have no more wit than I.—But let that pass.

I suppose, said I, that I am of so much consequence, however, as to vex him, if it be but to think he can't make a fool of such a one as I; and that is nothing at all, but a rebuke to the pride of his high condition, which he did not expect, and knows not how to put up with.

There is something in that, may be, said she; but, indeed, Pamela, he is very angry with you *too*; and calls you twenty perverse things; wonders at his own folly, to

have shewn you so much favour, as he calls it; which he
was first inclined to, he says, for his mother's sake, and
would have persisted to show you for your own, if you was
not your own enemy.

Nay, now I shan't love you, Mrs. Jervis, said I; you are
going to persuade me to ask to stay, though you know the
hazards I run.—No, said she, he says you *shall* go; for he
thinks it won't be for his reputation to keep you: but he
wished (don't speak of it for the world, Pamela), that he
knew a lady of birth, just such another as yourself, in
person and mind, and he would marry her to-morrow.

I coloured up to the ears at this word; but said, Yet, if
I was the lady of birth, and he would offer to be rude first,
as he has twice done to poor me, I don't know whether I
would have him: For *she* that can bear an insult of that
kind, I should think not worthy to be a gentleman's wife;
any more than *he* would be a gentleman that would offer it.

Nay, now, Pamela, said she, thou carriest thy notions a
great way. Well, dear Mrs. Jervis, said I very seriously,
for I could not help it, I am more full of fears than ever.
I have only to beg of you, as one of the best friends I have
in the world, to say nothing of my asking to stay. To say
my master likes me, when I know what end he aims at, is
abomination to my ears; and I shan't think myself safe till
I am at my poor father's and mother's.

She was a little angry with me, till I assured her that I
had not the least uneasiness on her account, but thought
myself safe under her protection and friendship. And so
we dropt the discourse for that time.

I hope to have finished this ugly waistcoat in two days;
after which I have only some linen to get up, and shall
then let you know how I contrive as to my passage; for
the heavy rains will make it sad travelling on foot: but
may be I may get a place to ——, which is ten miles of
the way, in farmer Nichols's close cart; for I can't sit a
horse well at all, and may be nobody will be suffered to see
me on upon the way. But I hope to let you know more

From, &c.

LETTER XXII.

My dear Father and Mother,—All my fellow-servants have now some notion that I am to go away; but can't imagine for what. Mrs. Jervis tells them, that my father and mother, growing in years, cannot live without me; and so I go home to them, to help to comfort their old age; but they seem not to believe it.

What they found it out by was, the butler heard him say to me, as I passed by him, in the entry leading to the hall, Who's that? Pamela, sir, said I. Pamela! said he, How long are *you* to stay here?—Only, please your honour, said I, till I have done the waistcoat; and it is almost finished.—You might, says he (very roughly indeed), have finished that long enough ago, I should have thought. Indeed, and please your honour, said I, I have worked early and late upon it; there is a great deal of work in it.—*Work in it!* said he; you mind your pen more than your needle; I don't want such idle sluts to stay in my house.

He seemed startled, when he saw the butler, as he entered the hall, where Mr. Jonathan stood. What do *you* here? said he.—The butler was as much confounded as I; for, never having been taxed so roughly, I could not help crying sadly; and got out of both their ways to Mrs. Jervis, and told my complaint. This love, said she, is the d——! In how many strange shapes does it make people show themselves! And in some the farthest from their hearts.

'So one, and then another, has been since whispering, Pray, Mrs. Jervis, are we to lose Mrs. Pamela? as they always call me—What has she done? And she tells them, as above, about going home to you.

She said afterwards to me, Well, Pamela, you have made our master, from the sweetest-tempered gentleman in the world, one of the most peevish. But you have it in your power to make him as sweet-tempered as ever; though I hope you'll never do it on his terms.

This was very good in Mrs. Jervis; but it intimated, that she thought as ill of his designs as I; and as she knew his mind more than I, it convinced me that I ought to get away as fast as I could.

My master came in, just now, to speak to Mrs. Jervis about household matters, having some company to dine with him to-morrow; and I stood up, and having been crying at his roughness in the entry, I turned away my face.

You may well, said he, turn away your cursed face; I wish I had never seen it!—Mrs. Jervis, how long is she to be about this waistcoat?

Sir, said I, if your honour had pleased, I would have taken it with me; and though it would be now finished in a few hours, I will do so still; and remove this hated poor Pamela out of your house and sight for ever.

Mrs. Jervis, said he, not speaking to me, I believe this little slut has the power of witchcraft, if ever there was a witch; for she enchants all that come near her. She makes even *you*, who should know better what the world is, think her an angel of light.

I offered to go away; for I believe he wanted me to ask to stay in my place, for all this his great wrath: and he said, Stay here! Stay here, when I bid you! and snatched my hand. I trembled, and said, I will! I will! for he hurt my fingers, he grasped me so hard.

He seemed to have a mind to say something to me; but broke off abruptly, and said, Begone! And away I tripped as fast as I could: and he and Mrs. Jervis had a deal of talk, as she told me; and among the rest, he expressed himself vexed to have spoken in Mr. Jonathan's hearing.

Now you must know, that Mr. Jonathan, our butler, is a very grave good sort of old man, with his hair as white as silver! and an honest worthy man he is. I was hurrying out with a flea in my ear, as the saying is, and going down stairs into the parlour, met him. He took hold of my hand (in a gentler manner, though, than my master) with both his; and he said, Ah! sweet, sweet Mrs. Pamela! what is it I

heard but just now!—I am sorry at my heart; but I am
sure I will sooner believe *anybody* in fault than *you*. Thank
you, Mr. Jonathan, said I; but as you value your place,
don't be seen speaking to such a one as me. I cried too;
and slipt away as fast as I could from him, for his own sake,
lest he should be seen to pity me.

And now I will give you an instance how much I am in
Mr. Longman's esteem also.

I had lost my pen somehow; and my paper being written
out, I stepped to Mr. Longman's, our steward's, office, to
beg him to give me a pen or two, and a sheet or two of
paper. He said, Ay, that I will, my sweet maiden! and
gave me three pens, some wafers, a stick of wax, and twelve
sheets of paper; and coming from his desk, where he was
writing, he said, Let me have a word or two with you, my
sweet little mistress: (for so these two good old gentlemen
often call me; for I believe they love me dearly:) I hear
bad news; that we are going to lose you: I hope it is not
true. Yes it is, sir, said I; but I was in hopes it would not
be known till I went away.

What a d—l, said he, ails our master of late! I never
saw such an alteration in any man in my life! He is pleased
with nobody as I see; and by what Mr. Jonathan tells me
just now, he was quite out of the way with you. What
could *you* have done to him, tro'? Only Mrs. Jervis is a
very good woman, or I should have feared *she* had been your
enemy.

No, said I, nothing like it. Mrs. Jervis is a just good
woman; and, next to my father and mother, the best friend
I have in the world.—Well, then, said he, it must be worse.
Shall I guess? You are too *pretty*, my sweet mistress, and,
may be, too *virtuous*. Ah! have I not hit it? No, good
Mr. Longman, said I, don't think anything amiss of my
master; he is cross and angry with me indeed, that's true;
but I may have given occasion for it, possibly; and because
I am desirous to go to my father and mother, rather than
stay here, perhaps he may think me ungrateful. But, you
know, sir, said I, that a father and mother's comfort is the

dearest thing to a good child that can be. Sweet excellence! said he, this becomes *you ;* but I know the world and
mankind too well; though I must hear, and see, and say
nothing. And so a blessing attend my little sweeting,
said he, wherever you go! And away went I with a courtesy
and thanks.

Now this pleases one, my dear father and mother, to be
so beloved.—How much better, by good fame and integrity,
is it to get every one's good word but *one*, than, by *pleasing
that one*, to make *every one else* one's enemy, and be an
execrable creature besides! I am, &c.

---o---

LETTER XXIII.

My dear Father and Mother,—We had a great many
neighbouring gentlemen, and their ladies, this day at dinner;
and my master made a fine entertainment for them: and
Isaac, and Mr Jonathan, and Benjamin waited at table:
And Isaac tells Mrs. Jervis that the ladies will by and by
come to see the house, and have the curiosity to see me; for,
it seems, they said to my master, when the jokes flew about,
Well, Mr. B——, we understand you have a servant-maid,
who is the greatest beauty in the county; and we promise
ourselves to see her before we go.

The wench is well enough, said he; but no such beauty
as you talk of, I'll assure ye. She was my mother's
waiting-maid, who, on her death-bed, engaged me to be
kind to her. She is young, and every thing is *pretty* that
is *young*.

Ay, ay, said one of the ladies, that's true; but if your
mother had *not* recommended her so strongly, there is so
much merit in beauty, that I make no doubt such a fine
gentleman would have wanted no inducement to be kind
to it.

They all laughed at my master: And he, it seems,
laughed for company; but said, I don't know how it is,

but I see with different eyes from other people; for I have heard much more talk of her prettiness than I think it deserves: She is well enough, as I said; but her greatest excellence is, that she is humble, and courteous, and faithful, and makes all her fellow-servants love her: My house-keeper, in particular, doats upon her; and you know, ladies, she is a woman of discernment: And, as for Mr. Longman, and Jonathan, here, if they thought themselves young enough, I am told, they would fight for her. Is it not true, Jonathan? Troth, sir, said he, an't please your honour, I never knew her peer, and all your honour's family are of the same mind. Do you hear now? said my master.—Well, said the ladies, we will make a visit to Mrs. Jervis by and by, and hope to see this paragon.

I believe they are coming; and will tell you the rest by and by. I wish they had come, and were gone. Why can't they make their game without me?

Well, these fine ladies have been here, and are gone back again. I would have been absent, if I could, and did step into the closet: so they saw me when they came in.

There were four of them, Lady Arthur at the great white house on the hill, Lady Brooks, Lady Towers, and the other, it seems, a countess, of some hard name, I forget what.

So, Mrs. Jervis, says one of the ladies, how do you do? We are all come to inquire after your health. I am much obliged to your ladyships, said Mrs. Jervis: Will your ladyships please to sit down? But, said the countess, we are not *only* come to ask after Mrs. Jervis's health neither; but we are come to see a rarity besides. Ah, says Lady Arthur, I have not seen your Pamela these two years, and they tell me she is grown wondrous pretty in that time.

Then I wished I had not been in the closet; for when I came out, they must needs know I heard them; but I have often found, that bashful bodies owe themselves a spite, and frequently confound themselves more, by endeavouring to avoid confusion.

Why, yes, says Mrs. Jervis, Pamela is very pretty indeed;

she's but in the closet there:—Pamela, pray step hither.
I came out, all covered with blushes, and they smiled at
one another.

The countess took me by the hand: Why, indeed, she
was pleased to say, report has not been too lavish, I'll
assure you. Don't be ashamed child (and stared full in
my face); I wish I had just such a face to be ashamed of.
Oh how like a fool I looked!

Lady Arthur said, Ay, my good Pamela, I say as her
ladyship says: Don't be so confused; though, indeed, it
becomes you too. I think your good lady departed made
a sweet choice of such a pretty attendant. She would have
been mighty proud of you, as she always was praising you,
had she lived till now.

Ah! madam, said Lady Brooks, do you think that so
dutiful a son as our neighbour, who always *admired* what
his mother *loved*, does not pride himself, for all what he
said at table, in such a pretty maiden?

She looked with such a malicious sneering countenance,
I can't abide her.

Lady Towers said with a free air (for it seems she is
called a wit), Well, Mrs. Pamela, I can't say I like you so
well as these ladies do; for I should never care, if you were
my servant, to have *you* and your *master* in the same house
together. Then they all set up a great laugh.

I know what I could have said, if I durst. But they are
ladies—and ladies may say anything.

Says Lady Towers, Can the pretty image speak, Mrs.
Jervis? I vow she has speaking eyes! Oh you little rogue,
said she, and tapped me on the cheek, you seem born to
undo, or to be undone!

God forbid, and please your ladyship, said I, it should
be *either!*—I beg, said I, to withdraw; for the sense
I have of my unworthiness renders me unfit for such a
presence.

I then went away, with one of my best courtesies; and
Lady Towers said, as I went out, Prettily said, I vow!—
And Lady Brooks said, See that shape! I never saw such

a face and shape in my life; why, she must be better descended than you have told me!

And so they run on for half an hour more in my praises, as I was told; and glad was I, when I got out of the hearing of them.

But, it seems, they went down with *such* a story to my master, and so full of *me*, that he had much ado to stand it; but as it was very little to my reputation, I am sure I could take no pride in it; and I feared it would make no better for me. This gives me another cause for wishing myself out of this house.

This is Thursday morning, and next Thursday I hope to set out; for I have finished my task, and my master is horrid cross! And I am vexed his crossness affects me so. If ever he had any kindness towards me, I believe he now hates me heartily.

Is it not strange, that love borders so much upon hate? But this wicked love is not like the true virtuous love, to be sure: *that* and *hatred* must be as far off as *light* and *darkness*. And how must this hate have been increased, if he had met with a base compliance, after his wicked will had been gratified?

Well, one may see by a little, what a great deal means. For if *innocence* cannot attract common civility, what must *guilt* expect, when novelty has ceased to have its charms, and changeableness had taken place of it? Thus we read in Holy Writ, that wicked Amnon, when he had ruined poor Tamar, hated her more than ever he loved her, and would have turned her out of door.

How happy am I, to be turned out of door, with that sweet companion 'my innocence!—Oh may that be always my companion! And while I presume not upon my own strength, and am willing to avoid the tempter, I hope the divine grace will assist me.

Forgive me, that I repeat in my letter part of my hourly prayer. I owe everything, next to God's goodness, to your piety and good examples, my dear parents, my dear *poor* parents! I say that word with pleasure; for your *poverty* is my *pride*, as your integrity shall be my imitation.

As soon as I have dined, I will put on my new clothes. I long to have them on. I know I shall surprise Mrs. Jervis with them; for she shan't see me till I am full dressed.—John is come back, and I'll soon send you some of what I have written.—I find he is going early in the morning; and so I'll close here, that I am

Your most dutiful DAUGHTER.

Don't lose your time in meeting me; because I am so uncertain. It is hard if, somehow or other, I can't get a passage to you. But may be my master won't refuse to let John bring me. I can ride behind him, I believe, well enough; for he is very careful, and very honest; and you know John as well as I; for he loves you both. Besides, may be, Mrs. Jervis can put me in some way.

—o—

LETTER XXIV.

DEAR FATHER AND MOTHER,—I shall write on, as long as I stay, though I should have nothing but silliness to write; for I know you divert yourselves on nights with what I write, because it is mine. John tells me how much you long for my coming; but he says, he told you he hoped something would happen to hinder it.

I am glad you did not tell him the occasion of my coming away; for *if* my fellow-servants should guess, it were better so, than to have it from you or me: Besides, I really am concerned, that my master should cast away a thought upon such a poor creature as me; for, besides the disgrace, it has quite turned his temper; and I begin to believe what Mrs. Jervis told me, that he likes me, and can't help it; and yet strives to conquer it; and so finds no way but to be cross to me.

Don't think me presumptuous and conceited; for it is more my concern than my pride, to see such a gentleman so demean himself, and lessen the regard he used to have in the eyes of all his servants, on my account.—But I am to tell you of my new dress to-day.

And so, when I had dined, upstairs I went, and locked myself into my little room. There I tricked myself up as well as I could in my new garb, and put on my round-eared ordinary cap; but with a green knot, however, and my home-spun gown and petticoat, and plain leather shoes; but yet they are what they call Spanish leather; and my ordinary hose, ordinary I mean to what I have been lately used to; though I shall think good yarn may do very well for every day, when I come home. A plain muslin tucker I put on, and my black silk necklace, instead of the French necklace my lady gave me; and put the ear-rings out of my ears; and when I was quite equipped, I took my straw hat in my hand, with its two blue strings, and looked about me in the glass, as proud as anything—To say truth, I never liked myself so well in my life.

Oh the pleasure of descending with ease, innocence, and resignation!—Indeed there is nothing like it! An humble mind, I plainly see, cannot meet with any very shocking disappointment, let fortune's wheel turn round as it will.

So I went down to look for Mrs. Jervis, to see how she liked me.

I met, as I was upon the stairs, our Rachel, who is the housemaid; and she made me a low courtesy, and I found did not know me. So I smiled, and went to the house-keeper's parlour; and there sat good Mrs. Jervis at work, making a shift: and, would you believe it? *she* did not know me at first; but rose up, and pulled off her spectacles; and said, Do you want *me*, forsooth? I could not help laughing, and said, Hey-day! Mrs. Jervis, what! don't you know me?—She stood all in amaze, and looked at me from top to toe: Why, you surprise me, said she; What! Pamela thus metamorphosed! How came this about?

As it happened, in stept my master; and my back being to him, he thought it was a stranger speaking to Mrs. Jervis, and withdrew again: and did not hear her ask, If his honour had any commands for her?—She turned me about and about, and I showed her all my dress, to my under-petticoat; and she said, sitting down, Why, I am all in amaze, I must sit down. What can all this mean? I told her, I had no clothes suitable to my condition when I returned to my father's; and so it was better to begin here, as I was soon to go away, that all my fellow-servants might see I knew how to suit myself to the state I was returning to.

Well, said she, I never knew the like of thee. But this sad preparation for going away (for now I see you are quite in earnest) is what I know not how to get over. Oh my dear Pamela, how can I part with you!

My master rung in the back-parlour, and so I withdrew, and Mrs. Jervis went to attend him. It seems, he said to her, I was coming in to let you know, that I shall go to Lincolnshire, and possibly to my sister Davers's, and be absent some weeks. But, pray, what pretty neat damsel was with you? She says, she smiled, and asked, If his honour did not know who it was? No, said he, I never saw her before. Farmer Nichols, or Farmer Brady, have neither of them such a tight prim lass for a daughter! have they?—Though I did not see her face neither, said he. If your honour won't be angry, said she, I will introduce her into your presence; for I think, says she, she outdoes our Pamela.

Now I did not thank her for this, as I told her afterwards (for it brought a great deal of trouble upon me, as well as crossness, as you shall hear.) That can't be, he was pleased to say. But if you can find an excuse for it, let her come in.

At that she stept to me, and told me, I must go in with her to her master; but, said she, for goodness sake, let him find you out; for he don't know you. Oh fie, Mrs. Jervis, said I, how could you serve me so? Besides, it looks too

free both *in me,* and *to him.* I tell you, said she, you shall
come in; and pray don't reveal yourself till he finds you
out.

So I went in, foolish as I was; though I must have been
seen by him another time, if I had not then. And she
would make me take my straw hat in my hand.

I dropt a low courtesy, but said never a word. I daresay he knew me as soon as he saw my face: but was as
cunning as Lucifer. He came up to me, and took me by
the hand, and said, Whose pretty maiden are you?—I
daresay you are Pamela's sister, you are so like her. So
neat, so clean, so pretty! Why, child, you far surpass your
sister Pamela!

I was all confusion, and would have spoken: but he took
me about the neck: Why, said he, you are very pretty,
child: I would not be so free with your *sister,* you may
believe; but I must kiss *you.*

Oh sir, said I, I am Pamela, indeed I am: indeed I am
Pamela, *her own self!*

He kissed me for all I could do; and said, Impossible!
you are a lovelier girl by half than Pamela; and sure I may
be innocently free with *you,* though I would not do her so
much favour.

This was a sad trick upon me, indeed, and what I could
not expect; and Mrs. Jervis looked like a fool as much as
I, for her officiousness.—At last I got away, and ran out of
the parlour, most sadly vexed, as you may well think.

He talked a good deal to Mrs. Jervis, and at last ordered
me to come in to him. Come in, said he, you little villain!
—for so he called me. (Good sirs! what a name was there!)
—Who is it you put your tricks upon? I was resolved never
to honour your unworthiness, said he, with so much notice
again; and so you must disguise yourself to attract me, and
yet pretend, like an hypocrite as you are——

I was out of patience then: Hold, good sir, said I; don't
impute disguise and hypocrisy to me, above all things; for
I hate them both, mean as I am. I have put on no disguise.—What a plague, said he, for that was his word, do

you mean then by this dress?—Why, and please your
honour, said I, I mean one of the honestest things in the
world. I have been in disguise, indeed, ever since my good
lady your mother took me from my poor parents. I came
to her ladyship so poor and mean, that these clothes I have
on, are a princely suit to those I had then: and her goodness
heaped upon me rich clothes, and other bounties: and as I
am now returning to my poor parents again so soon, I cannot wear those good things without being hooted at; and
so have bought what will be more suitable to my degree,
and be a good holiday-suit too, when I get home.

He then took me in his arms, and presently pushed me
from him. Mrs. Jervis, said he, take the little witch from
me; I can neither bear, nor forbear her—(strange words
these!)—But stay; you shan't go!—Yet begone!—No,
come back again.

I thought he was mad, for my share; for he knew not
what he would have. I was going, however; but he stept
after me, and took hold of my arm, and brought me in
again: I am sure he made my arm black and blue; for the
marks are upon it still. Sir, sir, said I, pray have mercy; I
will, I will come in!

He sat down, and looked at me, and, as I thought afterwards, as sillily as such a poor girl as I. At last, he said,
Well, Mrs. Jervis, as I was telling you, you may permit her
to stay a little longer, till I see if my sister Davers will
have her; if, meantime, she humble herself, and ask this
as a favour, and is sorry for her pertness, and the liberty
she has taken with my character out of the house, and in
the house. Your honour indeed told me so, said Mrs.
Jervis; but I never found her inclinable to think herself
in a fault. Pride and perverseness, said he, with a vengeance! Yet this is your doating-piece!—Well, for once,
I'll submit myself to tell you, hussy, said he to me, you
may stay a fortnight longer, till I see my sister Davers:
Do you hear what I say to you, statue? Can you neither
speak nor be thankful?—Your honour frights me so, said
I, that I can hardly speak: But I will venture to say, that

I have only to beg, as a favour, that I may go to my father and mother.—Why, fool, said he, won't you like to go to wait on my sister Davers? Sir, said I, I was once fond of that honour; but you were pleased to say, I might be in danger from her ladyship's nephew, or he from me.—D—d impertinence! said he; do you hear, Mrs. Jervis, do you hear, how she retorts upon me? Was ever such matchless assurance!——

I then fell a weeping; for Mrs. Jervis said, Fie, Pamela, fie!—And I said, My lot is very hard indeed; I am sure I would hurt nobody; and I have been, it seems, guilty of indiscretions, which have cost me my place, and my master's favour, and so have been turned away: and when the time is come, that I should return to my poor parents, I am not suffered to go quietly. Good your honour, what have I done, that I must be used worse than if I had robbed you?—Robbed me! said he, why so you have, hussy; you *have* robbed me. Who? I, sir? said I; have I robbed you? Why then you are a justice of peace, and may send me to gaol, if you please, and bring me to a trial for my life! If you can prove that I have robbed you, I am sure I ought to die.

Now I was quite ignorant of his meaning; though I did not like it, when it was afterwards explained, neither: And well, thought I, what will this come to at last, if poor Pamela is esteemed a thief! Then I thought in an instant, how I should show my face to my honest poor parents, if I was but suspected.

But, sir, said I, let me ask you but one question, and pray don't let me be called names for it; for I don't mean disrespectfully: Why, if I have done amiss, am I not left to be discharged by your housekeeper, as the other maids have been? And if Jane, or Rachel, or Hannah were to offend, would your honour stoop to take notice of them? And why should you so demean yourself to take notice of me? Pray, sir, if I have not been worse than others, why should I suffer more than others? and why should I not be turned away, and there's an end of it? For indeed I am not of consequence enough for my master to concern himself, and be angry about such a creature as me.

Do you hear, Mrs. Jervis, cried he again, how pertly I am interrogated by this saucy slut? Why, sauce-box, says he, did not my good mother desire me to take care of you? And have you not been always distinguished by me, above a common servant? And does your ingratitude upbraid me for this?

I said something mutteringly, and he vowed he would hear it. I begged excuse; but he insisted upon it. Why then, said I, if your honour must know, I said, That my good lady did not desire your care to extend to the *summer-house*, and her *dressing-room.*

Well, this was a little saucy, you'll say—And he flew into such a passion, that I was forced to run for it; and Mrs. Jervis said, It was happy I got out of the way.

Why what makes him provoke one so, then?—I'm almost sorry for it; but I would be glad to get away at any rate. For I begin to be more fearful now.

Just now Mr. Jonathan sent me these lines—(Bless me! what shall I do?)

‘ Dear Mrs. Pamela, Take care of yourself; for Rachel
‘ heard my master say to Mrs. Jervis, who, she believes,
‘ was pleading for you, Say no more, Mrs. Jervis; for by
‘ G—d I will have her! Burn this instantly.’

Oh pray for your poor daughter. I am called to go to bed by Mrs. Jervis, for it is past eleven; and I am sure she shall hear of it; for all this is owing to her, though she did not mean any harm. But I have been, and am, in a strange fluster; and I suppose too, she'll say, I have been full pert.

Oh my dear father and mother, power and riches never want advocates! But, poor gentlewoman, she cannot live without him: and he has been very good to her.

So good-night. May be I shall send this in the morning; but may be not; so won't conclude; though I can't say too often, that I am (though with great apprehension)

Your most dutiful DAUGHTER.

LETTER XXV.

MY DEAR PARENTS,—Oh let me take up my complaint, and say, Never was poor creature so unhappy, and so barbarously used, as poor Pamela! Indeed, my dear father and mother, my heart's just broke! I can neither write as I should do, nor let it alone, for to whom but you can I vent my griefs, and keep my poor heart from bursting! Wicked, wicked man!—I have no patience when I think of him!—But yet, don't be frightened—for—I hope—I hope, I am honest!—But if my head and my hand will let me, you shall hear all.—Is there no constable nor headborough, though, to take me out of his house? for I am sure I can safely swear the peace against him: But, alas! he is greater than any constable: he is a justice himself: Such a justice deliver me from!—But God Almighty, I hope, in time, will right me—For He knows the innocence of my heart!

John went your way in the morning; but I have been too much distracted to send by him; and have seen nobody but Mrs. Jervis or Rachel, and one I hate to see or be seen by: and indeed I hate now to see anybody. Strange things I have to tell you, that happened since last night, that good Mr. Jonathan's letter, and my master's harshness, put me into such a fluster; but I will not keep you in suspense.

I went to Mrs. Jervis's chamber; and, oh dreadful! my wicked master had hid himself, base gentleman as he is! in her closet, where she has a few books, and chest of drawers, and such like. I little suspected it; though I used, till this sad night, always to look into that closet and another in the room, and under the bed, ever since the summer-house trick; but never found anything; and so I did not do it then, being fully resolved to be angry with Mrs. Jervis for what had happened in the day, and so thought of nothing else.

I sat myself down on one side of the bed, and she on the

other, and we began to undress ourselves; but she on
that side next the wicked closet, that held the worst heart
in the world. So, said Mrs Jervis, you won't speak to
me, Pamela! I find you are angry with me. Why, Mrs.
Jervis, said I, so I am, a little; 'tis a folly to deny it.
You see what I have suffered by your forcing me in to my
master: and a gentlewoman of your years and experience
must needs know, that it was not fit for me to pretend
to be anybody else for my own sake, nor with regard to
my master.

But, said she, who would have thought it would have
turned out so? Ay, said I, little thinking who heard me,
Lucifer always is ready to promote his own work and workmen. You see presently what use he made of it, pretending
not to know me, on purpose to be free with me. And
when he took upon himself to know me, to quarrel with
me, and use me hardly: And you too, said I, to cry, Fie,
fie, Pamela! cut me to the heart: for that encouraged
him.

Do you think, my dear, said she, that I would encourage
him?—I never said so to you before; but, since you have
forced it from me, I must tell you, that, ever since you
consulted me, I have used my utmost endeavours to divert
him from his wicked purposes: and he has promised fair;
but, to say all in a word, he doats upon you; and I begin
to see it is not in his power to help it.

I luckily said nothing of the note from Mr. Jonathan;
for I began to suspect all the world almost: but I said, to
try Mrs. Jervis, Well then, what would you have me do?
You see he is for having me wait on Lady Davers now.

Why, I'll tell you freely, my dear Pamela, said she, and
I trust to your discretion to conceal what I say: my master
has been often desiring me to put you upon asking him
to let you stay——

Yes, said I, Mrs. Jervis, let me interrupt you: I will tell
you why I could not think of that: It was not the pride
of my *heart*, but the pride of my *honesty:* For what must
have been the case? Here my master has been very rude

to me, once and twice; and you say he cannot help it,
though he pretends to be sorry for it: Well, he has given
me warning to leave my place, and uses me very harshly;
perhaps to frighten me to his purposes, as he supposes I
would be fond of staying (as indeed I should, if I could be
safe; for I love you and all the house, and value him, if
he would act as my master). Well then, as I know his
designs, and that he owns he cannot help it; must I have
asked to stay, knowing he would attempt me again? for
all you could assure me of, was, he would do nothing by
force; so I, a poor weak girl, was to be left to my own
strength! And was not this to *allow* him to tempt me, as
one may say? and to encourage him to go on in his wicked
devices?—How then, Mrs. Jervis, could I ask or wish to
stay?

You say well, my dear child, says she; and you have a
justness of thought above your years; and for all these
considerations, and for what I have heard this day, after
you ran away (and I am glad you went as you did), I cannot persuade you to stay; and I shall be glad (which is
what I never thought I could have said), that you were
well at your father's; for if Lady Davers will entertain
you, she may as well have you from thence as here. There's
my good Mrs. Jervis! said I; God will bless you for your
good counsel to a poor maiden, that is hard beset. But
pray what did he say when I was gone? Why, says she,
he was very angry with you. But he would hear it! said
I: I think it was a little bold; but then he provoked me
to it. And had not my honesty been in the case, I would
not by any means have been so saucy. Besides, Mrs.
Jervis, consider it was the truth; if he does not love to
hear of the *summer-house,* and the *dressing-room,* why
should he not be ashamed to continue in the same mind?
But, said she, when you had muttered this to yourself, you
might have told him anything else. Well, said I, I cannot tell a wilful lie, and so there's an end of it. But I
find you now give him up, and think there's danger in
staying.—Lord bless me! I wish I was well out of the

house; so it was at the bottom of a wet ditch, on the wildest common in England.

Why, said she, it signifies nothing to tell you all he said; but it was enough to make me fear you would not be so safe as I could wish; and, upon my word, Pamela, I don't wonder he loves you; for, without flattery, you are a charming girl! and I never saw you look more lovely in my life than in that same new dress of yours. And then it was such a surprise upon us all!—I believe truly, you owe some of your danger to the lovely *appearance* you made. Then, said I, I wish the clothes in the fire: I expected *no* effect from them; but, if *any*, a quite contrary one.

Hush! said I, Mrs. Jervis, did you not hear something stir in the closet? No, silly girl, said she, your fears are always awake.—But indeed, said I, I think I heard something rustle.—May be, says she, the cat may be got there: but I hear nothing.

I was hush; but she said, Pr'ythee, my good girl, make haste to bed. See if the door be fast. So I did, and was thinking to look into the closet; but, hearing no more noise, thought it needless, and so went again and sat myself down on the bed-side, and went on undressing myself. And Mrs. Jervis, being by this time undressed, stepped into bed, and bid me hasten, for she was sleepy.

I don't know what was the matter, but my heart sadly misgave me: Indeed, Mr. Jonathan's note was enough to make it do so, with what Mrs. Jervis had said. I pulled off my stays, and my stockings, and all my clothes to an under-petticoat; and then hearing a rustling again in the closet, I said, Heaven protect us! but before I say my prayers, I must look into this closet. And so was going to it slip-shod, when, oh dreadful! out rushed my master in a rich silk and silver morning gown.

I screamed, and ran to the bed, and Mrs. Jervis screamed too; and he said, I'll do you no harm, if you forbear this noise; but otherwise take what follows.

Instantly he came to the bed (for I had crept into it, to Mrs. Jervis, with my coat on, and my shoes); and takin'

me in his arms, said, Mrs. Jervis, rise, and just step up
stairs, to keep the maids from coming down at this noise:
I'll do no harm to this rebel.

Oh, for Heaven's sake! for pity's sake! Mrs. Jervis, said
I, if I am not betrayed, don't leave me; and, I beseech
you, raise all the house. No, said Mrs. Jervis, I will not
stir, my dear lamb; I will not leave you. I wonder at
you, sir, said she; and kindly threw herself upon my coat,
clasping me round the waist: You shall not hurt this innocent, said she: for I will lose my life in her defence. Are
there not, said she, enough wicked ones in the world, for
your base purpose, but you must attempt such a lamb as
this?

He was desperate angry, and threatened to throw her
out of the window; and to turn her out of the house the
next morning. You need not, sir, said she; for I will not
stay in it. God defend my poor Pamela till to-morrow,
and we will both go together.—Says he, let me but expostulate a word or two with you, Pamela. Pray, Pamela,
said Mrs. Jervis, don't hear a word, except he leaves the
bed, and goes to the other end of the room. Ay, out of
the room, said I; expostulate to-morrow, if you must expostulate!

I found his hand in my bosom; and when my fright let
me know it, I was ready to die; and I sighed and screamed,
and fainted away. And still he had his arms about my
neck; and Mrs. Jervis was about my feet, and upon my
coat. And all in a cold dewy sweat was I. Pamela!
Pamela! said Mrs. Jervis, as she tells me since, O—h, and
gave another shriek, my poor Pamela is dead for certain!
And so, to be sure, I was for a time; for I knew nothing
more of the matter, one fit following another, till about
three hours after, as it proved to be, I found myself in
bed, and Mrs. Jervis sitting upon one side, with her wrap-
per about her, and Rachel on the other; and no master,
for the wicked wretch was gone. But I was so overjoyed,
that I hardly could believe myself; and I said, which were
my first words, Mrs. Jervis, Mrs. Rachel, can I be *sure* it

is you? Tell me! can I?—Where have I been? Hush, my
dear, said Mrs. Jervis; you have been in fit after fit. I
never saw anybody so frightful in my life!

By this I judged Rachel knew nothing of the matter;
and it seems my wicked master had, upon Mrs. Jervis's
second noise on my fainting away, slipt out, and, as if he
had come from his own chamber, disturbed by the screaming, went up to the maids' room (who, hearing the noise,
lay trembling, and afraid to stir), and bid them go down,
and see what was the matter with Mrs. Jervis and me.
And he charged Mrs. Jervis, and promised to forgive her
for what she had said and done, if she would conceal the
matter. So the maids came down, and all went up again,
when I came to myself a little, except Rachel, who stayed
to sit up with me, and bear Mrs. Jervis company. I believe they all guess the matter to be bad enough; though
they dare not say anything.

When I think of my danger, and the freedoms he actually took, though I believe Mrs. Jervis saved me from
worse, and she said she did (though what can I think, who
was in a fit, and knew nothing of the matter?) I am almost
distracted.

At first I was afraid of Mrs. Jervis; but I am fully satisfied she is very good, and I should have been lost but for
her; and she takes on grievously about it. What would
have become of me, had she gone out of the room, to still
the maids, as he bid her! He'd certainly have shut her
out, and then, mercy on me! what would have become of
your poor Pamela?

I must leave off a little; for my eyes and my head are
sadly bad.—This was a dreadful trial! This was the worst
of all! Oh, that I was out of the power of this dreadfully
wicked man! Pray for

Your distressed DAUGHTER.

———*o*———

LETTER XXVI.

MY DEAR FATHER AND MOTHER,—I did not rise till ten o'clock, and I had all the concerns and wishes of the family, and multitudes of inquiries about me. My wicked master went out early to hunt; but left word he would be in to breakfast. And so he was.

He came up to our chamber about eleven, and had nothing to do to be sorry; for he was our *master*, and so put on sharp anger at first.

I had great emotions at his entering the room, and threw my apron over my head, and fell a crying, as if my heart would break.

Mrs. Jervis, said he, since I know *you*, and you *me* so well, I don't know how we shall live together for the future. Sir, said she, I will take the liberty to say, what I think is best for both. I have so much grief, that you should attempt to do any injury to this poor girl, and especially in my chamber, that I should think myself accessory to the mischief, if I was not to take notice of it. Though my ruin, therefore, may depend upon it, I desire not to stay; but pray let poor Pamela and me go together. With all my heart, said he; and the sooner the better. She fell a crying. I find, says he, this girl has made a party of the whole house in her favour against me. Her innocence deserves it of us all, said she very kindly: and I never could have thought that the son of my dear good lady departed, could have so forfeited his honour, as to endeavour to destroy a virtue he ought to protect. No more of this, Mrs. Jervis! said he; I will not bear it. As for Pamela, she has a lucky knack of falling into fits, when she pleases. But the cursed yellings of you both made me not myself. I intended no harm to her, as I told you both, if you'd have left your squallings: And I did no harm neither, but to myself; for I raised a hornet's nest about my ears, that, as far as I know, may have stung to death my reputation. Sir, said Mrs. Jervis, then I beg Mr. Longman may take my accounts, and I will go away as soon as I can. As for Pamela, she is at her liberty, I hope, to go away next Thursday, as she intends?

I sat still; for I could not speak nor look up, and his presence discomposed me extremely; but I was sorry to hear myself the unhappy occasion of Mrs. Jervis's losing her place, and hope that may be still made up.

Well, said he, let Mr. Longman make up your accounts, as soon as you will; and Mrs. Jewkes (who is his house-keeper in Lincolnshire) shall come hither in your place, and won't be less obliging, I daresay, than *you* have been. Said she, I have never disobliged you till now; and let me tell you, sir, if you knew what belonged to your own reputa-tion or honour—No more, no more, said he, of these anti-quated topics. I have been no bad friend to you; and I shall always esteem you, though you have not been so faith-ful to my secrets as I could have wished, and have laid me open to this girl, which has made her more afraid of me than she had occasion. Well, sir, said she, after what passed yesterday, and last night, I think I went rather too far in favour of your injunctions than otherwise; and I should have deserved everybody's censure, as the basest of creatures, had I been capable of contributing to your lawless attempts. Still, Mrs. Jervis, still reflecting upon me, and all for imaginary faults! for what harm have I done the girl?—I won't bear it, I'll assure you. But yet, in respect to my mother, I am willing to part friendly with you: though you ought both of you to reflect on the freedom of your conversation, in relation to me; which I should have resented more than I do, but that I am conscious I had no business to demean myself so as to be in your closet, where I might have expected to hear a multitude of impertinence between you.

Well, sir, said she, you have no objection, I hope, to Pamela's going away on Thursday next? You are mighty solicitous, said he, about Pamela: But no, not I; let her go as soon as she will: She is a naughty girl, and has brought all this upon herself; and upon me more trouble than she can have had from me: But I have overcome it all, and will never concern myself about her.

I have a proposal made me, added he, since I have been out this morning, that I shall go near to embrace; and so wish only, that a discreet use may be made of what is past ; and there's an end of everything with me, as to Pamela, I'll assure you.

I clasped my hands together through my apron, overjoyed at this, though I was soon to go away: For, naughty as he has been to me, I wish his prosperity with all my heart, for my good old lady's sake.

Well, Pamela, said he, you need not now be afraid to speak to me; tell me what you lifted up your hands at? I said not a word. Says he, If you like what I have said, give me your hand upon it. I held my hand up through my apron; for I could not speak to him; and he took hold of it, and pressed it, though less hard than he did my arm the day before. What does the little fool cover her face for? said he: Pull your apron away; and let me see how you look, after your freedom of speech of me last night. No wonder you are ashamed to see me. You know you were very free with my character.

I could not stand this barbarous insult, as I took it to be, considering his behaviour to me; and I then spoke and said, Oh the difference between the minds of Thy creatures, good God! How shall some be cast down in their innocence, while others can triumph in their guilt!

And so saying, I went up stairs to my chamber, and wrote all this; for though he vexed me at his taunting, yet I was pleased to hear he was likely to be married, and that his wicked intentions were so happily overcome as to me; and this made me a little easier. And I hope I have passed the worst; or else it is very hard. And yet I shan't think myself at ease quite, till I am with you: For, methinks, after all, his repentance and amendment are mighty suddenly resolved upon. But the divine grace is not confined to space; and remorse may, and I hope has, smitten him to the heart at once, for his injuries to poor me! Yet I won't be too secure neither.

Having opportunity, I send now what I know will grieve you to the heart. But I hope I shall bring my next scribble myself; and so conclude, though half broken-hearted,

Your ever dutiful DAUGHTER.

---o---

LETTER XXVII.

DEAR FATHER AND MOTHER,—I am glad I desired you not to meet me, and John says you won't; for he told you he is sure I shall get a passage well enough, either behind some one of my fellow-servants on horseback, or by Farmer Nichols's means: but as to the chariot he talked to you of, I can't expect that favour, to be sure; and I should not care for it, because it would look so much above me. But Farmer Brady, they say, has a chaise with one horse, and we hope to borrow that, or hire it, rather than fail; though money runs a little lowish, after what I have laid out; but I don't care to say so here; though I warrant I might have what I would of Mrs. Jervis, or Mr. Jonathan, or Mr. Longman; but then how shall I pay it? you'll say: And, besides, I don't love to be beholden.

But the chief reason I'm glad you don't set out to meet me, is the uncertainty; for it seems I must stay another week still, and hope certainly to go Thursday after. For poor Mrs. Jervis will go at the same time, she says, and can't be ready before.

Oh! that I was once well with you!—Though he is very civil too at present, and not so cross as he was; and yet he is as vexatious another way, as you shall hear. For yesterday he had a rich suit of clothes brought home, which they call a birthday suit; for he intends to go to London against next birthday, to see the court; and our folks will have it he is to be made a lord.—I wish they may make him an honest man, as he was always thought; but I have not found it so, alas for me!

And so, as I was saying, he had these clothes come home, and he tried them on. And before he pulled them off, he sent for me, when nobody else was in the parlour with him : Pamela, said he, you are so neat and so nice in your own dress (Alack-a-day, I didn't know I was!) that you must be a judge of ours. How are these clothes made? Do they fit me?—I am no judge, said I, and please you honour; but I think they look very fine.

His waistcoat stood on end with silver lace, and he looked very grand. But what he did last has made me very serious, and I could make him no compliments. Said he, Why don't you wear your usual clothes? Though I think every-thing looks well upon you (for I still continue in my new dress). I said, I have no clothes, sir, I ought to call my own, but these: and it is no matter what such an one as I wears. Said he, Why you look very serious, Pamela. I see you can bear malice.—Yes, so I can, sir, said I, accord-ing to the occasion! Why, said he, your eyes always look red, I think. Are you not a fool to take my last freedom so much to heart? I am sure you, and that fool Mrs. Jervis, frightened me, by your hideous squalling, as much as I could frighten you. That is all we had for it, said I; and if you could be so afraid of your own servants knowing of your attempts upon a poor unworthy creature, that is under your protection while I stay, surely your honour ought to be more afraid of God Almighty, in whose presence we all stand, in every action of our lives, and to whom the greatest, as well as the least, must be accountable, let them think what they list.

He took my hand, in a kind of good-humoured mockery, and said, Well urged, my pretty preacher! When my Lincolnshire chaplain dies, I'll put thee on a gown and cassock, and thou'lt make a good figure in his place.—I wish, said I, a little vexed at his jeer, your honour's con-science would be your preacher, and then you would need no other chaplain. Well, well, Pamela, said he, no more of this unfashionable jargon. I did not send for you so much for your opinion of my new suit, as to tell you, you are welcome to stay, since Mrs. Jervis desires it, till she goes. I welcome! said I; I am sure I shall rejoice when I am out of the house!　.

Well, said he, you are an ungrateful baggage; but I am thinking it would be pity, with these fair soft hands, and that lovely skin (as he called it, and took hold of my hand), that you should return again to hard work, as you must if you go to your father's; and so I would advise her to take a house in London, and let lodgings to us members of parliament, when we come to town; and such a pretty daughter as you may pass for, will always fill her house, and she'll get a great deal of money.

I was sadly vexed at this barbarous joke; but being ready to cry before, the tears gushed out, and (endeavouring to get my hand from him, but in vain) I said, I can expect no better: Your behaviour, sir, to me, has been just of a piece with these words: Nay, I will say it, though you were to be ever so angry.—I angry, Pamela? No, no, said he, I have overcome all that; and as you are to go away, I look upon you now as Mrs. Jervis's guest while you both stay, and not as my servant; and so you may say what you will. But I'll tell you, Pamela, why you need not take this matter in such high disdain!—You have a very pretty romantic turn for virtue, and all that.—And I don't suppose but you'll hold it still: and nobody will be able to prevail upon you. But, my child (sneeringly he spoke it), do but consider what a fine opportunity you will then have for a tale every day to good mother Jervis, and what subjects for letter-writing to your father and mother, and what pretty preachments you may hold forth to the young gentlemen. Ad's my heart! I think it would be the best thing you and she could do.

You do well, sir, said I, to even your wit to such a poor maiden as me: but, permit me to say, that if you was not rich and great, and I poor and little, you would not insult me thus.—Let me ask you, sir, if you think this becomes your fine clothes and a master's station ? Why so serious, my pretty Pamela? said he: Why so grave? And would kiss me; but my heart was full, and I said, Let me alone; I *will* tell you, if you was a king, and insulted me as you have done, that you have forgotten to act like a gentleman: and I won't stay to be used thus: I will go to the next farmer's, and there wait for Mrs. Jervis, if she must go: and I'd have you know, sir, that I can stoop to the ordinariest work of your scullions, for all these nasty soft hands, sooner than bear such ungentlemanly imputations.

I sent for you, said he, in high good humour; but it is impossible to hold it with such an impertinent: however, I'll keep my temper. But while I see you here, pray don't put on those dismal grave looks: Why, girl, you should forbear them, if it were but for your pride-sake; for the family will think you are grieving to leave the house. Then, sir, said I, I will try to convince them of the contrary, as well as your honour; for I will endeavour to be more cheerful while I-stay, for that very reason.

Well, replied he, I will set this down by itself, as the first time that ever what I had advised had any weight with you. And I will add, said I, as the first advice you have given me of late, that was fit to be followed.—I wish, said he (I am almost ashamed to write it, impudent gentleman as he is!) I wish I had thee as *quick another way,* as thou art in thy repartees—And he laughed; and I snatched my hand from him, and I tripped away as fast as I could. Ah! thought I, married? I am sure it is time you were married, or, at this rate, no honest maiden ought to live with you.

Why, dear father and mother, to be sure he grows quite a rake! How easy it is to go from bad to worse, when once people give way to vice!

How would my poor lady, had she lived, have grieved to see it! but may be he would have been better *then !*— Though it seems he told Mrs. Jervis, he had an eye upon me in his mother's lifetime; and he intended to let me know as much, by the bye, he told her! Here is shamelessness for you! Sure the world must be near at an end! for all the gentlemen about are as bad as he almost, as far as I can hear!—And see the fruits of such bad examples! There is 'Squire Martin in the grove has had three lyings-in, it seems, in his house, in three months past; one by himself; and one by his coachman; and one by his wood-man; and yet he has turned none of them away. Indeed, how can he, when they but follow his own vile example? There is he, and two or three more such as he, within ten miles of us, who keep company, and hunt with our fine master, truly; and I suppose he is never the better for their examples. But, Heaven bless me, say I, and send me out of this wicked house!

But, dear father and mother, what sort of creatures must the womenkind be, do you think, to give way to such wickedness? Why, this it is that makes every one be thought of alike: And, alack-a-day! what a world we live in! for it is grown more a wonder that the men are *resisted*, than that the women *comply*. This, I suppose, makes me such a sauce-box, and bold-face, and a creature, and all because I won't be a sauce-box and bold-face indeed.

But I am sorry for these things; one don't know what arts and stratagems men may devise to gain their vile ends; and so I will think as well as I can of these poor undone creatures, and pity them. For you see, by my sad story, and narrow escapes, what hardships poor maidens go through, whose lot it is to go out to service, especially to houses where there is not the fear of God, and good rule kept by the heads of the family.

You see I am quite grown grave and serious; indeed it becomes the present condition of

                                    Your dutiful DAUGHTER.

———o———

LETTER XXVIII.

DEAR FATHER AND MOTHER,—John says you wept when you read my last letter, that he carried. I am sorry you let him see that; for they all mistrust already how matters are; and as it is no credit that I have been *attempted*, though it is that I have *resisted;* yet I am sorry they have cause to think so evil of my master from any of us.

Mrs. Jervis has made up her accounts with Mr. Longman, and will stay in her place. I am glad of it, for her own sake, and for my master's; for she has a good master of him; so indeed all have, but poor me—and he has a good housekeeper in her.

Mr. Longman, it seems, took upon him to talk to my master, how faithful and careful of his interests she was, and how exact in her accounts; and he told him, there was no comparison between her accounts and Mrs. Jewkes's, at the Lincolnshire estate.

He said so many fine things, it seems, of Mrs. Jervis, that my master sent for her in Mr. Longman's presence, and said Pamela might come along with her; I suppose to mortify me, that I must go while she was to stay: But as, when I go away, I am not to go with her, nor was she to go with me; so I did not matter it much; only it would have been creditable to such a poor girl, that the housekeeper would bear me company, if I went.

Said he to her, Well, Mrs. Jervis, Longman says you have made up your accounts with him with your usual fidelity and exactness. I had a good mind to make you an offer of continuing with me, if you can be a little sorry for your hasty words, which, indeed, were not so respectful as I have deserved at your hands. She seemed at a sad loss what to say, because Mr. Longman was there, and she could not speak of the occasion of those words, which was *me*.

Indeed, said Mr. Longman, I must needs say before

your face, that since I have known my master's family, I
have never found such good management in it, nor so
much love and harmony neither.   I wish the Lincolnshire
estate was as well served!—No more of that, said my
master; but Mrs. Jervis may stay, if she will: and here,
Mrs. Jervis, pray accept of this, which at the close of
every year's accounts I will present you with, besides your
salary, as long as I find your care so useful and agreeable.
And he gave her five guineas.—She made him a low
courtesy, and thanking him, looked to me, as if she would
have spoken to me.

He took her meaning, I believe; for he said,—Indeed I
love to encourage merit and obligingness, Longman; but
I can never be equally kind to those who don't deserve it
at my hands, as to those who do; and then he looked full
on me.   Longman, continued he, I said that girl might
come in with Mrs. Jervis, because they love to be always
together.   For Mrs. Jervis is very good to her, and loves
her as well as if she was her daughter.   But else—Mr.
Longman, interrupting him, said, *Good* to Mrs. Pamela!
Ay, sir, and so she is, to be sure! But everybody must be
good to her; for——

He was going on: but my master said, No more, no
more, Mr. Longman.   I see old men are taken with pretty
young girls, as well as other folks; and fair looks hide many
a fault, where a person has the art to behave obligingly.
Why, and please your honour, said Mr. Longman, everybody—and was going on, I believe, to say something more
in my praise; but he interrupted him, and said, Not a
word more of this Pamela.   I can't let her stay, I'll assure
you; not only for her own freedom of speech, but her
letter-writing of all the secrets of my family.   Ay, said the
good old man, I am sorry for that too!   But, sir,—No
more, I say, said my master; for my reputation is so well
known (mighty fine, thought I!) that I care not what anybody writes or says of *me:* But to tell you the truth (not
that it need go further), I think of changing my condition
soon; and, you know, young ladies of birth and fortune

will choose their own servants, and that's my chief reason
why Pamela can't stay. As for the rest, said he, the girl is
a good sort of body, take her altogether; though I must
needs say, a little pert, since my mother's death, in her
answers, and gives me two words for one; which I can't ·
bear; nor is there reason I should, you know, Longman.
No, to be sure, sir, said he; but 'tis strange, methinks, she
should be so mild and meek to every one of us in the house,
and forget herself so, where she should show most respect!
Very true, Mr. Longman, said he, but so it is, I'll assure
you; and it was from her pertness, that Mrs. Jervis and I
had the words: And I should mind it the less, but that the
girl (there she stands, I say it to her face) has wit and sense
above her years, and knows better.

I was in great pain to say something, but yet I knew not
what, before Mr. Longman; and Mrs. Jervis looked at me,
and walked to the window to hide her concern for me. At
last, I said, It is for you, sir, to say what you please; and
for *me* only to say, God bless your honour!

Poor Mr. Longman faltered in his speech, and was ready
to cry. Said my. insulting master to me, Why, pr'ythee,
Pamela, now, show thyself as thou art, before Longman.
Canst not give him a specimen of that pertness which thou
hast exercised upon me sometimes.

Did he not, my dear father and mother, deserve all the
truth to be told? Yet I overcame myself so far, as to say,
Well, your honour may play upon a poor girl, that you
know *can* answer you, but *dare* not.

Why, pr'ythee now, insinuator, said he, say the worst
you *can* before Longman and Mrs. Jervis. I challenge the
utmost of thy impertinence; and as you are going away,
and have the love of everybody, I would be a little justified
to my family, that you have no reason to complain of hardships from me, as I have pert saucy answers from you,
besides exposing me by your letters.

Surely, sir, said I, I am of no consequence equal to this,
in your honour's family, that such a great gentleman as
you should need to justify yourself about me. I am glad

Mrs. Jervis stays with your honour; and I know I have not *deserved* to stay; and, more than that, I don't *desire* to stay.

Ads-bobbers! said Mr. Longman, and ran to me; don't say so, don't say so, dear Mrs. Pamela! We all love you dearly; and pray down of your knees, and ask his honour pardon, and we will all become pleaders in a body, and I, and Mrs. Jervis too, at the head of it, to beg his honour's pardon, and to continue you, at least, till his honour marries. —No, Mr. Longman, said I, I cannot ask; nor will I stay, if I might. All I desire is, to return to my poor father and mother: and though I love you all, I won't stay.—Oh well-a-day, well-a-day! said the good old man, I did not expect this!—When I had got matters thus far, and had made all up for Mrs. Jervis, I was in hopes to have got a double holiday of joy for all the family, in your pardon too. Well, said my master, this is a little specimen of what I told you, Longman. You see there's a spirit you did not expect.

Mrs. Jervis told me after, that she could stay no longer, to hear me so hardly used; and must have spoken, had she stayed, what would never have been forgiven her; so she went out. I looked after her to go too; but my master said, Come, Pamela, give another specimen, I desire you, to Longman: I am sure you must, if you will but *speak*. Well, sir, said I, since it seems your greatness wants to be justified by my lowness, and I have no desire you should suffer in the sight of your family, I will say, on my bended knees (and so I kneeled down), that I have been a very faulty, and a very ungrateful creature to the *best* of masters: I have been very perverse and saucy; and have deserved nothing at your hands but to be turned out of your family with shame and disgrace. I, therefore, have nothing to say for myself, but that I am not *worthy* to stay, and so cannot wish to stay, and *will* not stay: And so God Almighty bless you, and you Mr. Longman, and good Mrs. Jervis, and every living soul of the family! and I will pray for you as long as I live!—And so I rose up, and was forced to lean upon my master's elbow-chair, or I should have sunk down.

The poor old man wept more than I, and said, Ads-bobbers, was ever the like heard! 'Tis too much, too much; I can't bear it. As I hope to live, I am quite melted. Dear sir, forgive her! The poor thing prays for you; she prays for us all! She owns her fault; yet *won't* be forgiven! I profess I know not what to make of it.

My master himself, hardened wretch as he was, seemed a little moved, and took his handkerchief out of his pocket, and walked to the window: What sort of a day is it? said he.—And then, getting a little more hard-heartedness, he said, Well, you may be gone from my presence, thou strange medley of inconsistence! but you shan't stay after your time in the house.

Nay, pray, sir, pray, sir, said the good old man, relent a little. Ads-heartikins! you young gentlemen are made of iron and steel, I think: I'm sure, said he, my heart's turned into butter, and is running away at my eyes. I never felt the like before.—Said my master, with an imperious tone, Get out of my presence, hussy! I can't bear you in my sight. Sir, said I, I'm going as fast as I can.

But, indeed, my dear father and mother, my head was so giddy, and my limbs trembled so, that I was forced to go holding by the wainscot all the way with both my hands, and thought I should not have got to the door: But when I did, as I hoped this would be my last interview with this terrible hard-hearted master, I turned about, and made a low courtesy, and said, God bless you, sir! God bless *you*, Mr. Longman! and I went into the lobby leading to the great hall, and dropt into the first chair; for I could get no farther a good while.

I leave all these things to your reflection, my dear parents; but I can write no more. My poor heart's almost broken! Indeed it is.—Oh when shall I get away!—Send me, good God, in safety, once more to my poor father's peaceful cot! —and there the worst that can happen will be joy in per-fection to what I now bear!—Oh pity

Your distressed DAUGHTER.

LETTER XXIX.

My dear Father and Mother,—I must write on, though I shall come so soon; for now I have hardly anything else to do. I have finished all that lay upon me, and only wait the good time of setting out. Mrs. Jervis said, I must be low in pocket, for what I had laid out; and so would have presented me with two guineas of her five; but I could not take them of her, because, poor gentlewoman, she pays old debts for her children, that were extravagant, and wants them herself. This, though, was very good in her.

I am sorry I shall have but little to bring with me; but I know *you* won't, you are so good!—and I will work the harder, when I come home, if I can get a little plain-work, or anything, to do. But all your neighbourhood is so poor, that I fear I shall want work, except, may be, Dame Mumford can help me to something, from any good family she is acquainted with.

Here, what a sad thing it is! I have been brought up wrong, as matters stand. For, you know, my good lady, now in heaven, loved singing and dancing; and, as she would have it, I had a voice, she made me learn both; and often and often has she made me sing her an innocent song, and a good psalm too, and dance before her. And I must learn to flower and draw too, and to work fine work with my needle; why, all this too I have got pretty tolerably at my finger's end, as they say; and she used to praise me, and was a good judge of such matters.

Well now, what is all this to the purpose, as things have turned about?

Why, no more nor less, than that I am like the grass-hopper in the fable, which I have read of in my lady's book, as follows :*—

---

* See the Æsop's Fables which have lately been selected and reformed from those of Sir R. L'Estrange, and the most eminent mythologists.

' As the ants were airing their provisions one winter, a
' hungry grasshopper (as suppose it was poor I) begged a
' charity of them. They told him, That he should have
' wrought in summer, if he would not have wanted in
' winter. Well, says the grasshopper, but I was not idle
' neither; for I sung out the whole season. Nay, then,
' said they, you'll e'en do well to make a merry year of it,
' and dance in winter to the tune you sung in summer.'

So I shall make a fine figure with my singing and my
dancing, when I come home to you! Nay, I shall be unfit
even for a *May-day* holiday-time; for these minuets, riga-
doons, and French dances, that I have been practising, will
make me but ill company for my milk-maid companions
that are to be. To be sure I had better, as things stand,
have learned to wash and scour, and brew and bake, and
such like. But I hope, if I can't get work, and can meet
with a place, to learn these soon, if anybody will have the
goodness to bear with me till I am able: For, notwithstanding what my master says, I hope I have an humble
and teachable mind; and, next to God's grace, that's all
my comfort: for I shall think nothing too mean that is
honest. It may be a little hard at first; but woe to my
proud heart, if I find it so on trial; for I will make it bend
to its condition, or break it.

I have read of a good bishop that was to be burnt for
his religion; and he tried how he could bear it, by putting
his fingers into the lighted candle: So I, t'other day, tried,
when Rachel's back was turned, if I could not scour a
pewter plate she had begun. I see I could do't by degrees:
it only blistered my hand in two places.

All the matter is, if I could get plain-work enough, I
need not spoil my fingers. But if I can't, I hope to make
my hands as red as a blood-pudding, and as hard as a
beechen trencher, to accommodate them to my condition.
—But I must break off; here's somebody coming.

'Tis only our Hannah with a message from Mrs. Jervis.—
But, hold, here's somebody else,—Well, it is only Rachel.

I am as much frighted, as were the city mouse and the country mouse, in the same book of fables, at everything that stirs. Oh! I have a power of these things to entertain you with in winter evenings, when I come home. If I can but get work, with a little time for reading, I hope we shall be very happy over our peat fires.

What made me hint to you, that I should bring but little with me, is this:

You must know, I did intend to do, as I have this afternoon: and that is, I took all my clothes, and all my linen, and I divided them into three parcels, as I had before told Mrs. Jervis I intended to do; and I said, It is now Monday, Mrs. Jervis, and I am to go away on Thursday morning betimes; so, though I know you don't doubt my honesty, I beg you will look over my poor matters, and let every one have what belongs to them; for, said I, you know I am resolved to take with me only what I can properly call my own.

Said she (I did not know her drift then; to be sure she meant well; but I did not thank her for it, when I did know it), Let your things be brought down in the green-room, and I will do anything you will have me do.

With all my heart, said I, green-room or anywhere; but I think you might step up, and see 'em as they lie.

However, I fetched 'em down, and laid them in three parcels, as before; and when I had done, I went down to call her up to look at them.

Now, it seems, she had prepared my master for this scene, unknown to me; and in this green-room was a closet, with a sash-door, and a curtain before it; for there she puts her sweet-meats and such things; and she did it, it seems, to turn his heart, as knowing what I intended, I suppose that he should make me take the things; for, if he had, I should have made money of them, to help us when we got together; for, to be sure, I could never have appeared in them.

Well, as I was saying, he had got, unknown to me, into this closet; I suppose while I went to call Mrs. Jervis: and

she since owned to me, it was at his desire, when she told
him something of what I intended, or else she would not
have done it : though I have reason, I am sure, to remember
the last closet-work.

So I said, when she came up, Here, Mrs. Jervis, is the
first parcel; I will spread it all abroad. These are the
things my good lady gave me.—In the first place, said I—
and so I went on describing the clothes and linen my lady
had given me, mingling blessings, as I proceeded, for her
goodness to me; and when I had turned over that parcel,
I said, Well, so much for the first parcel, Mrs. Jervis; that
was my lady's gifts.

Now I come to the presents of my dear virtuous master:
Hey, you know *closet* for that! Mrs. Jervis. She laughed,
and said, I never saw such a comical girl in my life! But
go on.   I will, Mrs. Jervis, said I, as soon as I have opened
the bundle; for I was as brisk and as pert as could be,
little thinking who heard me.

Now here, Mrs. Jervis, said I, are my ever worthy master's
presents; and then I particularised all those in the second
bundle.

After which, I turned to my own, and said,

Now, Mrs. Jervis, comes poor Pamela's bundle; and a
little one it is to the others.   First, here is a calico night-
gown, that I used to wear o' mornings. 'Twill be rather
too good for me when I get home; but I must have something.   Then there is a quilted calamanco coat, and a pair
of stockings I bought of the pedlar, and my straw hat with
blue strings; and a remnant of Scots cloth, which will make
two shirts and two shifts, the same I have on, for my poor
father and mother.   And here are four other shifts, one
the fellow to that I have on; another pretty good one,
and the other two old fine ones, that will serve me to turn
and wind with at home, for they are not worth leaving
behind me; and here are two pair of shoes, I have taken
the lace off, which I will burn, and may be will fetch
me some little matter at a pinch, with an old silver buckle
or two.

What do you laugh for, Mrs. Jervis? said I.—Why you
are like an April day; you cry and laugh in a breath.

Well, let me see; ay, here is a cotton handkerchief I
bought of the pedlar; there should be another somewhere.
Oh, here it is! and here too are my new-bought knit mittens:
and this is my new flannel coat, the fellow to that I have
on: and in this parcel, pinned together, are several pieces of
printed calico, remnants of silks, and such like, that, if good
luck should happen, and I should get work, would serve for
robins and facings, and such like uses. And here too are a
pair of pockets: they are too fine for me; but I have no
worse. Bless me, said I, I did not think I had so many
good things!

Well, Mrs. Jervis, said I, you have seen all my store, and
I will now sit down, and tell you a piece of my mind.

Be brief then, said she, my good girl: for she was afraid,
she said afterwards, that I should say too much.

Why then the case is this: I am to enter upon a point
of equity and conscience, Mrs. Jervis; and I must beg, if
you love me, you'd let me have my own way. Those
things there of my lady's, I can have no claim to, so as to
take them away; for she gave them me, supposing I was
to wear them in her service, and to do credit to her bountiful heart. But, since I am to be turned away, you
know, I cannot wear them at my poor father's; for I
should bring all the little village upon my back; and so I
resolve not to have *them.*

Then, Mrs. Jervis, said I, I have far less right to these
of my worthy master's: for you see what was his intention
in giving them to me. So they were to be the price of my
shame, and if I *could* make use of them, I should think I
should never prosper with them; and, besides, you know,
Mrs. Jervis, if I would not do the good gentleman's work,
why should I take his wages? So, in conscience, in honour,
in everything, I have nothing to say to thee, thou *second
wicked* bundle!

But, said I, come to my arms, my dear *third* parcel, the

companion of my poverty, and the witness of my honesty ; and may I never deserve the least rag that is contained in thee, when I forfeit a title to that innocence, that I hope will ever be the pride of my life! and then I am sure it will be my highest comfort at my death, when all the riches and pomps of the world will be worse than the vilest rags that can be worn by beggars! And so I hugged my *third* bundle.

But, said I, Mrs. Jervis (and she wept to hear me), one thing more I have to trouble you with, and that's all.

There are four guineas, you know, that came out of my good lady's pocket, when she died; that, with some silver, my master gave me: Now these same four guineas I sent to my poor father and mother, and they have broken them; but would make them up, if I would: and if you think it should be so, it shall. But pray tell me honestly your mind: As to the three years before my lady's death, do you think, as I had no wages, I may be supposed to be quits?—By quits, I cannot mean that my poor services should be equal to my lady's goodness; for that's impossible. But as all her learning and education of me, as matters have turned, will be of little service to me now; for it had been better for me to have been brought up to hard labour, to be sure; for that I must turn to at last, if I can't get a place (and you know, in places too, one is subject to such temptations as are dreadful to think of): so, I say, by quits I only mean, as I return all the good things she gave me, whether I may not set my little services against my keeping; because, as I said, my learning is not now in the question; and I am sure my dear good lady would have thought so, had she lived; but that too is now out of the question. Well then, if so, I would ask, Whether, in above this year that I have lived with my master, as I am resolved to leave all his gifts behind me, I may not have earned, besides my keeping, these four guineas, and these poor clothes here upon my back, and in my third bundle? Now tell me your mind freely, without favour or affection.

Alas! my dear girl, says she, you make me unable to speak to you at all: To be sure it will be the highest

affront that can be offered, for you to leave any of these
things behind you; and you must take all your bundles
with you, or my master will never forgive you.

Well, well, Mrs. Jervis, said I, I don't care; I have been
too much used to be snubbed and hardly treated by my
master of late. I have done him no harm; and I shall
always pray for him and wish him happy. But I don't
deserve these things; I know I don't. Then, I can't wear
them, if I should take them; so they can be of no use to
me: And I trust I shall not want the poor pittance, that
is all I desire to keep life and soul together. Bread and
water I can live upon, Mrs. Jervis, with content. Water I
shall get anywhere; and if I can't get me bread, I will
live like a bird in winter upon hips and haws, and at other
times upon pig-nuts and potatoes, or turnips, or anything.
So what occasion have I for these things?—But all I ask
is about these four guineas, and if you think I need not
return them, that is all I want to know.—To be sure, my
dear, you need not, said she; you have well earned them
by that waistcoat only. No, I think not *so*, in that only;
but in the linen, and other things, do you think I have?
Yes, yes, said she, and more. And my keeping allowed
for, I mean, said I, and these poor clothes on my back,
besides? Remember that, Mrs. Jervis. Yes my dear odd-
one, no doubt you have. Well then, said I, I am as happy
as a princess. I am quite as rich as I wish to be: and
once more, my dear third bundle, I will hug thee to my
bosom. And I beg you'll say nothing of all this till I am
gone, that my master mayn't be so angry, but that I may
go in peace; for my heart, without other matters, will be
ready to break to part with you all.

Now, Mrs. Jervis, said I, as to one matter more: and
that is my master's last usage of me, before Mr. Longman.
—Said she, Pr'ythee, dear Pamela, step to my chamber,
and fetch me a paper I left on my table. I have something
to show you in it. I will, said I, and stepped down; but
that was only a fetch, to take the orders of my master, I
found. It seems he said, he thought two or three times

to have burst out upon me; but he could not stand it, and wished I might not know he was there. But I tripped up again so nimbly (for there was no paper), that I just saw his back, as if coming out of that green-room, and going into the next to it, the first door that was open—I whipped in, and shut the door, and bolted it. O Mrs. Jervis! said I, what have you done by me?—I see I can't confide in anybody. I am beset on all hands. Wretched, wretched Pamela, where shalt thou expect a friend, if Mrs. Jervis joins to betray thee thus? She made so many protestations (telling me all, and that he owned I had made him wipe his eyes two or three times, and said she hoped it would have a good effect, and remembered me, that I had said nothing but what would rather move compassion than resentment), that I forgave her. But oh! that I was safe from this house! for never poor creature sure was so flustered as I have been so many months together!—I am called down from this most tedious scribble. I wonder what will next befall

Your dutiful DAUGHTER.

Mrs. Jervis says, she is sure I shall have the chariot to carry me home to you. Though this will look too great for me, yet it will show as if I was not turned away quite in disgrace. The travelling chariot is come from Lincolnshire, and I fancy I shall go in that; for the other is quite grand.

———o———

LETTER XXX.

MY DEAR FATHER AND MOTHER,—I write again, though, may be, I shall bring it to you in my pocket: for I shall have no writing, nor writing-time, I hope, when I come to you. This is Wednesday morning, and I shall, I hope, set out to you to-morrow morning; but I have had more trials and more vexations; but of another complexion too a little though all from the same quarter.

Yesterday my master, after he came from hunting, sent
for me. I went with great terror; for I expected he would
storm, and be in a fine passion with me for my freedom of
speech before: so I was resolved to begin first, with submis-
sion, to disarm his anger; and I fell upon my knees as soon
as I saw him; and said, Good sir, let me beseech you, as
you hope to be forgiven yourself, and for the sake of my
dear good lady your mother, who recommended me to you
with her last words, to forgive me all my faults; and only
grant me this favour, the last I shall ask you, that you
will let me depart your house with peace and quietress
of mind, that I may take such a leave of my dear fellow-
servants as befits me; and that my heart be not quite
broken.

He took me up, in a kinder manner than ever I had
known; and he said, Shut the door, Pamela, and come to
me in my closet: I want to have a little serious talk with
you.—How can I, sir, said I, how can I! and wrung my
hands. Oh pray, sir, let me go out of your presence, I
beseech you!—By the God that made me, said he, I'll do
you no harm. Shut the parlour door, and come to me in
my library.

He then went into his closet, which is his library, and
full of rich pictures besides; a noble apartment, though
called a closet, and next the private garden, into which it
has a door that opens. I shut the parlour door, as he bid
me; but stood at it irresolute. Place some confidence in
me, said he: Surely you may, when I have spoken thus
solemnly. So I crept towards him with trembling feet, and
my heart throbbing through my handkerchief. Come in,
said he, when I bid you. I did so. Pray, sir, said I, pity
and spare me. I will, said he, as I hope to be saved. He
sat down upon a rich settee; and took hold of my hand,
and said, Don't doubt me, Pamela. From this moment I
will no more consider you as my servant; and I desire
you'll not use me with ingratitude for the kindness I am
going to express towards you. This a little emboldened me;
and he said, holding both my hands between his, You have

too much wit and good sense not to discover, that I, in spite
of my heart, and all the pride of it, cannot but love you.
Yes, look up to me, my sweet-faced girl! I *must* say I love
you; and have put on a behaviour to you, that was much
against my heart, in♦hopes to frighten you from your
reservedness. You see I own it ingenuously; and don't
play your sex upon me for it.

I was unable to speak; and he, seeing me too much
oppressed with confusion to go on in that strain, said, Well,
Pamela, let me know in what situation of life is your father:
I know he is a poor man; but is he as low and as honest as
he was when my mother took you?

Then I could speak a little; and with a down look (and
I felt my face glow like fire), I said, Yes, sir, as *poor* and
as *honest* too; and that is my pride. Says he, I will do
something for him, if it be not your fault, and make all
your family happy. Ah, sir, said I, he is happier already
than ever he can be, if his daughter's innocence is to be the
price of your favour: and I beg you will not speak to me
on the *only* side that can wound me. I have no design of
that sort, said he. Oh sir, said I, tell me not so, tell me not
so!—'Tis easy, said he, for me to be the making of your
father, without injuring *you.* Well, sir, said I, if this can
be done, let me know how; and all I can do with innocence
shall be the study and practice of my life.—But, oh! what
can such a poor creature as I do, and do my duty?—Said he,
I would have you stay a week or fortnight only, and behave
yourself with kindness to me; I stoop to beg it of you, and
you shall see all shall turn out beyond your expectation.
I see, said he, you are going to answer otherwise than I
would have you; and I begin to be vexed I should thus
meanly sue; and so I will say, that your behaviour before
honest Longman, when I used you as I did, and you could
so well have vindicated yourself, has quite charmed me. And
though I am not pleased with all you said yesterday, while
I was in the closet, yet you have moved me more to admire
you than before; and I am awakened to see more worthiness in you, than ever I saw in any lady in the world. All

the servants, from the highest to the lowest, dote upon you, instead of envying you; and look upon you in so superior a light, as speaks what you ought to be. I have seen more of your letters than you imagine (This surprised me!), and am quite overcome with your charming manner of writing, so free, so easy, and many of your sentiments so much above your years, and your sex; and all put together, makes me, as I tell you, love you to extravagance. Now, Pamela, when I have stooped to acknowledge all this, oblige me only to stay another week or fortnight, to give me time to bring about some certain affairs, and you shall see how much you may find your account in it.

I trembled to find my poor heart giving way.—Oh, good sir, said I, spare a poor girl that cannot look up to you, and speak. My heart is full; and why should you wish to undo me?—Only oblige me, said he, to stay a fortnight longer, and John shall carry word to your father, that I will see him in the time, either here, or at the Swan in his village. Oh sir, said I, my heart will burst; but on my bended knees, I beg you to let me go to-morrow, as I designed : and don't offer to tempt a poor creature, whose whole will would be to do yours, if my virtue would permit!—I shall permit it, said he; for I intend no injury to you, God is my witness! Impossible! said I; I cannot, sir, believe you, after what has passed : how many ways are there to undo poor creatures! Good God, protect me this *one* time, and send me but to my dear father's cot in safety!—Strange, d——d fate! said he, that when I speak so solemnly, I can't be believed!—What *should* I believe, sir? said I, what *can* I believe? What have you said, but that I am to stay a fortnight longer? and what then is to become of me?—My pride of birth and fortune (d——n them both! said he, since they cannot obtain credit with you, but must add to your suspicions) will not let me descend all at once; and I ask you but a fortnight's stay, that, after this declaration, I may pacify those proud demands upon me.

Oh how my heart throbbed! and I began (for I did not know what I did) to say the Lord's prayer. None of your beads to me, Pamela! said he; thou art a perfect nun, I think.

But I said aloud, with my eyes lifted up to heaven, *Lead me not into temptation : but deliver me from evil*, oh my good God! He hugged me in his arms, and said, Well, my dear girl, then you stay this fortnight, and you shall see what I will do for you—I'll leave you a moment, and walk into the next room, to give you time to think of it, and to show you I have no design upon you. Well, this, I thought, did not look amiss.

He went out, and I was tortured with twenty different doubts in a minute; sometimes I thought that to stay a week or fortnight longer in this house to obey him, while Mrs. Jervis was with me, could do no great harm: But then, thought I, how do I know what I may be *able* to do? I have withstood his *anger;* but may I not relent at his *kindness?*— How shall I stand *that ?*—Well, I hope, thought I, by the same protecting grace in which I will always confide !—But then, what has he promised? Why, he will make my poor father and mother's life comfortable. Oh! said I to myself, that is a rich thought; but let me not dwell upon it, for fear I should indulge it to my ruin.—What can he do for *me*, poor girl as I am!—What can his greatness stoop to! He talks, thought I, of his pride of heart, and pride of condition; Oh these are in his *head*, and in his *heart* too, or he would not confess them to me at *such* an instant. Well then, thought I, this can be only to seduce me.—He has promised nothing.—But I am to *see* what he will do, if I stay a fortnight ; and this fortnight, thought I again, is no such great matter; and I shall see in a few days how he carries it.— But then, when I again reflected upon this distance between him and me, and his now open declaration of love, as he called it; and that after this he would talk with me on that subject *more plainly* than ever, and I shall be *less* armed, may be, to withstand him; and then I bethought myself, why, if he meant no dishonour, he should not speak before Mrs. Jervis ; and the odious frightful closet came again into

my head, and my narrow escape upon it; and how easy it
might be for him to send Mrs. Jervis and the maids out of
the way; and so that all the mischief he designed me might
be brought about in less than that time; I resolved to go
away and trust all to Providence, and nothing to myself.
And how ought I to be thankful for this resolution!—as
you shall hear.

But just as I have writ to this place, John sends me
word, that he is going this minute your way; and so I
will send you so far as I have written, and hope by to-
morrow night, to ask your blessings, at your own poor,
but happy abode, and tell you the rest by word of mouth;
and so I rest, till then, and for ever,

Your dutiful DAUGHTER.

—o—

LETTER XXXI.

DEAR FATHER AND MOTHER,—I will continue my
writing still, because, may be, I shall like to read it, when
I am with you, to see what dangers I have been enabled to
escape; and though I bring it along with me.

I told you my resolution, my happy resolution, as I have
reason to think it: and just then he came in again, with
great kindness in his looks, and said, I make no doubt,
Pamela, you will stay this fortnight to oblige me. I
knew not how to frame my words so as to deny, and yet
not make him storm. But, said I, Forgive, sir, your poor
distressed servant. I know I cannot possibly deserve any
favour at your hands, consistent with virtue; and I beg
you will let me go to my poor father. Why, said he, thou
art the veriest fool that I ever knew. I tell you I will see
your father; I'll send for him hither to-morrow, in my
travelling chariot, if you will; and I'll let him know what
I intend to do for *him* and *you*. What, sir, may I ask you,
can that be? Your honour's noble estate may easily make
him happy, and not unuseful, perhaps to *you*, in some

respect or other. But what price am I to pay for all
this?—You shall be happy as you can wish, said he, I do
assure you: And here I will now give you this purse, in
which are fifty guineas, which I will allow your father
yearly, and find an employ suitable to his liking, to
deserve *that* and *more:* Pamela, he shall never want,
depend upon it. I would have given you still more for
him, but that, perhaps, you'd suspect I intended it as a
design upon you.—Oh sir, said I, take back your guineas!
I will not touch one, nor will my father, I am sure, till he
knows what is to be done *for* them; and particularly what
is to become of *me.* Why then, Pamela, said he, suppose
I find a man of probity, and genteel calling, for a husband
for you, that shall make you a gentlewoman as long as you
live?—I want no husband, sir, said I; for now I began to
see him in all his black colours!—Yet being so much in his
power, I thought I would a little dissemble. But, said he,
you are so pretty, that go where you will, you can never
be free from the designs of some or other of our sex; and
I shall think I don't answer the care of my dying mother
for you, who committed you to me, if I don't provide you
a husband to protect your virtue and your innocence;
and a worthy one I have thought of for you.

Oh black, perfidious creature! thought I, what an implement art thou in the hands of Lucifer, to ruin the innocent heart!—Yet still I dissembled; for I feared much
both him and the place I was in. But whom, pray, sir,
have you thought of?—Why, said he, young Mr. Williams,
my chaplain, in Lincolnshire, who will make you happy.
Does he know, sir, said I, anything of your honour's intentions?—No, my girl, said he, and kissed me (much
against my will; for his very breath was now poison to
me), but his dependence upon my favour, and your beauty
and merit, will make him rejoice at my kindness to him.
Well, sir, said I, then it is time enough to consider of this
matter; and it cannot hinder me from going to my father's:
for what will staying a fortnight longer signify to this?
Your honour's care and goodness may extend to me *there,*

as well as *here ;* and Mr. Williams, and all the world, shall
know that I am not ashamed of my father's poverty.

He would kiss me again, and I said, If I am to think
of Mr. Williams, or anybody, I beg *you'll* not be so free
with me: that is not pretty, I'm sure. Well, said he, but
you stay this next fortnight, and in that time I'll have both
Williams and your father here; for I will have the match
concluded in my house; and when I have brought it on,
you shall settle it as you please together. Meantime take
and send only these fifty pieces to your father, as an
earnest of my favour, and I'll make you all happy.—Sir,
said I, I beg at least two hours to consider of this. I
shall, said he, be gone out in one hour; and I would have
you write to your father what I propose; and John shall
carry it on purpose; and he shall take the purse with him
for the good old man, if you approve it. Sir, said I, I will
then let you know in one hour my resolution. Do so, said
he; and gave me another kiss, and let me go.

Oh how rejoiced I had got out of his clutches!—So I
write you this, that you may see how matters stand; for I
am resolved to come away, if possible. Base, wicked,
treacherous gentleman as he is!

So here was a trap laid for your poor Pamela! I tremble
to think of it! Oh what a scene of wickedness was here laid
down for all my wretched life! Blackhearted wretch! how
I hate him!—For, at first, as you'll see by what I have
written, he would have made me believe other things; and
this of Mr. Williams, I suppose, came into his head after
he walked out from his closet, to give himself time to think
how to delude me better: but the covering was now too
thin, and easy to be seen through.

I went to my chamber, and the first thing I did was to
write to him; for I thought it was best not to see him
again, if I could help it; and I put it under his parlour
door, after I had copied it, as follows:

‘ HONOURED SIR,—Your last proposal to me convinces
‘ me, that I ought not to stay, but to go to my father, if it

' were but to ask his advice about Mr. Williams. And I
' am so set upon it, that I am not to be persuaded. So,
' honoured sir, with a thousand thanks for all favours, I
' will set out to-morrow early; and the honour you designed
' me, as Mrs. Jervis tells me, of your chariot, there will be
' no occasion for: because I can hire, I believe, Farmer
' Brady's chaise. So, begging you will not take it amiss,
' I shall ever be

' Your dutiful Servant.'

' As to the purse, sir, my poor father, to be sure, won't
' forgive me, if I take it, till he can know how to de-
' serve it: which is impossible.'

So he has just now sent Mrs. Jervis to tell me, that since
I am resolved to go, go I may, and the travelling chariot
shall be ready; but it shall be worse for me; for that he
will never trouble himself about me as long as he lives.
Well, so I get out of the house, I care not; only I should
have been glad I could, with innocence, have made you, my
dear parents, happy.

I cannot imagine the reason of it, but John, who I
thought was gone with my last, is but now going; and he
sends to know if I have anything else to carry. So I
break off to send you this with the former.

I am now preparing for my journey, and about taking
leave of my good fellow-servants: and if I have not time
to write, I must tell you the rest, when I am so happy as
to be with you.

One word more: I slip in a paper of verses, on my
going; sad poor stuff! but as they come from me, you'll
not dislike them, may be. I showed them to Mrs. Jervis,
and she liked them, and took a copy; and made me sing
them to her, and in the green-room too; but I looked into
the closet first. I will only add, that I am

Your dutiful DAUGHTER.

Let me just say, That he has this moment sent me five
guineas by Mrs. Jervis, as a present for my pocket:
So I shall be very rich; for as *she* brought them, I

thought I might take them. He says he won't see me: and I may go when I will in the morning; and Lincolnshire Robin shall drive me: but he is so angry, he orders that nobody shall go out at the door with me, not so much as into the coach-yard. Well! I can't help it, not I! But does not this expose himself more than me?

But John waits, and I would have brought this and the other myself; but he says, he has put it up among other things, and so can take both as well as one.

John is very good, and very honest; I am under great obligations to him. I'd give him a guinea, now I'm so rich, if I thought he'd take it. I hear nothing of my lady's clothes, and those my master gave me: for I told Mrs. Jervis, I would not take them; but I fancy, by a word or two that was dropped, they will be sent after me. Dear sirs! what a rich Pamela you'll have if they should! But as I can't wear them if they do, I don't desire them; and if I have them, will turn them into money, as I can have opportunity. Well, no more—I'm in a fearful hurry!

VERSES ON MY GOING AWAY.

I.

My fellow-servants dear, attend
To these few lines, which I have penn'd :
I'm sure they're from your honest friend,   .
    And wisher-well, poor PAMELA.

II.

I, from a state of low degree,
Was plac'd in this good family :
Too high a fate for humble me,
    The helpless, hopeless PAMELA.

III.

Yet though my happy lot was so,
Joyful, I homeward from it go,
No less content, when poor and low,
    Than here you find your PAMELA.

IV.

For what indeed is happiness,
But conscious innocence and peace?
And that's a treasure I possess;
  Thank Heaven that gave it PAMELA.

V.

My future lot I cannot know:
But this I'm sure, where'er I go,
Whate'er I am, whate'er I do,
  I'll be the grateful PAMELA.

VI.

No sad regrets my heart annoy,
I'll pray for all your peace and joy,
From master high to scullion boy,
  For all your loves to PAMELA.

VII.

One thing or two I've more to say;
God's holy will, be sure, obey;
And for our master always pray,
  As ever shall poor PAMELA.

VIII.

For, oh! we *pity* should the great,
Instead of envying their estate;
Temptations always on 'em wait,
  Exempt from which are such as we.

IX.

Their riches, gay deceitful snares,
Enlarge their fears, increase their cares:
Their servants' joy surpasses theirs;
  At least so judges PAMELA.

X.

Your parents and relations love:
Let them your duty ever prove;
And you'll be bless'd by Heav'n above,
  As will, I hope, poor PAMELA.

XI.

For if asham'd I e'er could be
Of my dear parents' low degree,
What lot had been too mean for me,
  Unbless'd, unvirtuous PAMELA.

XII.

Thrice happy may you ever be,
Each one in his and her degree;
And, sirs, whene'er you think of me,
       Pray for content to PAMELA.

XIII.

Pray for her wish'd content and peace;
And rest assur'd she'll never cease
To pray for all your joys' increase,
       .While life is lent to PAMELA.

XIV.

On God all future good depends:
Serve Him.   And so my sonnet ends,
With, thank ye, thank ye, honest friends,
       For all your loves to PAMELA.

HERE it is necessary the reader should know, that the fair
Pamela's trials were not yet over; but the worst were to
come, at a time when she thought them at an end, and that
she was returning to her father: for when her master found
her virtue was not to be subdued, and he had in vain tried
to conquer his passion for her, being a gentleman of pleasure
and intrigue, he had ordered his Lincolnshire coachman to
bring his travelling chariot from thence, not caring to trust
his Bedfordshire coachman, who, with the rest of the servants, so greatly loved and honoured the fair damsel; and
having given him instructions accordingly, and prohibited
the other servants, on pretence of resenting Pamela's behaviour, from accompanying her any part of the road, he
drove her five miles on the way to her father's; and then
turning off, crossed the country, and carried her onwards
towards his Lincolnshire estate.

It is also to be observed, that the messenger of her letters
to her father, who so often pretended business that way, was
an implement in his master's hands, and employed by him
for that purpose; and always gave her letters first to him,
and his master used to open and read them, and then send

them on; by which means, as he hints to her (as she
observes in one of her letters, p. 88), he was no stranger to
what she wrote. Thus every way was the poor virgin beset:
And the whole will show the base arts of designing men to
gain their wicked ends; and how much it behoves the fair
sex to stand upon their guard against artful contrivances,
especially when riches and power conspire against innocence
and a low estate.

A few words more will be necessary to make the sequel
better understood. The intriguing gentleman thought fit,
however, to keep back from her father her three last letters;
in which she mentions his concealing himself to hear her
partitioning out her clothes, his last effort to induce her to
stay a fortnight, his pretended proposal of the chaplain, and
her hopes of speedily seeing them, as also her verses; and
to send himself a letter to her father, which is as follows:

'GOODMAN ANDREWS,—You will wonder to receive a
'letter from me. But I think I am obliged to let you
'know, that I have discovered the strange correspondence
'carried on between you and your daughter, so injurious to
'my honour and reputation, and which, I think, you should
'not have encouraged, till you knew there were sufficient
'grounds for those aspersions, which she so plentifully
'casts upon me. Something possibly there might be in
'what she has written from time to time; but, believe me,
'with all her pretended simplicity and innocence, I never
'knew so much romantic invention as she is mistress of.
'In short, the girl's head's turned by romances, and such
'idle stuff, to which she has given herself up, ever since her
'kind lady's death. And she assumes airs, as if she was
'a mirror of perfection, and everybody had a design upon
'her.

'Don't mistake me, however; I believe her very honest
'and very virtuous; but I have found out also, that she is
'carrying on a sort of correspondence, or love affair, with
'a young clergyman, that I hope in time to provide for;
'but who, at present, is destitute of any subsistence but my

' favour: And what would be the consequence, can you
' think, of two young folks, who have nothing in the world
' to trust to of their own, to come together with a family
' multiplying upon them before they have bread to eat?

' For my part, I have too much kindness to them both,
' not to endeavour to prevent it, if I can; and for this
' reason I have sent her out of his way for a little while,
' till I can bring them both to better consideration; and I
' would not, therefore, have you be surprised you don't see
' your daughter so soon as you might possibly expect.

' Yet I do assure you, upon my honour, that she shall be
' safe and inviolate; and I hope you don't doubt me, not-
' withstanding any airs she may have given herself, upon
' my jocular pleasantry to her, and perhaps a little innocent
' romping with her, so usual with young folks of the two
' sexes, when they have been long acquainted, and grown
' up together; for pride is not my talent.

' As she is a mighty letter-writer, I hope she has had
' the duty to apprise you of her intrigue with the young
' clergyman; and I know not whether it meets with your
' countenance: But now she is absent for a little while (for
' I know he would have followed her to your village, if she
' had gone home; and there, perhaps, they would have
' ruined one another, by marrying), I doubt not I shall
' bring him to see his interest, and that he engages not
' before he know how to provide for a wife: And when that
' can be done, let them come together in God's name,
' for me.

' I expect not to be answered on this head, but by your
' good opinion, and the confidence you may repose in my
' honour: being

' Your hearty friend to serve you.'

' P.S.—I find my man John has been the manager of
' the correspondence, in which such liberties have
' been taken with *me*. I shall soon, in a manner that
' becomes me, let the saucy fellow know how much I
' resent his part of the affair. It is a hard thing, that

'a man of my character in the world should be use.
' thus freely by his own servants.'

It is easy to guess at the poor old man's concern, upon
reading this letter from a gentleman of so much consideration. He knew not what course to take, and had no
manner of doubt of his poor daughter's innocence, and
that foul play was designed her. Yet he sometimes hoped
the best, and was ready to believe the surmised correspondence between the clergyman and her, having not received
the letters she wrote, which would have cleared up that
affair.

But, after all, he resolved, as well to quiet his own as her
mother's uneasiness, to undertake a journey to the 'squire's ;
and leaving his poor wife to excuse him to the farmer who
employed him, he set out that very evening, late as it was ;
and travelling all night, found himself, soon after daylight,
at the gate of the gentleman, before the family was up :
and there he sat down to rest himself till he should see
somebody stirring.

The grooms were the first he saw, coming out to water
their horses ; and he asked, in so distressful a manner, what
was become of Pamela, that they thought him crazy ; and
said, Why, what have you to do with Pamela, old fellow ?
Get out of the horses' way.—Where is your master ? said
the poor man : Pray, gentlemen, don't be angry : my heart's
almost broken.—He never gives anything at the door,
I assure you, says one of the grooms ; so you lose your
labour.—I am not a beggar *yet*, said the poor old man ;
I want nothing of him, but my Pamela :—Oh my child !
my child !

I'll be hanged, says one of them, if this is not Mrs.
Pamela's father.—Indeed, indeed, said he, wringing his
hands, I am ; and weeping, Where is my child ? Where is
my Pamela ?—Why, father, said one of them, we beg your
pardon ; but she is gone home to you : How long have
you been come from home ?—Oh ! but last night, said he ;
I have travelled all night : Is the 'squire at home, or is he

c?—Yes, but he is not stirring though, said the groom, as yet. Thank God for that! said he; thank God for that! Then I hope I may be permitted to speak to him anon. They asked him to go in, and he stepped into the stable, and sat down on the stairs there, wiping his eyes, and sighing so sadly, that it grieved the servants to hear him.

The family was soon raised with a report of Pamela's father coming to inquire after his daughter; and the maids would fain have had him go into the kitchen. But Mrs. Jervis, having been told of his coming, arose, and hastened down to her parlour, and took him in with her, and there heard all his sad story, and read the letter. She wept bitterly, but yet endeavoured, before him, to hide her concern; and said, Well, Goodman Andrews, I cannot help weeping at your grief; but I hope there is no occasion. Let nobody see this letter, whatever you do. I daresay your daughter is safe.

Well, but, said he, I see *you*, madam, know nothing about her:—If all was right, so good a gentlewoman as you are, would not have been a stranger to this. To be sure you thought she was with me!

Said she, My master does not always inform his servants of his proceedings; but you need not doubt his honour. You have his hand for it: And you may see he can have no design upon her, because he is not from hence, and does not talk of going hence. Oh that is all I have to hope for! said he; that is all, indeed!—But, said he—and was going on, when the report of his coming had reached the 'squire, who came down, in his morning-gown and slippers, into the parlour, where he and Mrs. Jervis were talking.

What's the matter, Goodman Andrews? said he; what's the matter? Oh my child! said the good old man; give me my child! I beseech you, sir.—Why, I thought, says the 'squire, that I had satisfied you about her: Sure you have not the letter I sent you, written with my own hand. Yes, yes, but I have, sir, said he; and that brought me hither; and I have walked all night. Poor man, returned he, with great seeming compassion, I am sorry for it truly! Why, your daughter has made a strange racket in my family; and if I thought it would have disturbed you so much, I would have e'en let her gone home; but what I did was to serve *her*, and *you* too. She is very safe, I do assure you, Goodman Andrews; and you may take my honour for it, I would not injure her for the world. Do you think I would, Mrs Jervis? No, I hope not, sir, said she.—*Hope not!* said the poor man; so do I; but pray, sir, give me my child; that is all I desire; and I'll take care no clergyman shall come near her.

Why, London is a great way off, said the 'squire, and I can't send for her back presently. What, then, said he, have you sent my poor Pamela to London? I would not have it said so, replied the 'squire; but I assure you, upon my honour, she is quite safe and satisfied, and will quickly inform you of it by letter. She is in a reputable family, no less than a bishop's, and is to wait on his lady, till I get the matter over that I mentioned to you.

Oh how shall I know this? replied he.—What! said the 'squire, pretending anger, am I to be doubted? Do you believe I can have any view upon your daughter? And if I had, do you think I would take such methods as *these* to effect it? Why, surely, man, thou forgettest whom thou talkest to!—Oh, sir, said he, I beg your pardon! but consider my dear child is in the case; let me know but what bishop, and where; and I will travel to London on foot to see my daughter, and then shall be satisfied.

Why, Goodman Andrews, I think thou hast read romances as well as thy daughter, and thy head's turned with them. May I not have my word taken? Do you think, once more, I would offer anything dishonourable to your daughter? Is there anything looks like it? Pr'ythee, man, recollect a little who I am; and if I am not to be believed, what signifies talking?—Why, sir, said he, pray forgive me; but there is no harm to say, What bishop's, or whereabouts? What, and so you'd go troubling his lordship with your impertinent fears and stories! Will you be satisfied, if you have a letter from her within a week, it may be less, if she be not negligent, to assure you all is well with her? Why that, said the poor man, will be some comfort. Well, then, said the gentleman, I can't answer for her negligence, if she don't write: And if she should send a letter to you, Mrs. Jervis (for I desire not to see it; I have had trouble enough about her already), be sure you send it by a man and horse the moment you receive it. To be sure I will, answered she. Thank your honour, said the good man: And then I must wait with as much patience as I can for a week, which will be a year to me.

I tell you, said the gentleman, it must be her own fault if she don't write; for 'tis what I insisted upon, for my own reputation; and I shan't stir from this house, I assure you, till she is heard from, and that to your satisfaction. God bless your honour, said the poor man, as you say and mean truth! *Amen, Amen,* Goodman Andrews, said he: you see I am not afraid to say *Amen.* So, Mrs. Jervis, make the good man as welcome as you can; and let me have no uproar about the matter.

He then, whispering her, bid her give him a couple of guineas to bear his charges home; telling him, he should be welcome to stay there till the letter came, if he would, and be a witness, that he intended honourably, and not to stir from his house for one while.

The poor old man stayed and dined with Mrs. Jervis, with some tolerable ease of mind, in hopes to hear from his beloved daughter in a few days; and then accepting the present, returned for his own house, and resolved to be as patient as possible.

Meantime Mrs. Jervis, and all the family, were in the utmost grief for the trick put upon the poor Pamela; and she and the steward represented it to their master in as moving terms as they durst: but were forced to rest satisfied with his general assurances of intending her no harm; which, however, Mrs. Jervis little believed, from the pretence he had made in his letter, of the correspondence between Pamela and the young parson; which she knew to be all mere invention, though she durst not say so.

But the week after, they were made a little more easy by the following letter brought by an unknown hand, and left for Mrs. Jervis, which, how procured, will be shown in the sequel.

'Dear Mrs. Jervis,—I have *been vilely tricked, and,* ' instead of being driven by Robin to my dear father's, *I am* ' carried off, to where, I have no liberty to tell. However, I ' am at present not used hardly, *in the main;* and write to ' beg of you to let my dear father and mother (whose hearts ' must be well-nigh broken) know that I am well, and that ' I am, and, by the grace of God ever will be, their honest, ' as well as dutiful daughter, and

'Your obliged friend,
'Pamela Andrews.'

' I must neither send date nor place; but have most ' solemn assurances of honourable usage. *This is the* ' *only time my low estate has been troublesome to me,* ' *since it has subjected me to the frights I have under-* ' *gone. Love to your good self, and all my dear fellow-* ' *servants. Adieu! adieu! but pray for poor* Pamela.'

This, though it quieted not entirely their apprehensions, was shown to the whole family, and to the gentleman himself, who pretended not to know how it came; and Mrs. Jervis sent it away to the good old folks; who at first suspected it was forged, and not their daughter's hand; but, finding the contrary, they were a little easier to hear she was alive and honest: and having inquired of all their acquaintance what could be done, and no one being able to put them in a way how to proceed, with effect, on so extraordinary an occasion, against so rich and so resolute a gentleman; and being afraid to make matters worse (though they saw plainly enough, that she was in no bishop's family, and so mistrusted all the rest of his story), they applied themselves to prayers for their poor daughter, and for an happy issue to an affair that almost distracted them.

We shall now leave the honest old pair praying for their dear Pamela, and return to the account she herself gives of all this; having written it journal-wise, to amuse and employ her time, in hopes some opportunity might offer to send it to her friends; and, as was her constant view, that she might afterwards thankfully look back upon the dangers she had escaped, when they should be happily over-blown, as in time she hoped they would be; and that then she might examine, and either approve or repent of her own conduct in them.

— o —

LETTER XXXII.

OH MY DEAREST FATHER AND MOTHER!—Let me write, and bewail my miserable hard fate, though I have no hope how what I write can be conveyed to your hands!—I have now nothing to do, but write and weep, and fear and pray! But yet what can I hope for, when I seem to be devoted, as a victim to the will of a wicked violator of all the laws of God and man!—But, gracious Heaven, forgive me my rashness and despondency! Oh let me not sin against Thee; for Thou best knowest what is fittest for Thy poor hand-maid!—And as Thou sufferest not Thy poor creatures to be tempted above what they can bear, I will resign myself to Thy good pleasure: And still, I hope, desperate as my condition seems, that as these trials are not of my own seeking, nor the effects of my presumption and vanity, I shall be enabled to overcome them, and, in God's own good time, be delivered from them.

Thus do I pray imperfectly, as I am forced by my distracting fears and apprehensions; and oh join with me, my dear parents!—But, alas! how can you know, how can I reveal to you, the dreadful situation of your poor daughter! The unhappy Pamela may be undone (which God forbid, and sooner deprive me of life!) before you can know her hard lot!

Oh the unparalleled wickedness, stratagems, and devices, of those who call themselves gentlemen, yet pervert the design of Providence, in giving them ample means to do good, to their own everlasting perdition, and the ruin of poor oppressed innocence!

But now I will tell you what has befallen me; and yet, how shall you receive it? Here is no honest John to carry my letters to you! And, besides, I am watched in all my steps; and no doubt shall be, till my hard fate may ripen his wicked projects for my ruin. I will every day, however, write my sad state; and some way, perhaps, may be opened to send the melancholy scribble to you. But, alas! when you *know* it, what will it do but aggravate your troubles? For, oh! what can the abject poor do against the mighty rich, when they are determined to oppress?

Well, but I must proceed to write what I had hoped to tell you in a few hours, when I believed I should receive your grateful blessings, on my return to you from so many hardships.

I will begin with my account from the last letter I wrote you, in which I enclosed my poor stuff of verses; and continue it at times, as I have opportunity; though, as I said, I know not how it can reach you.

The long-hoped-for Thursday morning came, when I was to set out. I had taken my leave of my fellow-servants over-night; and a mournful leave it was to us all: for men, as well as women servants, wept much to part with me; and, for *my* part, I was overwhelmed with tears, and the affecting instances of their esteem. They all would have made me little presents, as tokens of their love; but I would not take anything from the lower servants, to be sure. But Mr. Longman would have me accept of several yards of Holland, and a silver snuff-box, and a gold ring, which he desired me to keep for his sake; and he wept over me; but said, I am sure so good a maiden God will bless; and though you return to your poor father again, and his low estate, yet Providence will find you out: Remember I tell you so; and *one* day, though I mayn't live to see it, you will be rewarded.

I said, O dear Mr. Longman! you make me too rich, and too mody; and yet I must be a beggar before my time: for I shall want often to be scribbling (little thinking it would be my only employment so soon), and I will beg you, sir, to favour me with some paper; and, as soon as I get home, I will write you a letter, to thank you for all your kindness to me; and a letter to good Mrs. Jervis too.

This was lucky; for I should have had none else, but at the pleasure of my rough-natured governess, as I may call her; but now I can write to ease my mind, though I can't send it to you; and write what I please, for she knows not how well I am provided: for good Mr. Longman gave me above forty sheets of paper, and a dozen pens, and a little phial of ink; which last I wrapped in paper, and put in my pocket; and some wax and wafers.

Oh, dear sir, said I, you have set me up. How shall I requite you? He said, By a kiss, my fair mistress! And I gave it very willingly; for he is a good old man.

Rachel and Hannah cried sadly when I took my leave; and Jane, who sometimes used to be a little crossish, and Cicely too, wept sadly, and said, they would pray for me; but poor Jane, I doubt, will forget *that*; for she seldom says her prayers for herself: More's the pity!

Then Arthur the gardener, our Robin the coachman, and Lincolnshire Robin too, who was to carry me, were very civil; and both had tears in their eyes; which I thought then very good-natured in Lincolnshire Robin, because he knew but little of me.—But since, I find he might well be concerned; for he had then his instructions, it seems, and knew how he was to be a means to entrap me.

Then our other three footmen, Harry, Isaac, and Benjamin, and grooms, and helpers, were very much affected likewise; and the poor little scullion-boy, Tommy, was ready to run over for grief.

They had got all together over-night, expecting to be differently employed in the morning; and they all begged to shake hands with me, and I kissed the maidens, and prayed to God to bless them all; and thanked them for all their love and kindnesses to me: and, indeed, I was forced to leave them sooner than I would, because I could not stand it: Indeed I could not. Harry (I could not have thought it; for he is a little wildish, they say) cried till he sobbed again. John, poor honest John, was not then come back from you. But as for the butler, Mr. Jonathan, he could not stay in company.

I thought to have told you a deal about this; but I have worse things to employ my thoughts.

Mrs. Jervis, good Mrs. Jervis, cried all night long; and I comforted her all I could: And she made me promise, that if my master went to London to attend parliament, or to Lincolnshire, I would come and stay a week with her: and she would have given me money; but I would not take it.

Well, next morning came, and I wondered I saw nothing of poor honest John; for I waited to take leave of him, and thank him for all his civilities to me and to you. But I suppose he was sent farther by my master, and so could not return; and I desired to be remembered to him.

And when Mrs. Jervis told me, with a sad heart, the chariot was ready with four horses to it, I was just upon sinking into the ground, though I wanted to be with you.

My master was above stairs, and never asked to see me. I was glad of it in the main; but he knew, false heart as he is, that I was not to be out of his reach.—Oh preserve me, Heaven, from his power, and from his wickedness!

Well, they were not suffered to go with me one step, as I writ to you before; for he stood at the window to see me go. And in the passage to the gate, out of his sight, there they stood all of them, in two rows; and we could say nothing on·both sides, but God bless you! and God bless you! But Harry carried my own bundle, my third bundle, as I was used to call it, to the coach, with some plumb-cake, and diet-bread, made for me over-night, and some sweet-meats, and six bottles of Canary wine, which Mrs. Jervis would make me take in a basket, to cheer our hearts now and then, when we got together, as she said. And I kissed all the maids again, and shook hands with the men again; but Mr. Jonathan and Mr. Longman were not there; and then I tripped down the steps to the chariot, Mrs. Jervis crying most sadly.

I looked up. when I got to the chariot, and I saw my master at the window, in his gown; and I courtesied three times to him very low, and prayed for him with my hands lifted up; for I could not speak; indeed I was not able: And he bowed his head to me, which made me then very glad he would take such notice of me; and in I stepped, and was ready to burst with grief: and could only, till Robin began to drive, wave my white handkerchief to them, wet with my tears: and, at last, away he drove, Jehu-like, as they say, out of the courtyard. And I too soon found I had cause for greater and deeper grief.

Well, said I to myself, at this rate I shall soon be with my dear father and mother; and till I had got, as I supposed, halfway, I thought of the good friends I had left: And when, on stopping for a little bait to the horses, Robin told me I was near halfway, I thought it was high time to wipe my eyes, and think to whom I was going; as then, alack for me! I thought. So I began to ponder what a meeting I should have with you; how glad you'd both be to see me come safe and innocent to you, after all my dangers: and so I began to comfort myself, and to banish the other gloomy side from my mind; though, too, it returned now and then; for I should be ungrateful not to love them for their love.

Well, I believe I set out about eight o'clock in the morning; and I wondered and wondered, when it was about two, as I saw by a church dial, in a little village as we passed through, that I was still more and more out of my knowledge. Hey-day, thought I, to drive this strange pace, and to be so long a going a little more than twenty miles, is very odd! But to be sure, thought I, Robin knows the way.

At last he stopped, and looked about him, as if he was at a loss for the road ; and I said, Mr. Robert, sure you are out of the way!—I'm afraid I am, said he. But it can't be much; I'll ask the first person I see. Pray do, said I ; and he gave his horses a mouthful of hay: and I gave him some cake, and two glasses of Canary wine; and stopped about half an hour in all. Then he drove on very fast again.

I had so much to think of, of the dangers I now doubted not I had escaped, of the loving friends I had left, and my best friends I was going to; and the many things I had to relate to you; that I the less thought of the way, till I was startled out of my meditations by the sun beginning to set, and still the man driving on, and his horses sweating and foaming; and then I began to be alarmed all at once, and called to him; and he said he had horrid ill luck, for he had come several miles out of the way, but was now right, and should get in still before it was quite dark. My heart began then to misgive me a little, and I was very much fatigued; for I had no sleep for several nights before, to signify; and at last I said, Pray, Mr. Robert, there is a town before us, what do you call it?—If we are so much out of the way, we had better put up there, for the night comes on apace: And, Lord protect me! thought I, I shall have new dangers, mayhap, to encounter with the *man*, who have escaped the *master*—little thinking of the base contrivance of the latter.—Says he, I am just there: 'Tis but a mile on one side of the town before us.—Nay, said I, I may be mistaken; for it is a good while since I was this way; but I am sure the face of the country here is nothing like what I remember it.

He pretended to be much out of humour with himself for mistaking the way, and at last stopped at a farmhouse, about two miles beyond the village I had seen; and it was then almost dark, and he alighted, and said, We must make shift here ; for I am quite out.

Lord, thought I, be good to the poor Pamela ! More trials still !—What will befall me next !

The farmer's wife, and maid, and daughter, came out;

and the wife said, What brings you this way at this time
of night, Mr. Robert? And with a lady too?—Then I
began to be frightened out of my wits; and laying middle
and both ends together, I fell a crying, and said, God give
me patience! I am undone for certain!—Pray, mistress,
said I, do you know 'Squire B——, of Bedfordshire?

The wicked coachman would have prevented the answering me; but the simple daughter said, Know his worship!
yes, surely! why he is my father's landlord.—Well, said I,
then I am undone; undone for ever!—Oh, wicked wretch!
what have I done to you, said I to the coachman, to serve
me thus?—Vile tool of a wicked master!—Faith, said the
fellow, I am sorry this task was put upon me: but I could
not help it. But make the best of it now; here are very
civil reputable folks; and you'll be safe here, I'll assure
you.—Let me get out, said I, and I'll walk back to the
town we came through, late as it is:—For I will not enter
here.

Said the farmer's wife, You'll be very well used here, I'll
assure you, young gentlewoman, and have better conveniences than anywhere in the village. I matter not conveniences, said I: I am betrayed and undone! As you
have a daughter of your *own*, pity me, and let me know if
your landlord, as you call him, be here!—No, I'll assure
you he is not, said she.

And then came the farmer, a good-like sort of man,
grave, and well-behaved; and spoke to me in such sort, as
made me a little pacified; and seeing no help for it, I went
in; and the wife immediately conducted me up stairs to
the best apartment, and told me, that was mine as long
as I stayed; and nobody should come near me but when I
called. I threw myself on the bed in the room, tired and
frightened to death almost; and gave way to the most
excessive fit of grief that I ever had.

The daughter came up, and said, Mr. Robert had given
her a letter to give me; and there it was. I raised myself,
and saw it was the hand and seal of the wicked wretch, my
master, directed to Mrs. Pamela Andrews.—This was a

little better than to have him here; 'houg. " ᴋopes (
must have been brought through the ir; fo.
I was.

The good woman (for I began to see 'ings a.
little reputable, and no guile appearing in the but ra
a face of grief for my grief) offered me a gla of
cordial water, which I accepted, for I was ready 'o sii.
and then I sat up in a chair a little, though very la tish .
and they brought me two candles, and lighted a brush ᴠod
fire; and said, if I called, I should be waited on instam :
and so left me to ruminate on my sad condition, and t.
read my letter, which I was not able to do presently. After
I had a little come to myself, I found it to contain these
words:

'DEAR PAMELA,—The passion I have for you, and your
' obstinacy, have constrained me to act by you in a manner
' that I know will occasion you great trouble and fatigue,
' both of mind and body. Yet, forgive me, my dear girl;
' for, although I have taken this step, I will, by all that's
' good and holy! use you honourably. Suffer not your
' fears to transport you to a behaviour that will be disre-
' putable to us both: for the place where you'll receive
' this is a farm that belongs to me; and the people civil,
' honest, and obliging.
  ' You will, by this time, be far on your way to the place
' I have allotted for your abode for a few weeks, till I
' have managed some affairs, that will make me show my-
' self to you in a much different light, than you may pos-
' sibly apprehend from this rash action: And to convince
' you, that I mean no harm, I do assure you, that the house
' you are going to shall be so much at your command,
' that even I myself will not approach it without leave
' from you. So make yourself easy; be discreet and
' prudent; and a happier turn shall reward these your
' troubles than you may at present apprehend.
  ' Meantime I pity the fatigue you will have, if this come
' to your hand in the place I have directed: and will write

...er to satisfy him, that nothing but what is
c shall be offered to you, by

ur passionate admirer (so I must style myself),

'————.

'Don't think hardly of poor Robin: You have so pos-
' sessed all my servants in your favour, that I find they
' had rather serve you than me; and 'tis reluctantly
' the poor fellow undertook this task; and I was
' forced to submit to assure him of my honourable
' intentions to you, which I am fully resolved to make
' good, if you compel me not to a contrary conduct.'

I but too well apprehended that the letter was only to
pacify me for the present; but as my danger was not so
immediate as I had reason to dread, and he had promised to
forbear coming to me, and to write to you, my dear parents,
to quiet your concern, I was a little more easy than before:
and I made shift to eat a little bit of boiled chicken they had
got for me, and drank a glass of my sack, and made each of
them do so too.

But after I had so done, I was again a little flustered;
for in came the coachman with the look of a hangman, I
thought, and *madamed* me up strangely; telling me, he
would beg me to get ready to pursue my journey by five in
the morning, or else he should be late in. I was quite
grieved at this; for I began not to dislike my company,
considering how things stood; and was in hopes to get a
party among them, and so to put myself into any worthy
protection in the neighbourhood, rather than go forward.

When he withdrew, I began to tamper with the farmer
and his wife. But, alas! they had had a letter delivered
them at the same time I had; so securely had Lucifer put
it into his head to do his work; and they only shook their
heads, and seemed to pity me; and so I was forced to give
over that hope.

However, the good farmer showed me his letter; which I
copied as follows: for it discovers the deep arts of this
wicked master; and how resolved he seems to be on my

ruin, by the pains he took to deprive me of all hopes of freeing myself from his power.

' FARMER NORTON,—I send to your house, *for one night* ' *only,* a young gentlewoman, much against her will, who ' has deeply embarked in a love affair, which will be her ruin, ' as well as the person's to whom she wants to betroth her- ' self. I have, *to oblige her father,* ordered her to be carried ' to one of my houses, where she will be well used, to try, ' if by absence, and expostulation with both, they can be ' brought to know their own interest: and I am sure you ' will use her kindly for my sake: for, excepting this matter, ' *which she will not own,* she does not want prudence and ' discretion. I will acknowledge any trouble you shall be ' at in this matter the first opportunity; and am

' Your Friend and Servant.'

He had said, too cunningly for me, that I would not *own* this pretended love affair; so that he had provided them not to believe me, say what I would; and as they were his tenants, who all love him (for he has some amiable qualities, and so he had need!), I saw all my plot cut out, and so was forced to say the less.

I wept bitterly, however; for I found he was too hard for me, as well in his contrivances as riches; and so had recourse again to my only refuge, comforting myself, that God never fails to take the innocent heart into His protection, and is alone able to baffle and confound the devices of the mighty. Nay, the farmer was so prepossessed with the contents of his letter, that he began to praise his care and concern for me, and to advise me against entertaining addresses without my friends' advice and consent; and made me the subject of a lesson for his daughter's improvement. So I was glad to shut up this discourse; for I saw I was not likely to be believed.

I sent, however, to tell my driver, that I was so fatigued, I could not get out so soon the next morning. But he insisted upon it, and said, It would make my day's journey the lighter; and I found he was a more faithful servant to his master, notwithstanding what he wrote of his reluctance, than I could have wished : I saw still more and more, that all was deep dissimulation, and contrivance worse and worse.

Indeed I might have shown them his letter to me, as a full confutation of his to them ; but I saw no probability of engaging them in my behalf: and so thought it signified little, as I was to go away so soon, to enter more particularly into the matter with them ; and besides, I saw they were not inclinable to let me stay longer, for fear of disobliging him : so I went to bed, but had very little rest : and they would make their servant-maid bear me company in the chariot five miles, early in the morning, and she was to walk back.

I had contrived in my thoughts, when I was on my way in the chariot, on Friday morning, that when we came into some town to bait, as he must do for the horses' sake, I would, at the inn, apply myself, if I saw I any way could, to the mistress of the inn, and tell her the case, and to refuse to go farther, having nobody but this wicked coach-man to contend with.

Well, I was very full of this project, and in great hopes, somehow or other, to extricate myself this way. But, oh ! the artful wretch had provided for even this last refuge of mine ; for when we came to put up at a large town on the way, to eat a morsel for dinner, and I was fully resolved to execute my project, who should be at the inn that he put up at, but the wicked Mrs. Jewkes, expecting me ! And her sister-in-law was the mistress of it ; and she had provided a little entertainment for me.

And this I found, when I desired, as soon as I came in, to speak with the mistress of the house. She came to me ; and I said, I am a poor unhappy young body, that want your advice and assistance ; and you seem to be a good sort of a gentlewoman, that would assist an oppressed innocent person. Yes, madam, said she, I hope you guess right ; and I have the happiness to know something of the matter before you speak. Pray call my sister Jewkes.—Jewkes! Jewkes! thought I; I have heard of that name; I don't like it.

Then the wicked creature appeared, whom I had never seen but once before, and I was terrified out of my wits. No stratagem, thought I, not *one*! for a poor innocent girl; but everything to turn out against me; that is hard indeed!

So I began to pull in my horns, as they say, for I saw I was now worse off than at the farmer's.

The naughty woman came up to me with an air of confidence, and kissed me: See, sister, said she, here's a charming creature! Would she not tempt the best lord in the land to run away with her? Oh frightful! thought I; here's an avowal of the matter at once: I am now gone, that's certain. And so was quite silent and confounded; and seeing no help for it (for she would not part with me out of her sight), I was forced to set out with her in the chariot; for she came thither on horseback with a man-servant, who rode by us the rest of the way, leading her horse: and now I gave over all thoughts of redemption, and was in a desponding condition indeed.

Well, thought I, here are strange pains taken to ruin a poor innocent, helpless, and even *worthless* young body. This plot is laid too deep, and has been too long hatching, to be baffled, I fear. But then I put my trust in God, who I knew was able to do everything for me, when all other possible means should fail: and in Him I was resolved to confide.

You may see—(Yet, oh! that kills me; for I know not whether *ever* you can see what I now write or no—Else you will see)—what sort of woman that Mrs. Jewkes is, compared to good Mrs. Jervis, by this:—

Every now and then she would be staring in my face, in the chariot, and squeezing my hand, and saying, Why, you are very pretty, my silent dear! And once she offered to kiss me. But I said, I don't like this sort of carriage, Mrs. Jewkes; it is not like two persons of one sex. She fell a laughing very confidently, and said, That's prettily said, I vow! Then thou hadst rather be kissed by the other sex? 'I fackins, I commend thee for that!

I was sadly teased with her impertinence and bold way; but no wonder; she was innkeeper's housekeeper, before she came to my master; and those sort of creatures don't want confidence, you know: and indeed she made nothing to talk boldly on twenty occasions; and said two or three times, when she saw the tears every now and then, as we rid, trickle down my cheeks, I was sorely hurt, truly, to have the handsomest and finest young gentleman in five counties in love with me!

So I find I am got into the hands of a wicked procuress; and if I was not safe with good Mrs. Jervis, and where everybody loved me, what a dreadful prospect have I now before me, in the hands of a woman that seems to delight in filthiness!

Oh, dear sirs! what shall I do! What shall I do!—Surely, I shall never be equal to all these things!

About eight at night, we entered the courtyard of this handsome, large, old, and lonely mansion, that looks made for solitude and mischief, as I thought, by its appearance, with all its brown nodding horrors of lofty elms and pines about it: and here, said I to myself, I fear, is to be the scene of my ruin, unless God protect me, who is all-sufficient!

I was very sick at entering it, partly from fatigue, and partly from dejection of spirits: and Mrs. Jewkes got me some mulled wine, and seemed mighty officious to welcome me thither; and while she was absent, ordering the wine, the wicked Robin came in to me, and said, I beg a thousand pardons for my part in this affair, since I see your grief and your distress; and I do assure you, that I am sorry it fell to my task.

Mighty well, Mr. Robert! said I; I never saw an execution but once, and then the hangman asked the poor creature's pardon, and wiped his mouth, as you do, and pleaded his duty, and then calmly tucked up the criminal. But I am no criminal, as you all know: And if I could have thought it my duty to obey a wicked master in his unlawful commands, I had saved you all the merit of this vile service.

I am sorry, said he, you take it so: but everybody don't think alike. Well, said I, you have done *your* part, Mr. Robert, towards my ruin, very faithfully; and will have cause to be sorry, may be, at the long run, when you shall see the mischief that comes of it.—Your eyes were open, and you knew I was to be carried to my father's, and that I was barbarously tricked and betrayed; and I can only, once more, thank you for your part of it. God forgive you!

So he went away a little sad. What have you said to Robin, madam? said Mrs. Jewkes (who came in as he went out): the poor fellow's ready to cry. I need not be afraid of *your* following his example, Mrs. Jewkes, said I: I have been telling him, that he has done *his* part to my ruin: and he now can't help it! So his repentance does *me* no good; I wish it may *him*.

I'll assure you, madam, said she, I should be as ready to cry as he, if I should do you any harm. It is not in *his* power to help it now, said I; but *your* part is to come, and you may choose whether you'll contribute to my ruin or not.—Why, look ye, look ye, madam, said she, I have a great notion of doing my duty to my master; and therefore you may depend upon it, if I can do *that*, and serve *you*, I will: but you must think, if *your* desire, and *his* will, come to clash once, I shall do as he bids me, let it be what it will.

Pray, Mrs. Jewkes, said I, don't *madam* me so: I am but a silly poor girl, set up by the gambol of fortune, for a May-game; and now am to be something, and now nothing, just as that thinks fit to sport with me: And let you and me talk upon a foot together; for I am a servant inferior to you, and so much the more, as I am turned out of place.

Ay, ay, says she, I understand something of the matter; you have so great power over my master, that you may soon be mistress of us all; and so I would oblige you, if I could. And I must and will call you madam; for I am instructed to show you all respect, I'll assure you.

Who instructed you so to do? said I. Who! my master,

to be sure, said she. Why, said I, how can that be? You
have not seen him lately. No, that's true, said she; but I
have been expecting you here some time (oh the deep laid
wickedness! thought I); and, besides, I have a letter of instructions by Robin; but, may be, I should not have said so
much. If you would show them to me, said I, I should be
able to judge how far I could, or could not, expect favour
from you, consistent with your duty to our master. I beg
your pardon, fair mistress, for that, said she; I am sufficiently instructed; and you may depend upon it, I will
observe my orders; and, so far as they will let me, so far
will I oblige you; and there's an end of it.

Well, said I, you will not, I hope, do an unlawful or
wicked thing, for any master in the world. Look ye, said
she, he is my master; and if he bids me do anything that
I *can* do, I think I *ought* to do it; and let him, who has his
power to command me, look to the *lawfulness* of it. Why,
said I, suppose he should bid you cut my throat, would you
do it? There's no danger of that, said she; but to be sure
I would not; for then I should be hanged! for that would
be murder. Well, said I, and suppose he should resolve to
ensnare a poor young creature, and ruin her, would you
assist him in that? For to rob a person of her virtue is
worse than cutting her throat.

Why now, says she, how strangely you talk! Are not
the two sexes made for one another? And is it not natural
for a gentleman to love a pretty woman? And suppose he
can obtain his desires, is that so bad as cutting her throat?
And then the wretch fell a laughing, and talked most im-
pertinently, and showed me, that I had nothing to expect
from her virtue or conscience: and this gave me great
mortification; for I was in hopes of working upon her by
degrees.

So we ended our discourse here, and I bid her show me
where I must lie.—Why, said she, lie where you list,
madam; I can tell you, I must lie with you for the present.
For the present! said I, and torture then wrung my heart!
—But is it in your *instructions*, that you must lie with me?

Yes, indeed, said she.—I am sorry for it, said I. Why, said she, I am wholesome, and cleanly too, I'll assure you. Yes, said I, I don't doubt that; but I love to lie by myself. How so? said she; was not Mrs. Jervis your bedfellow at t'other house?

Well, said I, quite sick of her, and my condition; you must do as you are instructed, I think. I can't help myself, and am a most miserable creature. She repeated her insufferable nonsense. Mighty miserable, indeed, to be so well beloved by one of the finest gentlemen in England!

---o---

I am now come down in my writing to this present SATURDAY, and a deal I have written.

My wicked bedfellow has very punctual orders, it seems; for she locks me and herself in, and ties the two keys (for there is a double door to the room) about her wrist, when she goes to bed. She talks of the house having been attempted to be broken open two or three times; whether to fright me, I can't tell; but it makes me fearful; though not so much as I should be, if I had not other and greater fears.

I slept but little last night, and got up, and pretended to sit by the window which looks into the spacious gardens; but I was writing all the time, from break of day, to her getting up, and after, when she was absent.

At breakfast she presented the two maids to me, the cook and housemaid, poor awkward souls, that I can see no hopes of, they seem so devoted to her and ignorance. Yet I am resolved, if possible, to find some way to escape, before this wicked master comes.

There are, besides, of servants, the coachman, Robert, a groom, a helper, a footman; all but Robert (and he is accessory to my ruin), strange creatures, that promise nothing; and all likewise devoted to this woman. The gardener looks like a good honest man; but he is kept at a distance, and seems reserved.

I wondered I saw not Mr. Williams the clergyman, but

would not ask after him, apprehending it might give some jealousy; but when I had beheld the rest, he was the only one I had hopes of; for I thought his cloth would set him above assisting in my ruin.—But in the afternoon he came; for it seems he has a little Latin school in the neighbouring village, which he attends; and this brings him in a little matter, additional to my master's favour, till something better falls, of which he has hopes.

He is a sensible sober young gentleman; and when I saw him I confirmed myself in my hopes of him; for he seemed to take great notice of my distress and grief (for I could not hide it;) though he appeared fearful of Mrs. Jewkes, who watched all our motions and words.

He has an apartment in the house; but is mostly at a lodging in the town, for a conveniency of his little school; only on Saturday afternoon and Sundays: and he preaches sometimes for the minister of the village, which is about three miles off.

I hope to go to church with him to-morrow: Sure it is not in her instructions to deny me! He can't have thought of *every* thing! And something may strike out for me there.

I have asked her, for a feint (because she shan't think I am so well provided), to indulge me with pen and ink, though I have been using my own so freely when her absence would let me; for I begged to be left to myself as much as possible. She says she will let me have it; but then I must promise not to send any writing out of the house, without her seeing it. I said, it was only to divert my grief when I was by myself, as I desired to be; for I loved writing as well as reading; but I had nobody to send to, she knew well enough.

No, not at *present*, may be, said she; but I am told you are a great writer; and it is in my instructions to see all you write: So, look you here, said she, I will let you have a pen and ink, and two sheets of paper: for this employment will keep you out of worse thoughts; but I must see them always when I ask, written or not written. That's very hard, said I; but may I not have to myself the closet in the room where we lie, with the key to lock up my things? I believe I may consent to that, said she; and I will set it in order for you, and leave the key in the door. And there is a spinnet too, said she; if it be in tune, you may play to divert you now and then; for I know my old lady learnt you: And below is my master's library: you may take out what books you will.

And, indeed, these and my writing will be all my amusement: for I have no work given me to do; and the spinnet, if in tune, will not find my mind, I am sure, in tune to play upon it. But I went directly and picked out some books from the library, with which I filled a shelf in the closet she gave me possession of: and from these I hope to receive improvement, as well as amusement. But no sooner was her back turned, than I set about hiding a pen of my own here, and another there, for fear I should come to be denied, and a little of my ink in a broken China cup, and a little in another cup; and a sheet of paper here and there among my linen, with a little of the wax, and a few wafers, in several places, lest I should be searched; and something, I thought, might happen to open a way for my deliverance, by these or some other means. Oh the pride, thought I, I shall have, if I can secure my innocence, and escape the artful wiles of this wicked master! For, if he comes hither, I am undone, to be sure! For this naughty woman will assist him, rather than fail, in the worst of his attempts; and he'll have no occasion to send her out of the way, as he would have done Mrs. Jervis once. So I must set all my little wits at work.

It is a grief to me to write, and not to be able to send to you what I write; but now it is all the diversion I have, and if God will favour my escape with my innocence, as I trust He graciously will, for all these black prospects, with what pleasure shall I read them afterwards!

I was going to say, Pray for your dutiful daughter, as I used; but, alas! you cannot know my distress, though I am sure I have your prayers: And I will write on as things happen, that if a way should open, my scribble may be ready to be sent: For what I do, must be at a jirk, to be sure.

Oh how I want such an obliging, honest-hearted man as John!

———◊———

I am now come to SUNDAY.

WELL, here is a sad thing! I am denied by this barbarous woman to go to church, as I had built upon I might: and she has huffed poor Mr. Williams all to pieces, for pleading for me. I find he is to be forbid the house, if she pleases. Poor gentleman! all his dependence is upon my master, who has a very good living for him, if the incumbent die; and he has kept his bed these four months, of old age and dropsy.

He pays me great respect, and I see pities me; and would, perhaps, assist my escape from these dangers: But I have nobody to plead for me; and why should I wish to ruin a poor gentleman, by engaging him against his interest? Yet one would do anything to preserve one's innocence; and Providence would, perhaps, make it up to *him!*

Oh judge (but how shall you see what I write!) of my distracted condition, to be reduced to such a pass as to a desire to lay traps for mankind! But he wants sadly to say something to me, as he whisperingly hinted.

The wretch (I think I will always call her the *wretch* henceforth) abuses me more and more. I was but talking to one of the maids just now, indeed a little to tamper with her by degrees; and she popt upon us, and said—Nay, madam, don't offer to tempt poor innocent country maidens from doing their duty. You wanted, I hear, she should take a walk with you. But I charge you, Nan, never stir with her, nor obey her, without letting me know it, in the smallest trifles.—I say, walk with you! and where would you go, I tro'? Why, barbarous Mrs. Jewkes, said I, only to look a little up the elm-walk, since you would not let me go to church.

Nan, said she, to show me how much they were all in her power, pull off madam's shoes, and bring them to me. I have taken care of her others.—Indeed she shan't, said I.—Nay, said Nan, but I must if my mistress bids me: so pray, madam, don't hinder me. And so indeed (would you believe it?) she took my shoes off, and left me barefoot: and, for my share, I have been so frighted at this, that I have not power even to relieve my mind by my tears. I am quite stupefied to be sure!—Here I was forced to leave off.

Now I will give you a picture of this wretch: She is a broad, squat, pursy, *fat thing*, quite ugly, if anything human can be so called; about forty years old. She has a huge hand, and an arm as thick as my waist, I believe. Her nose is fat and crooked, and her brows grow down over her eyes; a dead spiteful, grey, goggling eye, to be sure she has. And her face is flat and broad; and as to colour, looks like as if it had been pickled a month in saltpetre: I daresay she drinks:—She has a hoarse, man-like voice, and is as thick as she is long; and yet looks so deadly strong, that I am afraid she would dash me at her foot in an instant, if I was to vex her.—So that with a heart more ugly than her face, she frightens me sadly; and I am undone to be sure, if God does not protect me; for she is very, very wicked—indeed she is.

This is poor helpless spite in me:—But the picture is too near the truth notwithstanding. She sends me a message just now, that I shall have my shoes again, if I will accept of her company to walk with me in the garden.—To *waddle* with me, rather, thought I.

Well, 'tis not my business to quarrel with her downright. I shall be watched the narrower, if I do; and so I will go with the hated wretch.—Oh for my dear Mrs. Jervis! or, rather, to be safe with my dear father, and mother.

Oh! I am out of my wits for joy! Just as I have got my shoes on, I am told John, honest John, is come on &c.

horseback!—A blessing on his faithful heart! What joy is
this! But I'll tell you more by and by. I must not let her
know I am so glad to see this dear blessed John, to be
sure!—Alas! but he looks sad, as I see him out of the
window! What can be the matter!—I hope my dear
parents are well, and Mrs. Jervis, and Mr. Longman, and
everybody, my naughty master not excepted;—for I wish
him to live and repent of all his wickedness to poor me.

Oh dear heart! what a world do we live in!—I am now
come to take up my pen again: But I am in a sad taking
truly! Another puzzling trial, to be sure.

Here was John, as I said, and the poor man came to
me, with Mrs. Jewkes, who whispered, that I would say
nothing about the shoes, for my *own* sake, as she said.
The poor man saw my distress, by my red eyes, and my
hagged looks, I suppose; for I have had a sad time of it,
you must needs think; and though he would have hid it,
if he could, yet his own eyes ran over. O Mrs. Pamela!
said he; O Mrs. Pamela! Well, honest fellow-servant,
said I, I cannot help it at present: I am obliged to your
honesty and kindness, to be sure; and then he wept more.
Said I (for my heart was ready to break to see his grief;
for it is a touching thing to see a man cry), Tell me the
worst! Is my master coming? No, no, said he, and sobbed.
—Well, said I, is there any news of my poor father and
mother? How do they do?—I hope well, said he, I know
nothing to the contrary. There is no mishap, I hope, to
Mrs. Jervis or to Mr. Longman, or my fellow-servants!—
No—said he, poor man! with a long N—o, as if his heart
would burst. Well, thank God then! said I.

The man's a fool, said Mrs. Jewkes, I think: What ado
is here! Why, sure thou'rt in love, John. Dost thou not
see young madam is well? What ails thee, man? Nothing
at all, said he; but I am such a fool as to cry for joy to
see good Mrs. Pamela: But I have a letter for you.

I took it, and saw it was from my master; so I put it in
my pocket. Mrs. Jewkes, said I, you need not, I hope,

see this. No, no, said she, I see whose it is, well enough; or else, may be, I must have insisted on reading it.

And here is one for you, Mrs. Jewkes, said he; but yours, said he to me, requires an answer, which I must carry back early in the morning, or to-night, if I can.

You have no more, John, said Mrs. Jewkes, for Mrs. Pamela, have you? No, said he, I have not, but everybody's kind love and service. Ay, to us both, to be sure, said she. John, said I, I will read the letter, and pray take care of yourself; for you are a good man, God bless you! and I rejoice to see you, and hear from you all. But I longed to say more; only that nasty Mrs. Jewkes.

So I went up, and locked myself in my closet, and opened the letter; and this is a copy of it:

'MY DEAREST PAMELA,—I send purposely to you on an
' affair that concerns you very much, and me somewhat, but
' chiefly for your sake. I am conscious that I have pro-
' ceeded by you in such a manner as may justly alarm your
' fears, and give concern to your honest friends: and all
' my pleasure is, that I *can* and *will* make you amends for
' the disturbance I have given you. As I promised, I sent
' to your father the day after your departure, that he might
' not be too much concerned for you, and assured him of
' my honour to you; and made an excuse, such an one as
' ought to have satisfied him, for your not coming to him.
' But this was not sufficient, it seems; for he, poor man!
' came to me next morning, and set my family almost in
' an uproar about you.

' Oh, my dear girl! what trouble has not your obstinacy
' given me, and yourself too! I had no way to pacify him,
' but to promise that he should see a letter written from
' you to Mrs. Jervis, to satisfy him you are well.

' Now all my care in this case is for your aged parents,
' lest they should be touched with too fatal a grief; and
' for you, whose duty and affection for them I know to be
' so strong and laudable: for this reason I beg you will
' write a few lines to them, and let me prescribe the form;

' which I have done, putting myself as near as I can in
' your place, and expressing your sense, with a warmth
' that I doubt will have too much possessed you.

.' After what is done, and which cannot now be helped,
' but which, I assure you, shall turn out honourably for
' you, I expect not to be refused; because I cannot pos-
' sibly have any view in it, but to satisfy your parents;
' which is more *your* concern than *mine ;* and so I must
' beg you will not alter one tittle of the underneath. If
' you do, it will be impossible for me to send it, or that
' it should answer the good end I propose by it.

' I have promised, that I will not approach you without
' your leave. If I find you easy, and not attempting to
' dispute or avoid your present lot, I will keep to my word,
' although it is a difficulty upon me. Nor shall your re-
' straint last long: for I will assure you, that I am resolved
' very soon to convince you of my good intentions, and
' with what ardour I am

' Yours, &c.'

——o——

The letter he prescribed for me was as this :

' DEAR MRS. JERVIS,—I have, instead of being driven by
' Robin to my dear father's, been carried off, where I have
' no liberty to tell. However, at present, I am not used
' hardly; and I write to beg you to let my dear father and
' mother, whose hearts must be well-nigh broken, know
' that I am well; and that I am, and, by the grace of God,
' ever will be, their honest, as well as dutiful daughter, and
' Your obliged friend.'

' I must neither send date nor place; but have most
' solemn assurances of honourable usage.'

I knew not what to do on this most strange request and
occasion. But my heart bled so much for you, my dear
father, who had taken the pains to go yourself, and inquire
after your poor daughter, as well as for my dear mother,

that I resolved to write, and pretty much in the above form,* that it might be sent to pacify you, till I could let you, somehow or other, know the true state of the matter. And I wrote thus to my strange wicked master himself: ·

' Sir,—If you knew but the anguish of my mind, and
' how much I suffer by your dreadful usage of me, you
' would surely pity me, and consent to my deliverance.
' What have I done, that I should be the *only* mark of your
' cruelty? I can have no hope, no desire of living left me,
' because I cannot have the least dependence, after what
' has passed, upon your solemn assurances.—It is impossible
' they should be consistent with the dishonourable methods
' you take.

' Nothing but your promise of not seeing me here in my
' deplorable bondage, can give me the least ray of hope.

' Don't, I beseech you, drive the poor distressed Pamela
' upon a rock, that may be the destruction both of her soul
' and body! You don't know, sir, how dreadfully I *dare*,
' weak as I am of mind and intellect, when my virtue is in
' danger. And, oh! hasten my deliverance, that a poor un-
' worthy creature, below the notice of such a gentleman as
' you, may not be made the sport of a high condition, for
' no reason in the world, but because she is not able to de-
' fend herself, nor has a friend that can right her.

' I have, sir, in part to show my obedience to you, but
' indeed, I own, more to give ease to the minds of my poor
' distressed parents, whose poverty, one would think, should
' screen them from violences of this sort, as well as their
' poor daughter, followed pretty much the form you have
' prescribed for me, in the letter to Mrs. Jervis; and the
' alterations I have made (for I could not help a few) are of
' such a nature, as, though they show my concern a little,
' yet must answer the end you are pleased to say you pre-
' pose by this letter.

' For God's sake, good sir, pity my lowly condition, and
' my present great misery; and *let* me join with all the rest

* See p. 103; her alterations are in a different character.

' of your servants to bless that goodness, which you have
' extended to every one but the poor afflicted, heart-broken
' PAMELA.'

I thought, when I had written this letter, and that which
he had prescribed, it would look like placing a confidence in
Mrs. Jewkes, to show them to her; and I showed her, at
the same time, my master's letter to me; for I believed the
value he expressed for me, would give me credit with one
who professed in everything to serve him, right or wrong;
though I had so little reason, I fear, to pride myself in it:
and I was not mistaken; for it has seemed to influence her
not a little, and she is at present mighty obliging, and runs
over in my praises; but is the less to be minded, because
she praises as much the author of my miseries, and his
honourable intentions, as she calls them; for I see, that she
is capable of thinking, as I fear *he* does, that everything
that makes for his wicked will is honourable, though to the
ruin of the innocent. Pray God I may find it otherwise!
Though, I hope, whatever the wicked gentleman may
intend, that I shall be at last rid of her impertinent bold
way of talk, when she seems to think, from his letter, that
he means honourably.

———o———

I am now come to MONDAY, the 5th day of my bondage and misery.

I WAS in hope to have an opportunity to see John, and
have a little private talk with him, before he went away;
but it could not be. The poor man's excessive sorrow made
Mrs. Jewkes take it into her head, to think he loved me;
and so she brought up a message to me from him this
morning that he was going. I desired he might come up
to *my* closet, as I called it, and she came with him. The
honest man, as I thought him, was as full of concern as
before, at taking leave: and I gave him two letters, the one
for Mrs. Jervis, enclosed in another for my master: but
Mrs. Jewkes would see me seal them up, lest I should enclose

anything else.—I was surprised, at the man's going away, to see him drop a bit of paper, just at the head of the stairs, which I took up without being observed by Mrs. Jewkes: but I was a thousand times more surprised, when I returned to my closet, and opening it read as follows:

'GOOD MRS. PAMELA,—I 'am grieved to tell you how
' much you have been deceived and betrayed, and that by
' such a vile dog as I. Little did I think it would come to
' this. But I must say, if ever there was a rogue in the
' world, it is me. I have all along showed your letters to
' my master: he employed me for that purpose; and he
' saw every one, before I carried them to your father and
' mother; and then sealed them up, and sent me with them.
' I had some business that way, but not half so often as I
' pretended: and as soon as I heard how it was, I was ready
' to hang myself. You may well think I could not stand
' in your presence. Oh vile, vile wretch, to bring you to
' this! If you are ruined, I am the rogue that caused it.
' All the justice I can do you, is to tell you, you are in vile
' hands; and I am afraid will be undone in spite of all your
' sweet innocence; and I believe I shall never live, after I
' know it. If you can forgive me, you are exceeding good;
' but I shall never forgive myself, that's certain. Howsom-
' ever, it will do you no good to make this known; and
' mayhap I may live to do you service. If I can, I will: I
' am sure I ought.—Master kept your last two or three
' letters, and did not send them at all. I am the most
' abandoned wretch of wretches.

                                          'J. ARNOLD.'

  ' You see your undoing has been long hatching. Pray
    ' take care of your sweet self. Mrs. Jewkes is a
    ' devil: but in my master's t'other house you have not
    ' one false heart, but myself. Out upon me for a
    ' villain!'

My dear father and mother, when you come to this place, I make no doubt your hair will stand an end as mine

I

does!—Oh the deceitfulness of the heart of man!—This
John, that I took to be the honestest of men; that you
took for the same; that was always praising you to me, and
me to you, and for nothing so much as for our *honest* hearts;
this *very* fellow was all the while a vile hypocrite, and a perfidious wretch, and helping to carry on my ruin.

But he says so much of himself, that I will only sit down
with this sad reflection, That power and riches never want
tools to promote their vilest ends, and there is nothing so
hard to be known as the heart of man:—I can but pity the
poor wretch, since he seems to have great remorse, and I
believe it best to keep his wickedness secret. If it lies in
my way, I will encourage his penitence; for I may possibly
make some discoveries by it.

One thing I should mention in this place; he brought
down, in a portmanteau, all the clothes and things my lady
and master had given me, and moreover two velvet hoods,
and a velvet scarf, that used to be worn by my lady; but
I have no comfort in them, or anything else.

Mrs. Jewkes had the portmanteau brought into my closet,
and she showed me what was in it; but then locked it up,
and said, she would let me have what I would out of it,
when I asked; but if I had the key, it might make me want
to go abroad, may be; and so the confident woman put it
in her pocket.

I gave myself over to sad reflections upon this strange
and surprising discovery of John's, and wept much for him,
and for myself too; for now I see, as he says, my ruin has
been long hatching, that I can make no doubt what my
master's *honourable* professions will end in. What a heap
of hard names does the poor fellow call himself! But what
must they deserve, then, who set him to work? Oh what
has this wicked master to answer for, to be so corrupt himself, and to corrupt others, who would have been all innocent; and to carry on a poor plot, I am sure for a gentleman, to ruin a poor creature, who never did him harm, nor
wished him any; and who can still pray for his happiness,
and his repentance?

I can't but wonder what these *gentlemen*, as they are called, can think of themselves for these vile doings! John had *some* inducement; for he hoped to please his master, who rewarded him and was bountiful to him; and the same may be said, bad as she is, for this same odious Mrs. Jewkes. But what inducement has my master for taking so much pains to do the devil's work for him?—If he loves me, as 'tis falsely called, must he therefore lay traps for me, to ruin me, and make me as bad as himself? I cannot imagine what good the undoing of such a poor creature as I can procure him.—To be sure, I am a very worthless body. People, indeed, say I am handsome; but if I was so, should not a gentleman prefer an honest servant to a guilty harlot? And must he be *more* earnest to seduce me, because I dread of all things to be seduced, and would rather lose my life than my honesty?

Well, these are strange things to me! I cannot account for them, for my share; but sure nobody will say, that these fine gentlemen have any tempter but their own wicked wills!—This naughty master could run away from me, when he apprehended his servants might discover his vile attempts upon me in that sad closet affair; but is it not strange that he should not be afraid of the all-seeing eye, from which even that base plotting heart of his, in its most secret motions, could not be hid?—But what avail me these sorrowful reflections? He is and will be wicked, and designs me a victim to his lawless attempts, if the God in whom I trust, and to whom I hourly pray, prevent it not.

——o——

Tuesday and Wednesday.

I HAVE been hindered, by this wicked woman's watching me so close, from writing on Tuesday; and so I will put both these days together. I have been a little turn with her for an airing, in the chariot, and walked several times in the garden; but have always her at my heels.

Mr. Williams came to see us, and took a walk with us

once; and while her back was just turned (encouraged by
the hint he had before given me), I said, Sir, I see two tiles
upon that parsley-bed; might not one cover them with
mould, with a note between them, on occasion?—A good
hint, said he; let that sunflower by the back-door of the
garden be the place; I have a key to the door; for it is my
nearest way to the town.

So I was forced to begin. Oh what inventions will
necessity push us upon! I hugged myself at the thought;
and she coming to us, he said, as if he was continuing a
discourse we were in: No, not extraordinary pleasant.
What's that? what's that? said Mrs. Jewkes.—Only, said
he, the town, I'm saying, is not very pleasant. No, indeed,
said she, it is not; it is a poor town, to my thinking. Are
there any gentry in it? said I. And so we chatted on
about the town, to deceive her. But my deceit intended
no hurt to anybody.

We then talked of the garden, how large and pleasant,
and the like; and sat down on the tufted slope of the fine
fish-pond, to see the fishers play upon the surface of the
water; and she said, I should angle if I would.

I wish, said I, you'd be so kind to fetch me a rod and
baits. Pretty mistress! said she—I know better than that,
I'll assure you, at this time.—I mean no harm, said I,
indeed. Let me tell you, said she, I know none who have
their thoughts more about them than you. A body ought
to look to it where you are. But we'll angle a little to-
morrow. Mr. Williams, who is much afraid of her, turned
the discourse to a general subject. I sauntered in, and left
them to talk by themselves; but he went away to town,
and she was soon after me.

I had got to my pen and ink; and I said, I want some
paper, Mrs. Jewkes (putting what I was about in my
bosom): You know I have written two letters, and sent
them by John. (Oh how his name, poor guilty fellow,
grieves me!) Well, said she, you have some left; one
sheet did for those two letters. Yes, said I; but I used
half another for a cover, you know; and see how I have

scribbled the other half; and so I showed her a parcel of broken scraps of verses, which I had tried to recollect, and had written purposely that she might see, and think me usually employed to such idle purposes. Ay, said she, so you have; well, I'll give you two sheets more; but let me see how you dispose of them, either written or blank. Well, thought I, I hope still, Argus, to be too hard for thee. Now Argus, the poets say, had a hundred eyes, and was set to watch with them all, as she does.

She brought me the paper, and said, Now, madam, let me see you write something. I will, said I; and took the pen and wrote, ' I wish Mrs. Jewkes would be so ' good to me, as I would be to her, if I had it in my ' power.'—That's pretty now, said she; well, I hope I am ; but what then? ' Why then (wrote I) she would do me ' the favour to let me know, what I have done to be ' made her prisoner; and what she thinks is to become ' of me.' Well, and what then? said she. ' Why then, of ' consequence (scribbled I), she would let me see her in- ' structions, that I may know how far to blame, or to ' acquit her.'

Thus I fooled on, to show her my fondness for scribbling; for I had no expectation of any good from her; that so she might suppose I employed myself, as I said, to no better purpose at other times: for she will have it, that I am upon some plot, I am so silent, and love so much to be by myself. —She would have made me write on a little further. No, said I; you have not answered me. Why, said she, what can you doubt, when my master himself assures you of his honour? Ay, said I; but lay your hand to your heart, Mrs. Jewkes, and tell me, if you yourself believe him. Yes, said she, to be sure I do. But, said I, what do *you* call honour? Why, said she, what does *he* call honour, think you?—Ruin! shame! disgrace! said I, I fear.—Pho! pho! said she; if you have any doubt about it, he can best explain his own meaning:—I'll send him word to come and satisfy you, if you will.—Horrid creature! said I, all in a fright— Canst thou not stab me to the heart? I'd rather thou

wouldst, than say such another word!—But I hope there is
no such thought of his coming.

She had the wickedness to say, No, no; he don't intend
to come, as I know of—but if I was he, I would not be long
away. What means the woman? said I.—Mean! said she
(turning it off); why I mean, I would come if I was he, and
put an end to all your fears—by making you as happy as
you wish. It is out of his power, said I, to make *me* happy,
great and rich as he is! but by leaving me innocent, and
giving me liberty to go to my dear father and mother.

She went away soon after, and I ended my letter, in hopes
to have an opportunity to lay it in the appointed place. So
I went to her, and said; I suppose, as it is not dark, I may
take another turn in the garden. It is too late, said she;
but if you will go, don't stay; and, Nan, see and attend
madam, as she called me.

So I went towards the pond, the maid following me, and
dropt purposely my hussy: and when I came near the tiles, I
said, Mrs. Anne, I have dropt my hussy; be so kind as to look
for it; I had it by the pond side. She went back to look,
and I slipt the note between the tiles, and covered them as
quick as I could with the light mould, quite unperceived;
and the maid finding the hussy, I took it, and sauntered in
again, and met Mrs. Jewkes coming to see after me. What
I wrote was this:

'REVEREND SIR,—The want of an opportunity to speak
'my mind to you, I am sure will excuse this boldness in a
'poor creature that is betrayed hither, I have reason to
'think, for the worst of purposes. You know something,
'to be sure, of my story, my native poverty, which I am not
'ashamed of, my late lady's goodness, and my master's
'designs upon me. It is true he promises honour, and all
'that; but the honour of the wicked is disgrace and shame
'to the virtuous: And he may think he keeps his promises,
'according to the notions he may allow himself to hold;
'and yet, according to mine and every good body's, basely
'ruin me.

' I am so wretched, and ill-treated by this Mrs. Jewkes,
' and she is so ill-principled a woman, that, as I may soon
' want the opportunity which the happy hint of this day
' affords to my hopes, I throw myself at once upon your
' goodness, without the least reserve; for I cannot be worse
' than I am, should that fail me; which, I daresay, to your
' power, it will not: For I see it, sir, in your looks, I hope
' it from your cloth, and I doubt it not from your inclina-
' tion, in a case circumstanced as my unhappy one is. For,
' sir, in helping me out of my present distress, you perform
' all the acts of religion in one; and the highest mercy and
' charity, both to the body and soul of a poor wretch, that,
' believe me, sir, has, at present, not so much as in thought
' swerved from her innocence.

' Is there not some way to be found out for my escape,
' without danger to yourself? Is there no gentleman or
' lady of virtue in this neighbourhood, to whom I may fly,
' only till I can find a way to get to my poor father and
' mother? Cannot Lady Davers be made acquainted with
' my sad story, by your conveying a letter to her? My
' poor parents are so low in the world, they can do nothing
' but break their hearts for me; and that, I fear, will be the
' end of it.

' My master promises, if I will be easy, as he calls it, in
' my present lot, he will not come down without my con-
' sent. Alas! sir, this is nothing: For what's the promise
' of a person who thinks himself at liberty to act as he has
' done by me? If he comes, it must be to ruin me; and
' come to be sure he will, when he thinks he has silenced
' the clamours of my friends, and lulled me, as no doubt he
' hopes, into a fatal security.

' Now, therefore, sir, is all the time I have to work and
' struggle for the preservation of my honesty. If I stay
' till he comes, I am undone. You have a key to the back
' garden-door; I have great hopes from that. Study, good
' sir, and contrive for me. I will faithfully keep your secret.
' —Yet I should be loath to have you suffer for me!

' I say no more, but commit this to the happy tiles, in

' the bosom of that earth, where, I hope, my deliverance will
' take root, and bring forth such fruit, as may turn to my
' inexpressible joy, and your eternal reward, both here and
' hereafter: As shall ever pray,

> ' Your oppressed humble Servant.'

—o—

Thursday.

THIS completes a terrible week since my setting out, as I
hoped to see you, my dear father and mother. Oh how
different were my hopes then, from what they are now!
Yet who knows what these happy tiles may produce!

But I must tell you, first, how I have been beaten by
Mrs. Jewkes! It is very true!—And thus it came about:

My impatience was great to walk in the garden, to see
if anything had offered, answerable to my hopes. But this
wicked Mrs. Jewkes would not let me go without her;
and said, she was not at leisure. We had a great many
words about it; for I told her, it was very hard I could
not be trusted to walk by myself in the garden for a little
air, but must be dogged and watched worse than a thief.

She still pleaded her instructions, and said she was not
to trust me out of her sight: And you had better, said she,
be easy and contented, I assure you; for I have worse
orders than you have yet found. I remember, added she,
your asking Mr. Williams, if there were any gentry in the
neighbourhood? This makes me suspect you want to get
away to them, to tell your sad dismal story, as you call it.

My heart was at my mouth; for I feared, by that hint,
she had seen my letter under the tiles: oh how uneasy I
was! At last she said, Well, since you take on so, you
may take a turn, and I will be with you in a minute.

When I was out of sight of her window, I speeded
towards the hopeful place; but was soon forced to slacken
my pace by her odious voice: Hey-day, why so nimble,
and whither so fast? said she: What! are you upon a
wager? I stopt for her, till her pursy sides were waddled

up to me; and she held by my arm, half out of breath: So I was forced to pass by the dear place, without daring to look at it.

The gardener was at work a little farther, and so we looked upon him, and I began to talk about his art; but she said, softly, My instructions are, not to let you be so familiar with the servants. Why, said I, are you afraid I should confederate with them to commit a robbery upon my master? May be I am, said the odious wretch; for to rob him of yourself, would be the worst that could happen to him, in his opinion.

And pray, said I, walking on, how came I to be his property? What right has he in me, but such as a thief may plead to stolen goods?—Why, was ever the like heard? says she.—This is downright rebellion, I protest!—Well, well, lambkin (which the foolish often calls me), if I was in his place, he should not have his property in you long questionable. Why, what would you do, said I, if you were he?—Not stand shill-I-shall-I, as he does; but put you and himself both out of your pain.—Why, Jezebel, said I (I could not help it), would you ruin me by force? —Upon this she gave me a deadly slap upon my shoulder: Take that, said she; whom do you call Jezebel?

I was so surprised (for you never beat me, my dear father and mother, in your lives), that I was like one thunder-struck; and looked round, as if I wanted some-body to help me; but, alas! I had nobody; and said, at last, rubbing my shoulder, Is this also in your instruc-tions?—Alas! for me! am I to be beaten too? And so fell a crying, and threw myself upon the grass-walk we were upon.—Said she, in a great pet, I won't be called such names, I'll assure you. Marry come up! I see you have a spirit: You must and shall be kept under. I'll manage such little provoking things as you, I warrant ye! Come, come, we'll go in a'doors, and I'll lock you up, and you shall have no shoes, nor anything else, if this be the case.

I did not know what to do. This was a cruel thing to

me, and I blamed myself for my free speech; for now I
have given her some pretence: and oh! thought I, here I
have, by my malapertness, ruined the only project I had
left.

The gardener saw this scene: but she called to him,
Well, Jacob, what do you stare at? Pray mind what
you're upon. And away he walked, to another quarter,
out of sight.

Well, thought I, I must put on the dissembler a little, I
see. She took my hand roughly: Come, get up, said she,
and come in a'doors!—I'll Jezebel you, I will so!—Why,
dear Mrs. Jewkes, said I.—None of your dears, and your
coaxing! said she; why not Jezebel again?—She was in a
fearful passion, I saw, and I was out of my wits. Thought
I, I have often heard women blamed for their tongues; I
wish mine had been shorter. But I can't go in, said I,
indeed I can't!—Why, said she, can't you? I'll warrant I
can take such a thin body as you under my arm, and carry
you in, if you won't walk. You don't know my strength.
—Yes, but I do, said I, too well; and will you not use me
worse when I come in?—So I arose, and she muttered to
herself all the way, She to be a Jezebel with me, that had
used me so well! and such like.

When I came near the house, I said, sitting down upon
a settle-bench, Well, I will *not* go in, till you say you forgive me, Mrs. Jewkes.—If you will forgive my calling you
that name, I will forgive your beating me.—She sat down
by me, and seemed in a great pucker, and said, Well,
come, I will forgive you for this time; and so kissed me,
as a mark of reconciliation.—But pray, said I, tell me
where I am to walk and go, and give me what liberty you
can; and when I know the most you can favour me with,
you shall see I will be as content as I can, and not ask you
for more.

Ay, said she, this is something like: I wish I could give
you all the liberty you desire; for you must think it is
no pleasure to me to tie you to my petticoat, as it were,
and not let you stir without me.—But people that will do

their duties, must have some trouble; and what I do, is to serve as good a master, to be sure, as lives.—Yes, said I, to everybody but me! He loves you too well, to be sure, returned she; and that's the reason; so you *ought* to bear it. I say, *love!* replied I. Come, said she, don't let the wench see you have been crying, nor tell her any tales; for you won't tell them fairly, I am sure; and I'll send her, and you shall take another walk in the garden, if you will: May be it will get you a stomach to your dinner; for you don't eat enough to keep life and soul together. You are beauty to the bone, added the strange wretch, or you could not look so well as you do, with so little stomach, so little rest, and so much pining and whining for nothing at all. Well, thought I, say what thou wilt, so I can be rid of thy bad tongue and company: and I hope to find some opportunity now to come at my sunflower. But I walked the other way, to take that in my return, to avoid suspicion.

I forced my discourse to the maid; but it was all upon general things; for I find she is asked after everything I say and do. When I came near the place, as I had been devising, I said, Pray step to the gardener, and ask him to gather a salad for me to dinner. She called out, Jacob! Said I, He can't hear you so far off; and pray tell him, I should like a cucumber too, if he has one. When she had stept about a bow-shot from me, I popt down, and whipt my fingers under the upper tile, and pulled out a letter without direction, and thrust it in my bosom, trembling for joy. She was with me, before I could well secure it; and I was in such a taking that I feared I should discover myself. You seem frightened, madam, said she. Why, said I, with a lucky thought (alas! your poor daughter will make an intriguer by and by; but I hope an innocent one!) I stooped to smell at the sunflower, and a great nasty worm ran into the ground, that startled me; for I can't abide worms. Said she, Sunflowers don't smell. So I find, replied I. And then we walked in; and Mrs. Jewkes said: Well, you have made haste now.—You shall go another time.

I went up to my closet, locked myself in, and opening my letter, found in it these words:

' I am infinitely concerned for your distress. I most
' heartily wish it may be in my power to serve and save so
' much innocence, beauty, and merit. My whole depend-
' ence is upon Mr. B——, and I have a near view of being
' provided for by his favour to me. But yet I would
' sooner forfeit all my hopes in him (trusting in.God for
' the rest), than not assist you, if possible. I never looked
' upon Mr. B—— in the light he now appears in to me,
' in your case. To be sure, he is no professed debauchee.
' But I am entirely of opinion, you should, if possible, get
' out of his hands; and especially as you are in very bad
' ones in Mrs. Jewkes's.

' We have here the widow Lady Jones, mistress of a
' good fortune; and a woman of virtue, I believe. We
' have also old Sir Simon Darnford, and his lady, who is
' a good woman; and they have two daughters, virtuous
' young ladies. All the rest are but middling people, and
' traders, at best. I will try, if you please, either Lady
' Jones, or Lady Darnford, if they'll permit you to take
' refuge with them. I see no probability of keeping myself
' concealed in this matter; but will, as I said, risk all things
' to serve you; for I never saw a sweetness and innocence
' like yours; and your hard case has attached me entirely
' to you; for I know, as you so happily express, if I can
' serve you in this case, I shall thereby perform all the acts
' of religion in one.

' As to Lady Davers, I will convey a letter, if you
' please, to her; but it must not be from our post-house,
' I give you caution; for the man owes all his bread to
' Mr. B——, and his place too; and I believe, by some-
' thing that dropt from him, over a can of ale, has his
' instructions. You don't know how you are surrounded;
' all which confirms me in your opinion, that no honour is
' meant you, let what will be professed; and I am glad you
' want no caution on that head.

' Give me leave to say, that I had heard much in your
' praise; but, I think, greatly short of what you deserve,
' both as to person and mind: My eyes convince me of the
' one, your letter of the other. For fear of losing the
' present lucky opportunity, I am longer than otherwise I
' should be. But I will not enlarge, any further than to
' assure you that I am, to the best of my power,
' Your faithful friend and servant,
' ARTHUR WILLIAMS.'

' I will come once every morning, and once every evening,
' after school-time, to look for your letters. I'll come
' in, and return without going into the house, if I
' see the coast clear: otherwise, to avoid suspicion, I'll
' come in.'

I instantly, in answer to this pleasing letter, wrote as
follows:

' REVEREND SIR,—Oh how suited to your function, and
' your character, is your kind letter! God bless you for it!
' I now think I am beginning to be happy. I should be
' sorry to have you suffer on my account: but I hope it will
' be made up to you an hundredfold, by that God whom
' you so faithfully serve. I should be too happy, could I
' ever have it in my power to contribute in the least to it.
' But, alas! to serve me, must be for God's sake only; for I
' am poor and lowly in fortune; though in mind, I hope,
' too high to do a mean or unworthy deed to gain a king-
' dom. But I lose time.——
' Any way you think best, I should be pleased with; for
' I know not the persons, nor in what manner it is best to
' apply to them. I am glad of the hint you so kindly give
' me of the man at the post-house. I was thinking of
' opening a way for myself by letter, when I could have
' opportunity; but I see more and more that I am, indeed,
' strangely surrounded with dangers; and that there is no
' dependence to be made on my master's honour.
' I should think, sir, if either of those ladies would give

' leave, I might some way get out by favour of your key ;
' and as it is impossible, watched as I am, to know when
' it can be, suppose, sir, you could get one made by it,
' and put it, the next opportunity, under the sunflower ?
' —I am sure no time is to be lost, because it is rather my
' wonder, that she is not thoughtful about this key, than
' otherwise ; for she forgets not the minutest thing.   But,
' sir, if I had this key, I could, if these ladies would *not*
' shelter me, run away anywhere : and if I was once out
' of the house, they could have no pretence to force me
' again ; for I have done no harm, and hope to make my
' story good to any compassionate body ; and by this way
' *you* need not to be known.   Torture should not wring it
' from me, I assure you.

  ' One thing more, good sir.   Have you no correspondence
' with my master's Bedfordshire family ?   By that means,
' may be, I could be informed of his intention of coming
' hither, and when.   I enclose you a letter of a deceitful
' wretch ; for I can trust you with anything ; poor John
' Arnold.   Its contents will tell why I enclose it.   Perhaps,
' by his means, something may be discovered ; for he seems
' willing to atone for his treachery to me, by the intimation
' of future service.   I leave the hint to you to improve
' upon, and am,

         ' Reverend Sir,
      ' Your for ever obliged and thankful servant.'

  ' I hope, sir, by your favour, I could send a little packet,
   ' now and then, somehow, to my poor father and
   ' mother.   I have a little stock of money, about five
   ' or six guineas : Shall I put half in your hands, to
   ' defray the charge of a man and horse, or any other
   ' incidents ? '

  I had but just time to transcribe this, before I was called
to dinner; and I put that for Mr. Williams, with a wafer
in it, in my bosom, to get an opportunity to lay it in the
dear place.

  Oh, good sirs, of all the flowers in the garden, the sunflower,

sure, is the loveliest !—It is a propitious one to me! How
nobly my plot succeeds! But I begin to be afraid my writings may be discovered; for they grow large: I stitch them
hitherto in my under-coat, next my linen. But if this brute
should search me.—I must try to please her, and then she
won't.

Well, I am but just come off from a walk in the garden,
and have deposited my letter by a simple wile. I got some
horse-beans; and we took a turn in the garden, to angle, as
Mrs. Jewkes had promised me. She baited the hook, and I
held it, and soon hooked a lovely carp. Play it, play it,
said she: I did, and brought it to the bank. A sad thought
just then came into my head; and I took it, and threw it in
again; and oh the pleasure it seemed to have, to flounce in,
when at liberty!—Why this? says she. O Mrs. Jewkes!
said I, I was thinking this poor carp was the unhappy Pamela.
I was likening you and myself to my naughty master. As
we hooked and deceived the poor carp, so was I betrayed by
false baits; and when you said, Play it, play it, it went to
my heart, to think I should sport with the destruction of
the poor fish I had betrayed; and I could not but fling it in
again; and did you not see the joy with which the happy
carp flounced from us? Oh! said I, may some good merciful body procure me my liberty in the same manner; for to
be sure, I think my danger equal!

Lord bless thee! said she, what a thought is there!—
Well, I can angle no more, added I. I'll try *my* fortune,
said she, and took the rod. Do, answered I; and I will
plant life, if I can, while you are destroying it. I have
some horse-beans here, and will go and stick them in one
of the borders, to see how long they will be coming up; and
I will call them my garden.

So you see, dear father and mother (I hope now you will
soon see; for, may be, if I can't get away so soon myself, I
may send my papers somehow; I say you will see), that
this furnishes me with a good excuse to look after my garden
another time; and if the mould should look a little freshish,

it won't be so much suspected. She mistrusted nothing of this; and I went and stuck in here and there my beans, for about the length of five ells, of each side of the sunflower; and easily deposited my letter. And not a little proud am I of this contrivance. Sure something will do at last!

——o——

I HAVE just now told you a trick of mine; now I'll tell you a trick of this wicked woman's. She comes up to me: Says she, I have a bill I cannot change till to-morrow; and a tradesman wants his money most sadly: and I don't love to turn poor trades-folks away without their money: Have you any about you? I have a little, replied I: how much will do? Oh! said she, I want eight pounds. Alack! said I, I have but between five and six. Lend me that, said she, till to-morrow. I did so; and she went down stairs: and when she came up, she laughed, and said, Well, I have paid the tradesman. Said I, I hope you'll give it me again to-morrow. At that, the assurance, laughing loud, said, Why, what occasion have you for money? To tell you the truth, lambkin, I didn't want it. I only feared you might make a bad use of it; and *now* I can trust Nan with you a little oftener, especially as I have got the key of your portmanteau; so that you can neither corrupt her with money, nor fine things. Never did anybody look more silly than I.—Oh how I fretted, to be so foolishly outwitted!—And the more, as I had hinted to Mr. Williams, that I would put some in his hands to defray the charges of my sending to you. I cried for vexation.—And now I have not five shillings left to support me, if I *can* get away.—Was ever such a fool as I! I must be priding myself in my contrivances, indeed! said I. Was this your instructions, wolfkin? (for she called me lambkin). Jezebel, you mean, child! said she.—Well, I now forgive you heartily; let's buss and be friends.—Out upon you! said I; I cannot bear you!—But I durst not call her names again; for I dread her huge

paw most sadly. The more I think of this thing, the more
do I regret it, and blame myself.

This night the man from the post-house brought a letter
for Mrs. Jewkes, in which was one enclosed to me: She
brought it me up. Said she, Well, my good master don't
forget us. He has sent you a letter; and see what he writes
to me. So she read, That he hoped her fair charge was well,
happy, and contented. Ay, to be sure, said I, I can't
choose!—That he did not doubt her care and kindness to
me; that I was very dear to him, and she could not use me
too well; and the like. There's a master for you! said she:
sure you will love and pray for him. I desired her to read
the rest. No, no, said she, but I won't. Said I, Are there
any orders for taking my shoes away, and for beating me?
No, said she, nor about Jezebel neither. Well, returned I,
I cry truce; for I have no mind to be beat again. I thought,
said she, we had forgiven one another.

———o———

My letter is as follows :

'MY DEAR PAMELA,—I begin to repent already, that I
'have bound myself, by promise, not to see you till you give
'me leave; for I think the time very tedious. Can you
'place so much confidence in me, as to *invite* me down?
'Assure yourself, that your generosity shall not be thrown
'away upon me. I the rather would press this, as I am
'uneasy for your uneasiness; for Mrs. Jewkes acquaints me,
'that you take your restraint very heavily; and neither eat,
'drink, nor rest well; and I have too great an interest in
'your health, not to wish to shorten the time of this trial;
'which will be the consequence of my coming down to you.
'John, too, has intimated to me your concern, with a grief
'that hardly gave him leave for utterance; a grief that
'a little alarmed my tenderness for you. Not that I fear
'anything, but that your disregard to me, which yet my
'proud heart will hardly permit me to own, may throw

' you upon some rashness, that might encourage a daring
' hope : But how poorly do I descend, to be anxious about
' such a menial as he!—I will only say one thing, that
' if you will give me leave to attend you at the Hall (con-
' sider *who* it is that requests this from you as a *favour*), I
' solemnly declare, that you shall have cause to be pleased
' with this obliging mark of your confidence in me, and con-
' sideration for me ; and if I find Mrs. Jewkes has not behaved
' to you with the respect due to one I so dearly love, I will
' put it entirely into your power to discharge her the house,
' if you think proper ; and Mrs. Jervis, or who else you
' please, shall attend you in her place. This I say on a hint
' John gave me, as if you resented something from that
' quarter. Dearest Pamela, answer favourably this earnest
' request of one that cannot live without you, and on whose
' honour to you, you may absolutely depend ; and so much
' the more, as you place a confidence in it.—I am, and
' assuredly ever will be,

' Your faithful and affectionate, &c.

' You will be glad, I know, to hear your father and mother
' are well, and easy upon your last letter. That gave
' me a pleasure that I am resolved you shall not re-
' pent. Mrs. Jewkes will convey to me your answer.'

I but slightly read this letter for the present, to give way
to one I had hopes of finding by this time from Mr.
Williams. I took an evening turn, as I called it, in Mrs.
Jewkes' company ; and walking by the place, I said, Do
you think, Mrs. Jewkes, any of my beans can have struck
since yesterday ? She laughed, and said, You are a poor
gardener ; but I love to see you divert yourself. She passing on, I found my good friend had provided for me ; and,
slipping it in my bosom (for her back was towards me),
Here, said I (having a bean in my hand), is one of them ;
but it has not stirred. No, to be sure, said she, and turned
upon me a most wicked jest, unbecoming the mouth of a
woman, about planting, &c. When I came in, I hied to
my closet, and read as follows :

' I am sorry to tell you, that I have had a repulse from
' Lady Jones. She is concerned at your case, she says;
' but don't care to make herself enemies. I applied to
' Lady Darnford, and told her in the most pathetic manner
' I could your sad story, and showed her your more pathetic
' letter. I found her well disposed; but she would advise
' with Sir Simon, who by the by is not a man of an extra-
' ordinary character for virtue; but he said to his lady in
' my presence, Why, what is all this, my dear, but that our
' neighbour has a mind to his mother's waiting-maid! And
' if he takes care she wants for nothing, I don't see any
' great injury will be done her. He hurts no *family* by
' this:' (So, my dear father and mother, it seems that poor
people's honesty is to go for nothing) : ' And I think, Mr.
' Williams, you, of all men, should not engage in this affair,
' against your friend and patron. He spoke this in so deter-
' mined a manner, that the lady had done; and I had only to
' beg no notice should be taken of the matter as from *me*.

' I have hinted your case to Mr. Peters, the minister of
' this parish; but I am concerned to say, that he imputed
' selfish views to me, as if I would make an interest in
' your affections by my zeal. And when I represented the
' duties of our function, and the like, and protested my dis-
' interestedness, he coldly said, I was very good; but was
' a young man, and knew little of the world. And though
' it was a thing to be lamented, yet when he and I should
' set about to reform mankind in this respect, we should
' have enough upon our hands; for, he said, it was too
' common and fashionable a case to be withstood by a
' private clergyman or two: and then he uttered some re-
' flections upon the conduct of the present fathers of the
' church, in regard to the first personages of the realm, as
' a justification of his coldness on this score.

' I represented the different circumstances of your affair;
' that other women lived evilly by their own consent, but
' to serve you, was to save an innocence that had but few
' examples; and then I showed him your letter.

' He said it was prettily written; and he was sorry for

' you; and that your good intentions ought to be en-
' couraged: But what, said he, would you have *me* do,
' Mr. Williams? Why suppose, sir, said I, you give her
' shelter in your house, with your spouse and niece, till she
' can get to her friends.—What! and embroil myself with
' a man of Mr. B——'s power and fortune! No, not I,
' I'll assure you!—And I would have you consider what
' you are about. Besides, she owns, continued he, that he
' promises to do honourably by her; and her shyness will
' procure her good terms enough; for he is no covetous
' nor wicked gentleman, except in this case; and 'tis what
' all young gentlemen will do.

' I am greatly concerned for him, I assure you; but I
' am not discouraged by this ill success, let what will come
' of it, if I can serve you.

' I don't hear, as yet, that Mr. B—— is coming. I am
' glad of your hint as to that unhappy fellow John Arnold.
' Something, perhaps, will strike out from that, which may
' be useful. As to your packets, if you seal them up, and
' lay them in the usual place, if you find it not suspected,
' I will watch an opportunity to convey them; but if they
' are large, you had best be very cautious. This evil
' woman, I find, mistrusts me much.

' I just hear, that the gentleman is dying, whose living
' Mr. B—— has promised me. I have almost a scruple to
' take it, as I am acting so contrary to his desires; but I
' hope he will one day thank me for it. As to money,
' don't think of it at present. Be assured you may com-
' mand all in my power to do for you without reserve.

' I believe, when we hear he is coming, it will be best to
' make use of the key, which I shall soon procure you;
' and I can borrow a horse for you, I believe, to wait
' within half a mile of the back-door, over the pasture;
' and will contrive, by myself, or somebody, to have you
' conducted some miles distant, to one of the villages there-
' abouts; so don't be discomforted, I beseech you.—I am,
' excellent Mrs. Pamela,

'Your faithful friend, &c.'

I made a thousand sad reflections upon the former part of this honest gentleman's kind letter; and but for the hope he gave me at last, should have given up my case as quite desperate. I then wrote to thank him most grate-fully for his kind endeavours; to lament the little concern the gentry had for my deplorable case; the wickedness of the world, first to give way to such iniquitous fashions, and then plead the frequency of them, against the attempt to amend them; and how unaffected people were with the distresses of others. I recalled my former hint as to writ-ing to Lady Davers, which I feared, I said, would only serve to apprise her brother, that she knew his wicked scheme, and more harden him in it, and make him come down the sooner, and to be the more determined on my ruin; besides that it might make Mr. Williams guessed at, as a means of conveying my letter: And being very fearful, that if that good lady *would* interest herself in my behalf (which was a doubt, because she both loved and feared her brother), it would have no effect upon him; and that there-fore I would wait the happy event I might hope for from his kind assistance in the key, and the horse. I intimated my master's letter, begging to be permitted to come down: was fearful it might be sudden; and that I was of opinion no time was to be lost; for we might let slip all our opportunities; telling him the money trick of this vile woman, &c.

I had not time to take a copy of this letter, I was so watched. And when I had it ready in my bosom, I was easy. And so I went to seek out Mrs. Jewkes, and told her, I would have her advice upon the letter I had received from my master; which point of confidence in her pleased her not a little. Ay, said she, now this is something like: and we'll take a turn in the garden, or where you please. I pretended it was indifferent to me; and so we walked into the garden. I began to talk to her of the letter; but was far from acquainting her with all the contents; only that he wanted my consent to come down, and hoped she used me kindly, and the like. And I said, Now, Mrs. Jewkes, let me have your advice as to this. Why then, said she, I will give it you freely ; E'en send to him to come down. It will highly oblige him, and I daresay you'll fare the better for it. How the *better?* said I.—I daresay, you think yourself, that he intends my ruin.—I hate, said she, that foolish word, your *ruin!* Why, ne'er a lady in the land may live happier than you if you will, or be more honourably used.

Well, Mrs. Jewkes, said I, I shall not, at this time, dispute with you about the words *ruin* and *honourable :* for I find we have quite different notions of both : But now I will speak plainer than ever I did. Do you think he intends to make proposals to me as to a kept mistress, or kept slave rather, or do you not ?—Why, lambkin, said she, what dost thou think thyself ?—I fear, said I, he does. Well, said she, but if he does (for I know nothing of the matter, I assure you), you may have your own terms—I see that; for you may do anything with him.

I could not bear this to be spoken, though it was all I feared of a long time; and began to exclaim most sadly. Nay, said she, he may marry you, as far as I know.—No, no, said I, that cannot be.—I neither desire nor expect it. His condition don't permit me to have such a thought; and that, and the whole series of his conduct, convinces me of the contrary ; and you would have me invite him to come down, would you ?   Is not this to invite my ruin ?

'Tis what *I* would do, said she, in your place; and if it was to be as you *think,* I should rather be out of my pain, than live in continual frights and apprehensions, as you do. No, replied I, an *hour* of innocence is worth an *age* of guilt ; and were my life to be made ever so miserable by it, I should never forgive myself, if I were not to lengthen out to the longest minute my happy time of honesty.   Who knows what Providence may do for me !

Why, may be, said she, as he loves you so well, you may prevail upon him by your prayers and tears ; and for that reason, I should think, you'd better let him come down. Well, said I, I will write him a letter, because he expects

an answer, or may be he will make a pretence to come
down. How can it go?

I'll take care of that, said she; it is in my instructions.—
Ay, thought I, so I doubt, by the hint Mr. Williams gave
me about the post-house.

The gardener coming by, I said, Mr. Jacob, I have
planted a few beans, and I call the place my garden. It is
just by the door out yonder: I'll show it you; pray don't
dig them up. So I went on with him; and when we had
turned the alley, out of her sight, and were near the place,
said I, Pray step to Mrs. Jewkes, and ask her if she has any
more beans for me to plant? He smiled, I suppose at my
foolishness; and I popped the letter under the mould, and
stepped back, as if waiting for his return; which, being
near, was immediate; and she followed him. What should
I do with beans? said she,—and sadly scared me; for she
whispered me, I am afraid of some fetch! You don't use
to send on such simple errands.—What fetch? said I: It
is hard I can neither stir, nor speak, but I must be suspected.
—Why, said she, my master writes, that I must have all
my eyes about me; for though you are as innocent as a
dove, yet you are as cunning as a serpent. But I'll forgive
you, if you cheat *me*.

Then I thought of my money, and could have called her
names, had I dared: And I said, Pray, Mrs. Jewkes, now
you talk of forgiving me, if I cheat you, be so kind as to
pay me my money; for though I have no occasion for it,
yet I know you was but in jest, and intended to give it me
again. You shall have it in a proper time, said she; but,
indeed, I was in earnest to get it out of your hands, for fear
you should make an ill use of it. And so we cavilled upon
this subject, as we walked in, and I went up to write my
letter to my master; and, as I intended to show it her, I
resolved to write accordingly as to her part of it; for I made
little account of his offer of Mrs. Jervis to me, instead of
this wicked woman (though the most agreeable thing that
could have befallen me, except my escape from hence), nor

indeed anything he said. For to be honourable, in the just
sense of the word, he need not have caused me to be run
away with, and confined as I am.   I wrote as follows:

' HONOURED SIR,—When I consider how easily you
' might make me happy, since all I desire is to be permitted
' to go to my poor father and mother; when I reflect upon
' your former proposal to me, in relation to a certain person,
' not one word of which is now mentioned; and upon my
' being in that strange manner run away with, and still
' kept here a miserable prisoner; do you think, sir (pardon
' your poor servant's freedom; my fears make me bold; do
' you think, I say), that your general assurances of honour
' to me, can have the effect upon me, that, were it not for
' these things, all your words ought to have?—Oh, good sir!
' I too much apprehend, that *your* notions of honour and
' *mine* are very different from one another: and I have no
' other hopes but in your continued absence. If you have
' any proposals to make me, that are consistent with your
' honourable professions, in my *humble* sense of the word,
' a few lines will communicate them to me, and I will return
' such an answer as befits me. But, oh! what proposals
' can one in your high station have to make to one in my
' low one! I know what belongs to your degree too well,
' to imagine, that anything can be expected but sad tempta-
' tions, and utter distress, if you come down; and you know
' not, sir, when I am made desperate, what the wretched
' *Pamela dares to do!*

' Whatever rashness you may impute to me, I cannot help
' it; but I wish I may not be forced upon any, that other-
' wise would never enter into my thoughts. Forgive me,
' sir, my plainness; I should be loath to behave to my
' master unbecomingly; but I must needs say, sir, my
' innocence is so dear to me, that all other considerations
' are, and, I hope, shall ever be, treated by me as niceties,
' that ought, for that, to be dispensed with. If you mean
' honourably, why, sir, should you not let me know it
' plainly? Why is it necessary to imprison me, to convince

' me of it? And why must I be close watched, and at-
' tended, hindered from stirring out, from speaking to any-
' body, from going so much as to church to pray for you,
' who have been, till of late, so generous a benefactor to me?
' Why, sir, I humbly ask, why all this, if you mean honour-
' ably?—It is not for me to expostulate so freely, but in a
' case so near to me, with you, sir, so greatly my superior.
' Pardon me, I hope you will ; but as to *seeing you,* I can-
' not bear the dreadful apprehension. Whatever you have
' to propose, whatever you intend by me, let my assent be
' that of a free person, mean as I am, and not of a sordid
' slave, who is to be threatened and frightened into a com-
' pliance with measures, which your conduct to her seems
' to imply would be otherwise abhorred by her.—My restraint
' is indeed hard upon me: I am very uneasy under it.
' Shorten it, I beseech you, or—but I will not dare to say
' more, than that I am

' Your greatly oppressed unhappy servant.'

After I had taken a copy of this, I folded it up; and
Mrs. Jewkes, coming just as I had done, sat down by me ;
and said, when she saw me direct it, I wish you would tell
me if you have taken my advice, and consented to my
master's coming down. If it will oblige you, said I, I will
read it to you. That's good, said she ; then I'll love you
dearly.—Said I, Then you must not offer to alter one word.
I won't, replied she. So I read it to her, and she praised
me much for my wording it; but said she thought I pushed
the matter very close ; and it would better bear *talking* of,
than *writing* about. She wanted an explanation or two, as
about the proposal to a *certain person ;* but I said, she must
take it as she heard it. Well, well, said she, I make no doubt
you understand one another, and will do so more and more.
I sealed up the letter, and she undertook to convey it.

———o———

For my part, I knew it in vain to expect to have leave to
go to church now, and so I did not ask; and I was the
more indifferent, because, if I might have had permission,
the sight of the neighbouring gentry, who had despised
my sufferings, would have given me great regret and sorrow; and it was impossible I should have edified under
any doctrine preached by Mr. Peters: so I applied myself
to my private devotions.

Mr. Williams came yesterday, and this day, as usual,
and took my letter; but, having no good opportunity, we
avoided one another's conversation, and kept at a distance:
But I was concerned I had not the key; for I would not
have lost a moment in that case, had I been he, and he I.
When I was at my devotion, Mrs. Jewkes came up, and
wanted me sadly to sing her a psalm, as she had often on
common days importuned me for a song upon the spinnet:
but I declined it, because my spirits were so low I could
hardly speak, nor cared to be spoken to; but when she was
gone, I remembering the cxxxviith psalm to be a little touching, turned to it, and took the liberty to alter it, somewhat
nearer to my case. I hope I did not sin in it; but thus I
turned it:

I.

When sad I sat in B——n Hall,
  All guarded round about,
And thought of ev'ry absent friend,
  The tears for grief burst out.

II.

My joys and hopes all overthrown,
  My heart-strings almost broke,
Unfit my mind for melody,
  Much more to bear a joke.

III.

Then she to whom I pris'ner was,
  Said to me, tauntingly,
Now cheer your heart, and sing a song,
  And tune your mind to joy.

IV.

Alas ! said I, how can I frame
  My heavy heart to sing,
Or tune my mind, while thus enthrall'd
  By such a wicked thing !

V.

But yet, if from my innocence
  I, ev'n in thought, should slide,
Then let my fingers quite forget
  The sweet spinnet to guide.

VI.

And let my tongue within my mouth
  Be lock'd for ever fast,
If I rejoice, before I see
  My full deliv'rance past.

VII.

And thou, Almighty, recompense
  The evils I endure,
From those who seek my sad disgrace,
  So causeless, to procure.

VIII.

Remember, Lord, this Mrs. Jewkes
  When, with a mighty sound,
She cries, Down with her chastity,
  Down to the very ground !

IX.

Ev'n so shalt thou, O wicked one!
  At length to shame be brought,
And happy shall all those be call'd
  That my deliv'rance wrought.

X.

Yea, blessed shall the man be call'd
  That shames thee of thy evil,
And saves me from thy vile attempts,
  And thee, too, from the D——l.

—— *o* ——

Monday, Tuesday, Wednesday.

I WRITE now with a little more liking, though less opportunity, because Mr. Williams has got a large parcel of my papers, safe in his hands, to send them to you, as he has opportunity; so I am not quite uselessly employed; and I am delivered, besides, from the fear of their being found, if I should be searched, or discovered. I have been permitted to take an airing, five or six miles, with Mrs. Jewkes: But, though I know not the reason, she watches me more closely than ever; so that we have discontinued, by consent, for these three days, the sunflower correspondence.

The poor cook-maid has had a bad mischance; for she has been hurt much by a bull in the pasture, by the side of the garden, not far from the back-door. Now this pasture I am to cross, which is about half a mile, and then is a common, and near that a private horse-road, where I hope to find an opportunity for escaping, as soon as Mr. Williams can get me a horse, and has made all ready for me: for he has got me the key, which he put under the mould, just by the door, as he found an opportunity to hint to me.

He just now has signified, that the gentleman is dead whose living he has had hope of; and he came pretendedly to tell Mrs. Jewkes of it; and so could speak this to her before me. She wished him joy. See what the world is! One man's death is another man's joy. Thus we thrust out one another!—My hard case makes me serious. He found means to slide a letter into my hands, and is gone away: He looked at me with such respect and solemnness at parting, that Mrs. Jewkes said, Why, madam, I believe our young parson is half in love with you.—Ah! Mrs. Jewkes, said I, he knows better. Said she (I believe to sound me), Why, I can't see you can either of you do better; and I have lately been so touched for you, seeing how heavily you apprehend dishonour from my master, that I think it is a pity you should not have Mr. Williams.

I knew this must be a fetch of hers; because, instead of

being troubled for me, as she pretended, she watched me closer, and him too: and so I said, There is not the man living that I desire to marry. If I can but keep myself honest, it is all my desire: And to be a comfort and assistance to my poor parents, if it should be my happy lot to be so, is the very top of my ambition. Well, but, said she, I have been thinking very seriously, that Mr. Williams would make you a good husband; and as he will owe all his fortune to my master, he will be very glad, to be sure, to be obliged to him for a wife of his choosing: especially, said she, such a pretty one, and one so ingenious and genteelly educated.

This gave me a doubt, whether she knew of my master's intimation of that sort formerly; and I asked her, if she had reason to surmise that *that* was in view? No, she said; it was only her own thought; but it was very likely that my master had either that in view, or something better for me. But, if I approved of it, she would propose such a thing to her master directly; and gave a detestable hint, that I might take resolutions upon it, of bringing such an affair to effect. I told her I abhorred her vile insinuation; and as to Mr. Williams, I thought him a civil good sort of man; but as, on one side, he was above me; so, on the other, I said of all things I did not love a parson. So, finding she could make nothing of me, she quitted the subject.

I will open his letter by and by, and give you the contents of it; for she is up and down so much, that I am afraid of her surprising me.

Well, I see Providence has not abandoned me: I shall be under no necessity to make advances to Mr. Williams, if I was (as I am sure I am not) disposed to it. This is his letter:

' I KNOW not how to express myself, lest I should appear
' to you to have a selfish view in the service I would do you.
' But I really know but one effectual and honourable way

' to disengage yourself from the dangerous situation you
' are in. It is that of marriage with some person that
' you could make happy in your approbation. As for my
' own part, it would be, as things stand, my apparent ruin;
' and, worse still, I should involve you in misery too. But,
' yet, so great is my veneration for you, and so entire my
' reliance on Providence, upon so just an occasion, that I
' should think myself but too happy, if I might be accepted.
' I would, in this case, forego all my expectations, and be
' your conductor to some safe distance. But why do I say,
' *in this case?* That I will do, whether you think fit to
' reward me so eminently or not: And I will, the moment
' I hear of Mr. B——'s setting out (and I think now I
' have settled a very good method of intelligence of all his
' motions), get a horse ready, and myself to conduct you.
' I refer myself wholly to your goodness and direction; and
' am, with the highest respect,

> ' Your most faithful humble servant.

    ' Don't think this a sudden resolution. I always admired
    ' your hearsay character; and the moment I saw you,
    ' wished to serve so much excellence.'

What shall I say, my dear father and mother, to this
unexpected declaration? I want, now, more than ever, your
blessing and direction. But, after all, I have no mind to
marry: I had rather live with you. But yet, I would
marry a man who begs from door to door, and has no home
nor being, rather than endanger my honesty. Yet I cannot,
methinks, hear of being a wife.—After a thousand different
thoughts, I wrote as follows:

    ' REVEREND SIR,—I am greatly confused at the con-
    ' tents of your last. You are much too generous, and I
    ' can't bear you should risk all your future prospects for so
    ' unworthy a creature. I cannot think of your offer with-
    ' out equal concern and gratitude; for nothing, but to
    ' avoid my utter ruin, can make me think of a change of
    ' condition; and so, sir, you ought not to accept of such

' an involuntary compliance, as mine would be, were I,
' upon the last necessity, to yield to your very generous
' proposal. I will rely wholly upon your goodness to me,
' in assisting my escape; but shall not, on your account
' principally, *think* of the honour you propose for me, at
' present; and never, but at the pleasure of my parents;
' who, poor as they are, in such a weighty point, are as
' much entitled to my obedience and duty, as if they were
' ever so rich. I beg you, therefore, sir, not to think of
' anything from me, but everlasting gratitude, which will
' always bind me to be

' Your most obliged servant.'

—o—

Thursday, Friday, Saturday, the 14th,
15th, and 16th, of my bondage.

Mrs. Jewkes has received a letter, and is much civiller to
me, and Mr. Williams too, than she used to be. I wonder
I have not one in answer to mine to my master. I suppose I
put the matter too home to him; and he is angry. I am
not the more pleased with her civility; for she is horrid
cunning, and is not a whit less watchful. I laid a trap
to get at her instructions, which she carries in the bosom
of her stays; but it has not succeeded.

My last letter is come safe to Mr. Williams by the old
conveyance, so that he is not suspected. He has intimated,
that though I have not come so readily as he hoped into
his scheme, yet his diligence shall not be slackened, and he
will leave it to Providence and himself to dispose of him
as he shall be found to deserve. He has signified to me,
that he shall soon send a special messenger with the packet
to you, and I have added to it what has occurred since.

—o—

I AM just now quite astonished!—I hope all is right!—
but I have a strange turn to acquaint you with. Mr.
Williams and Mrs. Jewkes came to me both together; he
in ecstacies, she with a strange fluttering sort of air. Well,
said she, Mrs. Pamela, I give you joy! I give you joy!—
Let nobody speak but me! Then she sat down, as out of
breath, puffing and blowing. Why, everything turns as I
said it would! said she: Why, there is to be a match
between you and Mr. Williams! Well, I always thought it.
Never was so good a master!—Go to, go to, naughty, mistrustful Mrs. Pamela; nay, Mrs. Williams, said the forward
creature, I may as good call you: you ought on your
knees to beg his pardon a thousand times for mistrusting
him.

She was going on; but I said, Don't torture me thus, I
beseech you, Mrs. Jewkes. Let me know all!—Ah! Mr.
Williams, said I, take care, take care!—Mistrustful again!
said she: Why, Mr. Williams, show her your letter, and I
will show her mine: they were brought by the same hand.

I trembled at the thoughts of what this might mean; and
said, You have so surprised me, that I cannot stand, nor
hear, nor read! Why did you come up in such a manner to
attack such weak spirits? Said he, to Mrs. Jewkes, Shall
we leave our letters with Mrs. Pamela, and let her recover
from her surprise? Ay, said she, with all my heart; here is
nothing but flaming honour and good will! And so saying,
they left me their letters and withdrew.

My heart was quite sick with the surprise; so that I could
not presently read them, notwithstanding my impatience;
but, after a while, recovering, I found the contents thus
strange and unexpected:

'MR. WILLIAMS,—'The death of Mr. Fownes has now
' given me the opportunity I have long wanted, to make you
' happy, and that in a double respect: For I shall soon put
' you in possession of his living; and, if you have the art

' of making yourself well received, of one of the loveliest
' wives in England. She has not been used (as she has
' reason to think) according to her merit; but when she
' finds herself under the protection of a man of virtue and
' probity, and a happy competency to support life in the ·
' manner to which she has been of late years accustomed,
' I am persuaded she will forgive those seeming hardships
' which have paved the way to so happy a lot, as I hope it
' will be to you both. I have only to account for and
' excuse the odd conduct I have been guilty of, which I shall
' do when I see you: but as I shall soon set out for London,
' I believe it will not be yet this month. Meantime, if you
' can prevail with Pamela, you need not suspend for that
' your mutual happiness; only let me have notice of it first,
' and that she approves of it; which ought to be, in so
' material a point, entirely at her option; as I assure you,
' on the other hand, I would have it at yours, that nothing
' may be wanting to complete your happiness.

' I am your humble servant.'

Was ever the like heard?—Lie still, my throbbing heart,
divided as thou art, between thy hopes and thy fears!—But
this is the letter Mrs. Jewkes left with me:

'Mrs. Jewkes,—You have been very careful and dili-
' gent in the task, which, for reasons I shall hereafter
' explain, I had imposed upon you. Your trouble is now
' almost at an end; for I have written my intentions to Mr.
' Williams so particularly, that I need say the less here,
' because he will not scruple, I believe, to let you know the
' contents of my letter. I have only one thing to mention,
' that if you find what I have hinted to him in the least
' measure disagreeable to either, you assure them both, that
' they are at entire liberty to pursue their own inclinations.
' I hope you continue your civilities to the mistrustful,
' uneasy Pamela, who now will begin to think better of
' hers and

' Your friend, &c.'

I had hardly time to transcribe these letters, though, writing so much, I write pretty fast, before they both came up again in high spirits; and Mr. Williams said, I am glad at my heart, madam, that I was *beforehand* in my declarations to you: this generous letter has made me the happiest man on earth; and, Mrs. Jewkes, you may be sure, that if I can procure this fair one's consent, I shall think myself— I interrupted the good man, and said, Ah! Mr. Williams, take care, take care; don't let—There I stopt; and Mrs. Jewkes said, Still mistrustful!—I never saw the like in my life!—But I see, said she, I was not wrong, while my old orders lasted, to be wary of you both—I should have had a hard task to prevent you, I find; for, as the saying is, *Nought can restrain consent of twain.*

I doubted not her taking hold of his joyful indiscretion. —I took her letter, and said, Here, Mrs. Jewkes, is yours; I thank you for it; but I have been so long in a maze, that I can say nothing of this for the present. Time will bring all to light.—Sir, said I, here is yours: May everything turn to your happiness! I give you joy of my master's goodness in the living.—It will be *dying*, said he, not a *living*, without you.—Forbear, sir, said I; while I have a father and mother, I am not my own mistress, poor as they are; and I'll see myself quite at liberty, before I shall think myself fit to make a choice.

Mrs. Jewkes held up her eyes and hands, and said, Such art, such caution, such cunning, for thy years!—Well!— Why, said I (that he might be more on his guard, though I hope there cannot be deceit in this; 'twould be strange villany, and that is a hard word, if there should!) I have been so used to be made a fool of by fortune, that I hardly can tell how to govern myself; and am almost an infidel as to mankind. But I hope I may be wrong; henceforth, Mrs. Jewkes, you shall regulate my opinions as you please, and I will consult you in everything—(that I think proper, said I to myself)—for, to be sure, though I may forgive her, I can never love her.

She left Mr. Williams and me, a few minutes, together;

and I said, Consider, sir, consider what you have done.
'Tis impossible, said he, there can be deceit. I hope so,
said I; but what necessity was there for you to talk of
your *former* declaration? Let *this* be as it will, *that* could
do no good, especially before this woman. Forgive me,
sir; they talk of women's promptness of speech; but,
indeed, I see an honest heart is not always to be trusted
with itself in bad company.

He was going to reply, but though her task is said to be
ALMOST (I took notice of that word) at an end, she came
up to us again, and said: Well, I had a good mind to show
you the way to church to-morrow. I was glad of this,
because, though in my present doubtful situation I should
not have chosen it, yet I would have encouraged her
proposal, to be able to judge by her being in earnest or
otherwise, whether one might depend upon the rest. But
Mr. Williams again indiscreetly helped her to an excuse,
by saying, that it was now best to defer it one Sunday,
and till matters were riper for my appearance: and she
readily took hold of it, and confirmed his opinion.

After all, I hope the best: but if this should turn out
to be a plot, I fear nothing but a miracle can save me.
But, sure the heart of man is not capable of such black
deceit. Besides, Mr. Williams has it under his own hand,
and he dare not but be in earnest; and then again, though
to be sure he has been very wrong to me, yet his education,
and parents' example, have neither of them taught him
such very black contrivances. So I will hope for the best.

Mr. Williams, Mrs. Jewkes, and I, have been all three
walking together in the garden; and she pulled out her
key, and we walked a little in the pasture to look at the
bull, an ugly, grim, surly creature, that hurt the poor
cook-maid; who is got pretty well again. Mr. Williams
pointed at the sunflower, but I was forced to be very reserved to him; for the poor gentleman has no guard, no
caution at all.

We have just supped together, all three; and I cannot

yet think but all must be right.—Only I am resolved not to marry, if I can help it; and I will give no encouragement, I am resolved, at least, till I am with you.

Mr. Williams said, before Mrs. Jewkes, he would send a messenger with a letter to my father and mother.—I think the man has no discretion in the world: but I desire you will send no answer, till I have the pleasure and happiness which now I hope for soon, of seeing you. He will, in sending my packet, send a most tedious parcel of stuff, of my *oppressions,* my *distresses,* my *fears;* and so I will send this with it (for Mrs. Jewkes gives me leave to send a letter to my father, which looks well); and I am glad I can conclude, after all my sufferings, with my *hopes,* to be soon with you, which I know will give you comfort; and so I rest, begging the continuance of your prayers and blessings.

Your ever dutiful DAUGHTER.

—*o*—

MY DEAR FATHER AND MOTHER,—I have so much time upon my hands, that I must write on, to employ myself. The Sunday evening, where I left off, Mrs. Jewkes asked me, if I chose to lie by myself; I said, Yes, with *all* my heart, if she pleased. Well, said she, after to-night you shall. I asked her for more paper; and she gave me a bottle of ink, eight sheets of paper, which she said was all her store (for now she would get me to write for her to our master, if she had occasion), and six pens, with a piece of sealing wax. This looks mighty well.

She pressed me, when she came to bed, very much, to give encouragement to Mr. Williams, and said many things in his behalf; and blamed my shyness to him. I told her, I was resolved to give no encouragement, till I had talked to my father and mother. She said, he fancied I thought of somebody else, or I could never be so insensible. I assured her, as I could do very safely, that there was not a

man on earth I wished to have; and as to Mr. Williams,
he might do better by far; and I had proposed so much
happiness in living with my poor father and mother, that I
could not think of any scheme of life with pleasure, till
I had tried that. I asked her for my money; and she
said, it was above in her strong box, but that I should have
it to-morrow. All these things look well, as I said.

Mr. Williams would go home this night, though late,
because he would despatch a messenger to you with a letter
he had proposed from himself, and my packet. But pray
don't encourage him, as I said; for he is much too heady
and precipitate as to this matter, in my way of thinking;
though, to be sure, he is a very good man, and I am much
obliged to him.

—*o*—

Monday morning.

Alas-a-day! we have bad news from poor Mr. Williams.
He has had a sad mischance; fallen among rogues in his
way home last night: but by good chance has saved my
papers. This is the account he gives of it to Mrs. Jewkes.

‘ Good Mrs. Jewkes,—I have had a sore misfortune
‘ in going from you. When I had got as near the town as
‘ the dam, and was going to cross the wooden bridge, two
‘ fellows got hold of me, and swore bitterly they would kill
‘ me, if I did not give them what I had. They rummaged
‘ my pockets, and took from me my snuff-box, my seal-ring,
‘ and half a guinea, and some silver, and halfpence; also
‘ my handkerchief, and two or three letters I had in my
‘ pockets. By good fortune, the letter Mrs. Pamela gave
‘ me was in my bosom, and so that escaped: but they
‘ bruised my head and face, and cursing me for having no
‘ more money, tipped me into the dam, crying, Lie there,
‘ parson, till to-morrow! My shins and knees were bruised
‘ much in the fall against one of the stumps; and I had
‘ like to have been suffocated in water and mud. To be
‘ sure, I shan’t be able to stir out this day or two: for I am

'a frightful spectacle! My hat and wig I was forced to
'leave behind me, and go home, a mile and a half, with-
'out; but they were found next morning, and brought me,
'with my snuff-box, which the rogues must have dropped.
'My cassock is sadly torn, as is my band. To be sure, I
'was much frightened; for a robbery in these parts has
'not been known many years. Diligent search is making
'after the rogues. My humble respects to good Mrs.
'Pamela: if *she* pities my misfortunes, I shall be the
'sooner well, and fit to wait on her and you. This did
'not hinder me in writing a letter, though with great pain,
'as I do this (*To be sure this good man can keep no
'secret!*) and sending it away by a man and horse, this
'morning. I am, good Mrs. Jewkes,

> 'Your most obliged humble servant.

> 'God be praised it is no worse! And I find I have got
> 'no cold, though miserably wet from top to toe. My
> 'fright, I believe, prevented me from catching cold;
> 'for I was not rightly myself for some hours, and
> 'know not how I got home. I will write a letter of
> 'thanks this night, if I am able, to my kind patron,
> 'for his inestimable goodness to me. I wish I was
> 'enabled to say all I hope, with regard to the *better part*
> 'of his bounty to me, incomparable Mrs. Pamela.'

The wicked brute fell a laughing, when she had read
this letter, till her fat sides shook. Said she, I can but
think how the poor parson looked, after parting with his
pretty mistress in such high spirits, when he found himself
at the bottom of the dam! And what a figure he must cut
in his tattered band and cassock, and without a hat and
wig, when he got home. I warrant, added she, he was in
a sweet pickle!—I said, I thought it was very barbarous to
laugh at such a misfortune: but she replied, As he was safe,
she laughed; otherwise she would have been sorry: and
she was glad to see me so concerned for him—It looked
promising, she said.

I heeded not her reflections; but as I have been used to

causes for mistrusts, I cannot help saying that I don't like this thing : And their taking his letters most alarms me. —How happy it was they missed my packet ! I knew not what to think of it !—But why should I let every accident break my peace ? Yet it *will* do so, while I stay here.

Mrs. Jewkes is mightily at me, to go with her in the chariot, to visit Mr. Williams. She is so officious to bring on the affair between us, that, being a cunning, artful woman, I know not what to make of it : I have refused her absolutely ; urging, that except I intended to encourage his suit, I ought not to do it. And she is gone without me.

I have strange temptations to get away in her absence, for all these fine appearances. 'Tis sad to have nobody to advise with !—I know not what to do. But, alas for me ! I have no money, if I should, to buy anybody's civilities, or to pay for necessaries or lodgings. But I'll go into the garden, and resolve afterwards——

I have been in the garden, and to the back-door : and there I stood, my heart up at my mouth. I could not see I was watched ; so this looks well. But if anything should go bad afterwards, I should never forgive myself, for not taking this opportunity. Well, I will go down again, and see if all is clear, and how it looks out at the back-door in the pasture.

To be sure, there is witchcraft in this house ; and I believe Lucifer is bribed, as well as all about me, and is got into the shape of that nasty grim bull to watch me !— For I have been down again, and ventured to open the door, and went out about a bow-shot into the pasture ; but there stood that horrid bull, staring me full in the face, with fiery saucer eyes, as I thought. So I got in again, for fear he should come at me. Nobody saw me, however. —Do you think there are such things as witches and spirits ? If there be, I believe, in my heart, Mrs. Jewkes has got this bull of her side. But yet, what could I do without money, or a friend?—Oh this wicked woman! to trick me so! Every-thing, man, woman, and beast, is in a plot against your poor Pamela, I think!—Then I know not one step of the way, nor how far to any house or cottage; and whether I could gain protection, if I got to a house: And now the robbers are abroad too, I may run into as great danger as I want to escape; nay, greater much, if these promising appearances hold: And sure my master cannot be so black as that they should not!—What can I do?—I have a good mind to try for it once more; but then I may be pursued and taken; and it will be worse for me; and this wicked woman will beat me, and take my shoes away, and lock me up.

But, after all, if my master should mean *well*, he can't be angry at my fears, if I should escape; and nobody can blame me; and I can more easily be induced, with you, when all my apprehensions are over, to consider his pro-posal of Mr. Williams, than I could here; and he pretends, as you have read in his letter, he will leave me to my choice: Why then should I be afraid? I will go down again, I think! But yet my heart misgives me, because of the difficulties before me, in escaping; and being so poor and so friendless:—O good God! the preserver of the innocent! direct me what to do!

Well, I have just now a sort of strange persuasion upon me, that I ought to try to get away, and leave the issue to Providence. So, once more—I'll see, at least, if this bull be still there.

Alack-a-day! what a fate is this! I have not the courage to go, neither can I think to stay. But I must resolve. The gardener was in sight last time; so made me come up again. But I'll contrive to send him out of the way, if I can:—For if I never should have such another opportunity, I could not forgive myself. Once more I'll venture. God direct my footsteps, and make smooth my path and my way to safety!

Well, here I am, come back again! frightened, like a

fool, out of all my purposes! Oh how terrible everything
appears to me! I had got twice as far again, as I was
before, out of the back-door: and I looked and saw the
bull, as I thought, between me and the door; and another
bull coming towards me the other way: Well, thought I,
here is double witchcraft, to be sure! Here is the spirit
of my master in one bull, and Mrs. Jewkes's in the other.
And now I am gone, to be sure! Oh help! cried I, like a
fool, and ran back to the door, as swift as if I flew. When
I had got the door in my hand, I ventured to look back, to
see if these supposed bulls were coming; and I saw they
were only two poor cows, a grazing in distant places, that
my fears had made all this rout about. But as everything
is so frightful to me, I find I am not fit to think of my
escape: for I shall be as much frightened at the first strange
man that I meet with: and I am persuaded, that fear brings
one into more dangers, than the caution, that goes along
with it, delivers one from.

I then locked the door, and put the key in my pocket,
and was in a sad quandary; but I was soon determined;
for the maid Nan came in sight, and asked, if anything
was the matter, that I was so often up and down stairs?
God forgive me (but I had a sad lie at my tongue's end),
said I; Though Mrs. Jewkes is sometimes a little hard
upon me, yet I know not where I am without her: I go up,
and I come down to walk about in the garden; and, not
having her, know scarcely what to do with myself. Ay,
said the idiot, she is main good company, madam, no wonder
you miss her.

So here I am again, and here likely to be; for I have no
courage to help myself anywhere else. Oh why are poor
foolish maidens tried with such dangers, when they have
such weak minds to grapple with them!—I will, since it is
so, hope the best: but yet I cannot but observe how
grievously everything makes against me: for here are the
robbers; though I fell not into their hands myself, yet they
gave me as much terror, and had as great an effect upon

my fears, as if I had: And here is the bull; it has as
effectually frightened me, as if I had been hurt by it instead
of the cook-maid; and so these joined together, as I may
say, to make a very dastard of me. But my folly was the
worst of all, because that deprived me of my money: for
had I had *that*, I believe I should have ventured both the
bull and the robbers.

———o———

Monday afternoon.

So, Mrs. Jewkes is returned from her visit: Well, said she,
I would have you set your heart at rest; for Mr. Williams
will do very well again. He is not half so bad as he fancied.
Oh these scholars, said she, they have not the hearts of mice!
He has only a few scratches on his face; which, said she, I
suppose he got by grappling among the gravel at the bottom
of the dam, to try to find a hole in the ground, to hide
himself from the robbers. His shin and his knee are hardly
to be seen to ail anything. He says in his letter, he was a
frightful spectacle: He might be so, indeed, when he first
came in a doors; but he looks well enough now: and,
only for a few groans now and then, when he thinks of
his danger, I see nothing is the matter with him. So, Mrs.
Pamela, said she, I would have you be very easy about it.
I am glad of it, said I, for all your jokes, to Mrs. Jewkes.

Well, said she, he talks of nothing but you; and when
I told him I would fain have persuaded you to come with
me, the man was out of his wits with his gratitude to me:
and so has laid open all his heart to me, and told me all
that has passed, and was contriving between you two.
This alarmed me prodigiously; and the rather, as I saw, by
two or three instances, that his honest heart could keep
nothing, believing every one as undesigning as himself. I
said, but yet with a heavy heart, Ah! Mrs. Jewkes, Mrs.
Jewkes, this might have done with me, had he had anything that he could have told you of. But you know well
enough, that had we been disposed, we had no opportunity
for it, from your watchful care and circumspection. No,

said she, that's very true, Mrs. Pamela; not so much as for that declaration that he owned before me, he had found opportunity, for all my watchfulness, to make you. Come, come, said she, no more of these shams with me! You have an excellent head-piece for your years; but maybe I am as cunning as you.—However, said she, all is well now; because my *watchments* are now over, by my master's direction. How have you employed yourself in my absence?

I was so troubled at what might have passed between Mr. Williams and her, that I could not hide it; and she said, Well, Mrs. Pamela, since all matters are likely to be so soon and so happily ended, let me advise you to be a little less concerned at his discoveries: and make me your confidant, as he has done, and I shall think you have some favour for me, and reliance upon me; and perhaps you might not repent it.

She was so earnest, that I mistrusted she did this to pump me; and I knew how, now, to account for her kindness to Mr. Williams in her visit to him; which was only to get out of him what she could. Why, Mrs. Jewkes, said I, is all this fishing about for something, where there is nothing, if there be an end of your *watchments*, as you call them? Nothing, said she, but womanish curiosity, I'll assure you; for one is naturally led to find out matters, where there is such privacy intended. Well, said I, pray let me know what he has said; and then I'll give you an answer to your curiosity. I don't care, said she, whether you do or not; for I have as much as I wanted from him; and I despair of getting out of you anything you ha'n't a mind I should know, my little cunning dear.—Well, said I, let him have said what he would, I care not: for I am sure he can say no harm of me; and so let us change the talk.

I was the easier, indeed, because, for all her pumps, she gave no hints of the key and the door, &c., which, had he communicated to her, she would not have forborne giving me a touch of.—And so we gave up one another, as despairing to gain our ends of each other. But I am sure he must have said more than he should.—And I am the more apprehensive all is not right, because. she has now been actually, these two hours, shut up a writing; though she pretended she had given me up all her stores of papers, &c., and that I should write for her. I begin to wish I had ventured everything and gone off, when I might. Oh when will this state of doubt and uneasiness end !

She has just been with me, and says she shall send a messenger to Bedfordshire; and he shall carry a letter of thanks for me, if I will write it, for my master's favour to me. Indeed, said I, I have no thanks to give, till I am with my father and mother: and, besides, I sent a letter, as you know; but have had no answer to it. She said, she thought that his letter to Mr. Williams was sufficient; and the least I could do was to thank him, if but in two lines. No need of it, said I; for I don't intend to have Mr. Williams: What then is that letter to me?   Well, said she, I see thou art quite unfathomable!

I don't like all this. Oh my foolish fears of bulls and robbers !—For now all my uneasiness begins to double upon me. Oh what has this incautious man said ! That, no doubt, is the subject of her long letter.

I will close this day's writing, with just saying, that she is mighty silent and reserved, to what she was; and says nothing but No, or Yes, to what I ask. Something must be hatching, I doubt !—I the rather think so, because I find she does not keep her word with me, about lying by myself, and my money; to both which points she returned suspicious answers, saying, as to the one, Why, you are mighty earnest for your money; I shan't run away with it. And to the other, Good-lack! you need not be so willing, as I know of, to part with me for a bedfellow, till you are sure of one you *like better*. This cut me to the heart; and, at the same time, stopped my mouth.

—o—

MR WILLIAMS has been here; but we have had no opportunity to talk together: He seemed confounded at Mrs.
Jewkes's change of temper, and reservedness, after her kind
visit, and their freedom with one another, and much more
at what I am going to tell you. He asked, If I would take
a turn in the garden with Mrs. Jewkes and him. No, said
she, I can't go. Said he, May not Mrs. Pamela take a
walk?—No, said she; I desire she won't. Why, Mrs.
Jewkes? said he: I am afraid I have somehow disobliged
you. Not at all, replied she; but I suppose you will soon
be at liberty to walk together as much as you please: and
I have sent a messenger for my last instructions, about *this*
and *more* weighty matters; and when they come I shall
leave you to do as you both will; but, till then, it is no
matter how little you are together. This alarmed us both;
and he seemed quite struck of a heap, and put on, as I
thought, a self-accusing countenance. So I went behind
her back, and held my two hands together, flat, with a bit
of paper, I had, between them, and looked at him: and he
seemed to take me as I intended; intimating the renewing
of the correspondence by the tiles.

I left them both together, and retired to my closet to
write a letter for the tiles; but having no time for a copy,
I will give you the substance only.

I expostulated with him on his too great openness and
easiness to fall into Mrs. Jewkes's snares; told him my
apprehensions of foul play; and gave briefly the reasons
which moved me: begged to know what he had said; and
intimated, that I thought there was the highest reason to
resume our prospect of the escape by the back-door. I
put this in the usual place in the evening; and now wait
with impatience for an answer.

—o—

Thursday.

I have the following answer :

'DEAREST MADAM,—I am utterly confounded, and must
'plead guilty to all your just reproaches. I wish I were
'master of all but half your caution and discretion! I hope,
'after all, this is only a touch of this ill woman's temper,
'to show her power and importance: For I think Mr.
'B—— neither can nor dare deceive me in so black a
'manner. I would expose him all the world over if he did.
'But it is *not, cannot* be in him. I have received a letter
'from John Arnold, in which he tells me, that his master
'is preparing for his London journey; and believes, after-
'wards, he will come into these parts: But he says, Lady
'Davers is at their house, and is to accompany her brother
'to London, or meet him there, he knows not which. He
'professes great zeal and affection to your service: and I
'find he refers to a letter he sent me before, but which is
'not come to my hand. I *think* there can be no treachery;
'for it is a particular friend at Gainsborough, that I have
'ordered him to direct to; and this is come safe to my
'hands by this means; for well I know, I durst trust
'nothing to Brett, at the post-house here. This gives me
'a little pain; but I hope all will end well, and we shall
'soon hear, if it be necessary to pursue our former inten-
'tions. If it be, I will lose no time to provide a horse for
'you, and another for myself; for I can never do either
'God or myself better service, though I were to forego all
'my expectations for it here. I am

' Your most faithful humble servant.'

'I was too free indeed with Mrs. Jewkes, led to it by
'her dissimulation, and by her pretended concern to
'make me happy with you. I hinted, that I would
'not have scrupled to have procured your deliverance
'by any means; and that I had proposed to you, as
'the only honourable one, marriage with me. But I
'assured her, though she would hardly believe me, that

'you discouraged my application: which is too true!
'But not a word of the back-door key, &c.'

Mrs. Jewkes continues still sullen and ill-natured, and I
am almost afraid to speak to her. She watches me as close
as ever, and pretends to wonder why I shun her company
as I do.

I have just put under the tiles these lines inspired by my
fears, which are indeed very strong; and, I doubt, not
without reason.

'Sir,—Everything gives me additional disturbance. The
'missed letter of John Arnold's makes me suspect a plot.
'Yet am I loath to think myself of so much importance, as
'to suppose every one in a plot against me. Are you sure,
'however, the London journey is not to be a Lincolnshire
'one? May not John, who has been once a traitor, be so
'again?—Why *need* I be thus in doubt?—If I could have
'this horse, I would turn the reins on his neck, and trust
'to Providence to guide him for my safeguard! For I
'would not endanger you, now just upon the edge of your
'preferment. Yet, sir, I fear your fatal openness will make
'you suspected as accessory, let us be ever so cautious.

'Were my *life* in question, instead of my *honesty*, I
'would not wish to involve you, or anybody, in the least
'difficulty, for so worthless a poor creature. But oh, sir!
'my *soul* is of equal importance with the soul of a *princess;*
'though my quality is inferior to that of the meanest
'slave.

'Save then my innocence, good Heaven! and preserve
'my mind spotless; and happy shall I be to lay down my
'worthless life; and see an end to all my troubles and
'anxieties!

'Forgive my impatience: But my presaging mind bodes
'horrid mischiefs! Everything looks dark around me;
'and this woman's impenetrable sullenness and silence,
'without any apparent reason, from a conduct so very *con-*
'*trary,* bid me fear the worst.—Blame me, sir, if you think

' me wrong; and let me have your advice what to do;
' which will oblige

' Your most afflicted servant.'

———*o*———

Friday.

I HAVE this half angry answer; but, what is more to me
than all the letters in the world could be, yours, my dear
father, enclosed.

' MADAM,—I think you are too apprehensive by much;
' I am sorry for your uneasiness. You may depend upon
' me, and all I can do. But I make no doubt of the London
' journey, nor of John's contrition and fidelity. I have just
' received, from my Gainsborough friend, this letter, as I
' suppose, from your good father, in a cover, directed for me,
' as I had desired. I hope it contains nothing to add to
' your uneasiness. Pray, dearest madam, lay aside your
' fears, and wait a few days for the issue of Mrs. Jewkes's
' letter, and mine of thanks to Mr. B——. Things, I hope,
' *must* be better than you expect. Providence will not
' desert such piety and innocence: and be this your com-
' fort and reliance: Which is the best advice that can at
' present be given, by

' Your most faithful humble servant.'

N.B.—The father's letter was as follows :

' MY DEAREST DAUGHTER,—Our prayers are at length
' heard, and we are overwhelmed with joy. Oh what suffer-
' ings, what trials, hast thou gone through! Blessed be the
' Divine goodness, which has enabled thee to withstand so
' many temptations! We have not yet had leisure to read
' through your long accounts of all your hardships. I say
' *long*, because I wonder how you could find time and
' opportunity for them; but otherwise they are the delight
' of our spare hours; and we shall read them over and over,

' as long as we live, with thankfulness to God, who has
' given us so virtuous and so discreet a daughter. How
' happy is our lot in the midst of our poverty! Oh let none
' ever think children a burden to them; when the poorest
' circumstances can produce so much riches in a Pamela!
' Persist, my dear daughter, in the same excellent course;
' and we shall not envy the highest estate, but defy them to
' produce such a daughter as ours.

' I said, we had not read through all yours in course.
' We were too impatient, and so turned to the end; where
' we find your virtue within view of its reward, and your
' master's heart turned to see the folly of his ways, and the
' injury he had intended to our dear child : For, to be sure,
' my *dear*, he *would* have ruined you, if he could. But seeing
' your virtue, his heart is touched; and he has, no doubt,
' been awakened by your good example.

' We don't see that you can do any way so well, as to
' come into the present proposal, and make Mr. Williams,
' the worthy Mr. Williams! God bless him!—happy. And
' though we are poor, and can add no merit, no reputation,
' no fortune, to our dear child, but rather must be a disgrace
' to her, as the world will think ; yet I hope I do not sin in
' my pride, to say, that there is no good man, of a common
' degree (especially as your late lady's kindness gave you
' such good opportunities, which you have had the grace to
' improve), but may think himself happy in you. But, as
' you say, you had rather *not* marry at present, far be it
' from us to offer violence to your inclination! So much
' prudence as you have shown in all your conduct, would
' make it very wrong in us to mistrust it in this, or to offer
' to direct you in your choice. But, alas! my child, what
' can *we* do for you?—To partake our hard lot, and involve
' yourself into as hard a life, would not help *us*, but *add* to
' your afflictions. But it will be time enough to talk of these
things, when we have the pleasure you now put us in hope
of, of seeing you with us; which God grant. Amen, amen,
say

' Your most indulgent parents. Amen!

' Our humblest service and thanks to the worthy Mr.
' Williams. Again, we say, God bless him for ever!
' Oh what a deal we have to say to you! God give us a
' happy meeting! We understand the 'squire is setting
' out for London. He is a fine gentleman, and has wit
' at will. I wish he was as good. But I hope he will
' now reform.'

Oh what inexpressible comfort, my dear father, has your
letter given me!—You ask, *What* can you do for me?—
What is it you *cannot do* for your child!—You can give her
the advice she *has so much wanted*, and *still* wants, and will
always want: You can confirm her in the paths of virtue,
into which you first initiated her; and you can pray for her,
with hearts so sincere and pure, that are not to be met with
in palaces!—Oh! how I long to throw myself at your feet,
and receive from your own lips the blessings of such good
parents! But, alas! how are my prospects again over-
clouded, to what they were when I closed my last parcel!—
More trials, more dangers, I fear, must your poor Pamela
be engaged in: But through the Divine goodness, and your
prayers, I hope, at last, to get well out of all my difficulties;
and the rather, as they are not the effect of my own vanity
or presumption!

But I will proceed with my hopeless story. I saw Mr.
Williams was a little nettled at my impatience; and so I
wrote to assure him I would be as easy as I could, and
wholly directed by him; especially as my father, whose
respects I mentioned, had assured me my master was setting
out for London, which he must have somehow from his
own family: or he would not have written me word of it.

—*o*—

Saturday, Sunday.

MR. WILLIAMS has been here both these days, as usual; but is very indifferently received still by Mrs. Jewkes; and, to avoid suspicion, I left them together, and went up to my closet, most of the time he was here. He and she, I found by her, had a quarrel; and she seems quite out of humour with him; but I thought it best not to say anything: and he said, he would very little trouble the house, till he had an answer to his letter from Mr. B——. And she returned, The less, the better. Poor man! he has got but little by his openness, making Mrs. Jewkes his confidant, as she bragged, and would have had me to do likewise.

I am more and more satisfied there is mischief brewing; and shall begin to hide my papers, and be circumspect. She seems mighty impatient for an answer to her letter to my master.

—*o*—

Monday, Tuesday, the 25th and 26th days
of my heavy restraint.

STILL more and more strange things to write! A messenger is returned, and no wall is out! Oh wretched, wretched Pamela! What, at last, will become of me!—Such strange turns and trials sure never poor creature, of my years, experienced. He brought two letters, one to Mrs. Jewkes, and one to me: but, as the greatest wits may be sometimes mistaken, they being folded and sealed alike, that for me was directed to Mrs. Jewkes; and that for *her* was directed to me. But *both* are stark naught, abominably bad! She brought me up that directed for me, and said, Here's a letter for you: Long looked for is come at last. I will ask the messenger a few questions, and then I will read mine. So she went down, and I broke it open in my closet, and found it directed *To* Mrs. PAMELA ANDREWS. But when I opened it, it began, Mrs. Jewkes. I was quite confounded; but, thought I, this may be a lucky mistake; I may discover something: And so I read on these horrid contents:

   ' Mrs. Jewkes,—What you write me has given me no
' small disturbance. This wretched *fool's plaything*, no
' doubt, is ready to leap at *anything* that offers, rather than
' express the least sense of gratitude for all the benefits she
' has received from my family, and which I was determined
' more and more to heap upon her. I reserve her for my
' future resentment; and I charge you double your dili-
' gence in watching her, to prevent her escape. I send
' this by an honest Swiss, who attended me in my travels;
' a man I can trust; and so let him be your assistant: for
' the artful *creature* is enough to corrupt a nation by her
' seeming innocence and simplicity; and she may have got
' a party, perhaps, among my servants with you, as she
' has here. Even John Arnold, whom I confided in, and
' favoured more than any, has proved an execrable villain;
' and shall meet his reward for it.
   ' As to that *college novice*, Williams, I need not bid you
' take care he sees not this *painted bauble:* for I have
' ordered Mr. Shorter, my attorney, to throw him instantly
' into gaol, on an action of debt, for money he has had of
' me, which I had intended never to carry to account
' against him; for I know all his rascally practices, besides
' what you write me of his perfidious intrigue with that
' girl, and his acknowledged contrivances for her escape;
' when he knew not, for certain, that I designed her any
' mischief; and when, if he had been guided by a sense of
' piety, or compassion for injured innocence, as he pre-
' tends, he would have expostulated with me, as his func-
' tion, and my friendship for him, might have allowed him.
' But to enter into a vile intrigue with the *amiable gewgaw*,
' to favour her escape in so base a manner (to say nothing of
' his disgraceful practices against me, in Sir Simon Darnford's
' family, of which Sir Simon himself has informed me), is a
' conduct that, instead of preferring the ungrateful wretch,
' as I had intended, shall pull down upon him utter ruin.

' Monsieur Colbrand, my trusty Swiss, will obey you
' without reserve, if my other servants refuse.

' As for her denying that she encouraged his declaration,
' I believe it not. It is certain the *speaking picture*, with
' all that pretended innocence and bashfulness, would have
' run away with him. Yes, she would run away with a
' fellow that she had been acquainted with (and that not
' intimately, if you were as careful as you ought to be) but
' a few days; at a time when she had the strongest assur-
' ances of my honour to her.

' Well, I think, I now hate her perfectly; and though I
' will do nothing to her *myself*, yet I can bear, for the sake
' of my revenge, and my *injured honour* and *slighted love*,
' to see anything, even what *she most fears*, be *done to her* ;
' and then she may be turned loose to her evil destiny, and
' echo to the woods and groves her piteous lamentations for
' the loss of her fantastical innocence, which the romantic
' idiot makes such a work about. I shall go to London,
' with my sister Davers; and the moment I can disengage
' myself, which, perhaps, may be in three weeks from this
' time, I will be with you, and decide *her fate*, and put an
' end to your trouble. Meantime be doubly careful; for
' this innocent, as I have warned you, is full of con-
' trivances. I am

' Your friend.'

I had but just read this dreadful letter through, when
Mrs Jewkes came up in a great fright, guessing at the mistake, and that I had her letter; and she found me with it
open in my hand, just sinking away. What business, said
she, had you to read my letter? and snatched it from me.
You see, said she, looking upon it, it says Mrs. Jewkes, at
top: You ought, in manners, to have read no further. Oh
add not, said I, to my afflictions! I shall be soon out of all
your ways! This is too much! too much! I never can
support this—and threw myself upon the couch, in my
closet, and wept most bitterly. She read it in the next

room, and came in again afterwards. Why, this, said she, is a sad letter indeed: I am sorry for it: But I feared you would carry your niceties too far!—Leave me, leave me, Mrs. Jewkes, said I, for a while: I cannot speak nor talk.— Poor heart! said she; Well, I'll come up again presently, and hope to find you better. But here, take your own letter; I wish you well; but this is a sad mistake! And so she put down by me that which was intended for me: But I have no spirit to read it at present. Oh man! man! hard-hearted, cruel man! what mischiefs art thou not capable of, unrelenting persecutor as thou art!

I sat ruminating, when I had a little come to myself, upon the terms of this wicked letter; and had no inclina-tion to look into my own. The bad names, *fool's plaything, artful creature, painted bauble, gewgaw, speaking picture,* are hard words for your poor Pamela! and I began to think whether I was not indeed a very naughty body, and had not done vile things: But when I thought of his having dis-covered poor John, and of Sir Simon's base officiousness, in telling him of Mr. Williams, with what he had resolved against him in revenge for his goodness to me, I was quite dispirited; and yet still more about that fearful Colbrand, and what he could *see done to me ;* for then I was ready to gasp for breath, and my heart quite failed me. Then how dreadful are the words, that he will *decide my fate* in three weeks! Gracious Heaven, said I, strike me dead, before that time, with a thunderbolt, or provide some way for my escap-ing these threatened mischiefs! God forgive me, if I sinned!

At last, I took up the letter directed for Mrs. Jewkes, but designed for me; and I find *that* little better than the other. These are the hard terms it contains:

' WELL have you done, perverse, forward, artful, yet foolish
' Pamela, to convince me, before it was too late, how ill I
' had done to place my affections on so unworthy an object:
' I had vowed honour and love to your unworthiness, believ-
' ing you a mirror of bashful modesty and unspotted inno-
' cence; and that no perfidious designs lurked in so fair a

' bosom. But now I have found you out, you specious
' hypocrite! and I see, that though you could not repose the
' least confidence in one you had known for years, and who,
' under my good mother's misplaced favour for you, had
' grown up in a manner with you; when my passion, in
' spite of my pride, and the difference of our condition, made
' me stoop to a meanness that now I despise myself for; yet
' you could enter into an intrigue with a man you never
' knew till within these few days past, and resolve to run
' away with a stranger, whom your fair face, and insinuating
' arts, had bewitched to break through all the ties of honour
' and gratitude to me, even at a time when the happiness of
' his future life depended upon my favour.

' Henceforth, for Pamela's sake, whenever I see a lovely
' face, will I mistrust a deceitful heart: and whenever I
' hear of the greatest pretences to innocence, will I suspect
' some deep-laid mischief. You were determined to place no
' confidence in me, though I have solemnly, over and over,
' engaged my honour to you. What, though I had alarmed
' your fears in sending you one way, when you hoped to go
' another; yet, had I not, to convince you of my resolution
' to do justly by you (although with great reluctance, such
' then was my love for you), engaged not to come near you
' without your own consent? Was not this a voluntary
' demonstration of the generosity of my intention to you?
' Yet how have you requited me? The very first fellow that
' your charming face, and insinuating address, could influ-
' ence, you have practised upon, corrupted too, I may say
' (and even ruined, as the ungrateful wretch shall find), and
' thrown your *forward* self upon him. As, therefore, you
' would place no confidence in me, my honour owes you
' nothing; and, in a little time, you shall find how much you
' have erred, in treating, as you have done, a man who was
' once

' Your affectionate and kind friend.

' Mrs. Jewkes has directions concerning you: and if your
' lot is now harder than you might wish, you will bear

' it the easier, because your own rash folly has brought
' it upon you.'

Alas! for me, what a fate is mine, to be thus thought artful, and forward, and ungrateful; when all I intended was to
preserve my innocence; and when all the poor little shifts,
which his superior wicked wit and cunning have rendered
ineffectual, were forced upon me in my own necessary
defence!

When Mrs. Jewkes came up to me again, she found me
bathed in tears. She seemed, as I thought, to be moved to
some compassion; and finding myself now entirely in her
power, and that it is not for me to provoke her, I said, It is
now, I see, in vain for me to contend against my evil destiny,
and the superior arts of my barbarous master. I will resign
myself to the Divine will, and prepare to expect the worst.
But you see how this poor Mr. Williams is drawn in and
undone: I am sorry I am made the cause of *his* ruin. Poor,
poor man!—to be thus involved, and for my sake too!—
But if you'll believe me, said I, I gave no encouragement to
what he proposed, as to marriage; nor would he have proposed it, I believe, but as the only honourable way he
thought was left to save me: And his principal motive to
it at all, was virtue and compassion to one in distress.
What other view could he have? You know I am poor and
friendless. All I beg of you is, to let the poor gentleman
have notice of my master's resentment; and let him fly the
country, and not be thrown into gaol. This will answer
my master's end as well; for it will as effectually hinder him
from assisting me, as if he was in a prison.

Ask me, said she, to do anything that is in my power,
consistent with my duty and trust, and I will do it: for I
am sorry for you both. But, to be sure, I shall keep no
correspondence with him, nor let you. I offered to talk of
a duty superior to that she mentioned, which would oblige
her to help distressed innocence, and not permit her to go
the lengths enjoined by lawless tyranny; but she plainly

bid me be silent on that head ; for it was in vain to attempt to persuade her to betray her trust :--All I have to advise you, said she, is to be easy ; lay aside all your contrivances and arts to get away, and make me your friend, by giving me no reason to suspect you ; for I glory in my fidelity to my master : And you have both practised some strange sly arts, to make such a progress as he has owned there was between you, so seldom as I thought you saw one another ; and I must be more circumspect than I have been.

This doubled my concern ; for I now apprehended I should be much closer watched than before.

Well, said I, since I have, by this strange accident, dis-covered my hard destiny ; let me read over again that fearful letter of yours, that I may get it by heart, and with it feed my distress, and make calamity familiar to me. Then, said she, let me read yours again. I gave her mine, and she lent me hers ; and so I took a copy of it, with her leave ; because, as I said I would, by it, prepare myself for the worst. And when I had done, I pinned it on the head of the couch : This, said I, is the use I shall make of this wretched copy of your letter ; and here you shall always find it wet with my tears.

She said she would go down to order supper ; and insisted upon my company to it. I would have excused myself ; but she began to put on a commanding air, that I durst not oppose. And when I went down, she took me by the hand, and presented me to the most hideous monster I ever saw in my life. Here, Monsieur Colbrand, said she, here is *your* pretty ward and *mine ;* let us try to make her time with us easy. He bowed, and put on his foreign grimaces, and seemed to bless himself ; and, in broken English, told me, I was happy in de affections of de finest gentleman in de varld!—I was quite frightened, and ready to drop down ; and I will describe him to you, my dear father and mother, if now you will ever see this : and you shall judge if I had not reason, especially not knowing he was to be there, and being apprised, as I was, of his hated employment, to watch me closer.

He is a giant of a man for stature; taller by a good deal than Harry Mowlidge, in your neighbourhood, and large boned, and scraggy; and has a hand!—I never saw such an one in my life. He has great staring eyes, like the bull's that frightened me so; vast jaw-bones sticking out: eyebrows hanging over his eyes; two great scars upon his forehead, and one on his left cheek; and two large whiskers, and a monstrous wide mouth; blubber lips; long yellow teeth, and a hideous grin. He wears his own frightful long hair, tied up in a great black bag; a black crape neckcloth about a long ugly neck; and his throat sticking out like a wen. As to the rest, he was dressed well enough, and had a sword on, with a nasty red knot to it; leather garters, buckled below his knees; and a foot—near as long as my arm, I verily think.

He said, he fright de lady; and offered to withdraw; but she bid him not; and I told Mrs. Jewkes, That as she knew I had been crying, she should not have called me to the gentleman without letting me know he was there. I soon went up to my closet; for my heart ached all the time I was at table, not being able to look upon him without horror; and this brute of a woman, though she saw my distress, *before* this addition to it, no doubt did it on purpose to strike more terror into me. And indeed it had its effect; for when I went to bed, I could think of nothing but his hideous person, and my master's more hideous actions: and thought them too well paired; and when I dropt asleep, I dreamed they were both coming to my bedside, with the worst designs; and I jumped out of my bed in my sleep, and frightened Mrs. Jewkes; till, waking with the terror, I told her my dream; and the wicked creature only laughed, and said, All I feared was but a dream, as well as that; and when it was over, and I was well awake, I should laugh at it as such!

——o——

And now I am come to the close of Wednesday, the 27th day of
my distress.

POOR Mr. Williams is actually arrested, and carried away
to Stamford. So there is an end of all my hopes from
him, poor gentleman! His over-security and openness have
ruined us both! I was but too well convinced, that we
ought not to have lost a moment's time; but he was half
angry, and thought me too impatient; and then his fatal
confessions, and the detestable artifice of my master!—But
one might well think, that he who had so cunningly, and
so wickedly, contrived all his stratagems hitherto, that it
was impossible to avoid them, would stick at nothing to
complete them. I fear I shall soon find it so!

But one stratagem I have just invented, though a very
discouraging one to think of; because I have neither friends
nor money, nor know one step of the way, if I was out of
the house. But let bulls, and bears, and lions, and tigers,
and, what is worse, false, treacherous, deceitful men, stand
in my way, I cannot be in more danger than I am; and I
depend nothing upon his three weeks: for how do I know,
now he is in such a passion, and has already begun his
vengeance on poor Mr. Williams, that he will not change
his mind, and come down to Lincolnshire before he goes to
London?

My stratagem is this: I will endeavour to get Mrs.
Jewkes to go to bed without me, as she often does, while I
sit locked up in my closet; and as she sleeps very sound
in her first sleep, of which she never fails to give notice by
snoring, if I can but then get out between the two bars of
the window (for you know I am very slender, and I find I
can get my head through), then I can drop upon the leads
underneath, which are little more than my height, and
which leads are over a little summer-parlour, that juts out
towards the garden; and as I am light, I can easily drop
from them; for they are not high from the ground: then I
shall be in the garden; and then, as I have the key of the
back-door, I will get out. But I have another piece of

cunning still: Good Heaven, succeed to me my dangerous, but innocent devices!—I have read of a great captain, who, being in danger, leaped over-board into the sea, and his enemies, as he swam, shooting at him with bows and arrows, he unloosed his upper garment, and took another course, while they stuck that full of their darts and arrows; and so he escaped, and lived to triumph over them all. So what will I do, but strip off my upper petticoat, and throw it into the pond, with my neckhandkerchief! For to be sure, when they miss me, they will go to the pond first, thinking I have drowned myself: and so, when they see some of my clothes floating there, they will be all employed in dragging the pond, which is a very large one; and as I shall not, perhaps, be missed till the morning, this will give me opportunity to get a great way off; and I am sure I will run for it when I am out. And so I trust, that Providence will direct my steps to some good place of safety, and make *some* worthy body my friend; for sure, if I suffer ever so, I cannot be in more danger, nor in worse hands, than where I am; and with such avowed bad designs.

Oh my dear parents! don't be frightened when you come to read this!—But all will be over before you can see it; and so God direct me for the best! My writings, for fear I should not escape, I will bury in the garden; for, to be sure, I shall be searched and used dreadfully, if I can't get off. And so I will close here, for the present, to prepare for my plot. Prosper thou, O gracious Protector of oppressed innocence! this last effort of thy poor handmaid! that I may escape the crafty devices and snares that have begun to entangle my virtue; and from which, but by this one trial, I see no way of escaping. And oh! whatever becomes of me, bless my dear parents, and protect poor Mr. Williams from ruin! for he was happy before he knew me.

Just now, just now! I heard Mrs. Jewkes, who is in her cups, own to the horrid Colbrand, that the robbing of poor Mr. Williams was a contrivance of hers, and executed by the groom and a helper, in order to seize my letters upon him, which they missed. They are now both laughing at the dismal story, which they little think I overheard.—Oh how my heart aches! for what are not such wretches capable of! Can you blame me for endeavouring, through any danger, to get out of such clutches?

—o—

Past eleven o'clock.

MRS. JEWKES is come up, and gone to bed; and bids me not stay long in my closet, but come to bed. Oh for a dead sleep for the treacherous brute! I never saw her so tipsy, and that gives me hopes. I have tried again, and find I can get my head through the iron bars. I am now all prepared, as soon as I hear her fast; and now I'll seal up these, and my other papers, my last work: and to thy providence, O my gracious God! commit the rest.—Once more, God bless you both! and send us a happy meeting; if not here, in His heavenly kingdom. Amen.

—o—

Thursday, Friday, Saturday, Sunday, the 28th, 29th, 30th, and 31st days of my distress.

AND distress indeed! For here I am still; and everything has been worse and worse! Oh! the poor unhappy Pamela! —Without any hope left, and ruined in all my contrivances. But, oh! my dear parents, rejoice with me, even in this low plunge of my distress; for your poor Pamela has escaped from an enemy worse than any she ever met with; an enemy she never thought of before, and was hardly able to stand against: I mean, the weakness and presumption, both in one, of her own mind; which had well nigh, had not the divine grace interposed, sunk her into the lowest, last abyss of misery and perdition!

I will proceed, as I have opportunity, with my sad

relation: for my pen and ink (in my now doubly-secured closet) are all I have to employ myself with: and indeed I have been so weak, that, till yesterday evening, I have not been able to hold a pen.

I took with me but one shift, besides what I had on, and two handkerchiefs, and two caps, which my pocket held (for it was not for me to encumber myself), and all my stock of money, which was but five or six shillings, to set out for I knew not where; and got out of the window, not without some difficulty, sticking a little at my shoulders and hips; but I was resolved to get out, if possible. And it was farther from the leads than I thought, and I was afraid I had sprained my ankle; and when I had dropt from the leads to the ground, it was still farther off; but I did pretty well there, at least. I got no hurt to hinder me from pursuing my intentions. So being now on the ground, I hid my papers under a rose-bush, and covered them with mould, and there they still lie, as I hope. Then I hied away to the pond: The clock struck twelve, just as I got out; and it was a dark misty night, and very cold; but I felt it not then.

When I came to the pond side, I flung in my upper coat, as I had designed, and my neckhandkerchief, and a round-eared cap, with a knot; and then with great speed ran to the door, and took the key out of my pocket, my poor heart beating all the time against my bosom, as if it would have forced its way through it: and beat it well might! for I then, too late, found, that I was most miserably disappointed; for the wicked woman had taken off that lock, and put another on; so that my key would not open it. I tried, and tried, and feeling about, I found a padlock besides, on another part of the door. Oh then how my heart sunk! —I dropt down with grief and confusion, unable to stir or support myself, for a while. But my fears awakening my resolution, and knowing that my attempt would be as terrible for me as any other danger I could then encounter, I clambered up upon the ledges of the door, and upon the lock, which was a great wooden one; and reached the top

of the door with my hands; then, little thinking I could
climb so well, I made shift to lay hold on the top of the wall
with my hands; but, alas for me! nothing but ill luck!—
no escape for poor Pamela! The wall being old, the bricks
I held by gave way, just as I was taking a spring to get up;
and down came I, and received such a blow upon my head,
with one of the bricks, that it quite stunned me; and I
broke my shins and my ankle besides, and beat off the heel
of one of my shoes.

In this dreadful way, flat upon the ground, lay poor I,
for I believe five or six minutes; and then trying to get up,
I sunk down again two or three times; and my left hip and
shoulder were very stiff, and full of pain, with bruises; and,
besides, my head bled, and ached grievously with the blow I
had with the brick. Yet these hurts I valued not; but
crept a good way upon my feet and hands, in search of a
ladder, I just recollected to have seen against the wall two
days before, on which the gardener was nailing a nectarine
branch that was loosened from the wall: but no ladder
could I find, and the wall was very high. What now,
thought I, must become of the miserable Pamela!—Then I
began to wish myself most heartily again in my closet, and
to repent of my attempt, which I now censured as rash,
because it did not succeed.

God forgive me! but a sad thought came just then into
my head!—I tremble to think of it! Indeed my apprehensions of the usage I should meet with, had like to have
made me miserable for ever! Oh my dear, dear parents, forgive your poor child; but being then quite desperate, I
crept along, till I could raise myself on my staggering feet;
and away limped I!—What to do, but to throw myself into
the pond, and so put a period to all my griefs in this world!
—But, oh! to find them infinitely aggravated (had I not, by
the Divine grace, been withheld) in a miserable *eternity!*
As I have escaped this temptation (blessed be God for it!)
I will tell you my conflicts on this dreadful occasion, that
the Divine mercies may be magnified in my deliverance, that

I am yet on this side the dreadful gulf, from which there could have been no return.

It was well for me, as I have since thought, that I was so maimed, as made me the longer before I got to the water; for this gave me time to consider, and abated the impetuousness of my passions, which possibly might otherwise have hurried me, in my first transport of grief (on my seeing no way to escape, and the hard usage I had reason to expect from my dreadful keepers), to throw myself in. But my weakness of body made me move so slowly, that it gave time, as I said, for a little reflection, a ray of grace, to dart in upon my benighted mind; and so, when I came to the pond-side, I sat myself down on the sloping bank, and began to ponder my wretched condition; and thus I reasoned with myself.

Pause here a little, Pamela, on what thou art about, before thou takest the dreadful leap; and consider whether there be no way yet left, no hope, if not to escape from this wicked house, yet from the mischiefs threatened thee in it.

I then considered; and, after I had cast about in my mind everything that could make me hope, and saw no probability; a wicked woman, devoid of all compassion! a horrid helper, just arrived, in this dreadful Colbrand! an angry and resenting master, who now hated me, and threatened the most afflicting evils! and that I should, in all probability, be deprived even of the opportunity I now had before me, to free myself from all their persecutions!—What hast thou to do, distressed creature, said I to myself, but hrow thyself upon a merciful God (who knows how innocently I suffer), to avoid the merciless wickedness of those who are determined on my ruin?

And then, thought I (and oh! that thought was surely of the devil's instigation; for it was very soothing, and powerful with me), these wicked wretches, who now have no remorse, no pity on me, will then be moved to lament their misdoings; and when they see the dead corpse of the unhappy Pamela dragged out to these dewy banks, and lying breathless at their feet, they will find that remorse to soften

their obdurate heart, which, now, has no place there!—And
my master, my angry master, will then forget his resentments, and say, Oh, this is the unhappy Pamela! that I have
so causelessly persecuted and destroyed! Now do I see she
preferred her honesty to her life, will he say, and is no hypocrite, nor deceiver; but really was the innocent creature
she pretended to be! Then, thought I, will he, perhaps,
shed a few tears over the poor corpse of his persecuted
servant; and though he may give out, it was love and
disappointment; and that, perhaps (in order to hide his
own guilt), for the unfortunate Mr. Williams, yet will he be
inwardly grieved, and order me a decent funeral, and save me,
or rather *this part* of me, from the dreadful stake, and the
highway interment; and the young men and maidens all
around my dear father's will pity poor Pamela! But, oh! I
hope I shall not be the subject of their ballads and elegies;
but that my memory, for the sake of my dear father and
mother, may quickly slide into oblivion.

I was once rising, so indulgent was I to this sad way of
thinking, to throw myself in: but, again, my bruises made
me slow; and I thought, What art thou about to do,
wretched Pamela? How knowest thou, though the prospect be all dark to thy short-sighted eye, what God may
do for thee, even when all human means fail? God Almighty would not lay me under these sore afflictions, if He
had not given me strength to grapple with them, if I will
exert it as I ought: And who knows, but that the very
presence I so much dread of my angry and designing
master (for he has had me in his power before, and yet I
have escaped), may be better for me, than these persecuting
emissaries of his, who, for his money, are true to their
wicked trust, and are hardened by that, and a long habit
of wickedness, against compunction of heart? God *can*
touch his heart in an instant; and if this should *not* be
done, I can *then* but put an end to my life by some other
means, if I am so resolved.

But how do I know, thought I, that even *these bruises*
and *maims* that I have gotten, while I pursued only the

laudable escape I had meditated, may not kindly have
furnished me with the opportunity I am now tempted
with to precipitate myself, and of surrendering up my life,
spotless and unguilty, to that merciful Being who gave it!

Then, thought I, who gave thee, presumptuous as thou
art, a power over thy life? Who authorised thee to put an
end to it, when the weakness of thy mind suggests not to
thee a way to preserve it with honour? How knowest thou
what purposes God may have to serve, by the trials with
which thou art now exercised? Art thou to put a bound
to the divine will, and to say, Thus much will I bear, and
no more? And wilt thou *dare* to say, That if the trial
be augmented and continued, thou wilt sooner die than
bear it?

This act of despondency, thought I, is a sin, that, if I
pursue it, admits of no repentance, and can therefore hope
no forgiveness.—And wilt thou, to shorten thy transitory
griefs, *heavy* as they are, and *weak* as thou fanciest thyself,
plunge both body and soul into everlasting misery!
Hitherto, Pamela, thought I, thou art the innocent, the
suffering Pamela; and wilt thou, to avoid thy sufferings,
be the guilty aggressor? And, because wicked men perse-
cute thee, wilt thou fly in the face of the Almighty, and
distrust His grace and goodness, who can *still* turn all these
sufferings to benefits? And how do I know, but that God,
who sees all the lurking vileness of my heart, may have
permitted these sufferings on that very score, and to make
me rely solely on His grace and assistance, who, perhaps,
have too much prided myself in a vain dependence on my
own foolish contrivances?

Then, again, thought I, wilt thou suffer in *one* moment
all the good lessons of thy poor honest parents, and the
benefit of their example (who have persisted in doing their
duty with resignation to the divine will, amidst the extreme degrees of disappointment, poverty, and distress,
and the persecutions of an ungrateful world, and merciless
creditors), to be thrown away upon thee; and bring down,
as in all probability this thy rashness will, their grey hairs

with sorrow to the grave, when they shall understand, that
their beloved daughter, slighting the tenders of divine
grace, despairing of the mercies of a protecting God, has
blemished, in this *last act*, a *whole* life, which they had
hitherto approved and delighted in?

What then, presumptuous Pamela, dost thou *here?*
thought I: Quit with speed these perilous banks, and fly
from these curling waters, that seem, in their meaning
murmurs, this still night, to reproach thy rashness! Tempt
not God's goodness on the mossy banks, that have been
witnesses of thy guilty purpose; and while thou hast power
left thee, avoid the tempting evil, lest thy grand enemy,
now repulsed by divine grace, and due reflection, return
to the assault with a force that thy weakness may not be
able to resist! and let one rash moment destroy all the
convictions, which now have awed thy rebellious mind into
duty and resignation to the divine will!

And so saying, I arose; but was so stiff with my hurts,
so cold with the moist dew of the night, and the wet grass
on which I had sat, as also with the damps arising from so
large a piece of water, that with great pain I got from this
pond, which now I think of with terror; and bending my
limping steps towards the house, took refuge in the corner
of an outhouse, where wood and coals are laid up for
family use, till I should be found by my cruel keepers, and
consigned to a more wretched confinement, and worse
usage than I had hitherto experienced; and there behind a
pile of firewood I crept, and lay down, as you may imagine, with a mind just broken, and a heart sensible to
nothing but the extremest woe and dejection.

This, my dear father and mother, is the issue of your
poor Pamela's fruitless enterprise; and who knows, if I
had got out at the back-door, whether I had been at all
in a better case, moneyless, friendless, as I am, and in
a strange place:—But blame not your poor daughter too
much: Nay, if ever you see this miserable scribble, all

bathed and blotted with my tears, let your pity get the
better of your reprehension! But I know it will.—And I
must leave off for the present.—For, oh! my strength and
my will are at this time very far unequal to one another.—
But yet I will add, that though I should have praised God
for my deliverance, had I been freed from my wicked
keepers, and my designing master; yet I have more abundant reason to praise Him, that I have been delivered from
a worse enemy, *myself!*

I will conclude my sad relation.

It seems Mrs. Jewkes awaked not till daybreak; and
not finding me in bed, she called me; and, no answer
being returned, she relates, that she got out of bed, and
ran to my closet; and, missing me, searched under the
bed, and in another closet, finding the chamber-door as she
had left it, quite fast, and the key, as usual, about her
wrist. For if I could have got out of the chamber-door,
there were two or three passages, and doors to them all,
double-locked and barred, to go through into the great
garden; so that, to escape, there was no way, but out of
the window; and of that window, because of the summer-
parlour under it: for the other windows are a great way
from the ground.
     She says she was excessively frightened; and instantly
raised the Swiss, and the two maids, who lay not far off;
and finding every door fast, she said, I must be carried
away, as St. Peter was out of prison, by some angel. It is
a wonder she had not a worse thought!
     She says, she wept, and wrung her hands, and took on
sadly, running about like a mad woman, little thinking I
could have got out of the closet window, between the iron
bars; and, indeed, I don't know whether I could do so
again. But at last finding that casement open, they concluded it must be so; and ran out into the garden, and
found my footsteps in the mould of the bed which I dropt
down upon from the leads: And so speeded away all of

them; that is to say, Mrs. Jewkes, Colbrand, and Nan,
towards the back-door, to see if that was fast; while the
cook was sent to the out-offices to raise the men, and
make them get horses ready, to take each a several way to
pursue me.

But, it seems, finding that door double-locked and pad-
locked, and the heel of my shoe, and the broken bricks,
they verily concluded I was got away by some means over
the wall; and then, they say, Mrs. Jewkes seemed like a
distracted woman: Till, at last, Nan had the thought to
go towards the pond: and there seeing my coat, and cap,
and handkerchief, in the water, cast almost to the banks
by the agitation of the waves, she thought it was me; and,
screaming out, ran to Mrs. Jewkes, and said, O madam,
madam! here's a piteous thing!—Mrs. Pamela lies drowned
in the pond. Thither they all ran; and finding my clothes,
doubted not I was at the bottom; and they all, Swiss
among the rest, beat their breasts, and made most dismal
lamentations; and Mrs. Jewkes sent Nan to the men, to
bid them get the drag-net ready, and leave the horses, and
come to try to find the poor innocent! as she, it seems,
then called me, beating her breast, and lamenting my hard
hap; but most what would become of them, and what
account they should give to my master.

While every one was thus differently employed, some
weeping and wailing, some running here and there, Nan
came into the wood-house; and there lay poor I; so weak,
so low, and dejected, and withal so stiff with my bruises,
that I could not stir, nor help myself to get upon my feet.
And I said, with a low voice (for I could hardly speak),
Mrs. Ann! Mrs. Ann!—The creature was sadly frightened,
but was taking up a billet to knock me on the head, believing I was some thief, as she said; but I cried out, O Mrs.
Ann, Mrs. Ann, help me, for pity's sake, to Mrs. Jewkes!
for I cannot get up!—Bless me, said she, what! you,
madam!—Why, our hearts are almost broken, and we were
going to drag the pond for you, believing you had drowned
yourself. Now, said she, you'll make us all alive again!

And, without helping me, she ran away to the pond, and brought all the crew to the wood-house.—The wicked woman, as she entered, said, Where is she ?—Plague of her spells, and her witchcrafts ! She shall dearly repent of this trick, if my name be Jewkes ; and, coming to me, took hold of my arm so roughly, and gave me such a pull, as made me squeal out (my shoulder being bruised on that side), and drew me on my face. Oh cruel creature ! said I, if you knew what I have suffered, it would move you to pity me !

Even Colbrand seemed to be concerned, and said, Fie, madam, fie ! you see she is almost dead ! You must not be so rough with her. The coachman Robin seemed to be sorry for me too, and said, with sobs, What a scene is here ! Don't you see she is all bloody in her head, and cannot stir ?—Curse of her contrivances ! said the horrid creature ; she has frightened *me* out of my wits, I'm sure. How the d—l came you here ?—Oh ! said I, ask me now no questions, but let the maids carry me up to my prison ; and there let me die decently, and in peace ! For, indeed, I thought I could not live two hours.

The still more inhuman tigress said, I suppose you want Mr. Williams to pray by you, don't you ? Well, I'll send for my master this minute : let him come and watch you himself, for me ; for there's no such thing as holding you, I'm sure.

So the maids took me up between them, and carried me to my chamber ; and when the wretch saw how bad I was, she began a little to relent—while every one wondered (at which I had neither strength nor inclination to tell them) how all this came to pass, which they imputed to sorcery and witchcraft.

I was so weak, when I had got up stairs, that I fainted away, with dejection, pain, and fatigue ; and they undressed me, and got me to bed ; and Mrs. Jewkes ordered Nan to bathe my shoulder, and arm, and ancle, with some old rum warmed ; and they cut the hair a little from the back part of my head, and washed that ; for it was clotted with blood,

from a pretty long, but not a deep gash; and put a family
plaister upon it; for, if this woman has any good quality,
it is, it seems, in a readiness and skill to manage in cases
where sudden misfortunes happen in a family.

After this, I fell into a pretty sound and refreshing sleep,
and lay till twelve o'clock, tolerably easy, considering I was
very feverish, and aguishly inclined; and she took a deal
of care to fit me to undergo more trials, which I had hoped
would have been happily ended: but 'Providence did not
see fit.

She would make me rise about twelve: but I was so
weak, I could only sit up till the bed was made, and went
into it again; and was, as they said, delirious some part of
the afternoon.   But having a tolerable night on Thursday,
I was a good deal better on Friday, and on Saturday got
up, and ate a little spoon-meat, and my feverishness seemed
to be gone; and I was so mended by evening, that I begged
her indulgence in my closet, to be left to myself; which
she consented to, it being double-barred the day before, and
I assuring her, that all my contrivances, as she called them,
were at an end.   But first she made me tell the whole story
of my enterprise; which I did very faithfully, knowing now
that nothing could stand me in any stead, or contribute to
my safety and escape: And she seemed full of wonder at
my resolution; but told me frankly, that I should have
found it a hard matter to get quite off; for that she was
provided with a warrant from my master (who is a justice
of peace in this county as well as in the other) to get
me apprehended, if I *had* got away, on suspicion of wrong-
ing him, let me have been where I would.

Oh how deep-laid are the mischiefs designed to fall on
my devoted head!—Surely, surely, I cannot be worthy of
all this contrivance!—This too well shows me the truth of
what was hinted to me formerly at the other house, that
my master swore he would *have* me!   Oh preserve me,
Heaven! from being *his*, in his own wicked sense of the
adjuration!

I must add, that now the woman sees me pick up so fast,

she uses me worse, and has abridged me of paper, all but one sheet, which I am to show her, written or unwritten, on demand : and has reduced me to one pen : yet my hidden stores stand me in stead. But she is more and more snappish and cross; and tauntingly calls me Mrs. Williams, and any-thing she thinks will vex me.

——o——

Sunday afternoon.

MRS. JEWKES has thought fit to give me an airing, for three or four hours, this afternoon; and I am a good deal better : and should be much more so, if I knew for what I am reserved. But health is a blessing hardly to be coveted in my circumstances, since that but exposes me to the calamity I am in continual apprehensions of; whereas a weak and sickly state might possibly move compassion for me. Oh how I dread the coming of this angry and incensed master; though I am sure I have done him no harm !

Just now we heard, that he had like to have been drowned in crossing the stream, a few days ago, in pursuing his game. What is the matter, that with all his ill usage of me, I cannot hate him? To be sure, I am not like other people! He has certainly done enough to make me hate him; but yet, when I heard his danger, which was very great, I could not in my heart forbear rejoicing for his safety ; though his death would have ended my afflictions. Ungenerous master! if you knew this, you surely would not be so much my per-secutor ! But, for my late good lady's sake, I must wish him well ; and oh, what an angel would he be in my eyes yet, if he would cease his attempts, and reform !

Well, I hear by Mrs. Jewkes, that John Arnold is turned away, being detected in writing to Mr. Williams; and that Mr. Longman, and Mr. Jonathan the butler, have incurred his displeasure, for offering to speak in my behalf. Mrs. Jervis too is in danger; for all these three, probably, went together to beg in my favour; for now it is known where I am.

Mrs. Jewkes has, with the news about my master, received a letter; but she says the contents are too bad for me to know. They must be bad indeed, if they be worse than what I have already known.

Just now the horrid creature tells me, as a secret, that she has reason to think he has found out a way to satisfy my scruples: It is, by marrying me to this dreadful Colbrand, and buying me of him on the wedding-day, for a sum of money!—Was ever the like heard?—She says it will be my duty to obey my husband; and that Mr. Williams will be forced, as a punishment, to marry us; and that, when my master has paid for me, and I am surrendered up, the Swiss is to go home again, with the money, to his former wife and children; for, she says, it is the custom of those people to have a wife in every nation.

But this, to be sure, is horrid romancing! Yet, abominable as it is, it may possibly serve to introduce some plot now hatching!—With what strange perplexities is my poor mind agitated! Perchance, some sham-marriage may be designed, on purpose to ruin me: But can a husband sell his wife against her own consent?—And will such a bargain stand good in law?

———o———

Monday, Tuesday, Wednesday, the 32d, 33d,
and 34th days of my imprisonment.

NOTHING offers these days but squabblings between Mrs. Jewkes and me. She grows worse and worse to me. I vexed her yesterday, because she talked nastily; and told her she talked more like a vile London prostitute, than a gentleman's housekeeper; and she thinks she cannot use me bad enough for it. Bless me! she curses and storms at me like a trooper, and can hardly keep her hands off me. You may believe she must talk sadly, to make me say such harsh words: indeed it cannot be repeated; as she is a disgrace to her sex. And then she ridicules me, and laughs at my notions of honesty; and tells me, impudent creature as she is! what a fine bed-fellow I shall make for my master (and such-like), with such whimsical notions about me!—Do you think this is to be borne? And yet she talks worse than this, if possible! quite filthily! Oh what vile hands am I put into!

———*o*———

Thursday.

I HAVE now all the reason that can be, to apprehend my master will be here soon; for the servants are busy in setting the house to rights; and a stable and coach-house are cleaning out, that have not been used some time. I asked Mrs. Jewkes; but she tells me nothing, nor will hardly answer me when I ask her a question. Sometimes I think she puts on these strange wicked airs to me, purposely to make me wish for, what I dread most of all things, my master's coming down. *He* talk of love!—If he had any the least notion of regard for me, to be sure he would not give this naughty body such power over me:—And if he *does* come, where is his promise of not seeing me without I consent to it? But, it seems, *his honour owes me nothing!* So he tells me in his letter. And why? Because I am willing to keep mine. But, indeed, he says, *he hates me perfectly:* But it is plain he does, or I should not be left to the mercy of this woman: and, what is worse, to my woful apprehensions.

———*o*———

Friday, the 36th day of my imprisonment.

I TOOK the liberty yesterday afternoon, finding the gates open, to walk out before the house; and, ere I was aware, had got to the bottom of the long row of elms; and there I sat myself down upon the steps of a sort of broad stile, which leads into the road, and goes towards the town. And as I sat musing upon what always busies my mind, I saw a whole body of folks running towards me from the

house, men and women, as in a fright. At first I wondered
what was the matter, till they came nearer; and I found
they were all alarmed, thinking I had attempted to get off.
There was first the horrible Colbrand, running with his long
legs, well nigh two yards at a stride; then there was one of
the grooms, poor Mr. Williams's robber; then I spied Nan,
half out of breath, and the cook-maid after her! and lastly,
came waddling, as fast as she could, Mrs. Jewkes, exclaim-
ing most bitterly, as I found, against me. Colbrand said,
Oh how have you frighted us all!—And went behind me,
lest I should run away, as I suppose.

I sat still, to let them see I had no view to get away;
for, besides the improbability of succeeding, my last sad
attempt has cured me of enterprising again. And when
Mrs. Jewkes came within hearing, I found her terribly incensed, and raving about my contrivances. Why, said I,
should you be so concerned? Here I have sat a few
minutes, and had not the least thought of getting away, or
going farther; but to return as soon as it was duskish. She
would not believe me; and the barbarous creature struck
at me with her horrid fist, and, I believe, would have felled
me, had not Colbrand interposed, and said, He saw me
sitting still, looking about me, and not seeming to have
the least inclination to stir. But this would not serve:
She ordered the two maids to take me each by an arm, and
lead me back into the house, and up stairs; and there have
I been locked up ever since, without shoes. In vain have
I pleaded, that I had no design, as indeed I had not the
least; and last night I was forced to lie between her and
Nan; and I find she is resolved to make a handle of this
against me, and in her own behalf.—Indeed, what with her
usage, and my own apprehensions of still worse, I am quite
weary of my life.

Just now she has been with me, and given me my shoes,
and has laid her imperious commands upon me, to dress
myself in a suit of clothes out of the portmanteau, which I
have not seen lately, against three or four o'clock; for she

says, she is to have a visit from Lady Darnford's two daughters, who come purposely to see me; and so she gave me the key of the portmanteau. But I will not obey her; and I told her I would not be made a show of, nor see the ladies. She left me, saying, it would be worse for me, if I did not. But how can that be?

—— o ——

Five o'clock is come,

And no young ladies!—So that I fancy—But hold! I hear their coach, I believe. I'll step to the window.—I won't go down to them, I am resolved—

Good sirs! good sirs! What will become of me! Here is my master come in his fine chariot!—Indeed he is! What shall I do? Where shall I hide myself?—Oh! what shall I do? Pray for me! But oh! you'll not see this!—Now, good God of heaven, preserve me; if it be Thy blessed will!

—— o ——

Seven o'clock.

Though I dread to see him, yet do I wonder I have not. To be sure something is resolved against me, and he stays to hear all her stories. I can hardly write; yet, as I can do nothing else, I know not how to forbear!—Yet I cannot hold my pen—How crooked and trembling the lines!—I must leave off, till I can get quieter fingers!—Why should the guiltless tremble so, when the guilty can possess their minds in peace?

—— o ——

Saturday morning.

Now let me give you an account of what passed last night; for I had no power to write, nor yet opportunity till now.

This vile woman held my master till half an hour after seven; and he came hither about five in the afternoon. And then I heard his voice on the stairs, as he was coming up to me. It was about his supper; for he said, I shall choose a boiled chicken with butter and parsley.—And up he came!

He put on a stern and majestic air; and he can look very majestic when he pleases. Well, perverse Pamela, ungrateful runaway, said he, for my first salutation:—You do well, don't you, to give me all this trouble and vexation! I could not speak; but throwing myself on the floor, hid my face, and was ready to die with grief and apprehension.—He said, Well may you hide your face! well may you be ashamed to see me, vile forward one, as you are!—I sobbed and wept, but could not speak. And he let me lie, and went to the door, and called Mrs. Jewkes. —There, said he, take up that fallen angel!—Once I thought her as innocent as an angel of light: but I have now no patience with her. The little hypocrite prostrates herself thus, in hopes to move my weakness in her favour, and that I'll raise her from the floor myself. But I shall not touch her: No, said he, cruel gentleman as he was! let such fellows as Williams be taken in by her artful wiles! I know her now, and see she is for any fool's turn, that will be caught by her.

I sighed, as if my heart would break!—And Mrs. Jewkes lifted me up upon my knees; for I trembled so, I could not stand. Come, said she, Mrs. Pamela, learn to know your best friend; confess your unworthy behaviour, and beg his honour's forgiveness of all your faults. I was ready to faint: And he said, She is mistress of arts, I'll assure you; and will mimic a fit, ten to one, in a minute.

I was struck to the heart at this; but could not speak presently; only lifted up my eyes to heaven!—And at last made shift to say—God forgive you, sir!—He seemed in a great passion, and walked up and down the room, casting sometimes an eye upon me, and seeming as if he would have spoken, but checked himself—And at last he said,

When she has *acted* this her *first part* over, perhaps I will see her again, and she shall *soon* know what she has to trust to.

And so he went out of the room: And I was quite sick at heart!—Surely, said I, I am the wickedest creature that ever breathed! Well, said the impertinent, not so wicked as *that* neither; but I am glad you begin to see your faults. Nothing like being humble!—Come, I'll stand your friend, and plead for you, if you'll promise to be more dutiful for the future: Come, come, added the wretch, this may be all made up by to-morrow morning, if you are not a fool. —Begone, hideous woman! said I, and let not my afflictions be added to by thy inexorable cruelty, and unwomanly wickedness.

She gave me a push, and went away in a violent passion: And it seems, she made a story of this; and said, I had such a spirit, there was no bearing it.

I laid me down on the floor, and had no power to stir, till the clock struck nine; and then the wicked woman came up again. You must come down stairs, said she, to my master; that is, if you please, spirit!—Said I, I believe I cannot stand. Then, said she, I'll send Mons. Colbrand to carry you down.

I got up as well as I could, and trembled all the way down stairs: And she went before me into the parlour; and a new servant that he had waiting on him, instead of John, withdrew as soon as I came in: And, by the way, he had a new coachman too, which looked as if Bedfordshire Robin was turned away.

I thought, said he, when I came down, you should have sat at table with me, when I had not company; but when I find you cannot forget your original, but must prefer my menials to me, I call you down to wait on me while I sup, that I may have some talk with you, and throw away as little time as possible upon you.

Sir, said I, you do me honour to wait upon you:—And I never shall, I hope, forget my original. But I was forced to stand behind his chair, that I might hold by it. Fill me, said he, a glass of that Burgundy. I went to do it; but my hand shook so, that I could not hold the plate with the glass in it, and spilt some of the wine. So Mrs. Jewkes poured it for me, and I carried it as well as I could; and made a low courtesy. He took it, and said, Stand behind me, out of my sight!

Why, Mrs. Jewkes, said he, you tell me she remains very sullen still, and eats nothing. No, said she, not so much as will keep life and soul together.—And is always crying, you say, too? Yes, sir, answered she, I think she is, for one thing or another. Ay, said he, your young wenches will feed upon their tears; and their obstinacy will serve them for meat and drink. I think I never saw her look better though, in my life!—But, I suppose, she lives upon love. This sweet Mr. Williams, and her little villanous plots together, have kept her alive and well, to be sure: For mischief, love, and contradiction, are the natural aliments of a woman.

Poor I was forced to hear all this, and be silent; and indeed my heart was too full to speak.

And so you say, said he, that she had *another* project, but yesterday, to get away? She denies it herself, said she; but it had all the appearance of one. I'm sure she made me in a fearful pucker about it: And I am glad your honour is come, with all my heart; and I hope, whatever be your honour's intention concerning her, you will not be long about it; for you'll find her as slippery as an eel, I'll assure you.

Sir, said I, and clasped his knees with my arms, not knowing what I did, and falling on my knees, Have mercy on me, and hear me, concerning that wicked woman's usage of me——

He cruelly interrupted me, and said, I am satisfied she has done her duty: it signifies nothing what you say against Mrs. Jewkes. That you are here, little hypocrite as you are, pleading your cause before me, is owing to her care of you; else you had been with the parson.—Wicked girl! said he, to tempt a man to undo himself, as you have done him, at a time I was on the point of making him happy for his life!

I arose; but said with a deep sigh, I have done, sir!—I have done!—I have a strange tribunal to plead before. The poor sheep in the fable had such an one: when it was tried before the vulture, on the accusation of the wolf!

So, Mrs. Jewkes, said he, you are the wolf, I the vulture, and this the poor innocent lamb on her trial before us.—Oh! you don't know how well this innocent is read in reflection. She has wit at will, when she has a mind to display her own romantic innocence, at the price of other people's characters.

Well, said the aggravating creature, this is nothing to what she has called me: I have been a Jezebel, a London prostitute, and what not?—But I am contented with her ill names, now I see it is her fashion, and she can call your honour a vulture.

Said I, I had no thought of comparing my master—and was going to say on: but he said, Don't prate, girl!—No, said she, it don't become you, I am sure.

Well, said I, since I must not speak, I will hold my peace; but there is a righteous Judge, who knows the secrets of all hearts; and to Him I appeal.

See there! said he: now this meek, good creature is praying for fire from heaven upon us! Oh she can curse most heartily, in the spirit of Christian meekness, I'll assure you!—Come, saucy-face, give me another glass of wine.

So I did, as well as I could; but wept so, that he said, I suppose I shall have some of your tears in my wine!

When he had supped, he stood up, and said, Oh how happy for you it is, that you can, at will, thus make your speaking eyes overflow in this manner, without losing any of their brilliancy! You have been told, I suppose, that you are *most* beautiful in your tears!—Did you ever, said he to *her* (who all this while was standing in one corner of the parlour), see a more charming creature than this? Is it to be wondered at, that I demean myself thus to take notice of her?—See, said he, and took the glass with one hand, and turned me round with the other, what a shape! what a neck! what a hand! and what a bloom on that lovely face!—But who can describe the tricks and artifices, that lie lurking in her little, plotting, guileful heart! 'Tis no wonder the poor parson was infatuated with her.—I blame him less than I do her; for who could expect such artifice in so young a sorceress?

I went to the farther part of the room, and held my face against the wainscot; and in spite of all I could do to refrain crying, sobbed as if my heart would break. He said, I am surprised, Mrs. Jewkes, at the mistake of the letters you tell me of! But, you see, I am not afraid anybody should read what I write. I don't carry on private correspondences, and reveal every secret that comes to my knowledge, and then corrupt people to carry my letters against their duty, and all good conscience.

Come hither, hussy! said he: You and I have a dreadful reckoning to make. Why don't you come, when I bid you?—Fie upon it, Mrs. Pamela, said she. What! not stir, when his honour commands you to come to him!—Who knows but his goodness will forgive you?

He came to me (for I had no power to stir), and put his arms about my neck, and would kiss me; and said, Well, Mrs. Jewkes, if it were not for the thought of this cursed parson, I believe in my heart, so great is my weakness, that I could *yet* forgive this intriguing little slut, and take her to my bosom.

Oh, said the sycophant, you are very good, sir, very forgiving, indeed!—But come, added the profligate wretch, I hope you will be so good, as to take her to your bosom; and that, by to-morrow morning, you'll bring her to a better sense of her duty!

Could anything in womanhood be so vile? I had no patience: but yet grief and indignation choked up the passage of my words; and I could only stammer out a passionate exclamation to Heaven, to protect my inno-

cence. But the word was the subject of their ridicule.
Was ever poor creature worse beset!

He said, as if he had been considering whether he could
forgive me or not, No, I cannot yet forgive her neither.—
She has given me great disturbance; has brought great
discredit upon me, both abroad and at home; has corrupted
all my servants at the other house; has despised my honourable views and intentions to her, and sought to run away
with this ungrateful parson.—And surely I ought not to
forgive all this!—Yet, with all this wretched grimace, he
kissed me again, and would have put his hand into my
bosom; but I struggled, and said, I would *die* before I
would be used thus.—Consider, Pamela, said he, in a
threatening tone, consider where you are! and don't play
the fool: If you do, a more dreadful fate awaits you than
you expect. But take her upstairs, Mrs. Jewkes, and I'll
send a few lines to her to consider of; and let me have
your answer, Pamela, in the morning. Till then you have
to resolve: and after that your doom is fixed.—So I went
upstairs, and gave myself up to grief, and expectation of
what he would send: but yet I was glad of this night's
reprieve!

He sent me, however, nothing at all. And about twelve
o'clock, Mrs. Jewkes and Nan came up, as the night before,
to be my bed-fellows; and I would go to bed with some of
my clothes on: which they muttered at sadly; and Mrs.
Jewkes railed at me particularly. Indeed I would have sat
up all night, for fear, if she would have let me. For I had
but very little rest that night, apprehending this woman
would let my master in. She did nothing but praise him,
and blame me: but I answered her as little as I could.

He has Sir Simon Tell-tale, alias Darnford, to dine with
him to-day, whose family sent to welcome him into the
country; and it seems the old knight wants to see me; so
I suppose I shall be sent for, as Samson was, to make sport
for him.—Here I am, and must bear it all!

.'

Twelve o'clock, Saturday noon.

JUST now he has sent me up, by Mrs. Jewkes, the following proposals. So here are the honourable intentions all at
once laid open. They are, my dear parents, to make me a
vile kept mistress: which, I hope, I shall always detest the
thoughts of. But you'll see how they are accommodated
to what I should have most desired, could I have honestly
promoted it, your welfare and happiness. I have answered
them, as I am sure you'll approve; and I am prepared for
the worst: For though I fear there will be nothing omitted
to ruin me, and though my poor strength will not be able
to defend me, yet I will be innocent of crime in my intention, and in the sight of God; and to Him leave the aveng-
ing of all my wrongs, in His own good time and manner.
I shall write to you my answer against his articles; and
hope the best, though I fear the worst. But if I should
come home to you ruined and undone, and may not be able
to look you in the face; yet pity and inspirit the poor
Pamela, to make her little remnant of life easy; for long I
shall not survive my disgrace: and you may be assured it
shall not be my fault, if it be my misfortune.

———o———

' To Mrs. PAMELA ANDREWS.

' *The following* ARTICLES *are pro-*
' *posed to your serious considera-*
' *tion; and let me have an answer,*
' *in writing, to them, that I may*
' *take my resolutions accordingly.*
' *Only remember, that I will not be*
' *trifled with; and what you give*
' *for answer will absolutely decide*
' *your fate, without expostulation, or*
' *further trouble.*

This is my ANSWER.

Forgive, sir, the spirit your poor ser-
vant is about to show in her answer
to your ARTICLES. *Not to be warm,*
and in earnest, on such an occasion
as the present, would show a degree
of guilt, that, I hope, my soul abhors.
I will not trifle with you, nor act
like a person doubtful of her own
mind; for it wants not one moment's
consideration with me; and I there-
fore return the ANSWER *following,*
let what will be the consequence.

'I. If you can convince me that 'the hated parson has had no encour-'agement from you in his addresses; 'and that you have no inclination for 'him, in preference to me; then I 'will offer the following proposals to 'you, which I will punctually make 'good.

I. As to the first article, sir, it may behove me (that I may not deserve, in your opinion, the opprobrious terms of *forward* and *artful*, and such like) to declare solemnly, that Mr. Williams never had the least encouragement from me, as to what you hint; and I believe his principal motive was the apprehended duty of his function, quite contrary to his apparent interest, to assist a person he thought in dis-tress. You may, sir, the rather believe me, when I declare, that I know not the man breathing I would wish to marry; and that the only one I could honour more than another, is the gentleman, who, of all others, seeks my everlasting dishonour.

'II. I will directly make you a 'present of 500 *guineas*, for your own 'use, which you may dispose of to any 'purpose you please: and will give 'it absolutely into the hands of any 'person you shall appoint to receive 'it; and expect no favour in return, 'till you are satisfied in the posses-'sion of it.

II. As to your second proposal, let the consequence be what it will, I reject it with all my soul. Money, sir, is not my chief good: May God Al-mighty desert me, whenever it is! and whenever, for the sake of that, I can give up my title to that blessed hope which will stand me in stead, at a time when millions of gold will not purchase one happy moment of reflection on a past misspent life!

'III. I will likewise directly make 'over to you a purchase I lately made 'in Kent, which brings in 250*l. per* '*annum*, clear of all deductions. This 'shall be made over to you in full 'property for your life, and for the 'lives of any children to perpetuity, 'that you may happen to have: And 'your father shall be immediately put 'into possession of it in trust for these 'purposes: and the management of it 'will yield a comfortable subsistence 'to him, and your mother, for life; 'and I will make up any deficiencies, 'if such should happen, to that clear 'sum, and allow him 50*l.* per annum,

III. Your third proposal, sir, I re-ject for the same reason; and am sorry you could think my poor honest parents would enter into their part of it, and be concerned for the manage-ment of an estate, which would be owing to the prostitution of their poor daughter. Forgive, sir, my warmth on this occasion; but you know not the poor man, and the poor woman, my ever dear father and mother, if you think, that they would not much rather choose to starve in a ditch, or rot in a noisome dungeon, than accept of the fortune of a monarch, upon such wicked terms. I dare not say all that my full

‘ besides, for his life, and that of your
‘ mother, for his care and management
‘ of this your estate.

mind suggests to me on this grievous
occasion—But, indeed, sir, you know
them not ; nor shall the terrors of
death, in its most frightful form, I
hope, through God's assisting grace,
ever make me act unworthy of such
poor honest parents !

‘ IV. I will, moreover, extend my
‘ favour to any other of your relations,
‘ that you may think worthy of it, or
‘ that are valued by you.

IV. Your fourth proposal, I take
upon me, sir, to answer as the third.
If I have any friends that want the
favour of the great, may they *ever* want
it, if they are capable of desiring it on
unworthy terms !

‘ V. I will, besides, order patterns
‘ to be sent you for choosing four com-
‘ plete suits of rich clothes, that you
‘ may appear with reputation, as if
‘ you were my wife. And I will give
‘ you the two diamond rings, and two
‘ pair of ear-rings, and diamond neck-
‘ lace, that were bought by my mother,
‘ to present to Miss Tomlins, if the
‘ match that was proposed between
‘ her and me had been brought to
‘ effect : and I will confer upon you
‘ still *other* gratuities, as I shall find
‘ myself obliged, by your good beha-
‘ viour and affection.

V. Fine clothes, sir, become not
me ; nor have I any ambition to wear
them. I have greater pride in my
poverty and meanness, than I should
have in dress and finery. Believe me,
sir, I think such things less become
the humble-born Pamela, than the
rags your good mother raised me from.
Your rings, sir, your necklace, and
your ear-rings, will better befit ladies
of degree, than me : and to lose the
best jewel, my virtue, would be poorly
recompensed by those you propose to
give me. What should I think, when
I looked upon my finger, or saw in the
glass those diamonds on my neck, and
in my ears, but that they were the
price of my honesty ; and that I *wore*
those jewels outwardly, because I had
none inwardly.

‘ VI. Now, Pamela, will you see
‘ by this, what a value I set upon the
‘ free-will of a person *already* in my
‘ power ; and who, if these proposals
‘ are not accepted, shall find, that I
‘ have not taken all these pains, and
‘ risked my reputation, as I have done,
‘ without resolving to gratify my pas-
‘ sion for you, at all adventures ; and
‘ if you refuse, without making any
‘ terms at all.

VI. I know, sir, by woful experience, that I am in your power : I know
all the resistance I can make will be
poor and weak, and, perhaps, stand
me in little stead : I dread your *will*
to ruin me is as great as your *power:*
yet, sir, will I dare to tell you, that I
will make no free-will offering of my
virtue. All that I *can* do, poor as it
is, I *will* do, to convince you, that
your offers shall have no part in my

choice; and if I cannot escape the violence of man, I hope, by God's grace, I shall have nothing to reproach myself, for not doing all in my power to avoid my disgrace; and then I can safely appeal to the great God, my only refuge and protector, with this consolation, That my will bore no part in my violation.

' VII. You shall be mistress of my
' person and fortune, as much as if the
' foolish ceremony had passed. All
' my servants shall be yours; and you
' shall choose any two persons to
' attend yourself, either male or female,
' without any control of mine : and if
' your conduct be such, that I have
' reason to be satisfied with it, I know
' not (but will not engage for this) that
' I may, after a twelvemonth's cohabi-
' tation, marry you; for, if my love
' increases for you, as it has done for
' many months past, it will be impos-
' sible for me to deny you anything.

' And now, Pamela, consider well, it
' is in your power to oblige me on
' such terms, as will make yourself,
' and all your friends, happy : but
' this will be over this very day,
' irrevocably over; and you shall
' find all you would be thought to
' fear, without the least benefit aris-
' ing from it to yourself.

' And I beg you'll well weigh the
' matter, and comply with my pro-
' posals; and I will instantly set
' about securing to you the full effect
' of them : And let me, if you value
' yourself, experience a grateful re-
' turn on this occasion, and I'll for-
' give all that's past.'

VII. I have not once dared to look so high, as to such a proposal as your seventh article contains. Hence have proceeded all my little abortive arti-fices to escape from the confinement you have put me in; although you promised to be honourable to me. Your honour, well I know, would not let you stoop to so mean and so un-worthy a slave, as the poor Pamela : All I desire is, to be permitted to re-turn to my native meanness unviolated. What have I done, sir, to deserve it should be otherwise? For the obtain-ing of this, though I would not have *married* your chaplain, yet would I have *run away* with your meanest servant, if I had thought I could have got safe to my beloved poverty. I heard you once say, sir, That a certain great commander, who could live upon lentils, might well refuse the bribes of the greatest monarch : And I hope, as I can contentedly live at the meanest rate, and think not myself above the lowest condition, that I am also above making an exchange of my honesty for all the riches of the Indies. When I come to be proud and vain of gaudy apparel, and outside finery, then (which I hope will never be) may I rest my principal good in such vain trinkets and despise for them the more solid ornaments of a good fame, and a chas-tity inviolate !

———*0*———

Give me leave to say, sir, in answer to what you hint,
That you may in a twelvemonth's time marry me, on the
continuance of my good behaviour; that *this* weighs less
with me, if possible, than anything else you have said : for,
in the first place, there is an end of all merit, and all good
behaviour, on my side, if I have *now* any, the moment I
consent to your proposals: And I should be so far from
expecting such an honour, that I will pronounce, that I
should be most *unworthy* of it. What, sir, would the world
say, were you to marry your harlot ?—That a gentleman of
your rank in life should stoop, not only to the base-born
Pamela, but to a base-born prostitute ?—Little, sir, as I
know of the world, I am not to be caught by a bait so
poorly covered as this !

Yet, after all, dreadful is the thought, that I, a poor, weak,
friendless, unhappy creature, am too full in your power !
But permit me, sir, to pray, as I now write on my bended
knees, That before you resolve upon my ruin, you will weigh
well the matter. Hitherto, sir, though you have taken large
strides to this crying sin, yet are you on *this* side the
commission of it.—When once it is done, nothing can recall
it ! And where will be your triumph ?—What glory will
the spoils of such a weak enemy yield you ? Let me but
enjoy my poverty with honesty, is all my prayer; and I
will *bless* you, and *pray for* you, every moment of my life !
Think, oh think ! before it is yet too late ! what stings, what
remorse will attend your dying hour, when you come to
reflect, that you have ruined, perhaps soul and body, a
wretched creature, whose only pride was her virtue ! And
how pleased you will be, on the contrary, if in that tremendous moment you shall be able to acquit yourself of
this foul crime, and to plead in your own behalf, that you
suffered the earnest supplications of an unhappy wretch to
prevail with you to be innocent yourself, and let her remain
so !—May God Almighty, whose mercy so lately saved you
from the peril of perishing in deep waters (on which, I hope,
you will give me cause to congratulate you !) touch your
heart in my favour, and save *you* from this *sin*, and *me* from

this *ruin !*—And to Him do I commit my cause ; and to Him
will I give the glory, and night and day pray for you, if I
may be permitted to escape this great evil !——

Your poor oppressed, broken spirited servant.

I TOOK a copy of this for your perusal, my dear parents,
if I shall ever be so happy to see you again (for I hope my
conduct will be approved of by you) ; and at night, when
Sir Simon was gone, he sent for me down. Well, said he,
have you considered my proposals ? Yes, sir, said I, I have :
and there is my answer : But pray let me not see you read
it. Is it your bashfulness, said he, or your obstinacy, that
makes you not choose I should read it before you ?

I offered to go away ; and he said, Don't run from me ;
I won't read it till you are gone. But, said he, tell me,
Pamela, whether you comply with my proposals, or not ?
Sir, said I, you will see presently ; pray don't hold me ;
for he took my hand. Said he, Did you well consider
before you answered ?—I did, sir, said I. If it be not
what you think will please me, said he, dear girl, take it
back again, and reconsider it ; for if I have this as your
absolute answer, and I don't like it, you are undone ; for
I will not sue meanly, where I can command. I fear, said
he, it is not what I like, by your manner : and let me tell
you, that I cannot bear denial. If the terms I have
offered are not sufficient, I will augment them to two-
thirds of my estate ; for, said he, and swore a dreadful
oath, I cannot live without you : and, since the thing is
gone so far, *I will not !* And so he clasped me in his
arms in such a manner as quite frightened me ; and kissed
me two or three times.

I got from him, and run upstairs, and went to the
closet, and was quite uneasy and fearful.

In an hour's time he called Mrs. Jewkes down to him !
And I heard him very high in passion : and all about me !
And I heard her say, It was his own fault ; there would
be an end of all my complaining and perverseness, if he
was once resolved ; and other most impudent aggravations.

I am resolved not to go to bed this night, if I can help it!
—Lie still, lie still, my poor fluttering heart!—What will
become of me!

—*o*—

Almost twelve o'clock, Saturday night.

HE sent Mrs. Jewkes, about ten o'clock, to tell me to
come to him. Where? said I. I'll show you, said she.
I went down three or four steps, and saw her making to
his chamber, the door of which was open: So I said, I
cannot go there!—Don't be foolish, said she; but come;
no harm will be done to you!—Well, said I, if I die, I
cannot go there. I heard him say, Let her come, or it
shall be worse for her. I can't bear, said he, to speak to
her myself!—Well, said I, I cannot come, indeed I cannot;
and so I went up again into my closet, expecting to be
fetched by force.

But she came up soon after, and bid me make haste to
bed: Said I, I will not go to bed this night, that's certain!
—Then, said she, you shall be *made* to come to bed; and
Nan and I will undress you. I knew neither prayers nor
tears would move this wicked woman: So I said, I am sure
you will let master in, and I shall be undone! Mighty
piece of undone! she said: but he was too much exaspe-
rated against me, to be so familiar with me, she would
assure me!—Ay, said she, you'll be disposed of another
way soon, I can tell you for your comfort: and I hope
your *husband* will have your obedience, though nobody
else can have it. No husband in the world, said I, shall
make me do an unjust or base thing.—She said, That
would be soon tried; and Nan coming in, What! said I,
am I to have *two* bed-fellows again, these warm nights?
Yes, said she, slippery one, you are, till you can have *one
good one* instead of us. Said I, Mrs. Jewkes, don't talk
nastily to me: I see you are beginning again; and I shall
affront you, maybe; for next to bad actions, are bad
words; for they could not be spoken, if they were not in

the heart.—Come to bed, purity! said she. You are a
nonsuch, I suppose. Indeed, said I, I can't come to bed;
and it will do you no harm to let me stay all night in the
great chair. Nan, said she, undress my young lady. If
she won't let you, I'll help you; and, if neither of us can
do it quietly, we'll call my master to do it for us; though,
said she, I think it an office worthier of Monsieur Colbrand!—You are very wicked, said I. I know it, said
she; I am a Jezebel, and a London prostitute, you know.
You did great feats, said I, to tell my master all this poor
stuff; but you did not tell him how you beat me. No,
lambkin, said she (a word I had not heard a good while),
that I left for you to tell; and you was going to do it if
the *vulture* had not taken the *wolf's* part, and bid the
poor innocent *lamb* be silent!—Ay, said I, no matter for
your fleers, Mrs. Jewkes; though I can have neither justice nor mercy here, and cannot be heard in my defence,
yet a time will come, maybe, when I *shall* be heard, and
when your own guilt will strike you dumb.—Ay! spirit,
said she; and the vulture too! Must we both be dumb?
Why that, lambkin, will be pretty!—Then, said the
wicked one, you'll have all the talk to yourself?—Then
how will the tongue of the pretty lambkin bleat out *innocence*, and *virtue*, and *honesty*, till the whole trial be at an
end!—You're a wicked woman, that's certain, said I; and
if you thought anything of another world, could not talk
thus. But no wonder!—It shows what hands I'm got
into!—Ay, so it does, said she; but I beg you'll undress,
and come to bed, or I believe your innocence won't keep
you from *still worse* hands. I will come to bed, said I, if
you will let me have the keys in my own hand; not else,
if I can help it. Yes, said she, and then, hey for another
contrivance, another escape!—No, no, said I, all my contrivances are over, I'll assure you! Pray let me have the
keys, and I will come to bed. She came to me, and took
me in her huge arms, as if I was a feather: Said she, I do
this to show you what a poor resistance you can make
against me, if I please to exert myself; and so, lambkin,

don't say to your wolf, I *won't* come to bed!—And set me down, and tapped me on the neck: Ah! said she, thou art a pretty creature, 'tis true; but so obstinate! so full of spirit! if thy strength was but answerable to that, thou would'st run away with us all, and this great house too on thy back!—But, undress, undress, I tell you.

Well, said I, I see my misfortunes make you very merry, and very witty too: but I will *love* you, if you will humour me with the keys of the chamber-doors.—Are you *sure* you will love me? said she: Now speak your conscience! —Why, said I, you must not put it so close; neither would you, if you thought you had not given reason to doubt it!—But I will love you as well as I can!—I would not tell a wilful lie: and if I did, you would not believe me, after your hard usage of me. Well, said she, that's all fair, I own!—But, Nan, pray pull off my young lady's shoes and stockings.—No, pray don't, said I; I will come to bed presently, since I must.

And so I went to the closet, and scribbled a little about this idle chit-chat. And she being importunate, I was forced to go to bed; but with some of my clothes on, as the former night; and she let me hold the two keys; for there are two locks, there being a double door; and so I got a little sleep that night, having had none for two or three nights before.

I can't imagine what she means; but Nan offered to talk a little once or twice; and she snubbed her, and said, I charge you, wench, don't open your lips before me; and if you are asked any questions by Mrs. Pamela, don't answer her one word, while I am here!—But she is a lordly woman to the maid-servants; and that has always been her character: oh how unlike good Mrs. Jervis in everything!

—o—

A THOUGHT came into my head ; I meant no harm ; but
it was a little bold.   For, seeing my master dressing to go
to church ; and his chariot getting ready, I went to my
closet, and I writ,

The prayers of this congregation are earnestly desired for a gentleman of
great worth and honour, who labours under a temptation to exert his
great power to ruin a poor, distressed, worthless maiden :

And also,

The prayers of this congregation are earnestly desired by a poor distressed
creature, for the preservation of her virtue and innocence.

Mrs. Jewkes came up : Always writing ! said she ; and
would see it : And strait, all that ever I could say, carried
it down to my master.—He looked upon it, and said, Tell
her, she shall soon see how her prayers are answered ; she
is very bold : but as she has rejected all my favours, her
reckoning for all is not far off.   I looked after him out of
the window ; and he was charmingly dressed : To be sure
he is a handsome fine gentleman !—What pity his heart is
not as good as his appearance !   Why can't I hate him ?—
But don't be uneasy, if you should see this ; for it is impossible I should love him ; for his vices all *ugly him over*,
as I may say.

My master sends word, that he shall not come home to
dinner : I suppose he dines with this Sir Simon Darnford.
I am much concerned for poor Mr. Williams.   Mrs. Jewkes
says, he is confined still, and takes on much.   All his
trouble is brought upon him for my sake : This grieves me
much.   My master, it seems, will have his money from him.
This is very hard ; for it is three fifty pounds, he gave him,
as he thought, as a salary for three years that he has been
with him : but there was no agreement between them ; and
he absolutely depended on my master's favour.   To be sure,
it was the more generous of him to run these risks for the

sake of oppressed innocence: and I hope he will meet with his reward in due time. Alas for me! I dare not plead for him; that would raise my oppressor's jealousy more. And I have not interest to save myself!

——*o*——

Sunday evening.

Mrs. Jewkes has received a line from my master: I wonder what it is; for his chariot has come home without him. But she will tell me nothing; so it is in vain to ask her. I am so fearful of plots and tricks, I know not what to do!—Everything I suspect; for, now my disgrace is avowed, what can I think!—To be sure, the worst will be attempted! I can only pour out my soul in prayer to God, for His blessed protection. But, if I must suffer, let me not be long a mournful survivor!—Only let me not shorten my own time sinfully!——

This woman left upon the table, in the chamber, this letter of my master's to her; and I bolted myself in, till I had transcribed it. You'll see how tremblingly, by the lines. I wish poor Mr. Williams's release at any rate; but this letter makes my heart ache. Yet I have another day's reprieve, thank God!

' Mrs. Jewkes,—I have been so pressed on Williams's
' affair, that I shall set out this afternoon, in Sir Simon's
' chariot, and with Parson Peters', who is his intercessor,
' for Stamford; and shall not be back till to-morrow even-
' ing, if then. As to your ward, I am thoroughly incensed
' against her: She has withstood her time; and now, would
' she sign and seal to my articles, it is too late. I shall
' discover something, perhaps, by him; and will, on my
' return, let her know, that all her ensnaring loveliness shall
' not save her from the fate that awaits her. But let her
' know nothing of this, lest it put her fruitful mind upon
' plots and artifices. Be sure trust her not without another

' with you at night, lest she venture the window in her
' foolish rashness: for I shall require her at your hands.

' Yours, &c.'

I had but just finished taking a copy of this, and laid
the letter where I had it, and unbolted the door, when she
came up in a great fright, for fear I should have seen it;
but I being in my closet, and that lying as she left it,
she did not mistrust. Oh, said she, I was afraid you had
seen my master's letter here, which I carelessly left on the
table. I wish, said I, I had known that. Why sure, said
she, if you had, you would not have offered to read my
letters! Indeed, said I, I should, at this time, if it had
been in my way:—Do let me see it.—Well, said she, I
wish poor Mr. Williams well off: I understand my master
is gone to make up matters with him; which is very good.
To be sure, added she, he is a very good gentleman, and
very forgiving!—Why, said I, as if I had known nothing
of the matter, how can he make up matters with him? Is
not Mr. Williams at Stamford? Yes, said she, I believe so;
but Parson Peters pleads for him, and he is gone with him
to Stamford, and will not be back to-night: so we have
nothing to do, but to eat our suppers betimes, and go to
bed. Ay, that's pure, said I; and I shall have good rest
this night, I hope. So, said she, you might every night,
but for your own idle fears. You are afraid of your friends,
when none are near you. Ay, that's true, said I; for I
have not one near me.

So I have one more good honest night before me:
What the next may be I know not, and so I'll try to
take in a good deal of sleep, while I can be a little easy.
Therefore, here I say, Good night, my dear parents; for I
have no more to write about this night: and though his
letter shocks me, yet I will be as brisk as I can, that she
mayn't suspect I have seen it.

——o——

Tuesday night.

For the future, I will always mistrust most when appearances look fairest. Oh your poor daughter! what has she not suffered since what I wrote on Sunday night!—My worst trial, and my fearfullest danger! Oh how I shudder to write you an account of this wicked interval of time! For, my dear parents, will you not be too much frightened and affected with my distress, when I tell you, that his journey to Stamford was all abominable pretence! for he came home privately, and had well nigh effected all his vile purposes, and the ruin of your poor daughter! and that by such a plot as I was not in the least apprehensive of: And, oh! you'll hear what a vile and unwomanly part that wicked wretch, Mrs. Jewkes, acted in it!

I left off with letting you know how much I was pleased that I had one night's reprieve added to my honesty. But I had less occasion to rejoice than ever, as you will judge by what I have said already. Take, then, the dreadful story, as well as I can relate it.

The maid Nan is a little apt to drink, if she can get at liquor; and Mrs. Jewkes happened, or designed, as is too probable, to leave a bottle of cherry-brandy in her way, and the wench drank some of it more than she should; and when she came in to lay the cloth, Mrs. Jewkes perceived it, and fell a rating at her most sadly; for she has too many faults of her own, to suffer any of the like sort in anybody else, if she can help it; and she bid her get out of her sight, when we had supped, and go to bed, to sleep off her liquor, before we came to bed. And so the poor maid went muttering upstairs.

About two hours after, which was near eleven o'clock, Mrs. Jewkes and I went up to go to bed; I pleasing myself with what a charming night I should have. We locked both doors, and saw poor Nan, as I thought (but, oh! 'twas my abominable master, as you shall hear by and by), sitting fast asleep, in an elbow-chair, in a dark corner of the room, with her apron thrown over her head and neck. And Mrs.

Jewkes said, There is that beast of a wench fast asleep,
instead of being a-bed! I knew, said she, she had taken a
fine dose. I'll wake her, said I. No, don't, said she; let
her sleep on; we shall lie better without her. Ay, said I,
so we shall; but won't she get cold?

Said she, I hope you have no writing to-night. No,
replied I, I will go to bed with you, Mrs. Jewkes. Said she,
I wonder, what you can find to write about so much! and
am sure you have better conveniencies of that kind, and
more paper than I am aware of: and I had intended to
rummage you, if my master had not come down; for I
spied a broken tea-cup with ink, which gave me suspicion:
but as he is come, let him look after you, if he will; and if
you deceive him, it will be his own fault.

All this time we were undressing ourselves: And I fetched
a deep sigh! What do you sigh for? said she. I am
thinking, Mrs. Jewkes, answered I, what a sad life I live,
and how hard is my lot. I am sure, the thief that has
robbed is much better off than I, 'bating the guilt; and I
should, I think, take it for a mercy, to be hanged out of
the way, rather than live in these cruel apprehensions. So,
being not sleepy, and in a prattling vein, I began to give a
little history of myself, as I did, once before, to Mrs. Jervis;
in this manner:

Here, said I, were my poor honest parents; they took
care to instil good principles into my mind, till I was
almost twelve years of age; and taught me to prefer goodness and poverty to the highest condition of life; and they
confirmed their lessons by their own practice; for they
were, of late years, remarkably poor, and always as remarkably honest, even to a proverb: for, *As honest as goodman
Andrews*, was a byeword.

Well then, said I, comes my late dear good lady, and
takes a fancy to me, and said, she would be the making of
me, if I was a good girl; and she put me to sing, to dance,
to play on the spinnet, in order to divert her melancholy
hours; and also taught me all manner of fine needle-work;
but still this was her lesson, *My good Pamela, be virtuous,*

and keep the men at a distance. Well, so I was, I hope, and so I did; and yet, though I say it, they all loved me and respected me; and would do anything for me, as if I was a gentlewoman.

But, then, what comes next?—Why, it pleased God to take my good lady; and then comes my master: and what says he?—Why in effect, it is, *Be not virtuous, Pamela.*

So here I have lived about sixteen years in virtue and reputation; and all at once, when I come to know what is good, and what is evil, I must renounce all the good, all the whole sixteen years' innocence, which, next to God's grace, I owed chiefly to my parents, and my lady's good lessons and examples, and choose the evil; and so, in a moment's time, become the vilest of creatures! And all this, for what, I pray? Why, truly, for a pair of diamond earrings, a necklace, and a diamond ring for my finger; which would not become me: for a few paltry fine clothes, which, when I wore them, would make but my former poverty more ridiculous to everybody that saw me; especially when they knew the base terms I wore them upon. But, indeed, I was to have a great parcel of guineas besides; I forget how many; for had there been ten times more, they would have been not so much to me, as the honest six guineas you tricked me out of, Mrs. Jewkes.

Well, forsooth! but then I was to have I know not how many pounds a year for my life; and my poor father (there was the jest of it!) was to be the manager for the abandoned prostitute his daughter: and then (there was the jest again!) my kind, forgiving, virtuous master, would pardon me all my misdeeds!

Yes, thank him for nothing, truly. And what, pray, are all these violent misdeeds?—Why, they are for daring to adhere to the good lessons that were taught me; and not learning a new one, that would have reversed all my former: for not being contented when I was run away with, in order to be ruined; but contriving, if my poor wits had been able, to get out of danger, and preserve myself honest.

Then was he once jealous of poor John, though he knew John was his own creature, and helped to deceive me.

Then was he outrageous against poor Parson Williams! and him has his good, merciful master thrown into gaol; and for what? Why, truly, for that, being a divine, and a good man, he had the fear of God before his eyes, and was willing to forego all his expectations of interest, and assist an oppressed poor creature.

But, to be sure, I must be forward, bold, saucy, and what not! to dare to run away from certain ruin, and to strive to escape from an unjust confinement; and I must be married to the parson, nothing so sure!

He would have had but a poor catch of me, had I consented: but he, and *you* too, know I did not want to marry *anybody*. I only wanted to go to my poor parents, and to have my own liberty, and not to be confined by such an unlawful restraint; and which would not have been inflicted upon me, but only that I am a poor, destitute young body, and have no friend that is able to right me.

So, Mrs. Jewkes, said I, here is my history in brief. And I am a very unhappy young creature, to be sure!—And why am I so?—Why, because my master sees something in my person that takes his present fancy; and because I would not be undone.—Why, therefore to choose, I must, and I shall be undone!—And this is all the reason that can be given!

She heard me run on all this time, while I was undressing, without any interruption; and I said, Well, I must go to the two closets, ever since an affair of the closet at the other house, though he is so far off. And I have a good mind to wake this poor maid. No, don't, said she, I charge you. I am very angry with her, and she'll get no harm there; and if she wakes, she may come to bed well enough, as long as there is a candle in the chimney.

So I looked into the closet, and kneeled down in my own, as I used to do, to say my prayers, and this with my under-clothes in my hand, all undressed; and passed by the poor sleeping wench, as I thought, in my return. But, oh! little

did I think it was my wicked, wicked master, in a gown
and petticoat of hers, and her apron over his face and
shoulders. What meanness will not Lucifer make his
votaries stoop to, to gain their abominable ends!

Mrs. Jewkes, by this time, was got to bed, on the farther
side, as she used to be; and, to make room for the maid,
when she should awake, I got into bed, and lay close to her.
And I said, Where are the keys? though, said I, I am not
so much afraid to-night. Here, said the wicked woman,
put your arm under mine, and you shall find them about
my wrist, as they used to be. So I did, and the abominable
designer held my hand with her right hand, as my right arm
was under her left.

In less than a quarter of an hour, I said, There's poor
Nan awake; I hear her stir. Let us go to sleep, said she,
and not mind her: she'll come to bed, when she's quite
awake. Poor soul! said I, I'll warrant she will have the
head-ache finely to-morrow for this! Be silent, said she, and
go to sleep; you keep me awake; and I never found you in
so talkative a humour in my life. Don't chide me, said I;
I will but say one thing more: Do you think Nan could
hear me talk of my master's offers? No, no, said she; she
was dead asleep. I'm glad of that, said I; because I would
not expose my master to his common servants; and I knew
you were no stranger to his *fine* articles. Said she, I think
they were *fine* articles, and you were bewitched you did not
close with them: but let us go to sleep. So I was silent?
and the pretended Nan (oh wicked, base, villainous designer!
what a plot, what an unexpected plot was this!) seemed to
be awaking; and Mrs. Jewkes, abhorred creature! said,
Come, Nan:—what, are you awake at last?—Pr'ythee come
to bed; for Mrs. Pamela is in a talking fit, and won't go to
sleep one while.

At that, the pretended she came to the bedside; and,
sitting down in a chair, where the curtain hid her, began to
undress. Said I, Poor Mrs. Anne, I warrant your head
aches most sadly! How do you do?—She answered not a
word. Said the superlatively wicked woman, You know I

have ordered her not to answer you. And this plot, to be sure, was laid when she gave her these orders the night before.

I heard her, as I thought, breathe all quick and short: Indeed, said I, Mrs. Jewkes, the poor maid is not well. What ails you, Mrs. Anne? And still no answer was made.

But, I tremble to relate it! the pretended she came into bed, but trembled like an aspen-leaf; and I, poor fool that I was! pitied her much—but well might the barbarous deceiver tremble at his vile dissimulation, and base designs.

What words shall I find, my dear mother (for my father should not see this shocking part), to describe the rest, and my confusion, when the guilty wretch took my left arm, and laid it under his neck, and the vile procuress held my right; and then he clasped me round the waist!

Said I, is the wench mad? Why, how now, confidence! thinking still it had been Nan. But he kissed me with frightful vehemence; and then his voice broke upon me like a clap of thunder. Now, Pamela, said he, is the dreadful time of reckoning come, that I have threatened.—I screamed out in such a manner, as never anybody heard the like. But there was nobody to help me: and both my hands were secured, as I said. Sure never poor soul was in such agonies as I. Wicked man! said I; wicked abominable woman! O God! my God! this *time!* this *one time!* deliver me from this distress! or strike me dead this moment! And then I screamed again and again.

Says he, One word with you, Pamela; one word hear me but; and hitherto you see I offer nothing to you. Is this *nothing*, said I, to be in bed here? to hold my hands between you! I will hear, if you will instantly leave the bed, and take this villainous woman from me!

Said she (oh disgrace of womankind!), What you do, sir, do; don't stand dilly-dallying. She cannot exclaim worse than she has done: and she'll be quieter, when she knows the worst.

Silence! said he to her; I must say one word to you, Pamela! it is this: You see now you are in my power!—

You cannot get from me, nor help yourself: yet have I not offered anything amiss to you. But if you resolve not to comply with my proposals, I will not lose this opportunity: if you do, I will yet leave you.

Oh, sir, said I, leave me, leave me but, and I will do anything I ought to do.—Swear then to me, said he, that you will accept my proposals! and then (for this was all detestable grimace) he put his hand in my bosom. With struggling, fright, terror, I fainted away quite, and did not come to myself soon; so that they both, from the cold sweats that I was in, thought me dying.—And I remember no more, than that, when with great difficulty they brought me to myself, she was sitting on one side of the bed, with her clothes on; and he on the other with his, and in his gown and slippers.

Your poor Pamela cannot answer for the liberties taken with her in her deplorable state of death. And when I saw them there, I sat up in my bed, without any regard to what appearance I made, and nothing about my neck; and he soothing me, with an aspect of pity and concern, I put my hand to his mouth, and said, Oh tell me, yet tell me not, what have I suffered in this distress? And I talked quite wild, and knew not what; for, to be sure, I was on the point of distraction.

He most solemnly, and with a bitter imprecation, vowed that he had not offered the least indecency; that he was frightened at the terrible manner I was taken with the fit; that he should desist from his attempt; and begged but to see me easy and quiet, and he would leave me directly, and go to his own bed. Oh then, said I, take with you this most wicked woman, this vile Mrs. Jewkes, as an earnest that I may believe you!

And will you, sir, said the wicked wretch, for a fit or two, give up such an opportunity as this?—I thought you had known the sex better. She is now, you see, quite well again!

This I heard; more she might say; but I fainted away once more, at these words, and at his clasping his arms about me again. And, when I came a little to myself, I saw him sit there, and the maid Nan, holding a smelling-bottle to my nose, and no Mrs. Jewkes.

He said, taking my hand, Now will I vow to you, my dear Pamela, that I will leave you the moment I see you better, and pacified. Here's Nan knows, and will tell you, my concern for you. I vow to God, I have not offered any indecency to you: and, since I found Mrs. Jewkes so offensive to you, I have sent her to the maid's bed, and the maid shall lie with you to-night. And but promise me that you will compose yourself, and I will leave you. But, said I, will not Nan also hold my hand? And will not she let you come in again to me?—He said, By heaven! I will not come in again to-night. Nan, undress yourself, go to bed, and do all you can to comfort the dear creature: And now, Pamela, said he, give me but your hand, and say you forgive me, and I will leave you to your repose. I held out my trembling hand, which he vouchsafed to kiss; and I said, God forgive you, sir, as you *have been* just in my distress; and as you *will be* just to what you promise! And he withdrew, with a countenance of remorse, as I hoped; and she shut the doors, and, at my request, brought the keys to bed.

This, oh my dear parents! was a most dreadful trial. I tremble still to think of it; and dare not recall all the horrid circumstances of it. I hope, as he assures me, he was not guilty of indecency; but have reason to bless God, who, by disabling me in my faculties, empowered me to preserve my innocence; and, when all my strength would have signified nothing, magnified himself in my weakness.

I was so weak all day on Monday, that I could not get out of my bed. My master showed great tenderness for me; and I hope he is really sorry, and that this will be his last attempt; but he does not say so neither.

He came in the morning, as soon as he heard the door open: and I began to be fearful. He stopped short of the

bed, and said, Rather than give you apprehensions, I will
come no farther. I said, Your honour, sir, and your mercy,
is all I have to beg. He sat himself on the side of the
bed, and asked kindly, how I did!—begged me to be composed; said, I still looked a little wildly. And I said,
Pray, good sir, let me not see this infamous Mrs. Jewkes;
I doubt I cannot bear her sight. She shan't come near
you all this day, if you'll promise to compose yourself.
Then, sir, I will try. He pressed my hand very tenderly,
and went out. What a change does this show!—Oh may
it be lasting!—But, alas! he seems only to have altered
his method of proceeding; and retains, I doubt, his wicked
purpose.

On Tuesday, about ten o'clock, when my master heard
I was up, he sent for me down into the parlour. As soon
as he saw me, he said, Come nearer to me, Pamela. I did
so, and he took my hand, and said, You begin to look
well again: I am glad of it. You little slut, how did you
frighten me on Sunday night!

Sir, said I, pray name not that night; and my eyes overflowed at the remembrance, and I turned my head aside.

Said he, Place some little confidence in me: I know
what those charming eyes mean, and you shall not need to
explain yourself: for I do assure you, that as soon as I saw
you change, and a cold sweat bedew your pretty face, and
you fainted away, I quitted the bed, and Mrs. Jewkes did
so too. And I put on my gown, and she fetched her smelling-bottle, and we both did all we could to restore you;
and my passion for you was all swallowed up in the concern I had for your recovery; for I thought I never saw a
fit so strong and violent in my life: and feared we should
not bring you to life again; for what I saw you in once
before was nothing to it. This, said he, might be my folly,
and my unacquaintedness with what passion your sex *can*
show when they are in earnest. But this I repeat to you,
that your mind may be entirely comforted—whatever I
offered to you, was before you fainted away, and that, I am
sure, was innocent.

Sir, said I, that was very bad: and it was too plain you
had the worst designs. When, said he, I tell you the truth
in one instance, you may believe me in the other. I know
not, I declare, beyond this lovely bosom, your sex: but
that I did intend what you call the *worst* is most certain:
and though I would not too much alarm you now, I could
curse my weakness, and my folly, which makes me own,
that I love you beyond all your sex, and cannot live without you. But if I am master of myself, and my own
resolution, I will not attempt to force you to anything
again.

Sir, said I, you may easily keep your resolution, if you'll
send me out of your way, to my poor parents; that is all
I beg.

'Tis a folly to talk of it, said he. You must not, shall
not go! And if I could be assured you would not attempt
it, you should have better usage, and your confinement
should be made easier to you.

But to what end, sir, am I to stay? said I: You yourself seem not sure you can keep your own present good
resolutions; and do you think, if I was to stay, when I
could get away, and be safe, it would not look, as if either I
confided too much in my own strength, or would tempt my
ruin? And as if I was not in earnest to wish myself safe,
and out of danger?—And then, how long am I to stay?
And to what purpose? And in what light must I appear
to the world? Would not *that* censure me, although I
might be innocent? And you will allow, sir, that, if there
be anything valuable or exemplary in a good name, or
fair reputation, one must not despise the world's censure, if
one can avoid it.

Well, said he, I sent not for you on this account, just
now; but for two reasons. The first is, That you promise
me, that for a fortnight to come you will not offer to go
away without my express consent; and this I expect for
your own sake, that I may give you a little more liberty.
And the second is, that you will see and forgive Mrs.
Jewkes: she takes on much, and thinks that, as all her

fault was her obedience to me, it would be very hard to sacrifice her, as she calls it, to your resentment.

As to the first, sir, said I, it is a hard injunction, for the reasons I have mentioned. And as to the second, considering her vile, unwomanly wickedness, and her endeavours to instigate you more to ruin me, when your returning goodness seemed to have some compassion upon me, it is still harder. But, to show my obedience to your commands (for you know, my dear parents, I might as well make a merit of my compliance, when my refusal would stand me in no stead), I will consent to both; and to everything else, that you shall be pleased to enjoin, which I can do with innocence.

That's my good girl! said he, and kissed me: This is quite prudent, and shows me, that you don't take insolent advantage of my favour for you; and will, perhaps, stand you in more stead than you are aware of.

So he rung the bell, and said, Call down Mrs. Jewkes. She came down, and he took my hand, and put it into hers; and said, Mrs. Jewkes, I am obliged to you for all your diligence and fidelity to me; but Pamela, I must own, is not; because the service I employed you in was not so very obliging to her, as I could have wished she would have thought it: and you were not to favour her, but obey me. But yet I'll assure you, at the very first word, she has *once* obliged me, by consenting to be friends with you; and if she gives me no great cause, I shall not, perhaps, put you on such disagreeable service again.—Now, therefore, be you once more bed-fellows and board-fellows, as I may say, for some days longer; and see that Pamela sends no letters nor messages out of the house, nor keeps a correspondence unknown to me, especially with that Williams; and, as for the rest, show the dear girl all the respect that is due to one I must love, if she will deserve it, as I hope she will yet; and let her be under no unnecessary or harsh restraints. But your watchful care is not, however, to cease; and remember that you are not to disoblige me, to oblige her; and that I will not, cannot, yet part with her.

Mrs. Jewkes looked very sullen, and as if she would be glad still to do me a good turn, if it lay in her power.

I took courage then to drop a word or two for poor Mr. Williams; but he was angry with me for it, and said he could not endure to hear his name in *my* mouth; so I was forced to have done for that time.

All this time, my papers, that I buried under the rosebush, lay there still; and I begged for leave to send a letter to you. So I should, he said, if he might read it first. But this did not answer my design; and yet I would have sent you such a letter as he might see, if I had been sure my danger was over. But that I cannot; for he now seems to take another method, and what I am more afraid of, because, may be, he may watch an opportunity, and join force with it, on occasion, when I am least prepared: for now he seems to abound with kindness, and talks of love without reserve, and makes nothing of allowing himself in the liberty of kissing me, which he calls innocent; but which I do not like, and especially in the manner he does it: but for a master to do it at all to a servant has meaning too much in it, not to alarm an honest body.

—— o ——

Wednesday morning.

I find I am watched and suspected still very close; and I wish I was with you; but that must not be, it seems, this fortnight. I don't like this fortnight; and it will be a tedious and a dangerous one to me, I doubt.

My master just now sent for me down to take a walk with him in the garden: but I like him not at all, nor his ways; for he would have, all the way, his arm about my waist, and said abundance of fond things to me, enough to make me proud, if his design had not been apparent. After walking about, he led me into a little alcove, on the farther part of the garden; and really made me afraid of myself, for he began to be very teasing, and made me sit on his knee; and was so often kissing me, that I said, Sir, I

don't like to be here at all, I assure you. Indeed you make
me afraid!—And what made me the more so, was what he
once said to Mrs. Jewkes, and did not think I heard him,
and which, though always uppermost with me, I did not
mention before, because I did not know how to bring it in,
in my writing.

She, I suppose, had been encouraging him in his wickedness; for it was before the last dreadful trial: and I only
heard what he answered.

Said he, I will try *once* more; but I have begun wrong:
for I see terror does but add to her frost; but she is a
charming girl, and may be thawed by kindness; and I
should have melted her by love, instead of freezing her by
fear.

Is he not a wicked, sad man for this?—To be sure, I
blush while I write it. But I trust that that God, who has
delivered me from the paw of the lion and the bear; that is,
his and Mrs. Jewkes' violences, will soon deliver me from
this Philistine, that I may not *defy the commands of the
living God!*

But as I was saying, this expression coming into my
thoughts, I was of opinion, I could not be too much on my
guard, at all times: more especially when he took such
liberties: for he professed honour all the time with his
mouth, while his actions did not correspond. I begged
and prayed he would let me go: and had I not appeared
quite regardless of all he said, and resolved not to stay, if
I could help it, I know not how far he would have proceeded; for I was forced to fall down upon my knees.

At last he walked out with me, still bragging of his honour
and his love. Yes, yes, sir, said I, your honour is to destroy
mine: and your love is to ruin me; I see it too plainly.
But, indeed, I will not walk with you, sir, said I, any more.
Do you know, said he, whom you talk to, and where
you are?

You may believe I had reason to think him not so decent
as he should be; for I said, As to where I am, sir, I know
it too well; and that I have no creature to befriend me:

and, as to whom I talk to, sir, let me ask you, what you would have me answer?

Why, tell me, said he, what answer you would make? It will only make you angry, said I; and so I shall fare worse, if possible. I won't be angry, said he. Why then, sir, said I, you cannot be my late good lady's son; for she loved me, and taught me virtue. You cannot then be my master; for no master demeans himself so to his poor servant.

He put his arm round me, and his other hand on my neck, which made me more angry and bold: and he said, What then am I? Why, said I (struggling from him, and in a great passion), to be sure you are Lucifer himself, in the *shape* of my master, or you could not use me thus. These are too great liberties, said he, in anger; and I desire that you will not repeat them, for your own sake: For if you have no decency towards *me* I'll have none towards *you.*

I was running from him, and he said, Come back, when I bid you.—So, knowing every place was alike dangerous to me, and I had nobody to run to, I came back, at his call; and seeing him look displeased, I held my hands together, and wept, and said, Pray, sir, forgive me. No, said he, rather say, Pray, Lucifer, forgive me! And, now, since you take me for the devil, how can you expect any good from me?—How, rather, can you expect anything but the worst treatment from me?—You have given me a character, Pamela; and blame me not that I act up to it.

Sir, said I, let me beg you to forgive me: I am really sorry for my boldness; but indeed you don't use me like a gentleman: and how can I express my resentment, if I mince the matter, while you are so indecent?

Precise fool! said he, what indecencies have I offered you?—I was bewitched I had not gone through my purpose last Sunday night; and then your licentious tongue had not given the worst name to little puny freedoms, that show my love and my folly at the same time. But, begone, said he, taking my hand, and tossing it from him, and learn another conduct and more wit; and I will lay aside my foolish regard for you, and assert myself. Begone! said he, again, with a haughty air.

Indeed, sir, said I, I cannot go, till you pardon me, which I beg on my bended knees. I am truly sorry for my boldness,—but I see how you go on: you creep by little and little upon me; and now soothe me, and now threaten me; and if I should forbear to show my resentment, when you offer incivilities to me, would not that be to be lost by degrees? Would it not show, that I could bear anything from you, if I did not express all the indignation I *could* express, at the first approaches you make to what I dread? And have you not as good as avowed my ruin?—And have you once made me hope you will quit your purposes against me? How then, sir, can I act, but by showing my abhorrence of every step that makes towards my undoing? And what is left me but words?—And can these words be other than such strong ones, as shall show the detestation which, from the bottom of my heart, I have for every attempt upon my virtue? Judge for me, sir, and pardon me.

Pardon you! said he, what! when you don't repent? —When you have the boldness to justify yourself in your fault; why don't you say, you never will again offend me? I will endeavour, sir, said I, always to preserve that decency towards you which becomes me. But really, sir, I must beg your excuse for saying, That when you forget what belongs to decency in your actions, and when words are all that are left me, to shew my resentment of such actions, I will not promise to forbear the strongest expressions that my distressed mind shall suggest to me: nor shall your angriest frowns deter me, when my honesty is in question.

What, then, said he, do you beg pardon for? Where is the promise of amendment, for which I should forgive you? Indeed, sir, said I, I own that must absolutely depend on your usage of me: for I will bear anything you can inflict upon me with patience, even to the laying down of my life, to show my obedience to you in other cases; but I cannot be patient, I cannot be passive, when my virtue is at stake! It would be criminal in me, if I was.

He said, he never saw such a fool in his life. And he walked by the side of me some yards without saying a word, and seemed vexed; and at last walked in, bidding me attend him in the garden, after dinner. So having a little time, I went up, and wrote thus far.

——o——

Wednesday night.

If, my dear parents, I am not destined more surely than ever for ruin, I have now more comfort before me than ever I yet knew: and am either nearer my *happiness*, or my misery, than ever I was. God protect me from the latter, if it be His blessed will! I have now such a scene to open to you, that, I know, will alarm both your hopes and your fears, as it does mine. And this it is:—

After my master had dined, he took a turn into the stables to look at his stud of horses; and, when he came in, he opened the parlour-door, where Mrs. Jewkes and I sat at dinner; and, at his entrance, we both rose up; but he said, Sit still, sit still, and let me see how you eat your victuals, Pamela. Oh, said Mrs. Jewkes, very poorly, indeed, sir! No, said I, pretty well, sir, *considering*. None of your *considerings*, said he, pretty face; and tapped me on the cheek. I blushed, but was glad he was so good-humoured; but I could not tell how to sit before him, nor to behave myself. So he said, I know, Pamela, you are a nice carver: my mother used to say so. My lady, sir, said I, was very good to me in everything, and would always make me do the honours of her table for her, when she was with her few select friends that she loved. Cut up, said he, that chicken. I did so. Now, said he, and took a knife and fork, and put a wing upon my plate, let me see you eat that. Oh, sir, said I, I have eaten a whole breast of chicken already, and cannot eat so much. But he said, I must eat it for his sake, and he would teach me to eat heartily. So I did eat it; but was much confused at his so kind and unusual freedom and condescension. And good lack! you can't imagine how Mrs. Jewkes looked and stared, and how respectful she seemed to me, and called me *good madam*, I'll assure you, urging me to take a little bit of tart.

My master took two or three turns about the room, musing and thoughtful, as I had never before seen him; and at last he went out, saying, I am going into the garden: you know, Pamela, what I said to you before dinner. I rose, and courtesied, saying, I would attend his honour; and he said, Do, good girl!

Well, said Mrs Jewkes, I see how things will go. O madam, as she called me again, I am sure you are to be our mistress! And then I know what will become of me. Ah! Mrs. Jewkes, said I, if I can but keep myself virtuous, 'tis the most of my ambition; and, I hope, no temptation shall make me otherwise.

Notwithstanding I had no reason to be pleased with his treatment of me before dinner, yet I made haste to attend him; and I found him walking by the side of that pond, which for want of grace, and through a sinful despondence, had like to have been so fatal to me, and the sight of which, ever since, has been a trouble and reproach to me. And it was by the side of this pond, and not far from the place where I had that dreaded conflict, that my present hopes, if I am not to be deceived again, began to dawn: which I presume to flatter myself with being a happy omen for me, as if God Almighty would show your poor sinful daughter how well I did to put my affiance in his goodness, and not to throw away myself, because my ruin seemed inevitable, to my short-sighted apprehension.

So he was pleased to say, Well, Pamela, I am glad you are come of your own accord, as I may say: give me your hand. I did so; and he looked at me very steadily, and pressing my hand all the time, at last said, I will now talk to you in a serious manner.

You have a good deal of wit, a great deal of penetration

much beyond your *years*, and, as I thought, your *opportunities*. You are possessed of an open, frank, and generous mind; and a person so lovely, that you excel all your sex, in my eyes. All these accomplishments have engaged my affections so deeply, that, as I have often said, I cannot live without you; and I would divide, with all my soul, my estate with you, to make you mine upon my own terms. These you have absolutely rejected; and that, though in saucy terms enough, yet in such a manner as makes me admire you the more. Your pretty chit-chat to Mrs. Jewkes, the last Sunday night, so innocent, and so full of beautiful simplicity, half disarmed my resolution before I approached your bed : and I see you so watchful over your virtue, that though I hoped to find it otherwise, I cannot but confess my passion for you is increased by it. But now what shall I say farther, Pamela?—I will make you, though a party, my adviser in this matter, though not, perhaps, my definitive judge.

You know I am not a very abandoned profligate; I have hitherto been guilty of no very enormous or vile actions. This of seizing you, and confining you thus, may perhaps be one of the worst, at least to persons of real innocence. Had I been utterly given up to my passions, I should before now have gratified them, and not have shown that remorse and compassion for you, which have reprieved you, more than once, when absolutely in my power; and you are as inviolate a virgin as you were when you came into my house.

But what can I do? Consider the pride of my condition. I cannot endure the thought of marriage, even with a person of equal or superior degree to myself; and have declined several proposals of that kind. How then, with the distance between us in the world's judgment, can I think of making you my wife?—Yet I must have you; I cannot bear the thoughts of any other man supplanting me in your affections : and the very apprehension of that has made me hate the name of Williams, and use him in a manner unworthy of my temper.

Now, Pamela, judge for me; and, since I have told you,

thus candidly, my mind, and I see yours is big with some important meaning, by your eyes, your blushes, and that sweet confusion which I behold struggling in your bosom, tell me, with like openness and candour, what you think I ought to do, and what you would have me do.

It is impossible for me to express the agitations of my mind, on this unexpected declaration, so contrary to his former behaviour. His manner too had something so noble, and so sincere, as I thought, that, alas for me! I found I had need of all my poor discretion, to ward off the blow which this treatment gave to my most guarded thoughts. I threw myself at his feet; for I trembled, and could hardly stand: Oh, sir, said I, spare your poor servant's confusion! Oh spare the poor Pamela!—Speak out, said he, and tell me, when I bid you, what you think I ought to do? I cannot say what you *ought* to do, answered I : but I only beg you will not ruin me; and, if you think me virtuous, if you think me sincerely honest, let me go to my poor parents. I will vow to you, that I will never suffer myself to be engaged without your approbation.

Still he insisted upon a more explicit answer to his question, of what I thought he ought to do. And I said, As to *my* poor thoughts of what you ought to do, I must needs say, that indeed I think you ought to regard the world's opinion, and avoid doing anything disgraceful to your birth and fortune ; and, therefore, if you really honour the poor Pamela with your respect, a little time, absence, and the conversation of worthier persons of my sex, will effectually enable you to overcome a regard so unworthy your condition : And this, good sir, is the best advice I can offer.

Charming creature! lovely Pamela! said he (with an ardour that was never before so agreeable to me), this generous manner is of a piece with all the rest of your conduct. But tell me, still more explicitly, what you would advise me to, in the case.

Oh, sir! said I, take not advantage of my credulity, and these my weak moments : but were I the first lady in the

land, instead of the poor abject Pamela, I would, I *could*
tell you. But I can say no more——

Oh my dear father and mother! now I know you will
indeed be concerned for me;—for now I am for myself.—
And now I begin to be afraid I know too well the reason
why all his hard trials of me, and my black apprehensions,
would not let me hate him.

But be assured still, by God's grace, that I shall do
nothing unworthy of your Pamela; and if I find that he
is still capable of deceiving me, and that this conduct is
only put on to delude me more, I shall think nothing in
this world so vile, and so odious; and nothing, if he be
not the worst of his kind (as he says, and, I hope, he is
not), so desperately guileful, as the heart of man.

He generously said, I will spare your confusion, Pamela.
But I hope I may promise myself, that you can love me
preferably to any other man; and that no one in the world
has had any share in your affections; for I am very jealous
of what I love; and if I thought you had a secret whispering in your soul, that had not yet come up to a wish, for
any other man breathing, I should not forgive *myself* to
persist in my affection for you; nor *you*, if you did not
frankly acquaint me with it.

As I still continued on my knees, on the grass border
by the pond-side, he sat himself down on the grass by me,
and took me in his arms: Why hesitates my Pamela?
said he.—Can you not answer me with truth, as I wish?
If you cannot, speak, and I will forgive you.

Oh, good sir, said I, it is not *that;* indeed it is not: but
a frightful word or two that you said to Mrs. Jewkes, when
you thought I was not in hearing, comes cross my mind;
and makes me dread that I am in more danger than ever I
was in my life.

You have never found me a common liar, said he (too
fearful and foolish Pamela!)—nor will I answer how long
I may hold in my present mind; for my pride struggles
hard within me, I'll assure you; and if you doubt me, I
have no obligation to your confidence or opinion. But, at

present, I am really sincere in what I say: And I expect you will be so too; and answer directly my question.

I find, sir, said I, I know not myself; and your question is of such a nature, that I only want to tell you what I heard, and to have your kind answer to it; or else, what I have to say to your question, may pave the way to my ruin, and show a weakness that I did not believe was in me.

Well, said he, you may say what you have overheard; for, in not answering me directly, you put my soul upon the rack; and half the trouble I have had with *you* would have brought to my arms one of the finest ladies in England.

Oh, sir, said I, my virtue is as dear to me, as if I was of the highest quality; and my doubts (for which you know I have had too much reason) have made me troublesome. But now, sir, I will tell you what I heard, which has given me great uneasiness.

You talked to Mrs. Jewkes of having begun wrong with me, in trying to subdue me with terror, and of frost, and such like.—You remember it well:—And that you would, for the future, change your conduct, and try to *melt* me, that was your word, by kindness.

I fear not, sir, the grace of God supporting me, that any acts of kindness would make me forget what I owe to my virtue: but, sir, I may, I find, be made more miserable by such acts, than by terror; because my nature is too frank and open to make me wish to be ungrateful: and if I should be taught a lesson I never yet learnt, with what regret should I descend to the grave, to think that I could not hate my undoer: and that, at the last great day, I must stand up as an accuser of the poor unhappy soul, that I could wish it in my power to save!

Exalted girl! said he, what a thought is that!—Why, now, Pamela, you excel yourself! You have given me a hint that will hold me long. But, sweet creature, said he, tell me what is this lesson, which you never yet learnt, and which you are so afraid of learning?

If, sir, said I, you will again generously spare my confusion, I need not speak it: But this I will say, in answer to the question you seem most solicitous about, that I know not the man breathing that I would wish to be married to, or that ever I thought of with such an idea. I had brought my mind so to love poverty, that I hoped for nothing but to return to the best, though the poorest of parents; and to employ myself in serving God, and comforting them; and you know not, sir, how you disappointed those hopes, and my proposed honest pleasures, when you sent me hither.

Well then, said he, I may promise myself, that neither the parson, nor any other man, is any the least secret motive to your steadfast refusal of my offers? Indeed, sir, said I, you may; and, as you was pleased to ask, I answer, that I have not the least shadow of a wish, or thought, for any man living.

But, said he (for I am foolishly jealous, and yet it shows my fondness for you), have you not encouraged Williams to think you will have him? Indeed, sir, said I, I have not; but the very contrary. And would you not have had him, said he, if you had got away by his means? I had resolved, sir, said I, in my mind, otherwise; and he knew it; and the poor man—I charge you, said he, say not a word in his favour! You will excite a whirlwind in my soul, if you name him with kindness; and then you'll be borne away with the tempest.

Sir, said I, I have done:—Nay, said he, but do not have done; let me know the whole. If you have any regard for him, speak out; for it would end fearfully for _you_, for _me_, and for _him_, if I found that you disguised any secret of your soul from me, in this nice particular.

Sir, said I, if I have ever given you cause to think me sincere——Say then, said he, interrupting me with great vehemence, and taking both my hands between his, Say, that you now, in the presence of God, declare that you have not any the most hidden regard for Williams, or any other man.

Sir, said I, I do. As God shall bless me, and preserve

my innocence, I have not. Well, said he, I will believe you, Pamela; and in time, perhaps, I may better bear that man's name. And, if I am convinced that you are not prepossessed, my vanity makes me assured, that I need not to fear a place in your esteem, equal, if not preferable, to any man in England. But yet it stings my pride to the quick, that you was so easily brought, and at such a short acquaintance, to run away with that college novice!

Oh, good sir, said I, may I be heard one thing? And though I bring upon me your highest indignation, I will tell you, perhaps, the unnecessary and imprudent, but yet the whole truth.

My honesty (I am poor and lowly, and am not entitled to call it *honour*) was in danger. I saw no means of securing myself from your avowed attempts. You had showed you would not stick at little matters; and what, sir, could anybody have thought of my sincerity, in preferring that to all other considerations, if I had not escaped from these dangers, if I could have found any way for it? —I am not going to say anything for him; but, indeed, indeed, sir, I was the cause of putting him upon assisting me in my escape. I got him to acquaint me what gentry there were in the neighbourhood that I might fly to; and prevailed upon him—Don't frown at me, good sir; for I must tell you the whole truth—to apply to one Lady Jones; to Lady Darnford; and he was so good to apply to Mr. Peters, the minister: But they all refused me; and then it was he let me know, that there was no honourable way but marriage. That I declined; and he agreed to assist me for God's sake.

Now, said he, you are going—I boldly put my hand before his mouth, hardly knowing the liberty I took: Pray, sir, said I, don't be angry; I have just done—I would only say, that rather than have stayed to be ruined, I would have thrown myself upon the poorest beggar that ever the world saw, if I thought him honest.—And I hope, when you duly weigh all matters, you will forgive me, and not think me so bold, and so forward, as you have been pleased to call me.

Well, said he, even in this your last speech, which, let me tell you, shows more your honesty of heart than your prudence, you have not overmuch pleased me. But I *must* love you; and that vexes me not a little. But tell me, Pamela, for now the former question recurs: Since you so much prize your honour, and your virtue; since all attempts against that are so odious to you; and since I have avowedly made several of these attempts, do you think it is possible for you to love me *preferably* to any other of my sex?

Ah, sir! said I, and here my doubt recurs, that you may thus graciously use me, to take advantage of my credulity.

Still perverse and doubting! said he—Cannot you take me as I am at present? And that, I have told you, is sincere and undesigning, whatever I may be hereafter.

Ah, sir! replied I, what can I say? I have already said too much, if this dreadful *hereafter* should take place. Don't bid me say how well I can—And then, my face glowing as the fire, I, all abashed, leaned upon his shoulder, to hide my confusion.

He clasped me to him with great ardour, and said, Hide your dear face in my bosom, my beloved Pamela! your innocent freedoms charm me!—But then say, How well— what?

If you will be good, said I, to your poor servant, and spare her, I cannot say too much! But if not, I am doubly undone!—Undone indeed!

Said he, I hope my present temper will hold; for I tell you frankly, that I have known, in this agreeable hour, more sincere pleasure than I have experienced in all the guilty tumults that my desiring soul compelled me into, in the hopes of possessing you on my own terms. And, Pamela, you must pray for the continuance of this temper; and I hope your prayers will get the better of my temptations.

This. sweet goodness overpowered all my reserves. I threw myself at his feet, and embraced his knees: What pleasure, sir, you give me at these gracious words, is not lent your poor servant to express!—I shall be too much rewarded for all my sufferings, if this goodness hold! God grant it may, for your own soul's sake as well as mine. And oh! how happy should I be, if——

He stopt me, and said, But, my dear girl, what must we do about the world, and the world's censure?—Indeed, I cannot marry!

Now was I again struck all of a heap. However, soon recollecting myself, Sir, said I, I have not the presumption to hope such an honour. If I may be permitted to return in peace and safety to my poor parents, to pray for you there, it is all I at present request! This, sir, after all my apprehensions and dangers, will be a great pleasure to me. And, if I know my own poor heart, I shall wish you happy in a lady of suitable degree; and rejoice most sincerely in every circumstance that shall make for the happiness of my late good lady's most beloved son.

Well, said he, this conversation, Pamela, is gone farther than I intended it. You need not be afraid, at this rate, of trusting yourself with *me:* but it is I that ought to be doubtful of myself, when I am with *you.*—But, before I say anything farther on this subject, I will take my proud heart to task; and, till then, let everything be as if this conversation had never passed. Only, let me tell you, that the more confidence you place in me, the more you'll oblige me: but your doubts will only beget *cause* of doubts. And with this ambiguous saying, he saluted me with a more formal manner, if I may so say, than before, and lent me his hand; and so we walked toward the house, side by side, he seeming very thoughtful and pensive, as if he had already repented him of his goodness.

What shall I do, what steps take, if all this be designing! —Oh the perplexities of these cruel doubtings!—To be sure, if he be false, as I may call it, I have gone too far, much too far!—I am ready, on the apprehension of this, to bite my forward tongue (or rather to beat my more forward heart, that dictated to that poor machine) for what I have said. But sure, at least, he must be sincere for the *time!*—He could not be such a practised dissembler!—If he could, oh how desperately wicked is the heart of man!—And where could he learn all these barbarous arts?—If so, it must be native surely to the sex!—But, silent be my rash censurings; be hushed, ye stormy tumults of my disturbed mind! for have I not a father who is a man?—A man who knows no guile! who would do no wrong!—who would not deceive or oppress, to gain a kingdom!—How then can I think it is native to the sex? And I must also hope my good lady's son cannot be the *worst* of men!—If he is, hard the lot of the excellent woman that bore him!—But much harder the hap of your poor Pamela, who has fallen into such hands!—But yet I will trust in God, and hope the best: and so lay down my tired pen for this time.

—o—

Thursday morning.

SOMEBODY rapped at our chamber-door this morning, soon after it was light: Mrs. Jewkes asked, who it was? My master said, Open the door, Mrs. Jewkes! Oh, said I, for God's sake, Mrs. Jewkes, don't! Indeed, said she, but I must. Then, said I, and clung about her, let me slip on my clothes first. But he rapped again, and she broke from me; and I was frightened out of my wits, and folded myself in the bed-clothes. He entered, and said, What, Pamela, so fearful, after what passed yesterday between us! Oh, sir, sir, said I, I fear my prayers have wanted their wished effect! Pray, good sir, consider——He sat down on the bedside, and interrupted me; No need of your foolish fears; I shall say but a word or two, and go away.

After you went upstairs, said he, I had an invitation to a ball, which is to be this night at Stamford, on occasion of a wedding; and I am going to call on Sir Simon, and his lady and daughters; for the bride is a relation of theirs: so I shall not be at home till Saturday. I come, therefore, to caution *you*, Mrs. Jewkes, before Pamela (that she may not wonder at being closer confined, than for these three or four days past), that nobody sees her, nor delivers any letter to her, in that space; for a person has been seen lurking about, and inquiring after her, and I have been well informed, that either Mrs. Jervis, or Mr. Longman,' has written a letter, with a design of having it conveyed to her: And, said he, you must know, Pamela, that I have ordered Mr. Longman to give up his accounts, and have dismissed Jonathan and Mrs. Jervis, since I have been here; for their behaviour has been intolerable; and they have made such a breach between my sister Davers and me, as we shall never, perhaps, make up. Now, Pamela, I shall take it kindly in you, if you will confine yourself to your chamber pretty much, for the time I am absent, and not give Mrs. Jewkes cause of trouble or uneasiness; and the rather, as you know she acts by my orders.

Alas! sir, said I, I fear all these good people have suffered for my sake!—Why, said he, I believe so too; and there was never a girl of your innocence, that set a large family in such an uproar, surely.—But let that pass. You know both of you my mind, and, in part, the reason of it. I shall only say, that I have had such a letter from my sister, as I could not have expected; and, Pamela, said he, neither you nor I have reason to thank her, as you shall know, perhaps, at my return.—I go in my coach, Mrs. Jewkes, because I take Lady Darnford, and Mrs. Peters's niece, and one of Lady Darnford's daughters, along with me; and Sir Simon and his other daughter go in his chariot: so let all the gates be fastened; and don't take any airing in either of the chariots, nor let anybody go to the gate, without you, Mrs. Jewkes. I'll be sure, said she, to obey your honour.

I will give Mrs. Jewkes no trouble, sir, said I; and will keep pretty much in my chamber, and not stir so much as into the garden without her; to show you I will obey in everything I *can*. But I begin to fear—Ay, said he, more

plots and contrivances, don't you?—But I'll assure you, you
never had less reason; and I tell you the truth; for I am
really going to *Stamford this time;* and upon the occasion I
tell you. And so, Pamela, give me your hand, and one
kiss; and then I am gone.

I durst not refuse, and said, God bless you, sir, wherever
you go!—But I am sorry for what you tell me about your
servants!

He and Mrs. Jewkes had a little talk without the door;
and I heard her say, You may depend, sir, upon my care
and vigilance.

He went in his coach, as he said he should, and very
richly dressed, which looks as if what he said was likely:
but really I have been used to so many tricks, and plots,
and surprises, that I know not what to think. But I mourn
for poor Mrs. Jervis.—So here is Parson Williams; here's
poor naughty John; here is good Mrs. Jervis, and Mr.
Longman, and Mr. Jonathan, turned away for me!—Mr.
Longman is rich, indeed, and so need the less matter it;
but I know it will grieve him: and for poor Mr. Jonathan,
I am sure it will cut that good old servant to the heart.
Alas for me! what mischiefs am I the occasion of!—Or,
rather, my master, whose actions towards me have made so
many of my kind friends forfeit his favour, for my sake!

I am very sad about these things: If he really loved me,
methinks he should not be so angry, that his servants loved
me too.—I know not what to think!

— o —

Friday night.

I HAVE removed my papers from under the rose-bush; for I
saw the gardener begin to dig near that spot; and I was
afraid he would find them.

Mrs. Jewkes and I were looking yesterday through the
iron gate that fronts the elms; and a gipsy-like body made
up to us, and said; If, madam, you will give me some
broken victuals, I will tell you both your fortunes. I said,

Let us hear our fortunes, Mrs. Jewkes. She said, I don't
like these sort of people; but we will hear what she'll say
to us, however. I shan't fetch you any victuals, woman;
but I will give you some pence, said she.

But Nan coming out, she said, Fetch some bread, and
some of the cold meat, and you shall have your fortune told,
Nan.

This, you'll think, like some of my other matters, a very
trifling thing to write about. But mark the discovery of a
dreadful plot, which I have made by it. Oh, bless me!
What can I think of this naughty, this very naughty gentleman!—Now will I hate him most heartily. Thus it was:—

Mrs. Jewkes had no suspicion of the woman, the iron
gate being locked, and she on the outside, and we on the
inside; and so put her hand through. She said, muttering
over a parcel of cramp words, Why, madam, you will marry
soon, I can tell you. At that she seemed pleased, and said,
I am glad to hear that; and shook her fat sides with laughing. The woman looked most earnestly at *me*, all the time,
and as if she had meaning. Then it came into my head,
from my master's caution, that possibly this woman might
be employed to try to get a letter into my hands; and I was
resolved to watch all her motions. So Mrs. Jewkes said,
What sort of a man shall I have, pray?—Why, said she, a
man younger than yourself; and a very good husband he'll
prove.—I am glad of that, said she: and laughed again.
Come, madam, let us hear *your* fortune.

The woman came to me, and took my hand. Oh! said she,
I cannot tell your fortune: your hand is so white and fine,
I cannot see the lines: but, said she, and, stooping, pulled
up a little tuft of grass, I have a way for that; and so rubbed
my hand with the mould part of the tuft: Now, said she, I
can see the lines.

Mrs. Jewkes was very watchful of all her ways, and took
the tuft, and looked upon it, lest anything should be in that.
And then the woman said, Here is the line of Jupiter crossing the line of life; and Mars—Odd! my pretty mistress,

said she, you had best take care of yourself; for you are
hard beset, I'll assure you. You will never be married, I
can see; and will die of your first child. Out upon thee,
woman! said I, better thou hadst never come here.

Said Mrs. Jewkes, whispering, I don't like this: it looks
like a cheat: Pray, Mrs. Pamela, go in, this moment. So I
will, said I; for I have enough of fortune-telling. And in I
went.

The woman wanted sadly to tell me more, which made
Mrs. Jewkes threaten her, suspecting still the more; and
away the woman went, having told Nan her fortune, and
she would be drowned.

This thing ran strongly in all our heads; and we went, an
hour after, to see if the woman was lurking about, and took
Mr. Colbrand for our guard. Looking through the iron
gate, he spied a man sauntering about the middle of the walk;
which filled Mrs. Jewkes with still more suspicions; and she
said, Mr. Colbrand, you and I will walk towards this fellow,
and see what he saunters there for: And, Nan, do you and
madam stay at the gate.

So they opened the iron gate and walked down towards
the man; and guessing the woman, if employed, must mean
something by the tuft of grass, I cast my eye that way,
whence she pulled it, and saw more grass seemingly pulled up:
then I doubted not something was there for me; and I
walked to it, and standing over it, said to Nan, That's a
pretty sort of wild flower, that grows yonder, near the elm,
the fifth from us on the left; pray pull it for me. Said she,
It is a common weed. Well, said I, but pull it for me; there
are sometimes beautiful colours in a weed.

While she went on, I stooped, and pulled up a good hand-
ful of the grass, and in it a bit of paper, which I put instantly
in my bosom, and dropt the grass: and my heart went pit-a-
pat at the odd adventure. Said I, Let's go in, Mrs. Anne.
No, said she, we must stay till Mrs. Jewkes comes.

I was all impatience to read this paper: and when Colbrand and she returned, I went in. Said she, Certainly
there is some reason for my master's caution: I can make

nothing of this sauntering fellow; but, to be sure, there was some roguery in the gipsy. Well, said I, if there was, she lost her aim, you see! Ay, very true, said she; but that was owing to my watchfulness; and you was very good to go away, when I spoke to you.

I hastened upstairs to my closet, and found the billet to contain, in a hand that seemed disguised, and bad spelling, the following words:—

' Twenty contrivances have been thought of to let you
' know your danger; but all have proved in vain. Your
' friends hope it is not yet too late to give you this caution,
' if it reaches your hands. The 'squire is absolutely deter-
' mined to ruin you; and, because he despairs of any other
' way, he will pretend great love and kindness to you, and
' that he will marry you. You may expect a parson, for
' this purpose, in a few days; but it is a sly artful fellow of
' a broken attorney, that he has hired to personate a minister.
' The man has a broad face, pitted much with the small-pox,
' and is a very great companion. So take care of yourself.
' Doubt not this advice. Perhaps you'll have had but too
' much reason already to confirm you in the truth of it.
' From your zealous well-wisher,

'Somebody.'

Now, my dear father and mother, what shall we say of this truly diabolical master! Oh, how shall I find words to paint my griefs, and his deceit! I have as good as confessed I love him; but, indeed, it was on supposing him good.—⌄ This, however, has given him too much advantage. But now I will break this wicked forward heart of mine, if it will not be taught to hate him! Oh, what a black dismal heart must *he* have! So here is a plot to ruin me, and by my own consent too!—No wonder he did not improve his wicked opportunities (which I thought owing to remorse for his sin, and compassion for me), when he had such a project as *this* in reserve!—Here should I have been deluded with the hopes of a happiness that my highest ambition could have had aspired to!—But how dreadful must have been my lot, when

I had found myself an undone creature, and a guilty harlot, instead of a lawful wife! Oh! this is indeed too much, too much, for your poor Pamela to support! This is the worse, as I hoped all the worst was over; and that I had the pleasure of beholding a reclaimed man, and not an abandoned libertine. What *now* must your poor daughter do? Now all her hopes are dashed! And if this fails him, then comes, to be sure, my forced disgrace! for this shows he will never leave till he has ruined me!—Oh, the wretched, wretched Pamela!

—o—

Saturday noon, one o'clock.

My master is come home; and, to be sure, has been where he said. So *once* he has told truth; and this matter seems to be gone off without a plot: No doubt he depends upon his sham wicked marriage! He has brought a gentleman with him to dinner; and so I have not seen him yet.

—o—

Two o'clock.

I am very sorrowful, and still have greater reason; for, just now, as I was in my closet, opening the parcel I had hid under the rose-bush, to see if it was damaged by lying so long, Mrs. Jewkes came upon me by surprise, and laid her hands upon it; for she had been looking through the key-hole, it seems.

I know not what I shall do! For now he will see all my private thoughts of him and all my secrets, as I may say. What a careless creature I am!—To be sure I deserve to be punished.

You know I had the good luck, by Mr. Williams's means, to send you all my papers down to Sunday night, the 17th day of my imprisonment. But now these papers contain all my matters from that time, to Wednesday the 27th day of my distress: And which, as you may now, perhaps, never see, I will briefly mention the contents to you.

In these papers, then, are included, ' An account of Mrs.
' Jewkes's arts to draw me in to approve of Mr. Williams's
' proposal for marriage; and my refusing to do so; and
' desiring you not to encourage his suit to me. Mr
' Williams's being wickedly robbed, and a visit of hers to
' him; whereby she discovered all his secrets. How I was
' inclined to get off, while she was gone; but was ridicu-
' lously prevented by my foolish fears, &c. My having the
' key of the back-door. Mrs. Jewkes's writing to my master
' all the secrets she had discovered of Mr. Williams, and her
' behaviour to me and him upon it. Continuance of my
' correspondence with Mr. Williams by the tiles; begun in
' the parcel you had. My reproaches to him for his reveal--
' ing himself to Mrs. Jewkes; and his letter to me in answer,
' threatening to expose my master, if he deceived him;
' mentioning in it John Arnold's correspondence with him ;
' and a letter which John sent, and was intercepted, as it
' seems. Of the correspondence being carried on by a friend
' of his at Gainsborough. Of the horse he was to provide for
' me, and one for himself. Of what Mr. Williams had
' owned to Mrs. Jewkes; and of my discouraging his pro-
' posals. Then it contained a pressing letter of mine to him,
' urging my escape before my master came; with his half-
' angry answer to me. Your good letter to me, my dear
' father, sent to me by Mr. Williams's conveyance; in which
' you would have me encourage Mr. Williams, but leave it
' to me; and in which, fortunately enough, you take notice
' of my being uninclined to marry.—My earnest desire to be
' with you. The substance of my answer to Mr. Williams,
' expressing more patience, &c. A dreadful letter of my
' master to Mrs. Jewkes; which, by mistake, was directed to
' me; and one to me, directed by like mistake to her; and
' very free reflections of mine upon both. The concern I
' expressed for Mr. Williams's being taken in, deceived, and
' ruined. An account of Mrs. Jewkes's glorying in her
' wicked fidelity. A sad description I gave of Monsieur
' Colbrand, a person he sent down to assist Mrs. Jewkes in
' watching me. How Mr. Williams was arrested, and

' thrown into gaol; and the concern I expressed upon it; and
'.my free reflections on my master for it. A projected con-
' trivance of mine, to get away out of the window, and by
' the back-door; and throwing my petticoat and handkerchief
' into the pond to amuse them, while I got off: An attempt
' that had like to have ended very dreadfully for me! My
' further concern for Mr. Williams's ruin, on my account:
' And, lastly, my over-hearing Mrs. Jewkes brag of her
' contrivance to rob Mr. Williams, in order to get at my
' papers; which, however, he preserved, and sent safe to
' you.'

These, down to the execution of my unfortunate plot to
escape, are, to the best of my remembrance, the contents of
the papers which this merciless woman seized: For, how
badly I came off, and what followed, I still have safe, as I
hope, sewed in my under-coat, about my hips.

In vain were all my prayers and tears to her, to get her
not to show them to my master. For she said, It had now
come out, why I affected to be so much alone; and why I
was always writing. And she thought herself happy, she
said, she had found these; for often and often had she
searched every place she could think of, for writings, to no
purpose before. And she hoped, she said, there was nothing
in them but what *anybody* might see; for, said she, you
know you are *all innocence!*—Insolent creature! said I, I
am sure you are *all guilt!*—And so you must do your
worst; for now I can't help myself, and I see there is no
mercy to be expected from you.

Just now, my master being come up, she went to him
upon the stairs, and gave him my papers. There, sir, said
she; you always said Mrs. Pamela was a great writer; but
I never could get at anything of hers before. He took
them; and, without coming to me, went down to the
parlour again. And what with the gipsy affair, and what
with this, I could not think of going down to dinner; and
she told him that too; and so I suppose I shall have him
upstairs, as soon as his company is gone.

Saturday, six o'clock.

My master came up, and, in a pleasanter manner than I expected, said, So, Pamela, we have seized, it seems, your treasonable papers? Treasonable! said I, very sullenly. Ay, said he, I suppose so; for you are a great plotter: but I have not read them yet.

Then, sir, said I, very gravely, it will be truly honourable in you *not* to read them; but to give them to me again. To whom, says he, are they written?—To my father, sir; but I suppose you *see* to whom.—Indeed, returned he, I have not read three lines yet. Then, pray, sir, *don't* read them; but give them to me again. That I will not, said he, till I *have* read them. Sir, said I, you served me not well in the letters I used to write formerly: I think it was not worthy your character to contrive to get them in your hands, by that false John Arnold! for should such a gentleman as you mind what your poor servant writes?—Yes, said he, by all means, mind what such a servant as *my* Pamela writes.

Your Pamela! thought I. Then the sham marriage came into my head; and indeed it has not been out of it, since the gipsy affair.—But, said he, have you anything in these papers you would not have me see? To be sure, sir, said I, there is; for what one writes to one's father and mother, is not for everybody to see. Nor, said he, am I everybody.

Those letters, added he, that I did see by John's means, were not to your disadvantage, I'll assure you; for they gave me a very high opinion of your wit and innocence: And if I had not loved you, do you think I would have troubled myself about your letters?

Alas! sir, said I, great pride to me *that!* For they gave you such an opinion of my innocence, that you was resolved to ruin me. And what advantage have they brought *me?* —Who have been made a prisoner, and used as I have been between you and your housekeeper.

Why, Pamela, said he, a little seriously, why this behaviour, for my goodness to you in the garden?—This is not of a piece with your conduct and softness there, that quite charmed me in your favour: And you must not give me cause to think that you will be the more insolent, as you find me kinder. Ah! sir, said I, you know best your own heart and designs! But I fear I was too open-hearted then; and that you still keep your resolution to undo me, and have only changed the form of your proceedings.

When I tell you once again, said he, a little sternly, that you cannot oblige me more, than by placing some confidence in me, I will let you know, that these foolish and perverse doubts are the worst things you can be guilty of. But, said he, I shall possibly account for the cause of them, in these papers of yours; for I doubt not you have been sincere to your *father* and *mother,* though you begin to make *me* suspect you: For I tell you, perverse girl, that it is impossible you should be thus cold and insensible, after what has passed in the garden, if you were not prepossessed in some *other* person's favour: And let me add, that if I find it so, it shall be attended with such effects, as will make every vein in your heart bleed.

He was going away in wrath; and I said, One word, good sir, one word before you read them, since you *will* read them: Pray make allowances for all the harsh reflections that you will find in them, on your own conduct to me: And remember only, that they were not written for your sight; and were penned by a poor creature hardly used, and who was in constant apprehension of receiving from you the worst treatment that you could inflict upon her.

If that be all, said he, and there be nothing of *another* nature, that I cannot forgive, you have no cause for uneasiness; for I had as many instances of your saucy reflections upon me in your former letters, as there were lines; and yet, you see, I have never upbraided you on that score; though, perhaps, I wished you had been more sparing of your epithets, and your freedoms of that sort.

Well, sir, said I, since you *will,* you *must* read them; and I think I have no reason to be afraid of being found insincere, or having, in any respect, told you a falsehood;

because, though I don't remember all I wrote, yet I know
I wrote my heart; and that is not deceitful. And remember, sir, another thing, that I always declared I thought
myself right to endeavour to make my escape from this
forced and illegal restraint; and so you must not be angry
that I would have done so, if I could.

I'll judge you, never fear, said he, as favourably as you
deserve; for you have too powerful a pleader within me.
And so went downstairs.

About nine o'clock he sent for me down into the parlour.
I went a little fearfully; and he held the papers in his hand,
and said, Now, Pamela, you come upon your trial. Said
I, I hope I have a *just* judge to hear my cause. Ay, said
he, and you may hope for a *merciful* one too, or else I know
not what will become of you.

I expect, continued he, that you will answer me directly,
and plainly, to every question I shall ask you.—In the first
place, here are several love-letters between you and Williams.
Love-letters! sir, said I.—Well, call them what you will,
said he, I don't entirely like them, I'll assure you, with all
the allowances you desired me to make for you. Do you
find, sir, said I, that I encouraged his proposal, or do you
not? Why, said he, you discourage his address in appearance; but no otherwise than all your cunning sex do to
ours, to make us more eager in pursuing you.

Well, sir, said I, that is your comment; but it does not
appear so in the text. Smartly said! says he: Where a
d—l gottest thou, at these years, all this knowledge? And
then thou hast a memory, as I see by your papers, that nothing escapes. Alas! sir, said I, what poor abilities I have,
serve only to make me more miserable!—I have no pleasure
in my memory, which impresses things upon me, that I could
be glad never *were*, or everlastingly to *forget*.

Well, said he, so much for that.—But where are the
accounts (since you have kept so exact a journal of all that
has befallen you) *previous* to these here in my hand? My
father has them, sir, said I.—By whose means? said he.—

By Mr. Williams's, said I. Well answered, said he. But cannot you contrive to get me a sight of them? That would be pretty! said I. I wish I could have contrived to have kept those you have from your sight. Said he, I *must* see them, Pamela, or I shall never be easy; for I must know how this correspondence between you and Williams began: and if I *can* see them, it shall be better for you, if they answer what these give me hope they will.

I can tell you, sir, very faithfully, said I, what the beginning was; for I was bold enough to be the *beginner.* That won't do, said he; for though this may appear a punctilio to *you,* to *me* it is of high importance. Sir, said I, if you please to let me go to my father, I will send them to you by any messenger you shall send for them. Will you so? But I daresay, if you will write for them, they will send them to you, without the trouble of such a journey to yourself: and I beg you will.

I think, sir, said I, as you have seen all my *former* letters through John's baseness, and now *these,* through your faithful housekeeper's officious watchfulness, you *might* see all *the rest:* But I hope you will not desire it, till I can see how much my pleasing you in this particular will be of use to myself.

You must trust to my honour for that. But tell me, Pamela, said the sly gentleman, since I have seen these, would you have voluntarily shown me *those,* had they been in your possession?

I was not aware of this inference, and said, Yes, truly, sir, I think I should, if you commanded it. Well then, Pamela, said he, as I am sure you have found means to continue your journal, I desire, till the *former part* can come, that you will show me the *succeeding.*—Oh sir, sir, said I, have you caught me so?—But indeed you must excuse me there.

Why, said he, tell me truly, have you not continued your account till now? Don't ask me, sir, said I. But I insist upon your answer, replied he. Why then, sir, I will not tell an untruth; I have.—That's my good girl! said he, I love sincerity at my heart.—In *another,* sir, said I, I presume you

mean !—Well, said he, I'll allow you to be a little witty upon
me ; because it is *in you,* and you cannot help it : but you
will greatly oblige me, to show me voluntarily what you have
written.   I long to see the particulars of your plot, and your
disappointment, where your papers leave off : for you have
so beautiful a manner, that it is partly that, and partly my
love for you, that has made me desirous of reading all you
write ; though a great deal of it is against myself ; for
which you must expect to suffer a little : and as I have
furnished you with the subject, I have a title to see the fruits
of your pen.—Besides, said he, there is such a pretty air of
romance, as you relate them, in *your* plots, and *my* plots,
that I shall be better directed in what manner to wind up
the catastrophe of the pretty novel.

If I was your equal, sir, said I, I should say this is a very
provoking way of jeering at the misfortunes you have brought
upon me.

Oh, said he, the liberties you have taken with my character in your letters, sets us upon a par, at least in that respect.   Sir, I could not have taken those liberties, if you had
not given me the cause : and the *cause,* sir, you know, is before the *effect.*

True, Pamela, said he ; you chop logic very prettily.
What the deuce do we men go to school for ? If our wits
were equal to women's, we might spare much time and pains
in our education : for nature teaches your sex, what, in a
long course of labour and study, ours can hardly attain to.—
But, indeed, every lady is not a Pamela.

You delight to banter your poor servant, said I.

Nay, continued he, I believe I must assume to myself half
the merit of your wit, too ; for the innocent exercises you
have had for it, from me, have certainly sharpened your invention.

Sir, said I, could I have been without those *innocent*
exercises, as you are pleased to call them, I should have been
glad to have been as dull as a beetle. But then, Pamela,
said he, I should not have loved you so well. But then,
sir, I should have been safe, easy, and happy.—Ay, maybe

so, and maybe not; and the wife, too, of some clouterly ploughboy.

But then, sir, I should have been content and innocent; and that's better than being a princess, and not so. And maybe not, said he; for if you had had that pretty face, some of us keen fox-hunters should have found you out; and, in spite of your romantic notions (which then, too, perhaps, would not have had so strong a place in your mind), might have been more happy with the ploughman's wife, than I have been with my mother's Pamela. I hope, sir, said I, God would have given me more grace.

Well, but, resumed he, as to these writings of yours, that follow your fine plot, I *must* see them. Indeed, sir, you *must not*, if I can help it. Nothing, said he, pleases me better, than that, in all your arts, shifts, and stratagems, you have had a great regard to truth; and have, in all your little pieces of deceit, told very few *wilful* fibs. Now I expect you'll continue this laudable rule in your conversation with me.—Let me know then, where you have found supplies of pen, ink, and paper, when Mrs. Jewkes was so vigilant, and gave you but two sheets at a time?—Tell me truth.

Why, sir, little did I think I should have such occasion for them; but, when I went away from your house, I begged some of each of good Mr. Longman, who gave me plenty. Yes, yes, said he, it must be *good* Mr. Longman! All your confederates are good, every one of them: but such of my servants as have done their duty, and obeyed my orders, are painted out by you as black as devils! nay, so am I too, for that matter.

Sir, said I, I hope you won't be angry, but, saving yourself, do you think they are painted worse than they deserve? or worse than the parts they acted require?

You say, saving myself, Pamela; but is not that saving a mere compliment to me, because I am present, and you are in my hands? Tell me truly.—Good sir, excuse me; but I fancy I might ask you, why you should think so, if there was not a little bit of conscience that told you, there was but too much reason for it?

He kissed me, and said, I must either do thus, or be angry with you; for you are very saucy, Pamela.—But, with your bewitching chit-chat, and pretty impertinence, I will not lose my question. Where did you hide your paper, pens, and ink?

Some, sir, in one place, some in another; that I might have some left, if others should be found.—That's a good girl! said he; I love you for your sweet veracity. Now tell me where it is you hide your written papers, your saucy journal?—I must beg your excuse for that, sir, said I. But indeed, answered he, you will not have it: for I *will* know, and I will *see* them.—This is very hard, sir, said I; but I must say, you shall not, if I can help it.

We were standing most of this time; but he then sat down, and took me by both my hands, and said, Well said, my pretty Pamela, *if you can help it!* But I will not let you help it. Tell me, are they in your pocket? No, sir, said I; my heart up at my mouth. Said he, I know you won't tell a downright *fib* for the world: but for *equivoca-tion!* no Jesuit ever went beyond you. Answer me then, are they in neither of your pockets? No, sir, said I. Are they not, said he, about your stays? No, sir, replied I: But pray no more questions: for ask me ever so much, I will not tell you.

Oh, said he, I have a way for that. I can do as they do abroad, when the criminals won't confess; torture them till they do.—But pray, sir, said I, is this fair, just, or honest? I am no criminal; and I won't confess.

Oh, my girl! said he, many an innocent person has been put to the torture. But let me know where they are, and you shall escape the *question,* as they call it abroad.

Sir, said I, the torture is not used in England, and I hope you won't bring it up. Admirably said! said the naughty gentleman.—But I can tell you of as good a punishment. If a criminal won't plead with us, here in England, we press him to death, or till he does plead. And so now, Pamela, that is a punishment shall certainly be yours, if you won't tell without.

Tears stood in my eyes, and I said, This, sir, is very cruel and barbarous.—No matter, said he; it is but like your Lucifer, you know, in my shape! And, after I have done so many heinous things by you as *you* think, you have no great reason to judge so hardly of this; or, at least, it is but of a piece with the rest.

But, sir, said I (dreadfully afraid he had some notion they were about me), if you will be obeyed in this unreasonable manner, though it is sad tyranny, to be sure!—let me go up to them, and read them over again, and you shall see so far as to the end of the sad story that follows those you have.

I'll see them all, said he, down to this time, if you have written so far:—Or, at least, till within this week.—Then let me go up to them, said I, and see what I have written, and to what day, to show them to you; for you won't desire to see everything. But I will, replied he.—But say, Pamela, tell me truth: Are they *above?* I was much affrighted. He saw my confusion. Tell me truth, said he. Why, sir, answered I, I have sometimes hid them under the dry mould in the garden; sometimes in one place, sometimes in another; and those you have in your hand were several days under a rose-bush, in the garden. Artful slut! said he, what's this to my question?—Are they not *about* you?—If, said I, I must pluck them out of my hiding-place behind the wainscot, won't you see me?—Still more and more artful! said he—Is this an answer to my question? —I have searched every place above, and in your closet, for them, and cannot find them; so I *will* know where they are. Now, said he, it is my opinion they are about you; and I never undressed a girl in my life; but I will now begin to strip my pretty Pamela; and I hope I shall not go far before I find them.

I fell a crying, and said, I will not be used in this manner. Pray, sir, said I (for he began to unpin my handkerchief), consider! Pray, sir, do!—And pray, said he, do *you* consider. For I *will* see these papers. But maybe, said he, they are tied about your knees, with your garters, and stooped. Was ever anything so vile and so wicked?—I fell on my

knees, and said, What *can* I do? What *can* I do? If you'll
let me go up I'll fetch them to you. Will you, said he, on
your honour, let me see them uncurtailed, and not offer to
make them away; no not a single paper?—I will, sir.—On
your honour? Yes, sir. And so he let me go upstairs, crying
sadly for vexation to be so used. Sure nobody was ever so
served as I am!

I went to my closet, and there I sat me down, and could
not bear the thoughts of giving up my papers. Besides, I
must all undress me, in a manner, to untack them. So I
writ thus:

'SIR,—To expostulate with such an arbitrary gentleman,
'I know will signify nothing; and most hardly do you use
'the power you so wickedly have got over me. I have
'heart enough, sir, to do a deed that would make you regret
'using me thus; and I can hardly bear it, and what I am
'further to undergo. But a superior consideration withholds
'me; thank God, it does!—I will, however, keep my word,
'if you insist upon it when you have read this; but, sir, let
'me beg of you to give me time till to-morrow morning,
'that I may just run them over, and see what I put into
'your hands against me: and I will then give my papers to
'you, without the least alteration, or adding or diminishing:
'But I should beg still to be excused, if you please: But if
'not, spare them to me but till to-morrow morning: and
'this, so hardly am I used, shall be thought a favour, which
'I shall be very thankful for.'

I guessed it would not be long before I heard from him:
and he accordingly sent up Mrs. Jewkes for what I had
promised. So I gave her this note to carry to him. And he
sent word, that I must keep my promise, and he would give
me till morning; but that I must bring them to him without
his asking again.

So I took off my under-coat, and, with great trouble of
mind, unsewed them from it. And there is a vast quantity

of it. I will just slightly touch upon the subjects; because
I may not, perhaps, get them again for you to see.

They begin with an account of ' my attempting to get
' away out of the window first, and then throwing my pet-
' ticoat and handkerchief into the pond. How sadly I was
' disappointed, the lock of the back-door being changed.
' How, in trying to climb over the door, I tumbled down,
' and was piteously bruised; the bricks giving way, and
' tumbling upon me. How, finding I could not get off, and
' dreading the hard usage I should receive, I was so wicked
' as to think of throwing myself into the water. My sad
' reflections upon this matter. How Mrs. Jewkes used me
' upon this occasion, when she found me. How my master
' had like to have been drowned in hunting; and my con-
' cern for his danger, notwithstanding his usage of me. Mrs.
' Jewkes's wicked reports, to frighten me, that I was to be
' married to the ugly Swiss; who was to sell me on the
' wedding-day to my master. Her vile way of talking to
' me, like a London prostitute. My apprehensions of seeing
' preparations made for my master's coming. Her causeless
' fears that I was trying to get away again, when I had no
' thoughts of it; and my bad usage upon it. My master's
' dreadful arrival; and his hard, very hard treatment of me;
' and Mrs. Jewkes's insulting of me. His jealousy of Mr.
' Williams and me. How Mrs. Jewkes vilely instigated
' him to wickedness.' And down to here, I put into one
parcel, hoping that would content him. But for fear it
should not, I put into another parcel the following, viz.:

' A copy of his proposals to me, of a great parcel of gold,
' and fine clothes and rings, and an estate of I can't tell what
' a year ; and 50l. a year for the life of both you, my dear
' parents, to be his mistress; with an insinuation, that, may-
' be, he would marry me at the year's end: All sadly vile:
' With threatenings, if I did not comply, that he would ruin
' me, without allowing me anything. A copy of my answer,
' refusing all, with just abhorrence : But begging at last his

' goodness towards me, and mercy on me, in the most mov-
' ing manner I could think of. An account of his angry
' behaviour, and Mrs. Jewkes's wicked advice hereupon. His
' trying to get me to his chamber; and my refusal to go. A
' deal of stuff and chit-chat between me and the odious Mrs.
' Jewkes; in which she was very wicked and very insulting.
' Two notes I wrote, as if to be carried to church, to pray for
' his reclaiming, and my safety; which Mrs. Jewkes seized,
' and officiously showed him. A confession of mine, that,
' notwithstanding his bad usage, I could not hate him. My
' concern for Mr. Williams. A horrid contrivance of my
' master's to ruin me; being in my room, disguised in clothes
' of the maid's, who lay with me and Mrs. Jewkes. How
' narrowly I escaped (it makes my heart ache to think of it
' still!) by falling into fits. Mrs. Jewkes's detestable part in
' this sad affair. How he seemed moved at my danger, and
' forbore his abominable designs; and assured me he had
' offered no indecency. How ill I was for a day or two after;
' and how kind he seemed. How he made me forgive Mrs.
' Jewkes. How, after this, and great kindness pretended, he
' made rude offers to me in the garden, which I escaped.
' How I resented them.' Then I had written, ' How kindly
' he behaved himself to me; and how he praised me, and
' gave me great hopes of his being good at last. Of the too
' tender impression this made upon me; and how I began to
' be afraid of my own weakness and consideration for him,
' though he had used me so ill. How sadly jealous he was
' of Mr. Williams; and how I, as justly could, cleared myself
' as to his doubts on that score. How, just when he had
' raised me up to the highest hope of his goodness, he dashed
' me sadly again, and went off more coldly. My free reflec-
' tions upon this trying occasion.'

This brought down matters from Thursday, the 20th day
of my imprisonment, to Wednesday the 41st, and here I
was resolved to end, let what would come; for only Thursday,
Friday, and Saturday, remain to give an account of; and
Thursday he set out to a ball at Stamford; and Friday was
the gipsy story; and this is Saturday, his return from

Stamford. And truly, I shall have but little heart to write, if he is to see all.

So these two parcels of papers I have got ready for him against to-morrow morning. To be sure I have always used him very freely in my writings, and showed him no mercy; but yet he must thank himself for it; for I have only writ truth; and I wish he had deserved a better character at my hands, as well for his own sake as mine.—So, though I don't know whether ever you'll see what I write, I must say, that I will go to bed, with remembering you in my prayers, as I always do, and as I know you do me: And so, my dear parents, good night.

—o—

Sunday morning.

I REMEMBERED what he said, of not being obliged to ask again for my papers; and what I should be forced to do, and could not help, I thought I might as well do in such a manner as might show I would not disoblige on purpose: though I stomached this matter very heavily too. I had therefore got in readiness my two parcels; and he, not going to church in the morning, bid Mrs. Jewkes tell me he was gone into the garden.

I knew that was for me to go to him; and so I went: for how can I help being at his beck? which grieves me not a little, though he is my master, as I may say; for I am so wholly in his power, that it would do me no good to incense him; and if I refused to obey him in little matters, my refusal in greater would have the less weight. So I went down to the garden; but as he walked in one walk, I took another, that I might not seem too forward neither.

He soon 'spied me, and said, Do you expect to be courted to come to me? Sir, said I, and crossed the walk to attend him, I did not know but I should interrupt you in your meditations this good day.

Was that the case, said he, truly, and from your heart? Why, sir, said I, I don't doubt but you have very good thoughts sometimes; though not towards me. I wish, said he, I could avoid thinking so well of you as I do. But where are the papers?—I daresay you had them about you yesterday; for you say in those I have, that you will bury your writings in the garden, for fear you should be *searched*, if you did not escape. This, added he, gave me a glorious pretence to search you; and I have been vexing myself all night, that I did not strip you garment by garment, till I had found them. Oh fie, sir, said I; let me not be scared, with hearing that you had such a thought in earnest.

Well, said he, I hope you have not now the papers to give me; for I had rather find them myself, I'll assure you.

I did not like this way of talk; and thinking it best not to dwell upon it, said, Well, but, sir, you will excuse me, I hope, giving up my papers.

Don't trifle with me, said he; where are they?—I think I was very good to you last night, to humour you as I did. If you have either added or diminished, and have not strictly kept your promise, woe be to you! Indeed, sir, said I, I have neither added nor diminished. But there is the parcel that goes on with my sad attempt to escape, and the terrible consequences it had like to have been followed with. And it goes down to the naughty articles you sent me. And as you know all that has happened since, I hope these will satisfy you.

He was going to speak; but I said, to drive him from thinking of any more, And I must beg you, sir, to read the matter favourably, if I have exceeded in any liberties of my pen.

I think, said he, half smiling, you may wonder at my patience, that I can be so easy to read myself abused as I am by such a saucy slut.—Sir, said I, I have wondered you should be so desirous to see my bold stuff; and, for that very reason, I have thought it a very *good*, or a very *bad* sign. What, said he, is your *good* sign?—That it may have an effect upon your temper, at last, in my favour, when you see me so sincere. Your *bad* sign? Why, that if you can read my reflections and observations upon your treatment

of me, with tranquillity, and not be moved, it is a sign of a
very cruel and determined heart. Now, pray, sir, don't be
angry at my boldness in telling you so freely my thoughts.
You may, perhaps, said he, be least mistaken, when you
think of your bad sign. God forbid! said I.

So I took out my papers; and said, Here, sir, they are.
But if you please to return them, without breaking the seal,
it will be very generous : and I will take it for a great favour,
and a good omen.

He broke the seal instantly, and opened them : So much
for your *omen!* replied he. I am sorry for it, said I, very
seriously; and was walking away. Whither now? said he.
I was going in, sir, that you might have time to read them,
if you thought fit. He put them into his pocket, and said,
You have *more* than these. Yes, sir : but all they contain,
you know as well as *I.*—But I don't know, said he, the light
you put things in; and so give them me, if you have not a
mind to be searched.

Sir, said I, I can't stay, if you won't forbear that ugly
word.—Give me then no reason for it. Where are the
other papers? Why, then, unkind sir, if it must be so, here
they are. And so I gave him, out of my pocket, the second
parcel, sealed up, as the former, with this superscription;
From the naughty articles, down, through sad attempts, to
Thursday *the* 42d *day of my imprisonment.* This is last
Thursday, is it? Yes, sir; but now you *will* see what I
write, I will find some other way to employ my time : for
how can I write with any face, what must be for your perusal, and not for those I intended to read my melancholy
stories?

Yes, said he, I would have you continue your penmanship
by all means; and, I assure you, in the mind I am in, I
will not ask you for any after these; except anything very
extraordinary occurs. And I have another thing to tell you,
added he, that if you send for those from your father, and
let me read them, I may, very probably, give them all back
again to you. And so I desire you will do it.

This a little encourages me to continue my scribbling;

but, for fear of the worst, I will, when they come to any bulk, contrive some way to hide them, if I can, that I may protest I have them not about me, which, before, I could not say of a truth; and that made him so resolutely bent to try to find them upon me; for which I might have suffered frightful indecencies.

He led me, then, to the side of the pond; and sitting down on the slope, made me sit by him. Come, said he, this being the scene of part of your project, and where you so artfully threw in some of your clothes, I will just look upon that part of your relation. Sir, said I, let me then walk about, at a little distance; for I cannot bear the thought of it. Don't go far, said he.

When he came, as I suppose, to the place where I mentioned the bricks falling upon me, he got up, and walked to the door, and looked upon the broken part of the wall; for it had not been mended; and came back, reading on to himself, towards me; and took my hand, and put it under his arm.

Why, this, said he, my girl, is a very moving tale. It was a very desperate attempt, and, had you got out, you might have been in great danger; for you had a very bad and lonely way: and I had taken such measures, that, let you have been where you would, I should have had you.

You may see, sir, said I, what I ventured, rather than be ruined; and you will be so good as hence to judge of the sincerity of my profession, that my honesty is dearer to me than my life. Romantic girl! said he, and read on.

He was very serious at my reflections, on what God had enabled me to escape. And when he came to my reasonings about throwing myself into the water, he said, Walk gently before; and seemed so moved, that he turned away his face from me; and I blessed this good sign, and began not so much to repent at his seeing this mournful part of my story.

He put the papers in his pocket, when he had read my reflections, and thanks for escaping from *myself;* and said, taking me about the waist, Oh, my dear girl! you have

touched me sensibly with your mournful relation, and your
sweet reflections upon it. I should truly have been very
miserable had it taken effect. I see you have been used
too roughly; and it is a mercy you stood proof in that fatal
moment.

Then he most kindly folded me in his arms: Let us, say
I too, my Pamela, walk from this accursed piece of water;
for I shall not, with pleasure, look upon it again, to think
how near it was to have been fatal to my fair one. I
thought, added he, of terrifying you to my will, since I
could not move you by love; and Mrs. Jewkes too well
obeyed me, when the terrors of your return, after your disappointment, were so great, that you had hardly courage
to withstand them; but had like to have made so fatal a
choice, to escape the treatment you apprehended.

Oh, sir, said I, I have reason, I am sure, to bless my dear
parents, and my good lady, your mother, for giving me
something of a religious education; for, but for that, and
God's grace, I should, more than upon one occasion, have
attempted, at least, a desperate act: and I the less wonder
how poor creatures, who have not the fear of God before
their eyes, and give way to despondency, cast themselves
into perdition.

Come, kiss me, said he, and tell me you forgive me for
pushing you into so much danger and distress. If my
mind hold, and I can see those former papers of yours,
and that these in my pocket give me no cause to alter my
opinion, I will endeavour to defy the world and the world's
censures, and make my Pamela amends, if it be in the
power of my whole life, for all the hardships I have made
her undergo.

All this looked well; but you shall see how strangely it
was all turned. For this sham marriage then came into
my mind again; and I said, Your poor servant is far
unworthy of this great honour; for what will it be but to
create envy to herself, and discredit to you? Therefore, sir,
permit me to return to my poor parents, and that is all I
have to ask.

He was in a fearful passion then. And is it *thus,* said he, in my fond conceding moments, that I am to be despised and answered?—Precise, perverse, unseasonable Pamela! begone from my sight! and know as well how to behave in a hopeful prospect, as in a distressful state; and then, and not till then, shalt thou attract the shadow of my notice.

I was startled, and going to speak: but he stamped with his foot, and said, Begone! I tell you: I cannot bear this stupid romantic folly.

One word, said I; but one word, I beseech you, sir.

He turned from me in great wrath, and took down another alley, and so I went, with a very heavy heart; and fear I was too unseasonable, just at a time when he was so condescending: but if it was a piece of art of his side, as I apprehended, to introduce the sham-wedding (and, to be sure, he is very full of stratagem and art), I think I was not so much to blame.

So I went up to my closet; and wrote thus far, while he walked about till dinner was ready; and he is now sat down to it, as I hear by Mrs. Jewkes, very sullen, thoughtful, and out of humour; and she asks, What I have done to him?—Now, again, I dread to see him!—When will my fears be over?

—o—

Three o'clock.

Well, he continues exceeding wrath. He has ordered his travelling chariot to be got ready with all speed. What is to come next, I wonder!

Sure I did not say *so much !*—But see the lordliness of a high condition!—A poor body must not put in a word, when they take it into their heads to be angry! What a fine time a person of an equal condition would have of it, if she were even to marry such a one!—His poor dear mother spoiled him at first. Nobody must speak to him or contradict him, as I have heard, when he was a child;

and so he has not been used to be controlled, and cannot bear the least thing that crosses his violent will. This is one of the blessings attending men of high condition! Much good may do them with their pride of birth, and pride of fortune! say I:—All that it serves for, as far as I can see, is, to multiply their disquiets, and everybody's else that has to do with them.

So, so! where will this end?—Mrs. Jewkes has been with me from him, and she says, I must get out of the house this moment. Well, said I, but whither am I to be carried next? Why, home, said she, to your father and mother. And can it be? said I; No, no, I doubt I shall not be so happy as that!—To be sure some bad design is on foot again! To be sure it is!—Sure, sure, said I, Mrs. Jewkes, he has not found out some other housekeeper *worse than you!* She was very angry, you may well think. But I know she can't be made worse than she is.

She came up again. Are you ready? said she. Bless me, said I, you are very hasty! I have heard of this not a quarter of an hour ago. But I shall be soon ready; for I have but little to take with me, and no kind friends in this house to take leave of, to delay me. Yet, like a fool, I can't help crying. Pray, said I, just step down, and ask, if I may not have my papers.

So, I am quite ready now, against she comes up with an answer; and so I will put up these few writings in my bosom, that I have left.

I don't know what to think—nor how to judge; but I shall never believe I am with you, till I am on my knees before you, begging both your blessings. Yet I am sorry he is so *angry* with me! I thought I did not say *so much.*

There is, I see, the chariot drawn out, the horses too, the grim Colbrand going to get on horseback. What will be the end of all this?

—-o—

WELL, where this will end, I cannot say. But here I am, at a little poor village, almost such a one as yours! I shal learn the name of it by and by: and Robin assures me, he has orders to carry me to you, my dear father and mother. Oh that he may say truth, and not deceive me again! But having nothing else to do, and I am sure I shall not sleep a wink to-night, if I was to go to bed, I will write my time away, and take up my story where I left off, on Sunday afternoon.

Mrs. Jewkes came up to me, with this answer about my papers: My master says, he will not read them yet, lest he should be moved by anything in them to alter his resolution. But if he should think it worth while to read them, he will send them to you, afterwards, to your father's. But, said she, here are your guineas that I borrowed: for all is over now with you, I find.

She saw me cry, and said, Do you repent?—Of what? said I.—Nay, I can't tell, replied she; but, to be sure, he has had a taste of your satirical flings, or he would not be so angry. Oh! continued she, and held up her hand, thou hast a spirit!—But I hope it will now be brought down.— I hope so too, said I.

Well, added I, I am ready. She lifted up the window, and said, I'll call Robin to take your portmanteau: Bag and baggage! proceeded she, I'm glad you're going. I have no words, said I, to throw away upon *you*, Mrs. Jewkes; but, making her a very low courtesy, I most heartily thank you for all your *virtuous* civilities to me. And so adieu; for I'll have no portmanteau, I'll assure you, nor anything but these few things that I brought with me in my hand-kerchief, besides what I have on. For I had all this time worn my own bought clothes, though my master would have had it otherwise often: but I had put up paper, ink, and pens, however.

So down I went, and as I passed by the parlour, she

stepped in, and said, Sir, you have nothing to say to the girl before she goes? I heard him reply, though I did not see him, Who bid you say, *the girl*, Mrs. Jewkes, in that manner? She has offended only me.

I beg your honour's pardon, said the wretch; but if I was your honour, she should not, for all the trouble she has cost you, go away scot-free. No more of this, as I *told you before*, said he: What! when I have such proof, that her virtue is all her pride, shall I rob her of that?—No, added he, let her go, perverse and foolish as she is; but she *deserves* to go honest, and she *shall* go so!

I was so transported with this unexpected goodness, that I opened the door before I knew what I did; and said, falling on my knees at the door, with my hands folded, and lifted up, Oh thank you, thank your honour, a million of times!—May God bless you for this instance of your goodness to me! I will pray for you as long as I live, and so shall my dear father and mother. And, Mrs. Jewkes, said I, I will pray for *you* too, poor wicked wretch that you are!

He turned from me, and went into his closet, and shut the door. He need not have done so; for I would not have gone nearer to him!

Surely I did not say *so much*, to incur all this displeasure.

I think I was loath to leave the house. Can you believe it?—What could be the matter with me, I wonder?—I felt something so strange, and my heart was so lumpish!—I wonder what ailed me!—But this was so *unexpected!*—I believe that was all!—Yet I am very strange still. Surely, surely, I cannot be like the old murmuring Israelites, to long after the onions and garlic of Egypt, when they had suffered there such heavy bondage?—I'll take thee, oh lumpish, contradictory, ungovernable heart! to severe task, for this thy strange impulse, when I get to my dear father's and mother's; and if I find anything in thee that should not be, depend upon it thou shalt be humbled, if strict abstinence, prayer, and mortification, will do it!

But yet, after all, this last goodness of his has touched me too sensibly. I wish I had not heard it, almost; and yet, methinks, I am glad I did; for I should rejoice to think the best of him, for *his own* sake.

Well, and so I went out to the chariot, the same that brought me down. So, Mr. Robert, said I, here I am again! a poor sporting-piece for the great! a mere tennis-ball of fortune! You have your orders, I hope. Yes, madam, said he. Pray, now, said I, don't madam me, nor stand with your hat off to such a one as I. Had not my master, said he, *ordered* me not to be wanting in respects to you, I would have shown you all I could. Well, said I, with my heart full, that's very kind, Mr. Robert.

Mr. Colbrand, mounted on horseback, with pistols before him, came up to me, as soon as I got in, with *his* hat off too. What, monsieur! said I, are *you* to go with me?—Part of the way, he said, to see you safe. I *hope* that's kind too, in you, Mr. Colbrand, said I.

I had nobody to wave my handkerchief to now, nor to take leave of; and so I resigned myself to my contempla-tions, with this strange wayward heart of mine, that I never found so ungovernable and awkward before.

So away drove the chariot!—And when I had got out of the elm-walk, and into the great road, I could hardly think but I was in a dream all the time. A few hours before, in my master's arms almost, with twenty kind things said to me, and a generous concern for the misfortunes he had brought upon me; and only by *one* rash half-word exas-perated against me, and turned out of doors, at an hour's warning; and all his kindness changed to hate! And I now, from three o'clock to five, several miles off! But if I am going to you, all will be well again, I hope.

Lack-a-day, what strange creatures are men! *gentlemen,* I should say, rather! For, my dear deserving good mother, though poverty be both your lots, has had better hap, and you are, and have always been, blest in one another!—Yet this pleases me too; he was so good, he would not let Mrs. Jewkes speak ill of me, and scorned to take her odious unwomanly advice. Oh, what a black heart has this poor wretch! So I need not rail against *men* so much; for my

master, bad as I have thought him, is not half so bad as
this woman.—To be sure she must be an atheist!—Do you
think she is not?——

We could not reach further than this little poor place and
sad alehouse, rather than inn; for it began to be dark, and
Robin did not make so much haste as he might have done;
and he was forced to make hard shift for his horses.

Mr. Colbrand, and Robert too, are very civil. I see he
has got my portmanteau lashed behind the coach. I did
not desire it; but I shall not come quite empty.

A thorough riddance of me, I see!—Bag and baggage!
as Mrs. Jewkes says. Well, my story surely would furnish
out a surprising kind of novel, if it was to be well told.

Mr. Robert came up to me, just now, and begged me to
eat something: I thanked him; but said, I could not eat.
I bid him ask Mr. Colbrand to walk up; and he came; but
neither of them would sit; nor put their hats on. What
mockado is this, to such a poor soul as I! I asked them, if
they were at liberty to tell me the truth of what they were
to do with me? If not, I would not desire it.—They both
said, Robin was ordered to carry me to my father's; and
Mr. Colbrand was to leave me within ten miles, and then
strike off for the other house, and wait till my master arrived
there. They both spoke so solemnly, that I could not but
believe them.

But when Robin went down, the other said, he had a
letter to give me next day at noon, when we baited, as we
were to do, at Mrs. Jewkes's relation's.—May I not, said I,
beg the favour to see it to-night? He seemed so loath to
deny me, that I have hopes I shall prevail on him by and by.

Well, my dear father and mother, I have got the letter,
on great promises of secrecy, and making no use of it. I
will try if I can open it without breaking the seal, and will
take a copy of it by and by; for Robin is in and out: there
being hardly any room in this little house for one to be long
alone. Well, this is the letter :—

' When these lines are delivered to you, you will be far
' on your way to your father and mother, where you have
' so long desired to be; and, I hope, I shall forbear thinking
' of you with the least shadow of that fondness my foolish
' heart had entertained for you : I bear you, however, no ill
' will; but the end of my detaining you being over, I would
' not that you should tarry with me an hour more than
' needed, after the ungenerous preference you gave, at a
' time that I was inclined to pass over all other considera-
' tions, for an honourable address to you; for well I found
' the tables entirely turned upon me, and that I was in far
' more danger from *you* than you were from *me ;* for I was
' just upon resolving to defy all the censures of the world,
' and to make you my wife.

' I will acknowledge another truth: That, had I not
' parted with you as I did, but permitted you to stay till I
' had read your journal, reflecting, as I doubt not I shall
' find it, and till I had heard your bewitching pleas in your
' own behalf, I feared I could not trust myself with my own
' resolution. And this is the reason, I frankly own, that I
' have determined·not to see you, nor hear you speak ; for
' well I know my weakness in your favour.

' But I will get the better of this fond folly : Nay, I hope
' I have already done it, since it was likely to cost me so
' dear. And I write this to tell you, that I wish you well
' with all my heart, though you have spread such mischief
' through my family.—And yet I cannot but say that I could
' wish you would not think of marrying in haste; and,
' particularly, that you would not have this cursed Williams.
' —But what is all this to me now ?—Only, my weakness
' makes me say, That as I had already looked upon you as
' *mine,* and you have so soon got rid of your first husband ;
' so you will not refuse, to my *memory,* the decency that
' every common person observes, to pay a twelvemonth's
' compliment, though but a *mere* compliment, to my ashes.

' Your papers shall be faithfully returned you ; and I have
' paid so dear for my curiosity in the affection they have
' riveted upon me for you, that you would look upon

' yourself amply revenged if you knew what they have
' cost me.

' I thought of writing only a few lines; but I have run
' into length. I will now try to recollect my scattered
' thoughts, and resume my reason; and shall find trouble
' enough to replace my affairs, and my own family, and to
' supply the chasms you have made in it: For, let me tell
' you, though I can forgive *you*, I never can my *sister*, nor
' my domestics; for my vengeance must be wreaked some-
' where.

' I doubt not your prudence in forbearing to expose me
' any more than is necessary for your own justification; and
' for *that* I will suffer myself to be accused by you, and will
' also accuse myself, if it be needful. For I am, and will
' ever be,

' Your affectionate well-wisher.'

This letter, when I expected some new plot, has affected
me more than anything of *that* sort could have done. For
here is plainly his great value for me confessed, and his
rigorous behaviour accounted for in such a manner, as
tortures me much. And all this wicked gipsy story is, as it
seems, a forgery upon us both, and has quite ruined me:
For, oh my dear parents, forgive me! but I found, to my
grief, before, that my heart was too partial in his favour;
but *now* with so much openness, so much affection; nay, so
much *honour* too (which was all I had before doubted, and
kept me on the reserve), I am quite overcome. This was a
happiness, however, I had no reason to expect. But, to be
sure, I must own to you, that I shall never be able to think
of anybody in the world but him.—Presumption! you will
say; and so it is: But love is not a voluntary thing: *Love*,
did I say?—But come, I hope not:—At least it is not, I
hope, gone so far as to make me *very* uneasy: For I know
not *how* it came, nor *when* it began; but crept, crept it has,
like a thief, upon me; and before I knew what was the
matter, it looked like love.

I wish, since it is too late, and my lot determined, that

I had not had this letter, nor heard him take my part to that vile woman; for then I should have blessed myself in having escaped so happily his designing arts upon my virtue: but *now* my poor mind is all topsy-turvied, and I have made an escape to be more a prisoner.

But I hope, since thus it is, that all will be for the best; and I shall, with your prudent advice, and pious prayers, be able to overcome this weakness.—But, to be sure, my dear sir, I will keep a longer time than a twelvemonth, as a *true* widow, for a compliment, and *more* than a compliment, to your ashes! Oh the dear word!—How kind, how moving, how affectionate is the word! Oh why was I not a duchess, to show my gratitude for it! But must labour under the weight of an obligation, even had this happiness befallen me, that would have pressed me to death, and which I never could return by a whole life of faithful love, and cheerful obedience.

Oh forgive your poor daughter!—I am sorry to find this trial so sore upon me; and that all the weakness of my weak sex, and tender years, who never before knew what it was to be so touched, is come upon me, and too mighty to be withstood by me.—But time, prayer, and resignation to God's will, and the benefits of your good lessons, and examples, I hope, will enable me to get over this so heavy a trial.

Oh my treacherous, treacherous heart! to serve me thus! and give no notice to me of the mischiefs thou wast about to bring upon me!—But thus foolishly to give thyself up to the proud invader, without ever consulting thy poor mistress in the least! But thy punishment will be the *first* and the *greatest;* and well deservest thou to smart, oh perfidious traitor! for giving up so weakly thy *whole self,* before a summons came; and to one, too, who had used me so hardly; and when, likewise, thou hadst so well maintained thy post against the most violent and avowed, and, therefore, as I thought, more dangerous attacks!

After all, I must either not show you this my weakness, or tear it out of my writing. *Memorandum:* to consider of this, when I get home.

We are just come in here, to the inn kept by Mrs.
Jewkes's relation. The first compliment I had, was in a
very impudent manner, How I liked the 'squire?—I could
not help saying, Bold, forward woman! Is it for *you*, who
keep an inn, to treat passengers at this rate? She was but
in jest, she said, and asked pardon: And she came, and
begged excuse again, very submissively, after Robin and
Mr. Colbrand had talked to her a little.

The latter here, in great form, gave me, before Robin,
the letter which I had given him back for that purpose.
And I retired, as if to read it; and so I did; for I think I
can't read it too often; though, for my peace of mind's
sake, I might better try to forget it. I am sorry, methinks,
I cannot bring you back a sound heart; but, indeed, it is
an honest one, as to anybody but me; for it has deceived
nobody else: Wicked thing that it is!

More and more surprising things still——

Just as I had sat down, to try to eat a bit of victuals, to
get ready to pursue my journey, came in Mr. Colbrand, in
a mighty hurry. O madam! madam! said he, here be de
groom from de 'Squire B——, all over in a lather, man
and horse! Oh how my heart went pit-a-pat! What now,
thought I, is to come next! He went out, and presently
returned with a letter for me, and another, enclosed, for
Mr. Colbrand. This seemed odd, and put me all in a
trembling. So I shut the door; and never, sure, was the
like known! found the following agreeable contents:—

‘ In vain, my Pamela, do I find it to struggle against my
‘ affection for you. I must needs, after you were gone,
‘ venture to entertain myself with your Journal, when I.
‘ found Mrs. Jewkes's bad usage of you, after your dreadful
‘ temptations and hurts; and particularly your generous
‘ concern for me, on hearing how narrowly I escaped drown-
‘ ing (though my death would have been your *freedom*, and
‘ I had made it your *interest* to wish it); and your most

' agreeable confession in another place, that, notwithstand-
' ing all my hard usage of you, you could not *hate* me; and
' that expressed in so sweet, so soft, and so innocent a
' manner, that I flatter myself you may be brought to *love*
' me (together with the other parts of your admirable
' Journal): I began to repent my parting with you; but,
' God is my witness! for no unlawful end, as *you* would call
' it; but the very contrary: and the rather, as all this was
' improved in your favour, by your behaviour at leaving my
' house: For, oh! that melodious voice praying for me at
' your departure, and thanking me for my rebuke to Mrs.
' Jewkes, still hangs upon my ears, and delights my
' memory. And though I went to bed, I could not rest;
' but about two got up, and made Thomas get one of the
' best horses ready, in order to set out to overtake you,
' while I sat down to write this to you.

' Now, my dear Pamela, let me beg of you, on the receipt
' of this, to order Robin to drive you back again to my
' house. I would have set out myself, for the pleasure of
' bearing you company back in the chariot; but am really
' indisposed; I believe, with vexation that I should part
' thus with my soul's delight, as I now find you are, and
' must be, in spite of the pride of my own heart.

' You cannot imagine the obligation your return will lay
' me under to your goodness; and yet, if you will not so far
' favour me, you shall be under no restraint, as you will
' see by my letter enclosed to Colbrand; which I have not
' sealed, that you may read it. But spare me, my dearest
' girl! the confusion of following you to your father's;
' which I must do, if you persist to go on; for I find I can-
' not live a day without you.

' If you are the generous Pamela I imagine you to be
' (for hitherto you have been all goodness, where it has *not*
' been merited), let me see, by this new instance, the further
' excellence of your disposition; let me see you can forgive
' the man who loves you more than himself; let me see, by
' it, that you are not prepossessed in any other person's
' favour: And one instance more I would beg, and then I

' am all gratitude; and that is, that you would despatch
' Monsieur Colbrand with a letter to your father, assuring
' him that all will end happily; and to desire, that he will
' send to you, at my house, the letters you found means, by
' Williams's conveyance, to send him. And when I have all
' my proud, and, perhaps, *punctilious* doubts answered, I
' shall have nothing to do, but to make you happy, and be
' so myself. For I must be

' Yours, and only yours.

' Monday morn, near three o'clock.'

Oh my exulting heart! how it throbs in my bosom, as if
it would reproach me for so lately upbraiding it for giving
way to the love of so dear a gentleman!—But take care
thou art not too credulous neither, oh fond believer! Things
that we wish, are apt to gain a too ready credence with us.
This sham marriage is not yet cleared up: Mrs. Jewkes, the
vile Mrs. Jewkes! may yet instigate the mind of this
master: his pride of heart, and pride of condition, may
again take place: And a man that could in so *little* a space,
first love me, then hate, then banish me his house, and send
me away disgracefully; and now send for me again, in such
affectionate terms, may *still* waver, may *still* deceive thee.
Therefore will I not acquit thee yet, oh credulous, fluttering,
throbbing mischief! that art so ready to believe what thou
wishest! And I charge thee to keep better guard than thou
hast lately done, and lead me not to follow too implicitly
thy flattering and desirable impulses. Thus foolishly
dialogued I with my heart; and yet, all the time, this heart
is Pamela.

I opened the letter to Monsieur Colbrand; which was
in these words:—

' MONSIEUR,—I am sure you'll excuse the trouble I give
' you. I have, for good reasons, changed my mind; and I
' have besought it, as a favour, that Mrs. Andrews will
' return to me the moment Tom reaches you. I hope, for
' the reasons I have given her, she will have the goodness

' to oblige me. But, if not, you are to order Robin to
' pursue his directions, and set her down at her father's
' door. If she *will* oblige me in her return, perhaps she'll
' give you a letter to her father, for some papers to be
' delivered to you for her; which you'll be so good, in that
' case, to bring to her *here:* But if she will *not* give you
' such a letter, you'll return with her to me, if she please to
' favour me so far; and that with all expedition, that her
' health and safety will permit; for I am pretty much indis-
' posed; but hope it will be but slight, and soon go off.
' I am

'Yours, &c.

' On second thoughts, let Tom go forward with Mrs.
' Andrews's letter, if she pleases to give one; and you
' return with her, for her safety.'

Now this is a dear generous manner of treating me. Oh
how I love to be generously used!—Now, my dear parents,
I wish I could consult you for your opinions, how I should
act. Should I go back, or should I not?—I doubt he has
got too great hold in my heart, for me to be easy presently,
if I should refuse: And yet this gipsy information makes
me fearful.

Well, I will, I think, trust in his generosity! Yet is it
not too great a trust?—especially considering how I have
been used!—But then that was while he avowed his bad
designs; and now he gives great hope of his good ones.
And I *may be* the means of making many happy, as well
as myself, by placing a generous confidence in him.

And then, I think, he might have sent to Colbrand, or
to Robin, to carry me back, whether I would or not. And
how different is his behaviour to that! And would it not
look as if I was *prepossessed*, as he calls it, if I don't oblige
him; and as if it was a silly female piece of pride, to make
him follow me to my father's; and as if I would use him
hardly in *my* turn, for his having used me ill in *his?* Upon
the whole, I resolved to obey him; and if he uses me ill

afterwards, double will be his ungenerous guilt!—Though hard will be my lot, to have my credulity so justly blamable, as it will then seem. For, to be sure, the world, the *wise* world, that never is wrong itself, judges always by events. And if he should use me ill, then I shall be blamed for trusting him: If well, oh then I did right, to be sure!—But how would my censurers act in my case, before the event justifies or condemns the action, is the question?

Then I have no notion of obliging by halves; but of doing things with a grace, as one may say, where they are to be done; and so I wrote the desired letter to you, assuring you, that I had before me happier prospects than ever I had; and hoped all would end well: And that I begged you would send me, by the bearer, Mr. Thomas, my master's groom, those papers, which I had sent you by Mr. Williams's conveyance: For that they imported me much, for clearing up a point in my conduct, that my master was desirous to know, before he resolved to favour me, as he had intended.— But you will have *that* letter, before you can have *this:* for I would not send you this without the preceding; which now is in my master's hands.

And so, having given the letter to Mr. Thomas for him to carry to you, when he had baited and rested after his great fatigue, I sent for Monsieur Colbrand, and Robin, and gave to the former his letter; and when he had read it, I said, You see how things stand. I am resolved to return to our master; and as he is not so well as were to be wished, the more haste you make the better: and don't mind my fatigue, but consider only yourselves, and the horses. Robin, who guessed the matter, by his conversation with Thomas (as I suppose), said, God bless you, madam, and reward you, as your obligingness to my good master deserves; and may we all live to see you triumph over Mrs. Jewkes!

I wondered to hear him say so; for I was always careful of exposing my master, or even that naughty woman, before the common servants. But yet I question whether Robin would have said this, if he had not guessed, by

Thomas's message, and my resolving to return, that I might stand well with his master. So selfish are the hearts of poor mortals, that they are ready to change as favour goes!

So they were not long getting ready; and I am just setting out, back again : and I hope I shall have no reason to repent it.

Robin put on very vehemently; and when we came to the little town, where we lay on Sunday night, he gave his horses a bait, and said, he would push for his master's that night, as it would be moonlight, if I should not be too much fatigued : because there was no place between that and the town adjacent to his master's, fit to put up at, for the night. But Monsieur Colbrand's horse beginning to give way, made a doubt between them : wherefore I said (hating to lie on the road), if it could be done, I should bear it well enough, I hoped ; and that Monsieur Colbrand might leave his horse, when it failed, at some house, and come into the chariot. This pleased them both ; and, about twelve miles short, he left the horse, and took off his spurs and holsters, &c., and, with abundance of ceremonial excuses, came into the chariot; and I sat the easier for it ; for my bones ached sadly with the jolting, and so many miles travelling in so few hours, as I have done, from Sunday night, five o'clock. But, for all this, it was eleven o'clock at night, when we came to the village adjacent to my master's ; and the horses began to be very much tired, and Robin too : but I said, It would be pity to put up only three miles short of the house.

So about one we reached the gate; but everybody was a-bed. But one of the helpers got the keys from Mrs. Jewkes, and opened the gates ; and the horses could hardly crawl into the stable. And I, when I went to get out of the chariot, fell down, and thought I had lost the use of my limbs.

Mrs. Jewkes came down with her clothes huddled on, and lifted up her hands and eyes, at my return ; but showed more care of the horses than of me. By that time the two maids came; and I made shift to creep in, as well as I could.

It seems my poor master was very ill indeed, and had been upon the bed most part of the day; and Abraham (who succeeded John) sat up with him. And he was got into a fine sleep, and heard not the coach come in, nor the noise we made; for his chamber lies towards the garden, on the other side of the house. Mrs. Jewkes said, He had a feverish complaint, and had been blooded; and, very prudently, ordered Abraham, when he awaked, not to tell him I was come, for fear of surprising him, and augmenting his fever; nor, indeed, to say anything of me, till she herself broke it to him in the morning, as she should see how he was.

So I went to bed with Mrs. Jewkes, after she had caused me to drink almost half a pint of burnt wine, made very rich and cordial, with spices; which I found very refreshing, and set me into a sleep I little hoped for.

—*o*—

Tuesday morning.

GETTING up pretty early, I have written thus far, while Mrs. Jewkes lies snoring in bed, fetching up her last night's disturbance. I long for her rising, to know how my poor master does. 'Tis well for *her* she can sleep so purely. No love, but for herself, will ever break her rest, I am sure. I am deadly sore all over, as if I had been soundly beaten. I did not think I could have lived under such fatigue.

Mrs. Jewkes, as soon as she got up, went to know how my master did, and he had had a good night; and, having drank plentifully of sack whey, had sweated much; so that his fever had abated considerably. She said to him, that he must not be surprised, and she would tell him news. He asked, What? And she said, I was come. He raised himself up in his bed; Can it be? said he—What, already! —She told him I came last night. Monsieur Colbrand coming to inquire of his health, he ordered him to draw

near him, and was highly pleased with the account he gave
him of the journey, my readiness to come back, and my
willingness to reach home that night. And he said, Why,
these tender fair ones, I think, bear fatigue better than us
men. But she is very good, to give me such an instance of
her readiness to oblige me. Pray, Mrs. Jewkes, said he,
take great care of her health! and let her lie a-bed all day.
She told him I had been up these two hours. Ask her, said
he, if she will be so good as to make me a visit: If she
won't, I'll rise, and go to her. Indeed, sir, said she, you
must be still; and I'll go to her. But don't urge her too
much, said he, if she be unwilling.

She came to me, and told me all the above; and I said,
I would most willingly wait upon him; for, indeed, I longed
to see him, and was much grieved he was so ill.—So I went
down with her. Will she come? said he, as I entered the
room. Yes, sir, said we; and she said, at the first word,
Most willingly.—Sweet excellence! said he.

As soon as he saw me, he said, Oh, my beloved Pamela!
you have made me quite well. I'm concerned to return
my acknowledgments to you in so unfit a place and manner; but will you give me your hand? I did, and he kissed
it with great eagerness. Sir, said I, you do me too much
honour!—I am sorry you are so ill.—I can't be ill, said
he, while you are with me. I am very well already.

Well, said he, and kissed my hand again, you shall not
repent this goodness. My heart is too full of it to express
myself as I ought. But I am sorry you have had such a
fatiguing time of it.—Life is no life without you! If you
had refused me, and yet I had hardly hopes you would
oblige me, I should have had a severe fit of it, I believe;
for I was taken very oddly, and knew not what to make of
myself: but now I shall be well instantly. You need not,
Mrs. Jewkes, added he, send for the doctor from Stamford,
as we talked yesterday; for this lovely creature is my doctor,
as her absence was my disease.

He begged me to sit down by his bed-side, and asked
me, if I had obliged him with sending for my former

packet? I said I had, and hoped it would be brought. He said it was doubly kind.

I would not stay long because of disturbing him. And he got up in the afternoon, and desired my company; and seemed quite pleased, easy, and much better. He said, Mrs. Jewkes, after this instance of my good Pamela's obligingness in her return, I am sure we ought to leave her entirely at her own liberty; and pray, if she pleases to take a turn in our chariot, or in the garden, or to the town, or wherever she will, let her be left at liberty, and asked no questions; and do you do all in your power to oblige her. She said she would, to be sure.

He took my hand, and said, One thing I will tell you, Pamela, because I know you will be glad to hear it, and yet not care to ask me: I had, before you went, taken Williams's bond for the money; for how the poor man had behaved I can't tell, but he could get no bail; and if I have no fresh reason given me, perhaps I shall not exact the payment; and he has been some time at liberty, and now follows his school; but, methinks, I could wish you would not see him at present.

Sir, said I, I will not do anything to disoblige you wilfully; and I am glad he is at liberty, because I was the occasion of his misfortunes. I durst say no more, though I wanted to plead for the poor gentleman; which, in gratitude, I thought I ought, when I could do him service. I said, I am sorry, sir, Lady Davers, who loves you so well, should have incurred your displeasure, and that there should be any variance between your honour and her; I hope it was not on my account. He took out of his waistcoat pocket, as he sat in his gown, his letter-case, and said, Here, Pamela, read *that* when you go upstairs, and let me have your thoughts upon it; and that will let you into the affair.

He said he was very heavy of a sudden, and would lie down, and indulge for that day; and if he was better in the morning, would take an airing in the chariot. And so I took my leave for the present, and went up to my closet,

and read the letter he was pleased to put into my hands;
which is as follows :—

'BROTHER,— I am very uneasy at what I hear of you;
'and must write, whether it please you or not, my *full*
'mind. I have had some people with me, desiring me to
'interpose with you; and they have a greater regard for
'your honour, than, I am sorry to say it, you have your-
'self. Could I think, that a brother of mine would so
'meanly run away with my late dear mother's waiting-
'maid, and keep her a prisoner from all her friends, and
'to the disgrace of your own? But I thought, when you
'would not let the wench come to me on my mother's
'death, that you meant no good.—I blush for you, I'll
'assure you. The girl was an innocent, good girl; but I
'suppose that's over with her now, or soon will. What
'can you mean by this, let me ask you? Either you will
'have her for a kept mistress, or for a wife. If the former,
'there are enough to be had without ruining a poor wench
'that my mother loved, and who really was a very good
'girl : and of *this* you may be ashamed. As to the *other*,
'I daresay you don't think of it; but if you *should*, you
'would be utterly inexcusable. Consider, brother, that
'ours is no upstart family; but is as ancient as the best in
'the kingdom! and, for several hundreds of years, it has
'never been known, that the heirs of it have disgraced
'themselves by unequal matches : And you know you
'have been sought to by some of the best families in the
'nation, for your alliance. It might be well enough, if you
'were descended of a family of yesterday, or but a remove or
'two from the dirt you seem so fond of. But, let me tell
'you, that I, and all mine, will renounce you for ever, if
'you can descend so meanly; and I shall be ashamed to be
'called your sister. A handsome man, as you are, in your
'person; so happy in the gifts of your mind, that every-
'body courts your company; and possessed of such a noble
'and clear estate; and very rich in money besides, left you
'by the best of fathers and mothers, with such ancient

' blood in your veins, untainted! for *you* to throw away
' yourself thus, is intolerable; and it would be very wicked in
' you to ruin the wench too. So that I beg you will restore
' her to her parents, and give her 100*l.* or so, to make her
' happy in some honest fellow of her own degree; and that
' will be doing something, and will also oblige and pacify

' Your much grieved sister.

   ' If I have written too sharply, consider it is my love
   ' to you, and the shame you are bringing upon your-
   ' self; and I wish this may have the effect upon you,
   ' intended by your very loving sister.'

This is a sad letter, my dear fathe and mother; and
one may see how poor people are despised by the proud
and the rich! and yet we were al' on a foot originally:
And many of these gentry, that brag of their ancient blood,
would be glad to have it as wholesome, and as *really*
untainted, as ours!—Surely these proud people never think
what a short stage life is; and that, with all their vanity,
a time is coming, when they shall be obliged to submit to
be on a level with us: And true said the philosopher, when
he looked upon the skull of a king, and that of a poor man,
that he saw no difference between them. Besides, do they
not know, that the richest of princes, and the poorest of
beggars, are to have one great and tremendous Judge, at
the last day; who will not distinguish between them,
according to their circumstances in life?—But, on the
contrary, may make their condemnations the greater, as
their neglected opportunities were the greater? Poor
souls! how do I pity their pride!—Oh keep me, Heaven!
from *their* high condition, if my mind shall ever be tainted
with *their* vice! or polluted with so cruel and inconsiderate
a contempt of the humble estate which they behold with
so much scorn!

But, besides, how do these gentry know, that, supposing
they could trace back their ancestry for one, two, three,
or even five hundred years, that then the original stems of

these poor families, though they have not kept such elaborate records of their good-for-nothingness, as it often
proves, were not still deeper rooted?—And how can they
be assured, that one hundred years hence, or two, some of
those now despised upstart families may not revel in their
estates, while their descendants may be reduced to the
others' dunghills!—And, perhaps, such is the vanity, as well
as changeableness, of human estates, in *their* turns set up
for pride of family, and despise the others!

These reflections occurred to my thoughts, made serious
by my master's indisposition, and this proud letter of the
lowly Lady Davers, against the *high-minded* Pamela.
Lowly, I say, because she could *stoop* to such vain *pride;*
and *high-minded* I, because I hope I am too *proud* ever
to do the like!—But, after all, poor wretches that we be!
we scarce know what we *are*, much less what we *shall be!*
—But, once more pray I to be kept from the sinful pride
of a high estate.

On this occasion I recall the following lines, which
I have read; where the poet argues in a much better
manner:—

" —————— Wise Providence
Does various parts for various minds dispense :
The *meanest slaves*, or those who *hedge* and *ditch*,
Are useful, by their sweat, to feed the *rich*.
The *rich*, in due return, impart their store ;
Which comfortably feeds the lab'ring *poor*.
Nor let the *rich* the *lowest slave* disdain :
He's *equally* a *link* of Nature's *chain :*
Labours to the *same end*, joins in *one view :*
And *both alike* the *will divine* pursue ;
And, at the last, are levell'd, *king* and *slave*,
Without distinction, in the silent grave."

———*o*———

My master sent me a message just now, that he was so much better, that he would take a turn, after breakfast, in the chariot, and would have me give him my company. I hope I shall know how to be humble, and comport myself as I should do, under all these favours.

Mrs. Jewkes is one of the most obliging creatures in the world; and I have such respects shown me by every one, as if I was as great as Lady Davers.—But now, if this should all end in the sham marriage!—It cannot be, I hope. Yet the pride of greatness and ancestry, and suchlike, is so strongly set out in Lady Davers's letter, that I cannot flatter myself to be so happy as all these desirable appearances make for me. Should I be now deceived, I should be worse off than ever. But I shall see what light this new honour will procure me!—So I'll get ready. But I won't, I think, change my garb. Should I do it, it would look as if I would be nearer on a level with him: and yet, should I not, it might be thought a disgrace to him: but I will, I think, open the portmanteau, and, for the first time since I came hither, put on my best silk night-gown. But then that will be making myself a sort of right to the clothes I had renounced; and I am not yet quite sure I shall have no other crosses to encounter. So I will go as I am; for, though ordinary, I am as clean as a penny, though I say it. So I'll e'en go as I am, except he orders otherwise. Yet Mrs. Jewkes says, I ought to dress as fine as I can.—But I say, I think not. As my master is up, and at breakfast, I will venture down to ask him how he will have me be.

Well, he is kinder and kinder, and, thank God, purely recovered!—How charmingly he looks, to what he did yesterday! Blessed be God for it!

He arose, and came to me, and took me by the hand, and would set me down by him; and he said, My charming girl seemed going to speak. What would you say?—

Sir, said I (a little ashamed), I think it is too great an honour to go into the chariot with you. No, my dear Pamela, said he; the *pleasure* of your company will be greater than the *honour* of mine; and so say no more on that head.

But, sir, said I, I shall disgrace you to go thus. You would grace a prince, my fair one, said the good, kind, kind gentleman! in that dress, or any you shall choose: And you look so pretty, that, if you shall not catch cold in that round-eared cap, you shall go just as you are. But, sir, said I, then you'll be pleased to go a bye-way, that it mayn't be seen you do so much honour to your servant. Oh, my good girl! said he, I doubt you are afraid of yourself being talked of, more than me: for I hope by degrees to take off the world's wonder, and teach them to expect what is to follow, as a due to my Pamela.

Oh the dear good man! There's for you, my dear father and mother!—Did I not do well now to come back?—Oh could I get rid of my fears of this sham marriage (for all this is not yet inconsistent with that frightful scheme), I should be too happy!

So I came up, with great pleasure, for my gloves; and now wait his kind commands. Dear, dear sir! said I to myself, as if I was speaking to him, for God's sake let me have no more trials and reverses; for I could not bear it now, I verily think!

As last the welcome message came, that my master was ready; and so I went down as fast as I could; and he, before all the servants, handed me in, as if I was a lady; and then came in himself. Mrs. Jewkes begged he would take care he did not catch cold, as he had been ill. And I had the pride to hear his new coachman say, to one of his fellow-servants, They are a charming pair, I am sure! 'tis pity they should be parted!—Oh, my dear father and mother! I fear your girl will grow as proud as anything! And, especially, you will think I have reason to guard against it, when you read the kind particulars I am going to relate.

He ordered dinner to be ready by two; and Abraham,

who succeeds John, went behind the coach. He bid Robin drive gently, and told me, he wanted to talk to me about his sister Davers, and other matters. Indeed, at first setting out he kissed me a little too often, that he did; and I was afraid of Robin's looking back, through the fore-glass, and people seeing us, as they passed; but he was exceedingly kind to me, in his words, as well. At last, he said,

You have, I doubt not, read, over and over, my sister's saucy letter; and find, as I told you, that you are no more obliged to her than I am. You see she intimates, that some people had been with her; and who should they be, but the officious Mrs. Jervis, and Mr. Longman, and Jonathan! and so that has made me take the measures I did in dismissing them my service.—I see, said he, you are going to speak on their behalfs; but your time is not come to do that, if ever I shall permit it.

My sister, says he, I have been beforehand with; for I have renounced her. I am sure I have been a kind brother to her; and gave her to the value of 3000*l*. more than her share came to by my father's will, when I entered upon my estate. And the woman, surely, was beside herself with passion and insolence, when she wrote me such a letter; for well she knew I would not bear it. But you must know, Pamela, that she is much incensed, that I will give no ear to a proposal of hers, of a daughter of my Lord ——, who, said he, neither in person, or mind, or acquirements, even with all her opportunities, is to be named in a day with my Pamela. But yet you see the plea, my girl, which I made to you before, of the pride of condition, and the world's censure, which, I own, sticks a little too close with me still: for a woman shines not forth to the public as man; and the world sees not your excellences and perfections: If it did, I should entirely stand acquitted by the severest censures. But it will be taken in the lump; that here is Mr. B——, with such and such an estate, has married his mother's waiting-maid: not considering there is not a lady in the kingdom that can out-do her, or better support the

condition to which she will be raised, if I should marry her.
And, said he, putting his arm round me, and again kissing
me, I pity my dear girl too, for *her* part in this censure;
for, here will she have to combat the pride and slights of
the neighbouring gentry all around us. Sister Davers, you
see, will never be reconciled to you. The other ladies will
not visit you; and you will, with a merit superior to them
all, be treated as if unworthy their notice. Should I now
marry my Pamela, how will my girl relish all this? Won't
these be cutting things to my fair one? For, as to me, I
shall have nothing to do, but, with a good estate in possession, to brazen out the matter of my former pleasantry on
this subject, with my companions of the chase, the green,
and the assemblée; stand their rude jests for once or twice,
and my fortune will create me always respect enough, I
warrant you. But, I say, what will my poor girl do, as to
her part, with her own sex? For some company you must
keep. My station will not admit it to be with my servants;
and the ladies will fly your acquaintance; and still, though
my wife, will treat you as my mother's waiting-maid.—
What says my girl to this?

You may well guess, my dear father and mother, how
transporting these kind, these generous and condescending
sentiments were to me!—I thought I had the harmony of
the spheres all around me; and every word that dropped
from his lips was as sweet as the honey of Hybla to me.—
Oh! sir, said I, how inexpressibly kind and good is all this!
Your poor servant has a much greater struggle than this to
go through, a more knotty difficulty to overcome.

What is that? said he, a little impatiently: I will not
forgive your doubts now.—No, sir, said I, I cannot doubt;
but it is, how I shall *support*, how I shall *deserve* your goodness to me.—Dear girl! said he, and hugged me to his
breast, I was afraid you would have made me angry again;
but that I would not be, because I see you have a grateful
heart; and this your kind and cheerful return, after such
cruel usage as you had experienced in my house, enough to
make you detest the place, has made me resolve to bear any-

thing in you, but doubts of my honour, at a time when I am pouring out my soul, with a true and affectionate ardour, before you.

But, good sir, said I, my greatest concern will be for the rude jests you will have yourself to encounter with, for thus stooping beneath yourself. For, as to *me*, considering my lowly estate, and little merit, even the slights and reflections of the ladies will be an honour to me: and I shall have the pride to place more than half their ill will to their envy at my happiness. And if I can, by the most cheerful duty, and resigned obedience, have the pleasure to be agreeable to you, I shall think myself but too happy, let the world say what it will.

He said, You are very good, my dearest girl! But how will you bestow your time, when you will have no visits to receive or pay? No parties of pleasure to join in? No card-tables to employ your winter evenings; and even, as the taste is, half the day, summer and winter? And you have often played with my mother too, and so know how to perform a part there, as well as in the other diversions: and I'll assure you, my girl, I shall not desire you to live without such amusements, as *my wife* might expect, were I to marry a lady of the first quality.

Oh, sir, said I, you are all goodness! How shall I bear it?—But do you think, sir, in such a family as yours, a person whom you shall honour with the name of mistress of it, will not find useful employments for her time, without looking abroad for any others?

In the first place, sir, if you will give me leave, I will myself look into such parts of the family economy, as may not be beneath the rank to which I shall have the honour of being exalted, if any such there can be; and this, I hope, without incurring the ill will of any *honest* servant.

Then, sir, I will ease you of as much of your family accounts, as I possibly can, when I have convinced you, that I am to be trusted with them; and you know, sir, my late good lady made me her treasurer, her almoner, and everything.

Then, sir, if I must needs be visiting or visited, and the ladies won't honour me so much, or even if they *would* now and then, I will visit, if your goodness will allow me so to do, the sick poor in the neighbourhood around you; and administer to their wants and necessities, in such matters as may not be hurtful to your estate, but comfortable to them; and entail upon you their blessings, and their prayers for your dear health and welfare.

Then I will assist your housekeeper, as I used to do, in the making jellies, comfits, sweetmeats, marmalades, cordials; and to pot, and candy, and preserve for the uses of the family; and to make, myself, all the fine linen of it for yourself and me.

Then, sir, if you will sometimes indulge me with your company, I will take an airing in your chariot now and then: and when you shall return home from your diversions on the green, or from the chase, or where you shall please to go, I shall have the pleasure of receiving you with duty, and a cheerful delight; and, in your absence, count the moments till you return; and you will, maybe, fill up some part of my time, the sweetest by far! with your agreeable conversation, for an hour or two now and then; and be indulgent to the impertinent overflowings of my grateful heart, for all your goodness to me.

The breakfasting-time, the preparations for dinner, and sometimes to entertain your chosen friends, and the company you shall bring home with you, *gentlemen,* if not *ladies,* and the supperings, will fill up a great part of the day in a very necessary manner.

And, maybe, sir, now and then a good-humoured lady will drop in; and, I hope, if they do, I shall so behave myself, as not to *add* to the disgrace you will have brought upon yourself: for, indeed, I will be very circumspect, and try to be as discreet as I can; and as humble too, as shall be consistent with your honour.

Cards, 'tis true, I can play at, in all the usual games that our sex delight in; but this I am not fond of, nor shall ever desire to play, unless to induce such ladies, as you may wish

to see, not to abandon your house for want of an amusement
they are accustomed to.

Music, which our good lady taught me, will fill up some
intervals, if I should have any.

And then, sir, you know, I love reading and scribbling;
and though all the latter will be employed in the family
accounts, between the servants and me, and me and your
good self: yet reading, at proper times, will be a pleasure to
me, which I shall be unwilling to give up, for the best company in the world, except yours. And oh, sir! that will
help to polish my mind, and make me worthier of your
company and conversation; and, with the explanations you
will give me, of what I shall not understand, will be a sweet
employment, and improvement too.

But one thing, sir, I ought not to forget, because it is the
chief: My duty to God will, I hope, always employ some
good portion of my time, with thanks for His superlative
goodness to me; and to pray for *you* and *myself*: for *you*,
sir, for a blessing on you, for your great goodness to such
an unworthy creature: for *myself*, that I may be enabled
to discharge my duty to you, and be found grateful for all
the blessings I shall receive at the hands of Providence, by
means of your generosity and condescension.

With all this, sir, said I, can you think I shall be at a
loss to pass my time? But, as I know, that every slight to
me, if I come to be so happy, will be, in some measure, a
slight to you, I will beg of you, sir, not to let me go very
fine in dress; but appear only so, as that you may not be
ashamed of it after the honour I shall have of being called
by your worthy name: for well I know, sir, that nothing so
much excites the envy of my own sex, as seeing a person
above them in appearance, and in dress. And that would
bring down upon me an hundred *saucy things*, and *low-born
brats*, and I can't tell what!

There I stopped; for I had prattled a great deal too much
so early: and he said, clasping me to him, Why stops my
dear Pamela?—Why does she not proceed? I could dwell
"pon your words all the day long; and you shall be the

directress of your own pleasures, and your own time, so sweetly do you choose to employ it: and thus shall I find some of my own bad actions atoned for by your exemplary goodness, and God will bless *me* for *your* sake.

Oh, said he, what pleasure you give me in this sweet foretaste of *my* happiness! I will now defy the saucy, busy censurers of the world; and bid them know *your* excellence, and *my* happiness, before they, with unhallowed lips, presume to judge of *my* actions, and *your* merit!—And let me tell you, my Pamela, that I can add my hopes of a still more pleasing amusement, and what your bashful modesty would not permit you to hint; and which I will no otherwise touch upon, lest it should seem, to your nicety, to detract from the present purity of my good intentions, than to say, I hope to have superadded to all these, such an employment, as will give me a view of perpetuating my happy prospects, and my family at the same time; of which I am almost the only male.

I blushed, I believe; yet could not be displeased at the decent and charming manner with which he insinuated this distant hope: And, oh! judge for me, how my heart was affected with all these things!

He was pleased to add another charming reflection, which showed me the noble sincerity of his kind professions. I do own to you, my Pamela, said he, that I love you with a purer flame than ever I knew in my whole life; a flame to which I was a stranger; and which commenced for you in the garden; though you, unkindly, by your unseasonable doubts, nipped the opening bud, while it was too tender to bear the cold blasts of slight or negligence. And I know more sincere joy and satisfaction in this sweet hour's conversation with you, than all the guilty tumults of my former passion ever did, or (had even my attempts succeeded) ever could have afforded me.

Oh, sir, said I, expect not words from your poor servant, equal to these most generous professions. Both the means, and the will, I now see, are given to you, to lay me under an everlasting obligation. How happy shall I be, if, though

I cannot be worthy of all this goodness and condescension,
I can prove myself not entirely unworthy of it! But I can
only answer for a grateful heart; and if ever I give you
cause, wilfully (and you will generously allow for *involun-*
tary imperfections), to be disgusted with me, may I be an
outcast from your house and favour, and as much repudiated,
as if the law had divorced me from you!

But, sir, continued I, though I was so unseasonable as I
was in the garden, you would, I flatter myself, had you *then*
heard me, have pardoned my imprudence, and owned I had
some cause to fear, and to wish to be with my poor father
and mother: and this I the rather say, that you should not
think me capable of returning insolence for your goodness;
or appearing foolishly ungrateful to you, when you was so
kind to me.

Indeed, Pamela, said he, you gave me great uneasiness;
for I love you too well not to be jealous of the least appearance of your indifference to me, or preference to any other
person, not excepting your parents themselves. This made
me resolve not to hear you; for I had not got over my
reluctance to marriage; and a little weight, you know,
turns the scale, when it hangs in an equal balance. But
yet, you see, that though I could part with you, while my
anger held, yet the regard I had then newly professed for
your virtue, made me resolve not to offer to violate it; and
you have seen likewise, that the painful struggle I under-
went when I began to reflect, and to read your moving
journal, between my desire to recall you, and my doubt
whether you would return (though yet I resolved not to
force you to it), had like to have cost me a severe illness:
but your kind and cheerful return has dispelled all my fears,
and given me hope, that I am not indifferent to you; and
you see how your presence has chased away my illness.

I bless God for it, said I; but since you are so good as
to encourage me, and will not despise my weakness, I will
acknowledge, that I suffered more than I could have
imagined, till I experienced it, in being banished your
presence in so much anger; and the more still was I

affected, when you answered the wicked Mrs. Jewkes so
generously in my favour, at my leaving your house. For
this, sir, awakened all my reverence for you; and you saw
I could not forbear, not knowing what I did, to break
boldly in upon you, and acknowledge your goodness on my
knees. 'Tis true, my dear Pamela, said he, we have sufficiently tortured one another; and the only comfort that
can result from it, will be, reflecting upon the matter coolly
and with pleasure, when all these storms are overblown
(as I hope they now are), and we sit together secured in
each other's good opinion, recounting the uncommon gradations by which we have ascended to the summit of that
felicity, which I hope we shall shortly arrive at.

Meantime, said the good gentleman, let me hear what
my dear girl would have said in her justification, could I
have trusted myself with her, as to her fears, and the reason
of her wishing herself from me, at a time that I had begun
to show my fondness for her, in a manner that I thought
would have been agreeable to her and virtue.

I pulled out of my pocket the gipsy letter; but I said,
before I showed it to him, I have this letter, sir, to show
you, as what, I believe, you will allow must have given me
the greatest disturbance: but, first, as I know not who is
the writer, and it seems to be in a disguised hand, I would
beg it as a favour, that, if you guess who it is, which I
cannot, it may not turn to their prejudice, because it
was written, very probably, with no other view, than to
serve me.

He took it, and read it. And it being signed *Somebody*,
he said, Yes, this is indeed from *Somebody;* and, disguised
as the hand is, I know the writer: Don't you see, by the
setness of some of these letters, and a little secretary cut
here and there, especially in that *c*, and that *r*, that it is
the hand of a person bred in the law-way? Why, Pamela,
said he, 'tis old Longman's hand: an officious rascal as he
is!—But I have done with him. Oh, sir, said I, it would be
too insolent in me to offer (so much am I myself overwhelmed with your goodness), to defend anybody that you

are angry with: yet, sir, so far as they have incurred your
displeasure for my sake, and for no other want of duty or
respect, I could wish—But I dare not say more.

But, said he, as to the letter and the information it contains:—Let me know, Pamela, when you received this?
On the Friday, sir, said I, that you were gone to the wedding
at Stamford.—How could it be conveyed to you, said he,
unknown to Mrs. Jewkes, when I gave her such a strict
charge to attend you, and you had promised me, that you
would not throw yourself in the way of such intelligence?
For, said he, when I went to Stamford, I knew, from a
private intimation given me, that there would be an attempt
made to see you, or give you a letter, by somebody, if not
to get you away; but was not certain from what quarter,
whether from my sister Davers, Mrs. Jervis, Mr. Longman,
or John Arnold, or your father; and as I was then but
struggling with myself, whether to give way to my honourable inclinations, or to free you, and let you go to your
father, that I might avoid the danger I found myself in of
the former (for I had absolutely resolved never to wound
again even your ears with any proposals of a contrary nature);
that was the reason I desired you to permit Mrs. Jewkes to
be so much on her guard till I came back, when I thought
I should have decided this disputed point within myself,
between my pride and my inclinations.

This, good sir, said I, accounts well to me for your conduct in that case, and for what you said to me and Mrs.
Jewkes on that occasion: And I see more and more how
much I may depend upon your honour and goodness to me.
—But I will tell you all the truth. And then I recounted
to him the whole affair of the gipsy, and how the letter was
put among the loose grass, &c. And he said, The man who
thinks a thousand dragons sufficient to watch a woman,
when her inclination takes a contrary bent, will find all too
little; and she will engage the stones in the street, or the
grass in the field, to act for her, and help on her correspondence. If the mind, said he, be not engaged, I see there
is hardly any confinement sufficient for the body; and you

have told me a very pretty story; and, as you never gave me any reason to question your veracity, even in your severest trials, I make no doubt of the truth of what you have now mentioned: and I will, in my turn, give you such a proof of mine, that you shall find it carry a conviction with it.

You must know, then, my Pamela, that I had actually formed such a project, so well informed was this old rascally *Somebody!* and the time was fixed for the very person described in this letter to be here; and I had thought he should have read some part of the ceremony (as little as was possible, to deceive you) in my chamber; and so I hoped to have you mine upon terms that *then* would have been much more agreeable to me than real matrimony. And I did not in haste intend you the mortification of being undeceived; so that we might have lived for years, perhaps, very lovingly together; and I had, at the same time, been at liberty to confirm or abrogate it as I pleased.

Oh, sir, said I, I am out of breath with the thoughts of my danger! But what good angel prevented the execution of this deep-laid design?

Why, *your* good angel, Pamela, said he; for when I began to consider, that it would have made *you* miserable, and *me* not happy; that if you should have a dear little one, it would be out of my own power to legitimate it, if I should wish it to inherit my estate; and that, as I am almost the last of my family, and most of what I possess must descend to a strange line, and disagreeable and unworthy persons; notwithstanding that I might, in this case, have issue of my own body; when I further considered your untainted virtue, what dangers and trials you had undergone by my means, and what a world of troubles I had involved you in, only because you were beautiful and virtuous, which had excited all my passion for you; and reflected also upon your tried prudence and truth! I, though I doubted not effecting this my last plot, resolved to overcome myself; and, however I might suffer in struggling with my affection for you, to part with you, rather than to betray you under so black a veil. Besides, said he, I remember how much I had exclaimed against and censured an action of this kind, that had been attributed to one of the first men of the law, and of the kingdom, as he afterwards became; and that it was but treading in a path that another had marked out for me; and, as I was assured, with no great satisfaction to himself, when he came to reflect; my foolish pride was a little piqued with this, because I loved to be, if I went out of the way, my own original, as I may call it. On all these considerations it was, that I rejected this project, and sent word to the person, that I had better considered of the matter, and would not have him come, till he heard further from me: And, in this suspense I suppose, some of your confederates, Pamela (for we have been a couple of plotters, though your virtue and merit have procured you faithful friends and partisans, which my money and promises could hardly do), one way or other got knowledge of it, and gave you this notice; but, perhaps, it would have come too late, had not your white angel got the better of my black one, and inspired me with resolutions to abandon the project, just as it was to have been put into execution. But yet I own, that, from these appearances, you were but too well justified in your fears, on this odd way of coming at this intelligence; and I have only one thing to blame you for, that though I was resolved not to *hear* you in your own defence, yet, as you have so ready a talent at your pen, you might have cleared your part of this matter up to me by a line or two; and when I had known what seeming good grounds you had for pouring cold water on a young flame, that was just then rising to an honourable expansion, should not have imputed it, as I was apt to do, to unseasonable insult for my tenderness to you, on one hand; to perverse nicety, on the other; or to (what I was most alarmed by, and concerned for) prepossession for some other person: And this would have saved us both much fatigue, I of mind, you of body.

And, indeed, sir, said I, of *mind* too; and I could not

better manifest this, than by the cheerfulness with which I obeyed your recalling me to your presence.

Ay, that, my dear Pamela, said he, and clasped me in his arms, was the kind, the inexpressibly kind action, that has riveted my affections to you, and obliges me, in this free and unreserved manner, to pour my whole soul into your bosom.

I said, I had the less merit in this my return, because I was driven by an irresistible impulse to it; and could not help it, if I would.

This, said he, (and honoured me by kissing my hand), is engaging, indeed: if I may hope, that my Pamela's gentle inclination for her persecutor was the strongest motive to her return; and I so much value a voluntary love in the person I would wish for my wife, that I would have even prudence and interest hardly named in comparison with it: And can you return me sincerely the honest compliment I now make you?—In the *choice* I have made, it is impossible I should have any view to my *interest*. Love, *true* love, is the *only* motive by which *I* am induced. And were I not what I am, could you give me the *preference* to any other you know in the world, notwithstanding what has passed between us? Why, said I, should your so much obliged Pamela refuse to answer this kind question? Cruel as I have thought you, and dangerous as your views to my honesty have been; you, sir, are the only person living that ever was more than indifferent to me: and before I knew this to be what I blush now to call it, I could not hate you, or wish you ill, though, from my soul, the attempts you made were shocking, and most distasteful to me.

I am satisfied, my Pamela, said he; nor shall I want to see those papers that you have kindly written for to your father; though I still wish to see them too, for the sake of the sweet manner in which you relate what has passed, and to have before me the whole series of your sufferings, that I may learn what degree of kindness may be sufficient to recompense you for them.

In this manner, my dear father and mother, did your happy daughter find herself blessed by her generous master! An ample recompense for all her sufferings did I think this sweet conversation only. A hundred tender things he expressed besides, that though they never can escape my memory, yet would be too tedious to write down. Oh, how I blessed God, and, I hope, ever shall, for all His gracious favours to His unworthy handmaid! What a happy change is this! And who knows but my kind, my generous master, may put it in my power, when he shall see me not quite unworthy of it, to be a means, without injuring him, to dispense around me, to many persons, the happy influences of the condition to which I shall be, by his kind favour, exalted? Doubly blest shall I be, in particular, if I can return the hundredth part of the obligations I owe to such honest good parents, to whose pious instructions and examples, under God, I owe all my present happiness, and future prospects.—Oh the joy that fills my mind on these proud hopes! on these delightful prospects!—It is too mighty for me, and I must sit down to ponder all these things, and to admire and bless the goodness of that Providence, which has, through so many intricate mazes, made me tread the paths of innocence, and so amply rewarded me for what it has itself enabled me to do! All glory to God alone be ever given for it, by your poor enraptured daughter!——

I will now continue my most pleasing relation.

As the chariot was returning home from this sweet airing, he said, From all that has passed between us in this pleasing turn, my Pamela will see, and will believe, that the trials of her virtue are all over from me: But, perhaps, there will be some few yet to come of her patience and humility. For I have, at the earnest importunity of Lady Darnford, and her daughters, promised them a sight of my beloved girl: And so I intend to have their whole family, and Lady Jones, and Mrs. Peters's family, to dine with me once in a few days.

And, since I believe you would hardly choose, at present, to grace the table on the occasion, till you can do it in your own right, I should be glad you would not refuse coming down to us if I should desire it; for I would preface our nuptials, said the dear gentleman!—oh what a sweet word was that!—with their good opinion of your merits: and to see you, and your sweet manner, will be enough for that purpose; and so, by degrees, prepare my neighbours for what is to follow: And they already have your character from me, and are disposed to admire you.

Sir, said I, after all that has passed, I should be unworthy, if I could not say, that I *can* have no will but yours: And however awkwardly I shall behave in such company, weighed down with the sense of your obligations on one side, and my own unworthiness, with their observations on the other, I will not scruple to obey you.

I am obliged to you, Pamela, said he, and pray be only dressed as you are; for since they know your condition, and I have told them the story of your present dress, and how you came by it, one of the young ladies begs it as a favour, that they may see you just as you are: and I am the rather pleased it should be so, because they will perceive you owe nothing to dress, but make a much better figure with your own native stock of loveliness, than the greatest ladies arrayed in the most splendid attire, and adorned with the most glittering jewels.

Oh, sir, said I, your goodness beholds your poor servant in a light greatly beyond her merit! But it must not be expected, that others, ladies especially, will look upon me with *your* favourable eyes: but, nevertheless, I should be best pleased to wear always this humble garb, till you, for your own sake, shall order it otherwise: for, oh, sir, said I, I hope it will be always my pride to glory most in your goodness! and it will be a pleasure to me to show every one, that, with respect to my happiness in this life, I am entirely the work of your bounty; and to let the world see from what a lowly original you have raised me to honours, that the greatest ladies would rejoice in.

Admirable Pamela! said he; excellent girl!—Surely thy
sentiments are superior to those of all thy sex!—I might
have *addressed* a hundred fine ladies; but never, surely,
could have had reason to *admire* one as I do you.

As, my dear father and mother, I repeat these generous
sayings, only because they are the effect of my master's
goodness, being far from presuming to think I deserve one
of them; so I hope you will not attribute it to my vanity;
for I do assure you, I think I ought rather to be more
humble, as I am more *obliged:* for it must be always a sign
of a poor condition, to receive obligations one cannot repay;
as it is of a rich mind, when it can confer them without
expecting or *needing* a return. It is, on one side, the state
of the human creature, compared, on the other, to the
Creator; and so, with due deference, may his beneficence
be said to be God-like, and that is the highest that can be
said.

The chariot brought us home at near the hour of two;
and, blessed be God, my master is pure well, and cheerful;
and that makes me hope he does not repent him of his late
generous treatment of me. He handed me out of the
chariot, and to the parlour, with the same goodness, that
he showed when he put me into it, before several of the
servants. Mrs. Jewkes came to inquire how he did.
Quite well, Mrs. Jewkes, said he; quite well: I thank God,
and this good girl, for it!—I am glad of it, said she; but
I hope you are not the worse for my care, and *my* doctor-
ing of you!—No, but the better, Mrs. Jewkes, said he; you
have much obliged me by both.

Then he said, Mrs. Jewkes, you and I have used this
good girl very hardly.—I was afraid, sir, said she, I should
be the subject of her complaints.—I assure you, said he,
she has not opened her lips about you. We have had a
quite different subject to talk of; and I hope she will forgive us both: You especially she must; because you have
done nothing but by my orders. But I only mean, that the
necessary consequence of those orders has been very grievous

to my Pamela: And now comes our part to make her
amends, if we can.

Sir, said she, I always said to madam (as she called me),
that you was very good, and very forgiving. No, said he,
I have been stark naught; and it is she, I hope, will be very
forgiving. But all this preamble is to tell you, Mrs. Jewkes,
that now I desire you'll study to oblige her, as much as (to
obey me) you was forced to disoblige her before. And
you'll remember, that in everything she is to be her own
mistress.

Yes, said she, and mine too, I suppose, sir? Ay, said
the generous gentleman, I believe it will be so in a little
time.—Then, said she, I know how it will go with me! And
so put her handkerchief to her eyes.—Pamela, said my
master, comfort poor Mrs. Jewkes.

This was very generous, already to seem to put her in
my power: and I took her by the hand, and said, I shall
never take upon me, Mrs. Jewkes, to make a bad use of
any opportunities that may be put into my hands by my
generous master; nor shall I ever wish to do you any dis-
service, if I might: for I shall consider, that what you have
done, was in obedience to a will which it will become me
also to submit to: and so, if the *effects* of our obedience
may be different, yet as they proceed from *one* cause, *that*
must be always reverenced by me.

See there, Mrs. Jewkes, said my master, we are both in
generous hands; and indeed, if Pamela did not pardon you,
I should think she but half forgave me, because you acted
by my instructions.—Well, said she, God bless you both
together, since it must be so; and I will double my diligence to oblige my lady, as I find she will soon be.

Oh, my dear father and mother! now pray for me on
another score; for fear I should grow too proud, and be
giddy and foolish with all these promising things, so soothing to the vanity of my years and sex. But even to this
hour can I pray, that God would remove from me all these
delightful prospects, if they were likely so to corrupt my

mind, as to make me proud and vain, and not acknowledge, with thankful humility, the blessed Providence which has so visibly conducted me through the dangerous paths I have trod, to this happy moment.

My master was pleased to say, that he thought I might as well dine with him, since he was alone: But I begged he would excuse me, for fear, as I said, such excess of goodness and condescension, all at once, should turn my head; and that he would, by slower degrees, bring on my happiness, lest I should not know how to bear it.

Persons that doubt themselves, said he, seldom do amiss: And if there was any fear of what you say, you could not have it in your thoughts: for none but the presumptuous, the conceited, and the thoughtless, err capitally. But, nevertheless, said he, I have such an opinion of your prudence, that I shall generally think what you do right, because it is *you* that do it.

Sir, said I, your kind expressions shall not be thrown away upon me, if I can help it; for they will task me with the care of endeavouring to deserve your good opinion, and your approbation, as the best rule of my conduct.

Being then about to go up stairs, Permit me, sir, said I (looking about me with some confusion, to see that nobody was there), thus on my knees to thank you, as I often wanted to do in the chariot, for all your goodness to me, which shall never, I hope, be cast away upon me. And so I had the boldness to kiss his hand.

I wonder, since, how I came to be so forward. But what could I do?—My poor grateful heart was like a too full river, which overflows its banks: and it carried away my fear and my shamefacedness, as that does all before it on the surface of its waters!

He clasped me in his arms with transport, and condescendingly kneeled by me, and kissing me, said, Oh, my dear obliging good girl, on my knees, as you on yours, I vow to you everlasting truth and fidelity! and may God but bless us both with half the pleasures that seem to lie before us, and we shall have no reason to envy the felicity of the greatest princes!—Oh, sir, said I, how shall I support so much goodness! I am poor, indeed, in *everything*, compared to you! and how far, very far, do you, in every generous way, leave me behind you!

He raised me, and, as I bent towards the door, led me to the stairs foot, and saluting me there again, left me to go up to my closet, where I threw myself on my knees in raptures of joy, and blessed that gracious God, who had thus changed my distress to happiness, and so abundantly rewarded me for all the sufferings I had passed through.— And oh, how light, how very light, do all those sufferings *now* appear, which *then* my repining mind made so grievous to me!—Hence, in every state of life, and in all the changes and chances of it, for the future, will I trust in Providence, who knows what is best for us, and frequently turns the very evils we most dread, to be the causes of our happiness, and of our deliverance from greater.—My experiences, young as I am, as to this great point of reliance on God, are strong, though my judgment in general may be weak and uninformed: but you'll excuse these reflections, because they are your beloved daughter's; and, so far as they are not amiss, derive themselves from the benefit of yours and my late good lady's examples and instructions.

I have written a vast deal in a little time; and shall only say, to conclude this delightful Wednesday, That in the afternoon my good master was so well, that he rode out on horseback, and came home about nine at night; and then stepped up to me, and, seeing me with pen and ink before me in my closet, said, I come only to tell you I am very well, my Pamela: and since I have a letter or two to write, I will leave you to proceed in yours, as I suppose that was your employment (for I had put by my papers at his coming up), and so he saluted me, bid me good night, and went down; and I finished up to this place before I went to bed. Mrs. Jewkes told me, if it was more agreeable to me, she would lie in another room; but I said, No, thank you, Mrs. Jewkes; pray let me have your company. And she made me a fine courtesy, and thanked me.—How times are altered!

THIS morning my master came up to me, and talked with me on various subjects, for a good while together, in the most kind manner. Among other things, he asked me, if I chose to order any new clothes against my marriage. (Oh how my heart flutters when he mentions this subject so freely!) I said, I left everything to his good pleasure, only repeated my request, for the reasons aforegiven, that I might not be too fine.

He said, I think, my dear, it shall be very private: I hope you are not afraid of a sham marriage; and pray get the service by heart, that you may see nothing is omitted. I glowed between shame and delight. Oh how I felt my cheeks burn!

I said, I feared nothing, I apprehended nothing, but my own unworthiness. Said he, I think it shall be done within these fourteen days, from this day, at this house. Oh how I trembled! but not with grief, you may believe.—What says my girl? Have you to object against any day of the next fourteen: because my affairs require me to go to my other house, and I think not to stir from this till I am happy with you?

I have no will but yours, said I (all glowing like the fire, as I could feel): But, sir, did you say in the *house?* Ay, said he; for I care not how privately it be done; and it must be very public if we go to church. It is a *holy rite,* sir, said I; and would be better, methinks, in a *holy place.*

I see (said he, most kindly) my lovely maid's confusion; and your trembling tenderness shows I ought to oblige you all I may. Therefore I will order my own little chapel, which has not been used for two generations, for anything but a lumber-room, because our family seldom resided here long together, to be cleared and cleaned, and got ready for the ceremony, if you dislike your own chamber or mine.

Sir, said I, that will be better than the chamber, and I hope it will never be lumbered again, but kept to the use for which, as I *presume,* it has been consecrated. Oh yes, said he, it has been consecrated, and that several ages ago, in my great great grandfather's time, who built that and the good old house together.

But now, my good girl, if I do not too much add to your sweet confusion, shall it be in the *first* seven days, or the *second* of this fortnight? I looked down, quite out of countenance. Tell me, said he.

In the second, if you please, sir, said I.—As *you* please, said he most kindly; but I should thank you, Pamela, if you would choose the first. I'd *rather*, sir, if you please, said I, have the second. Well, said he, be it so; but don't defer it till the last day of the fourteen.

Pray, sir, said I, since you embolden me to talk on this important subject, may I not send my dear father and mother word of my happiness?—You may, said he; but charge them to keep it secret, till you or I direct the contrary. And I told you, I would see no more of your papers; but I meant, I would not without your consent: but if you will show them to me (and now I have no other motive for my curiosity, but the pleasure I take in reading what you write), I shall acknowledge it as a favour.

If, sir, said I, you will be pleased to let me write over again one sheet, I will; though I had relied upon your word, and not written them for your perusal. What is that? said he: though I cannot consent to it beforehand: for I more desire to see them, because they are your true sentiments at *the time*, and because they were *not* written for my perusal. Sir, said I, what I am loath you should see, are very severe reflections on the letter I received by the gipsy, when I apprehended your design of the sham marriage; though there are other things I would not have you see; but that is the worst. It can't be worse, said he, my dear sauce-box, than I have seen already; and I will allow your treating me in ever so black a manner, on that occasion, because it must have a very black appearance to you.—Well, sir, said I, I think I will obey you before night. But don't alter a word, said he. I won't, sir, replied I, since you order it.

While we were talking, Mrs. Jewkes came up, and said

Thomas was returned. Oh, said my master, let him bring
up the papers: for he hoped, and so did I, that you had
sent them by him. But it was a great balk, when he came
up and said, Sir, Mr. Andrews did not care to deliver them;
and would have it, that his daughter was forced to write
that letter to him: and, indeed, sir, said he, the old gentleman took on sadly, and would have it that his daughter was
undone, or else, he said, she would not have turned back,
when on her way (as I told him she did, said Thomas),
instead of coming to them. I began to be afraid now that
all would be bad for me again.

Well, Tom, said he, don't mince the matter; tell me,
before Mrs. Andrews, what they said. Why, sir, both he
and Goody Andrews, after they had conferred together upon
your letter, madam, came out, weeping bitterly, that grieved
my very heart; and they said, Now all was over with their
poor daughter; and either she had written that letter by
compulsion, or had yielded to your honour; so they said;
and was, or would be ruined!

My master seemed vexed, as I feared. And I said, Pray,
sir, be so good as to excuse the fears of my honest parents!
They cannot know your goodness to me.

And so (said he, without answering me), they refused to
deliver the papers? Yes, and please your honour, said
Thomas, though I told them, that you, madam, of your
own accord, on a letter I had brought you, very cheerfully
wrote what I carried: But the old gentleman said, Why,
wife, there are in these papers twenty things nobody should
see but ourselves, and especially not the 'squire. Oh the
poor girl has had so many stratagems to struggle with! and
now, at last, she has met with one that has been too hard
for her. And can it be possible for us to account for her
setting out to come to us, and in such post haste, and, when
she had got above half-way, to send us this letter, and to go
back again of her own accord, as you say: when we know
that all her delight would have been to come to us, and to
escape from the perils she had been so long contending with?
And then, and please your honour, he said, he could not

bear this; for his daughter was ruined, to be sure, before now. And so, said Thomas, the good old couple sat themselves down, and, hand-in-hand, leaning upon each other's shoulder, did nothing but lament.—I was piteously grieved, said he; but all I could say could not comfort them; nor would they give me the papers; though I told them I should deliver them only to Mrs. Andrews herself. And so, and please your honour, I was forced to come away without them.

My good master saw me all bathed in tears at this description of your distress and fears for me; and he said, I would not have you take on so. I am not angry with your father in the main; he is a good man; and I would have you write out of hand, and it shall be sent by the post to Mr. Atkins, who lives within two miles of your father, and I'll enclose it in a cover of mine, in which I'll desire Mr. Atkins, the moment it comes to his hand, to convey it safely to your father or mother: and say nothing of their sending their papers, that it may not make them uneasy; for I want not now to see them on any other score than that of mere curiosity; and that will do at any time. And so saying, he saluted me before Thomas, and with his own handkerchief wiped my eyes; and said to Thomas, The good old folks are not to be blamed in the main. They don't know my honourable intentions by their dear daughter; who, Tom, will, in a little time, be your mistress; though I shall keep the matter private some days, and would not have it spoken of by my servants out of my house.

Thomas said, God bless your honour! You know best. And I said, Oh, sir, you are all goodness!—How kind is this, to forgive the disappointment, instead of being angry, as I feared you would! Thomas then withdrew. And my master said, I need not remind you of writing out of hand, to make the good folks easy: and I will leave you to yourself for that purpose; only send me down such of your papers, as you are willing I should see, with which I shall entertain myself for an hour or two. But, one thing, added he, I forgot to tell you: The neighbouring gentry I men-

tioned will be here to-morrow to dine with me, and I have
ordered Mrs. Jewkes to prepare for them. And *must* I,
sir, said I, be shown to them? Oh yes, said he; that's the
chief reason of their coming. And you'll see nobody equal
to yourself: don't be concerned.

I opened my papers, as soon as my master had left me;
and laid out those beginning on the Thursday morning he
set out for Stamford, 'with the morning visit he made me
' before I was up, and the injunctions of watchfulness, &c.,
' to Mrs. Jewkes; the next day's gipsy affair, and my reflec-
' tions, in which I called him *truly diabolical*, and was other-
' wise very severe, on the strong appearances the matter
' had then against him. His return on Saturday, with the
' dread he put me in, on the offering to search me for my
' papers which followed those he had got by Mrs. Jewkes's
' means. My being forced to give them up. His carriage
' to me after he had read them, and questions to me. His
' great kindness to me on seeing the dangers I had escaped
' and the troubles I had undergone. And how I unseason-
' ably, in the midst of his goodness, expressed my desire of
' being sent to you, having the intelligence of a sham
' marriage, from the gipsy, in my thoughts. How this
' enraged him, and made him turn me that very Sunday
' out of his house, and send me on my way to you. The
' particulars of my journey, and my grief at parting with
' him; and my free acknowledgment to you, that I found,
' unknown to myself, I had begun to love him, and could
' not help it. His sending after me, to beg my return; but
' yet generously leaving me at my liberty, when he might
' have forced me to return whether I was willing or not.
' My resolution to oblige him, and fatiguing journey back.
' My concern for his illness on my return. His kind recep-
' tion of me, and showing me his sister Davers's angry letter,
' against his behaviour to me, desiring him to set me free,
' and threatening to renounce him as a brother, if he should
' degrade himself by marrying me. My serious reflections
' on this letter, &c.' (all which, I hope, with the others, you

will shortly see). And this carried matters down to Tuesday night last.

All that followed was so kind on his side, being our chariot conference, as above, on Wednesday morning, and how good he has been ever since, that I thought I would go no further; for I was a little ashamed to be so very open on that tender and most grateful subject; though his great goodness to me deserves all the acknowledgments I can possibly make.

And when I had looked these out, I carried them down myself into the parlour to him; and said, putting them into his hands, Your allowances, good sir, as heretofore; and if I have been too open and free in my reflections or declarations, let my fears on one side, and my sincerity on the other, be my excuse. You are very obliging, my good girl, said he. You have nothing to apprehend from my thoughts, any more than from my actions.

So I went up, and wrote the letter to you, briefly acquainting you with my present happiness, and my master's goodness, and expressing the gratitude of heart, which I owe to the kindest gentleman in the world, and assuring you, that I should soon have the pleasure of sending back to you, not only those papers, but all that succeeded them to this time, as I know you delight to amuse yourself in your leisure hours with my scribble: And I said, carrying it down to my master, before I sealed it, Will you please, sir, to take the trouble of reading what I write to my dear parents? Thank you, Pamela, said he, and set me on his knee, while he read it; and seemed much pleased with it; and giving it me again, You are very happy, said he, my beloved girl, in your style and expressions: and the affectionate things you say of me are inexpressibly obliging; and again, with this kiss, said he, do I confirm for truth all that you have promised for my intentions in this letter.— Oh what halcyon days are these! God continue them!—A change would kill me quite.

He went out in his chariot in the afternoon; and in the evening returned, and sent me word, he would be glad of my company for a little walk in the garden; and down I went that very moment.

He came to meet me. So, says he, how does my dear girl do now?—Whom do you think I have seen since I have been out?—I don't know, sir, said I. Why, said he, there is a turning in the road, about five miles off, that goes round a meadow, that has a pleasant foot-way, by the side of a little brook, and a double row of limes on each side, where now and then the gentry in the neighbourhood walk, and angle, and divert themselves.—I'll show it you next opportunity.—And I stept out of my chariot, to walk across this meadow, and bid Robin meet me with it on the further part of it: And whom should I 'spy there, walking, with a book in his hand, reading, but your humble servant Mr. Williams! Don't blush, Pamela, said he.—As his back was towards me, I thought I would speak to the man: and, before he saw me, I said, How do you, old acquaintance? (for, said he, you know we were of one college for a twelvemonth). I thought the man would have jumped into the brook, he gave such a start at hearing my voice, and seeing me.

Poor man! said I. Ay, said he, but not too much of your poor man, in that soft accent, neither, Pamela.—Said I, I am sorry my voice is so startling to you, Mr. Williams. What are you reading? Sir, said he, and stammered with the surprise, it is the French Telemachus; for I am about perfecting myself, if I can, in the French tongue.—Thought I, I had rather so, than perfecting my Pamela in it.—You do well, replied I.—Don't you think that yonder cloud may give us a small shower? and it did a little begin to wet.—He said, he believed not much.

If, said I, you are for the village, I'll give you a cast; for I shall call at Sir Simon's on my return from the little round I am taking. He asked me if it was not too great a favour?—No, said I, don't talk of that; let us walk to the further opening there, and we shall meet my chariot.

So, Pamela, continued my master, we fell into conversation as we walked. He said he was very sorry he had incurred my displeasure; and the more, as he had been told, by Lady Jones, who had it from Sir Simon's family, that I had a more honourable view than at first was apprehended. I said, We fellows of fortune, Mr. Williams, take sometimes a little more liberty with the world than we ought to do; wantoning, very probably, as you contemplative folks would say, in the sunbeams of a dangerous affluence; and cannot think of confining ourselves to the common paths, though the safest and most eligible, after all. And you may believe I could not very well like to be supplanted in a view that lay next my heart; and that by an old acquaintance, whose good, before this affair, I was studious to promote.

I would only say, sir, said he, that my *first* motive was entirely such as became my function: And, very politely, said my master, he added, And I am very sure, that however inexcusable I might seem in the progress of the matter, yourself, sir, would have been sorry to have it said, you had cast your thoughts on a person, that nobody could have wished for but yourself.

Well, Mr. Williams, said I, I see you are a man of gallantry, as well as religion: But what I took most amiss was, that, if you thought me doing a wrong thing, you did not expostulate with me upon it, as your function might have allowed you to do; but immediately determined to counterplot me, and attempt to secure to yourself a prize you would have robbed me of, and that from my own house. But the matter is at an end, and I retain not any malice upon it; though you did not *know* but I might, at last, do honourably by her, as I actually intend.

I am sorry for *myself*, sir, said he, that I should so unhappily incur your displeasure; but I rejoice for her sake in your honourable intentions: give me leave only to say, that if you make Miss Andrews your lady, she will do credit to your choice with everybody that sees her, or comes to know her; and, for person and mind both, you may challenge the county.

In this manner, said my master, did the parson and I

confabulate; and I set him down at his lodgings in the village. But he kept your secret, Pamela; and would not own, that you gave any encouragement to his addresses.

Indeed, sir, said I, he could not say that I did; and I hope you believe me. I do, I do, said he: but 'tis still my opinion, that if, when I saw plots set up against my plots, I had not discovered the parson as I did, the correspondence between you might have gone to a length that would have put our present situation out of both our powers.

Sir, said I, when you consider, that my utmost presumption could not make me hope for the honour you now seem to design me; that I was so hardly used, and had no prospect before me but dishonour, you will allow that I should have seemed very little in earnest in my professions of honesty, if I had not endeavoured to get away: but yet I resolved not to think of marriage; for I never saw the man I could love, till your goodness emboldened me to look up to you.

I should, my dear Pamela, said he, make a very ill compliment to my vanity, if I did not believe you; though, at · the same time, justice calls upon me to say, that it is, some things considered, beyond my merit.

There was a sweet, noble expression for your poor daughter, my dear father and mother!—And from my master too!

I was glad to hear this account of the interview between Mr. Williams and himself; but I dared not to say so. I hope in time he will be reinstated in his good graces.

He was so good as to tell me, he had given orders for the chapel to be cleared. Oh how I look forward with inward joy, yet with fear and trembling!

— *o* —

ABOUT twelve o'clock came Sir Simon, and his lady and two daughters; and Lady Jones, and a sister-in-law of hers; and Mr. Peters, and his spouse and niece. Mrs. Jewkes, who is more and more obliging, was much concerned I was not dressed in some of my best clothes, and made me many compliments.

They all went into the garden for a walk, before dinner; and, I understood, were so impatient to see me, that my master took them into the largest alcove, after they had walked two or three turns, and stept himself to me. Come, my Pamela, said he, the ladies can't be satisfied without seeing you, and I desire you'll come. I said, I was ashamed; but I would obey him. Said he, The two young ladies are dressed out in their best attire; but they make not such an appearance as my charming girl in this ordinary garb.—Sir, said I, shan't I follow you thither? For I can't bear you should do me so much honour. Well, said he, I'll go before you. And he bid Mrs. Jewkes bring a bottle of sack, and some cake. So he went down to them.

This alcove fronts the longest gravel-walk in the garden, so that they saw me all the way I came, for a good way: and my master told me afterwards, with pleasure, all they said of me.

Will you forgive the little vain slut, your daughter, if I tell you all, as he was pleased to tell me? He said, 'spying me first, Look, there, ladies, comes my pretty rustic!—They all, I saw, which dashed me, stood at the windows, and in the door-way, looking full at me.

My master told me, that Lady Jones said, She is a charming creature, I see that at this distance. And Sir Simon, it seems, who has been a sad rake in his younger days, swore he never saw so easy an air, so fine a shape, and so graceful a presence.—The Lady Darnford said, I was a sweet girl. And Mrs. Peters said very handsome things. Even the parson said, I should be the pride of the county. Oh, dear sirs! all this was owing to the light my good master's favour placed me in, which made me shine out in their eyes beyond my deserts. He said the young ladies blushed, and envied me.

When I came near, he saw me in a little confusion, and was so kind as to meet me: Give me your hand, said he, my good girl; you walk too fast (for, indeed, I wanted to be out of their gazing). I did so, with a courtesy, and he led me up the steps of the alcove, and, in a most gentleman-like manner, presented me to the ladies, and they all saluted me, and said, They hoped to be better acquainted with me: and Lady Darnford was pleased to say, I should be the flower of their neighbourhood. Sir Simon said, Good neighbour, by your leave; and saluting me, added, Now will I say, that I have kissed the loveliest maiden in England. But, for all this, methought I owed him a grudge for a tell-tale, though all had turned out so happily. Mr. Peters very gravely followed his example, and said, like a bishop, God bless you, fair excellence! Said Lady Jones, Pray, dear madam, sit down by me: and they all sat down: But I said, I would stand, if they pleased. No, Pamela, said my master: pray sit down with these good ladies, my neigh-bours:—They will indulge it to you, for *my* sake, till they know you better; and for *your own*, when they are acquainted with you. Sir, said I, I shall be proud to deserve their indulgence.

They all so gazed at me, that I could not look up; for I think it is one of the distinctions of persons of condition, and well-bred people, to put bashful bodies out of counten-ance. Well, Sir Simon, said my master, what say you now to my pretty rustic?—He swore a great oath, that he should better know what to say to me if he was as young as him-self. Lady Darnford said, You will never leave, Sir Simon.

Said my master, You are a little confused, my good girl, and out of *breath;* but I have told all my kind neighbours here a good deal of your story, and your excellence. Yes, said Lady Darnford, my dear neighbour, as I *will* call you; we that are here present have all heard of your uncommon story. Madam, said I, you have then heard what must make your kind allowance for me very necessary. No, said Mrs. Peters, we have heard what will always make you valued as an honour to our sex, and as a worthy pattern for all the young ladies in the county. You are very good, madam, said I, to make me able to look up, and to be thankful for the honour you are pleased to do me.

Mrs. Jewkes came in with the canary, brought by Nan, to the alcove, and some cakes on a silver salver; and I said, Mrs. Jewkes, let me be your assistant; I will serve the ladies with the cake. And so I took the salver, and went round to the good company with it, ending with my master. The Lady Jones said, She never was served with such a grace, and it was giving me too much trouble. O madam, said I, I hope my good master's favour will never make me forget, that it is my duty to wait upon his friends.—*Master,* sweet one! said Sir Simon, I hope you won't always call Mr. B—— by that name, for fear it should become a fashion for all our ladies to do the like through the county. I, sir, said I, shall have many reasons to continue this style, which cannot affect your good ladies.

Sir Simon, said Lady Jones, you are very arch upon us: but I see very well, that it will be the interest of all the gentlemen, to bring their ladies into an intimacy with one that can give them such a good example. I am sure then, madam, said I, it must be after I have been polished and improved by the honour of such an example as yours.

They all were very good and affable; and the young Lady Darnford, who had wished to see me in this dress, said, I beg your pardon, dear miss, as she called me; but I had heard how sweetly this garb became you, and was told the history of it; and I begged it, as a favour, that you might oblige us with your appearance in it. I am much obliged to your ladyship, said I, that your kind prescription was so agreeable to my choice. Why, said she, *was* it your choice then?—I am glad of that: though I am sure your person must *give,* and not *take,* ornament from any dress.

You are very kind, madam, said I: but there will be the less reason to fear I should forget the high obligations I

should have to the kindest of gentlemen, when I can delight
to show the humble degree from which his goodness had
raised me.—My dear Pamela, said my master, if you proceed
at this rate, I must insist upon your first seven days. You
know what I mean. Sir, said I, you are all goodness!

They drank a glass of sack each, and Sir Simon would
make me do so too, saying, It will be a reflection, madam,
upon all the ladies, if you don't do as they. No, Sir Simon,
said I, that can't be, because the ladies journey hither makes
a glass of canary a proper cordial for them: but I won't
refuse; because I will do myself the honour of drinking
good health to you, and to all this worthy company.

Said good Lady Darnford, to my master, I hope, sir, we
shall have Mrs. Andrews's company at table. He said, very
obligingly, Madam, it is her time now; and I will leave it
to her choice. If the good ladies, then, will forgive me, sir,
said I, I had rather be excused. They all said, I must not
be excused. I begged I might. Your reason for it, my
dear Pamela? said my master: since the ladies request it,
I wish you would oblige them. Sir, replied I, your goodness
will make me, every day, worthier of the honour the ladies
do me; and when I can persuade myself that I am more
worthy of it than at present, I shall with great joy embrace
all the opportunities they will be pleased to give me.

Mrs. Peters whispered Lady Jones, as my master told me
afterwards: Did you ever see such excellence, such prudence,
and discretion? Never in my life, said the other good lady.
She will adorn, she was pleased to say, her distinction. Ay,
says Mrs. Peters, she would adorn any station in life.

My good master was highly delighted, generous gentleman as he is! with the favourable opinion of the ladies;
and I took the more pleasure in it, because their favour
seemed to lessen the disgrace of his stooping so much
beneath himself.

Lady Darnford said, We will not oppress you; though
we could almost blame your too punctilious exactness: but
if we excuse Miss Andrews from dinner, we must insist upon
her company at the card-table, and at a dish of tea; for we

intend to pass the whole day with you, sir, as we told you. What say you to that, Pamela? said my master. Sir, replied I, whatever you and the ladies please, I will cheerfully do. They said, I was very obliging. But Sir Simon rapt out an oath, and said, That *they* might dine together, if they would; but *he* would dine with me, and nobody else: for, said he, I say, sir, as Parson Williams said (by which I found my master had told them the story), You must not think you have chosen one that nobody can like but yourself.

The young ladies said, If I pleased they would take a turn about the garden with me. I answered, I would very gladly attend them; and so we three, and Lady Jones's sister-in-law, and Mr. Peters's niece, walked together. They were very affable, kind, and obliging; and we soon entered into a good deal of familiarity; and I found Miss Darnford a very agreeable person. Her sister was a little more on the reserve; and I afterwards heard, that, about a year before, she would fain have had my master make his addresses to her: but though Sir Simon is reckoned rich, she was not thought sufficient fortune for him. And now, to have him look down so low as me, must be a sort of mortification to a poor young lady!—And I pitied her.—Indeed I did! —I wish all young persons of my sex could be as happy as I am like to be.

My master told me afterwards, that I left the other ladies, and Sir Simon and Mr. Peters, full of my praises: so that they could hardly talk of anything else; one launching out upon my complexion, another upon my eyes, my hand, and, in short, for you'll think me sadly proud, upon my whole person and behaviour; and they all magnified my readiness and obligingness in my answers, and the like: And I was glad of it, as I said, for my good master's sake, who seemed quite pleased and rejoiced. God bless him for his goodness to me!

Dinner not being ready, the young ladies proposed a tune upon the spinnet. I said, I believed it was not in tune. They said, they knew it was but a few months ago.

If it is, said I, I wish I had known it; though indeed,
ladies, added I, since you know my story, I must own, that
my mind has not been long in tune, to make use of it. So
they would make me play upon it, and sing to it; which I
did, a song my dear good lady made me learn, and used to
be pleased with, and which she brought with her from
Bath: and the ladies were much taken with the song, and
were so kind as to approve my performance: And Miss
Darnford was pleased to compliment me, that I had all the
accomplishments of my sex. I said, I had had a good lady,
in my master's mother, who had spared no pains nor cost
to improve me. She said, she wished Mr. B—— could be
prevailed upon to give a ball on an approaching [happy
occasion, that we might have a dancing-match, &c.—But
I can't say I do; though I did not say so: for these occasions, I think, are too solemn for the principals, at least
of our sex, to take part in, especially if they have the same
thoughts of that solemnity that I have: For, indeed,
though I have before me a prospect of happiness, that may
be envied by ladies of high rank, yet I must own to you,
my dear parents, that I have something very awful upon
my mind, when I think of the matter; and shall, more and
more, as it draws nearer and nearer. This is the song:

I.

Go, happy paper, gently steal,
    And underneath her pillow lie;
There, in soft dreams, my love reveal,
That love which I must still conceal,
    And, wrapt in awful silence, die.

II.

Should flames be doom'd thy hapless fate,
    To atoms thou wouldst quickly turn:
My pains may bear a longer date;
For should I live, and should she hate,
    In endless torments I should burn.

III.

Tell fair AURELIA, she has charms,
    Might in a hermit stir desire.

T' attain the heav'n that's in her arms,
I'd quit the world's alluring harms,
   And to a cell, content, retire.

IV.

Of all that pleas'd my ravish'd eye,
  Her beauty should supply the place ;
Bold Raphael's strokes, and Titian's dye,
Should but in vain presume to vie
  With her inimitable face.

V.

No more I'd wish for Phœbus' rays,
  To gild the object of my sight ;
Much less the taper's fainter blaze :
Her eyes should measure out my days ;
  And when she slept, it should be night.

—o—

                                About four o'clock.

My master just came up to me, and said, If you should see Mr. Williams below, do you think, Pamela, you should not be surprised?—No, sir, said I, I hope not. Why should I? Expect, said he, a stranger then, when you come down to us in the parlour ; for the ladies are preparing themselves for the card-table, and they insist upon your company.—You have a mind, sir, said I, I believe, to try all my courage. Why, said he, does it want courage to see him? No, sir, said I, not at all. But I was grievously dashed to see all those strange ladies and gentlemen ; and now to see Mr. Williams before them, as some of them refused his application for me, when I wanted to get away, it will a little shock me, to see them smile, in recollecting what has passed of that kind. Well, said he, guard your heart against surprises, though you shall see, when you come down, a man that I can allow you to love dearly ; though hardly preferably to me.

This surprises me much. I am afraid he begins to be jealous of me. What will become of me (for he looked very seriously), if any turn should happen now!—My heart aches! I know not what's the matter. But I will go down as brisk as I can, that nothing may be imputed to me. Yet I wish this Mr. Williams had not been there now, when they are all there; because of their fleers at him and me. Otherwise I should be glad to see the poor gentleman; for, indeed, I think him a good man, and he has suffered for my sake.

So, I am sent for down to cards. I'll go: but wish I may continue their good opinions of me: for I shall be very awkward. My master, by his serious question, and bidding me guard my heart against surprises, though I should see, when I came down, a man he can allow me to love dearly, though hardly better than himself, has quite alarmed me, and made me sad!—I hope he loves me!— But whether he does or not, I am in for it now, over head and ears, I doubt, and can't help loving him; 'tis a folly to deny it. But to be sure I can't love any man preferably to him. I shall soon know what he means.

Now, my dear mother, must I write to *you*. Well might my good master say so mysteriously as he did, about guarding my heart against surprises. I never was so surprised in my life; and never could see a man I loved so dearly!— Oh my dear mother, it was my dear, dear father, and not Mr. Williams, that was below ready to receive and to bless your daughter! and both my master and he enjoined me to write how the whole matter was, and what my thoughts were on this joyful occasion.

I will take the matter from the beginning, that Providence directed his feet to this house, to this time, as I have had it from Mrs. Jewkes, from my master, my father, the ladies, and my own heart and conduct, as far as I know of both; because they command it, and you will be pleased with my relation : and so, as you know how I came by the connection, will make one uniform relation of it.

It seems, then, my dear father and you were so uneasy to know the truth of the story which Thomas had told you, that fearing I was betrayed, and quite undone, he got leave of absence, and set out the day after Thomas was there; and so, on Friday morning, he got to the neighbouring town; and there he heard, that the gentry in the neighbourhood were at my master's, at a great entertainment. [He put on a clean shirt and neckcloth (which he brought in his pocket) at an alehouse there, and got shaved; and so, after he had eaten some bread and cheese, and drank a can of ale, he set out for my master's house, with a heavy heart, dreading for me, and in much fear of being browbeaten. He had, it seems, asked, at the alehouse, what family the 'squire had down here, in hopes to hear something of me: And they said, A housekeeper, two maids, and, at present, two coachmen, and two grooms, a footman, and a helper. Was that all? he said. They told him, there was a young creature there, belike who *was*, or *was to be*, his mistress, or somewhat of that nature; but had been his mother's waiting-maid. This, he said, grieved his heart, and confirmed his fears.

So he went on, and about three o'clock in the afternoon came to the gate; and, ringing there, Sir Simon's coachman went to the iron gate; and he asked for the housekeeper; though, from what I had written, in his heart he could not abide her. She sent for him in, little thinking who he was, and asked him, in the little hall, what his business with her was?—Only, madam, said he, whether I cannot speak one word with the 'squire? No, friend, said she; he is engaged with several gentlemen and ladies. Said he, I have business with his honour of greater consequence to me than either life or death; and tears stood in his eyes.

At that she went into the great parlour, where my master was talking very pleasantly with the ladies; and she said, Sir, here is a good tight old man, that wants to see you on business of life and death, he says, and is very earnest. Ay, said he, who can that be?—Let him stay in the little hall, and I'll come to him presently. They all seemed to stare; and Sir Simon said, No more nor less, I daresay, my good friend, but a bastard-child. If it is, said Lady Jones, bring it in to us. I will, said he.

Mrs. Jewkes tells me, my master was much surprised when he saw who it was; and she much more, when my dear father said,—Good God! give me patience! but, as great as you are, sir, I must ask for my child! and burst out into tears. (Oh what trouble have I given you both!) My master said, taking him by the hand, Don't be uneasy, Goodman Andrews; your daughter is in the way to be happy.

This alarmed my dear father, and he said, What! then, is she dying? And trembled, he could scarce stand. My master made him sit down, and sat down by him, and said, No; God be praised! she is very well: And pray be comforted; I cannot bear to see you thus apprehensive; but she has written you a letter to assure you, that she has reason to be well satisfied, and happy.

Ah, sir! said he, you told me once she was in London, waiting on a bishop's lady, when all the time she was a severe prisoner here.—Well, that's all over now, Goodman Andrews, said my master: but the times are altered; for now the sweet girl has taken me prisoner; and in a few days I shall put on the most agreeable fetters that ever man wore.

Oh, sir! said he, you are too pleasant for my griefs. My heart's almost broke. But may I not see my poor child? You shall presently, said he; for she is coming down to us; and since you won't believe *me*, I hope you will *her*.

I will ask you, good sir, said he, but one question till then, that I may know how to look upon her when I see her. Is she honest? Is she virtuous?—As the new-born babe, Mr. Andrews, said my good master; and in twelve days time, I hope, will be my wife.

Oh flatter me not, good your honour, said he: It cannot be! it cannot be!—I fear you have deluded her with strange hopes; and would make me believe impossibilities!—Mrs. Jewkes, said he, do you tell my dear Pamela's good father, when I go out, all you know concerning me, and your mistress that is to be. Mean time, make much of him, and set out what you have; and let him drink a glass of what he likes best. If this be wine, added he, fill me a bumper.

She did so; and he took my father by the hand, and said, Believe me, good man, and be easy; for I can't bear to see you tortured in this cruel suspense: Your dear daughter is the beloved of my soul. I am glad you are come: for you'll see us all in the same story. And here's your dame's health; and God bless you both, for being the happy means of procuring for me so great a blessing! And so he drank a bumper to this most obliging health.

What do I hear? It cannot surely be, said my father. And your honour is too good, I hope, to mock a poor old man.—This ugly story, sir, of the bishop, runs in my head. —But you say I shall see my dear child—And I shall see her honest.—If not, poor as I am, I would not own her.

My master bid Mrs. Jewkes not to let me know yet, that my father was come; and went to the company, and said, I have been agreeably surprised: Here is honest old Goodman Andrews come full of grief to see his daughter; for he fears she is seduced; and tells me, good honest man, that, poor as he is, he will not own her, if she be not virtuous. Oh, said they all, with one voice almost, Dear sir! shall we not see the good old man you have so praised for his plain good sense, and honest heart? If, said he, I thought Pamela would not be too much affected with the surprise, I would make you all witness to their first interview; for never did daughter love a father, or a father a daughter, as they two do one another. Miss Darnford, and all the ladies, and the gentlemen too, begged it might be so. But was not this very cruel, my dear mother? For well might they think I should not support myself in such an agreeable surprise.

He said, kindly, I have but one fear, that the dear girl may be too much affected. Oh, said Lady Darnford, we'll all help to keep up her spirits. Says he, I'll go up, and prepare her; but won't tell her of it. So he came up to me, as I have said, and amused me about Mr. Williams, to half prepare me for some surprise; though that could not

have been anything to this: and he left me, as I said, in
that suspense, at his mystical words, saying, He would send
to me, when they were going to cards.

My master went from me to my father, and asked if
he had eaten anything. No, said Mrs. Jewkes; the good
man's heart is so full, he cannot eat, nor do anything, till
he has seen his dear daughter. That shall soon be, said my
master. I will have you come in with me; for she is going
to sit down with my guests, to a game at quadrille; and I
will send for her down. Oh, sir, said my father, don't,
don't let me; I am not fit to appear before your guests;
let me see my daughter by myself, I beseech you. Said he,
They all know your honest character, Goodman Andrews,
and long to see you, for Pamela's sake.

So he took my father by the hand, and led him in
against his will, to the company. They were all very good.
My master kindly said, Ladies and gentlemen, I present to
you one of the honestest men in England, my good Pamela's
father. Mr. Peters went to him, and took him by the hand,

and said, We are all glad to see you, sir; you are the
happiest man in the world in a daughter; whom we never
saw before to-day, but cannot enough admire.

Said my master, This gentleman, Goodman Andrews, is
the minister of the parish; but is not young enough for
Mr. Williams. This airy expression, my poor father said,
made him fear, for a moment, that all was a jest.—Sir
Simon also took him by the hand, and said, Ay, you have a
sweet daughter, *Honesty;* we are all in love with her. And
the ladies came, and said very fine things: Lady Darnford
particularly, That he might think himself the happiest man
in England, in such a daughter. If, and please you,
madam, said he, she be but virtuous, 'tis all in all: For all
the rest is accident. But I doubt his honour *has been too
much upon the jest with me.* No, said Mrs. Peters, we are
all witnesses, that he intends very honourably by her.—It is
some comfort, said he, and wiped his eyes, that such good
ladies say so—But I wish I could see her.

They would have had him sit down by them; but he

would only sit behind the door, in the corner of the room, so that one could not soon see him as one came in ; because the door opened against him, and hid him almost. The ladies all sat down ; and my master said, Desire Mrs. Jewkes to step up, and tell Mrs. Andrews the ladies wait for her. So down I came.

Miss Darnford rose, and met me at the door, and said, Well, Miss Andrews, we longed for your company. I did not see my dear father ; and it seems his heart was too full to speak ; and he got up, and sat down three or four times successively, unable to come to me, or to say anything. The ladies looked that way : but I would not, supposing it was Mr. Williams. And they made me sit down between Lady Darnford and Lady Jones ; and asked me, what we should play at ? I said, At what your ladyships please. I wondered to see them smile, and look upon me, and to that corner of the room ; but I was afraid of looking that way, for fear of seeing Mr. Williams ; though my face was that way too, and the table before me.

Said my master, Did you send your letter away to the post-house, my good girl, for your father ? To be sure, sir, said I, I did not forget that : I took the liberty to desire Mr. Thomas to carry it. What, said he, I wonder, will the good old couple say to it ? Oh, sir, said I, your goodness will be a cordial to their dear honest hearts ! At that, my dear father, not able to contain himself, nor yet to stir from the place, gushed out into a flood of tears, which he, good soul ! had been struggling with, it seems ; and cried out, Oh my dear child !

I knew the voice, and, lifting up my eyes, and seeing my father, gave a spring, overturned the table, without regard to the company, and threw myself at his feet : Oh my father ! my father ! said I, can it be ?—Is it you ? Yes, it is ! it is ! —Oh bless your happy——daughter ! I would have said, and down I sunk. .

My master seemed concerned—I feared, said he, that the surprise would be too much for her spirits ; and all the ladies ran to me, and made me drink a glass of water ; and

I found myself encircled in the arms of my dearest father.
—Oh tell me, said I, everything! How long have you been
here? When did you come? How does my honoured
mother? And half a dozen questions more, before he could
answer one.

They permitted me to retire with my father; and then I
poured forth all my vows and thanksgivings to God for this
additional blessing; and confirmed all my master's goodness to his scarce-believing amazement. And we kneeled
together, blessing God, and one another, for several ecstatic
minutes : and my master coming in soon after, my dear
father said, Oh, sir, what a change is this! May God reward
and bless you, both in this world and the next!

May God bless us all! said he. But how does my sweet
girl? I have been in pain for you—I am sorry I did not
apprise you beforehand.

Oh, sir, said I, it was you; and all you do must be good—
But this was a blessing so unexpected!——

Well, said he, you have given pain to all the company.
They will be glad to see you, when you can; for you have
spoiled all their diversion; and yet painfully delighted them
at the same time. Mr. Andrews, added he, do you make
this house your own; and the longer you stay, the more
welcome you'll be. After you have a little composed yourself, my dear girl, step in to us again. I am glad to see you
so well already. And so he left us.

See you, my dear father, said I, what goodness there is in
this once naughty master! Oh pray for him! and pray for
me, that I may deserve it!

How long has this happy change been wrought, my dear
child?—Oh, said I, several happy days!—I have written
down everything; and you'll see, from the depth of misery,
what God has done for your happy daughter!

Blessed be His name! said he. But do you say he will
marry you? Can it be, that such a brave gentleman will
make a lady of the child of such a poor man as I? Oh the
divine goodness! How will your poor dear mother be able
to support these happy tidings! I will set out to-morrow,

to acquaint her with them: for I am but half happy, till the dear good woman shares them with me!—To be sure, my dear child, we ought to go into some far country to hide ourselves, that we may not disgrace you by our poverty!

Oh, my dear father, said I, now you are unkind for the first time! Your poverty has been my glory, and my riches; and I have nothing to brag of, but that I ever thought it an honour, rather than a disgrace; because you were always so honest, that your child might well boast of such a parentage!

In this manner, my dear mother, did we pass the happy moments, till Miss Darnford came to me, and said, How do you do, dear madam? I rejoice to see you so well! Pray let us have your company. And yours too, good Mr. Andrews, taking his hand.

This was very obliging, I told her; and we went to the great parlour; and my master took my father by the hand, and made him sit down by him, and drink a glass of wine with him. Meantime, I made my excuses to the ladies, as well as I could, which they readily granted me. But Sir Simon, after his comical manner, put his hands on my shoulders: Let me see, let me see, said he, where your wings grow; for I never saw anybody fly like you.—Why, said he, you have broken Lady Jones's shins with the table. Show her else, madam.

His pleasantry made them laugh. And I said, I was very sorry for my extravagancy: and if it had not been my master's doings, I should have said, it was a fault to permit me to be surprised, and put out of myself, before such good company. They said, All was very excusable; and they were glad I suffered no more by it.

They were so kind as to excuse me at cards, and played by themselves; and I went by my master's commands and sat on the other side, in the happiest place I ever was blest with, between two of the dearest men in the world to me, and each holding one of my hands:—my father, every now and then, with tears, lifting up his eyes, and saying, Could I ever have hoped this!

I asked him, If he had been so kind as to bring the papers with him? He said, He had; and looked at me, as who should say, Must I give them to you now?—I said, Be pleased to let me have them. He pulled them from his pocket; and I stood up, and, with my best duty, gave them into my master's hands. He said, Thank you, Pamela. Your father shall take all with him, to see what a sad fellow I have been, as well as the present happier alteration. But I must have them all again, for the writer's sake.

The ladies and gentlemen would make me govern the tea-table, whatever I could do; and Abraham attended me, to serve the company. My master and my father sat together, and drank a glass or two of wine instead of tea, and Sir Simon joked with my master, saying, I warrant you would not be such a woman's man, as to drink tea, for ever so much, with the ladies. But your time's coming, and I doubt not you'll be made as comfortable as I.

My master was very urgent with them to stay supper; and at last they complied, on condition that I would grace the table, as they were pleased to call it. I begged to be excused. My master said, Don't be excused, Pamela, since the ladies desire it: And besides, said he, we won't part with your father; and so you may as well stay with us.

I was in hopes my father and I might sup by ourselves, or only with Mrs. Jewkes. And Miss Darnford, who is a most obliging young lady, said, We will not part with you, indeed we won't.

When supper was brought in, Lady Darnford took me by the hand, and said to my master, Sir, by your leave; and would have placed me at the upper end of the table. Pray, pray, madam, said I, excuse me; I cannot do it, indeed I cannot. Pamela, said my master, to the great delight of my good father, as I could see by his looks, oblige Lady Darnford, since she desires it. It is but a little before your time, you know.

Dear, good sir, said I, pray don't command it! Let me sit by my father, pray! Why, said Sir Simon, here's ado indeed! Sit down at the upper end, as you should do; and your father shall sit by you, there. This put my dear father upon difficulties. And my master said, Come, I'll place you all: and so put Lady Darnford at the upper end, Lady Jones at her right hand, and Mrs. Peters on the other; and he placed me between the two young ladies; but very genteelly put Miss Darnford below her younger sister; saying, Come, miss, I put you here, because you shall hedge in this little cuckow; for I take notice, with pleasure, of your goodness to her; and, besides, all you very young ladies should sit together. This seemed to please both sisters; for had the youngest miss been put there, it might have piqued her, as matters have been formerly, to be placed below me; whereas Miss Darnford giving place to her youngest sister, made it less odd she should to me; especially with that handsome turn of the dear man, as if I was a cuckow, and to be hedged in.

My master kindly said, Come, Mr. Andrews, you and I will sit together. And so took his place at the bottom of the table, and set my father on his right hand; and Sir Simon would sit on his left. For, said he, parson, I think the petticoats should sit together; and so do you sit down by that lady (his sister). A boiled turkey standing by me, my master said, Cut up that turkey, Pamela, if it be not too strong work for you, that Lady Darnford may not have too much trouble. So I carved it in a trice, and helped the ladies. Miss Darnford said, I would give something to be so dexterous a carver. O madam, said I, my late good lady would always make me do these things, when she entertained her female friends, as she used to do on particular days.

Ay, said my master, I remember my poor mother would often say, if I, or anybody at table, happened to be a little out in carving, I'll send up for my Pamela, to show you how to carve. Said Lady Jones, Mrs. Andrews has every accomplishment of her sex. She is quite wonderful for her years. Miss Darnford said, And I can tell you, madam, that she plays sweetly upon the spinnet, and sings as sweetly to it; for she has a fine voice. Foolish! said Sir Simon; who,

that hears her speak, knows not that? And who that sees
her fingers, believes not that they were made to touch any
key? O parson! said he, 'tis well you're by, or I should
have had a blush from the ladies. I hope not, Sir Simon,
said Lady Jones; for a gentleman of your politeness would
not say anything that would make ladies blush.—No, no,
said he, for the world: but if I had, it would have been, as
the poet says,

'They blush, because they understand.'

When the company went away, Lady Darnford, Lady
Jones, and Mrs. Peters, severally invited my master, and me
with him, to their houses; and begged he would permit me,
at least, to come before we left those parts. And they said,
We hope, when the happy knot is tied, you will induce Mr.
B—— to reside more among us. We were always glad, said
Lady Darnford, when he was here; but now shall have
double reason. Oh what grateful things were these to the
ears of my good father!

When the company was gone, my master asked my father
if he smoked? He answered, No. He made us both sit
down by him, and said, I have been telling this sweet girl,
that in fourteen days, and two of them are gone, she must
fix on one to make me happy. And have left it to her to
choose either one of the first or last seven. My father held
up his hands, and eyes; God bless your honour! said he, is
all I can say. Now, Pamela, said my master, taking my
hand, don't let a little wrong-timed bashfulness take place,
without any other reason, because I should be glad to go to
Bedfordshire as soon as I could; and I would not return till
I carry my servants there a mistress, who should assist me to
repair the mischiefs she has made in it.

I could not look up for confusion. And my father said,
My dear child, I need not, I am sure, prompt your obedience in whatever will most oblige so good a gentleman.
What says my Pamela? said my master: She does not use
to be at a loss for expressions. Sir, said I, were I too sudden,
it would look as if I doubted whether you would hold in

your mind, and was not willing to give you time for reflection : but otherwise, to be sure I ought to resign myself
implicitly to your will.

Said he, I want not time for reflection : for I have often
told you, and that long ago, I could not live without you :
and my pride of condition made me both tempt and terrify
you to other terms ; but your virtue was proof against all
temptations, and was not to be awed by terrors : Wherefore,
as I could not conquer my passion for you, I corrected myself, and resolved, since you would not be mine upon my
terms, you should upon your own : and now I desire you
not on any other, I assure you : and I think the sooner it is
done the better. What say you, Mr. Andrews? Sir, said
he, there is so much goodness on your side, and, blessed be
God ! so much prudence on my daughter's, that I must be
quite silent. But when it is done, I and my poor wife shall
have nothing to do, but to pray for you both, and to look
back, with wonder and joy, on the ways of Providence.

This, said my master, is Friday night; and suppose, my
girl, it be next Monday, Tuesday, Wednesday, or Thursday
morning?—Say, my Pamela.

Will you, sir, said I, excuse me till to-morrow for an
answer? I will, said he ; and touched the bell, and called for
Mrs. Jewkes. Where, said he, does Mr. Andrews lie to-
night? You'll take care of him. He's a very good man ;
and will bring a blessing upon every house he sets his
foot in.

My dear father wept for joy ; and I could not refrain keeping him company. And my master, saluting me, bid us
good-night, and retired. And I waited upon my dear father,
and was so full of prattle, of my master's goodness, and my
future prospects, that I believed afterwards I was turned all
into tongue : but he indulged me, and was transported with
joy ; and went to bed, and dreamed of nothing but Jacob's
ladder, and angels ascending and descending, to bless him
and his daughter.

I AROSE early in the morning; but found my father was up before me, and was gone to walk in the garden. I went to him: and with what delight, with what thankfulness, did we go over every scene of it, that had before been so dreadful to me! The fish pond, the back-door, and every place. Oh what reason had we for thankfulness and gratitude!

About seven o'clock my good master joined us, in his morning gown and slippers; and looking a little heavy, I said, Sir, I fear you had not good rest last night. That is your fault, Pamela, said he. After I went from you, I must needs look into your papers, and could not leave them till I had read them through; and so 'twas three o'clock before I went to sleep. I wish, sir, said I, you had had better entertainment. The worst part of it, said he, was what I had brought upon myself; and you have not spared me. Sir, said I—He interrupting me, said, Well, I forgive you. You had too much reason for it. But I find, plainly enough, that if you had got away, you would soon have been Williams's wife: and I can't see how it could well have been otherwise. Indeed, sir, said I, I had no notion of it, or of being any-body's. I believe so, said he; but it must have come as a thing of course; and I see your father was for it. Sir, said he, I little thought of the honour your goodness would confer upon her; and I thought that would be a match above what we could do for her, a great deal. But when I found she was not for it, I resolved not to urge her; but leave all to her own prudence.

I see, said he, all was sincere, honest, and open; and I speak of it, if it had been done, as a thing that could hardly well be avoided; and I am quite satisfied. But, said he, I must observe, as I have a hundred times, with admiration, what a prodigious memory, and easy and happy manner of narration, this excellent girl has! And though she is full of her pretty tricks and artifices, to escape the snares I had laid for her, yet all is innocent, lovely, and uniformly beautiful. You are exceedingly happy in a daughter; and

I hope I shall be so in a wife.—Or, said my father, may she not have that honour! I fear it not, said he; and I hope I shall deserve it of her.

But, Pamela, said my master, I am sorry to find in some parts of your journal, that Mrs. Jewkes carried her orders a little too far: and I the more take notice of it, because you have not complained to me of her behaviour, as she might have expected for some parts of it; though a good deal was occasioned by my strict orders.—But she had the insolence to strike my girl, I find. Sir, said I, I was a little provoking, I believe; but as we forgave one another, I was the less entitled to complain of her.

Well, said he, you are very good; but if you have any particular resentment, I will indulge it so far, as that she shall hereafter have nothing to do where you are. Sir, said I, you are so kind, that I ought to forgive everybody; and when I see that my happiness is brought about by the very means that I thought then my greatest grievance, I ought to bless those means, and forgive all that was disagreeable to me at the same time, for the great good that hath issued from it.—That, said he, and kissed me, is sweetly considered! and it shall be my part to make you amends for what you have suffered, that you may still think lighter of the one, and have cause to rejoice in the other.

My dear father's heart was full; and he said, with his hands folded, and lifted up, Pray, sir, let me go—let me go—to my dear wife, and tell her all these blessed things, while my heart holds; for it is ready to burst with joy! Good man! said my master—I hope to hear this honest heart of yours speaking at your lips. I enjoin you, Pamela, to continue your relation, as you have opportunity; and though your father be here, write to your mother, that this wondrous story be perfect, and we, your friends, may read and admire you more and more. Ay, pray, pray do, my child, said my father; and this is the reason that I write on, my dear mother, when I thought not to do it, because my father could tell you all that passed while he was here.

My master took notice of my psalm, and was pleased to commend it; and said, That I had very charitably turned the last verses, which, in the original, were full of heavy curses, to a wish that showed I was not of an implacable disposition: though my then usage might have excused it, if I had. But, said he, I think you shall sing it to me to-morrow.

After we have breakfasted, added he, if you have no objection, Pamela, we'll take an airing together; and it shall be in the coach, because we'll have your father's company. He would have excused himself; but my master would have it so: but he was much ashamed, because of the meanness of his appearance.

My master would make us both breakfast with him on chocolate; and he said, I would have you, Pamela, begin to dress as you used to do; for now, at least, you may call your *two other bundles* your own; and if you want anything against the approaching occasion, private as I design it, I'll send to Lincoln for it, by a special messenger. I said, My good lady's bounty, and his own, had set me much above my degree, and I had very good things of all sorts; and I did not desire any other, because I would not excite the censure of the ladies. That would be a different thing, he was pleased to say, when he publicly owned his nuptials, after we came to the other house. But, at present, if I was satisfied, he would not make words with me.

I hope, Mr. Andrews, said he, to my father, you'll not leave us till you see the affair over, and then you'll be *sure* I mean honourably: and, besides, Pamela will be induced to set the day sooner. Oh, sir, said he, I bless God I have no reason to doubt your meaning honourably: and I hope you'll excuse me, if I set out on Monday morning, very early, to my dear wife, and make her as happy as I am.

Why, Pamela, says my good master, may it not be performed on Tuesday? And then your father, maybe, will stay.—I should have been glad to have had it to-morrow, added he; but I have sent Monsieur Colbrand for a licence, that you may have no scruple unanswered; and he can't

very well be back before to-morrow night, or Monday
morning.

This was most agreeable news. I said, Sir, I know my
dear father will want to be at home : and as you was so
good to give me a fortnight from last Thursday, I should be
glad you would be pleased to indulge me still to some day
in the second seven.

Well, said he, I will not be too urgent ; but the sooner
you fix, the better. Mr. Andrews, we must leave something
to these Jephthah's daughters, in these cases, he was pleased
to say : I suppose the little bashful folly, which, in the
happiest circumstances, may give a kind of regret to quit
the maiden state, and an awkwardness at the entrance into
a new one, is a reason with Pamela ; and so she shall name
her day. Sir, said he, you are all goodness.

I went up soon after, and new dressed myself, taking
possession, in a happy moment, I hope, of my *two bundles,*
as my good master was pleased to call them (alluding to
my former division of those good things my lady and himself bestowed upon me) ; and so put on fine linen, silk shoes,
and fine white cotton stockings, a fine quilted coat, a delicate green Mantea silk gown and coat, a French necklace,
and a laced cambric handkerchief, and clean gloves ; and,
taking my fan in my hand, I, like a little proud hussy, looked
in the glass, and thought myself a gentlewoman once more ;
but I forgot not to return due thanks, for being able to put
on this dress with so much comfort.

Mrs. Jewkes would help to dress me, and complimented
me highly, saying, among other things, That now I looked
like a lady indeed : and as, she said, the little chapel was
ready, and divine service would be read in it to-morrow, she
wished the happy knot might then be tied. Said she, Have
you not seen the chapel, madam, since it has been cleaned
out ? No, said I ; but are we to have service in it to-morrow,
do you say ?—I am glad of that ; for I have been a sad
heathen lately, sore against my will !—But who is to officiate?
—Somebody, replied she, Mr. Peters will send. You tell
me very good news, said I, Mrs. Jewkes : I hope it will

never be a lumber-room again.—Ay, said she, I can tell you more good news; for the two Misses Darnford, and Lady Jones, are to be here at the opening of it; and will stay and dine with you. My master, said I, has not told me that. You must alter your style, madam, said she: It must not be *master* now, sure!—Oh, returned I, this is a language I shall never forget: he shall always be my master; and I shall think myself more and more his servant.

My poor father did not know I went up to dress myself; and he said his heart misgave him when he saw me first, for fear I was made a fool of, and that here was some fine lady that was to be my master's true wife. And he stood in admiration, and said, Oh, my dear child, how well will you become your happy condition! Why you look like a lady already! I hope, my dear father, said I, and boldly kissed him, I shall always be your dutiful daughter, whatever my condition be.

My master sent me word he was ready; and when he saw me, said, Dress as you will, Pamela, you're a charming girl! and so handed me to the coach, and would make my father and me sit both on the foreside, and sat backwards, over against me; and bid the coachman drive to the meadow; that is, where he once met Mr. Williams.

The conversation was most agreeable to me, and to my dear father, as we went; and he more and more exceeded in goodness and generosity; and, while I was gone up to dress, he had presented my father with twenty guineas; desiring him to buy himself and my mother such apparel as they should think proper; and lay it all out: but I knew not this till after we came home; my father having had no opportunity to tell me of it.

He was pleased to inform me of the chapel being got in tolerable order; and said, it looked very well; and against he came down next, it should be all new white-washed, and painted and lined; and a new pulpit-cloth, cushion, desk, &c., and that it should always be kept in order for the future. He told me the two Misses Darnford, and Lady Jones, would dine with him on Sunday: And, with their

servants and mine, said he, we shall make a tolerable congregation. And, added he, have I not well contrived to
show you that the chapel is really a little house of God, and
has been consecrated, before we solemnise our nuptials in
it?—Oh, sir, replied I, your goodness to me is inexpressible!
Mr. Peters, said he, offered to come and officiate in it; but
would not stay to dine with me, because he has company at
his own house: and so I intend that divine service shall be
performed in it by one to whom I shall make some yearly
allowance, as a sort of chaplain.—You look serious, Pamela,
added he: I know you think of your friend Williams.
Indeed, sir, said I, if you won't be angry, I did. Poor man!
I am sorry I have been the cause of his disobliging you.

When we came to the meadow, where the gentry have
their walk sometimes, the coach stopt, and my master
alighted, and led me to the brook-side, and it is a very
pretty summer walk. He asked my father, If he chose to
walk out, or go on in the coach to the farther end? He,
poor man, chose to go on in the coach, for fear, he said,
any gentry should be walking there; and he told me, he was
most of the way upon his knees in the coach, thanking God
for His gracious mercies and goodness; and begging a blessing upon my good master and me.

I was quite astonished, when we came into the shady
walk, to see Mr. Williams there. See there, said my master,
there's poor Williams, taking his solitary walk again, with
his book. And, it seems, it was so contrived; for Mr. Peters
had been, as I since find, desired to tell him to be in that
walk at such an hour in the morning.

So, old acquaintance, said my master, again have I met
you in this place? What book are you now reading? He
said, it was Boileau's Lutrin. Said my master, You see I
have brought with me my little fugitive, that would have
been: While you are perfecting yourself in French, I am
trying to learn English; and hope soon to be master of it.

Mine, sir, said he, is a very beautiful piece of French:
but your English has no equal.

You are very polite, Mr. Williams, said my master: And

he that does not think as you do, deserves no share in her.
Why, Pamela, added he, very generously, why so strange,
where you have once been so familiar? I do assure you
both, that I mean not, by this interview, to insult Mr.
Williams, or confound you. Then I said, Mr. Williams, I
am very glad to see you well; and though the generous
favour of my good master has happily changed the scene,
since you and I last saw one another, I am nevertheless very
glad of an opportunity to acknowledge, with gratitude, your
good intentions, not so much to serve me, as *me*, but as a
person that then had great reason to believe herself in distress. And I hope, sir, added I, to my master, your goodness will permit me to say this.

You, Pamela, said he, may make what acknowledgments
you please to Mr. Williams's good intentions; and I would
have you speak as you think: but I do not apprehend
myself to be quite so much obliged to those intentions.

Sir, said Mr. Williams, I beg leave to say, I knew well,
that, by education, you was no libertine; nor had I reason
to think you so by inclination; and, when you came to
reflect, I hoped you would not be displeased with me. And
this was no small motive to me, at first, to do as I did.

Ay, but Mr. Williams, said my master, could you think
I should have had reason to thank you, if, loving one person
above all her sex, you had robbed me of her, and married
her yourself?—And then, said he, you are to consider, that
she was an old acquaintance of mine, and a quite new one
to you; that I had sent her down to my own house, for
better securing her; and that you, who had access to my
house, could not effect your purpose, without being guilty,
in some sort, of a breach of the laws of hospitality and
friendship. As to my designs upon her, I own they had not
the best appearance; but still I was not answerable to Mr.
Williams for those; much less could you be excused to
invade a property so very dear to me, and to endeavour to
gain an interest in her affections, when you could not be
certain that matters would not turn out as they have
actually done.

I own, said he, that some parts of my conduct seem exceptionable, as you state it. But, sir, I am but a young man. I meant no harm. I had no interest, I am sure, to incur your displeasure; and when you think of everything, and the inimitable graces of person, and perfections of mind, that adorn this excellent lady (so he called me), you will, perhaps, find your generosity allow something as an extenuation of a fault, which your anger would not permit as an excuse.

I have done, said my master; nor did I meet you here to be angry with you. Pamela knew not that she should see you: and now you are both present, I would ask you, Mr. Williams, if, now you know my honourable designs towards this good girl, you can really be *almost*, I will not say *quite*, as well pleased with the friendship of my wife, as you could be with the favour of Mrs. Andrews?

Sir, said he, I will answer you truly. I think I could have preferred, with her, any condition that could have befallen me, had I considered only *myself*. But, sir, I was very far from having any encouragement to expect her *favour;* and I had much more reason to believe, that, if she could have hoped for your goodness, her heart would have been too much pre-engaged to think of anybody else. And give me leave further to say, sir, that, though I tell you sincerely my thoughts, were I only to consider *myself;* yet, when I consider *her good*, and *her merit*, I should be highly ungenerous, were it put to my *choice*, if I could not wish her in a condition so much superior to what I could raise her to, and so very answerable to her merit.

Pamela, said my master, you are obliged to Mr. Williams, and ought to thank him: he has distinguished well. But, as for *me*, who had like to have lost you by his means, I am glad the matter was not left to his *choice*. Mr. Williams, added he, I give you Pamela's hand, because I know it will be pleasing to her, in token of her friendship and esteem for you; and I give you mine, that I will not be your enemy: but yet I must say, that I think I owe this proper manner of your thinking more to your disappointment, than to the generosity you talk of.

Mr. Williams kissed my hand, as my master gave it him; and my master said, Sir, you will go home and dine with me, and I'll show you my little chapel; and do you, Pamela, look upon yourself at liberty to number Mr. Williams in the list of your friends.

How generous, how noble, was this! Mr. Williams (and so had I) had tears of pleasure in his eyes. I was silent: But Mr. Williams said, Sir, I shall be taught, by your generosity, to think myself inexcusably wrong, in every step I took, that could give you offence; and my future life shall show my respectful gratitude.

We walked on till we came to the coach, where was my dear father. Pamela, said my master, tell Mr. Williams who that good man is. O Mr. Williams! said I, it is my dear father! and my master was pleased to say, One of the honestest men in England: Pamela owes everything that she is to be, as well as her being, to him; for, I think, she would not have brought me to this, nor made so great resistance, but for the good lessons, and religious education, she had imbibed from him.

Mr. Williams said, taking my father's hand, You see, good Mr. Andrews, with inexpressible pleasure, no doubt, the fruits of your pious care; and now are in a way, with your beloved daughter, to reap the happy effects of it.—I am overcome, said my dear father, with his honour's goodness: But I can only say, I bless *God*, and bless *him*.

Mr. Williams and I being nearer the coach than my master, and he offering to draw back, to give way to him, he kindly said, Pray, Mr. Williams, oblige Pamela with your hand; and step in yourself. He bowed, and took my hand; and my master made him step in, and sit next me, all that ever he could do; and sat himself over against him, next my father, who sat against me.

And he said, Mr. Andrews, I told you yesterday that the divine you saw was *not* Mr. Williams; I now tell you, this gentleman *is*: and though I have been telling him, I think

not *myself* obliged to his intentions; yet I will own that
Pamela and *you* are; and though I won't promise to love
him, I would have you.

Sir, said Mr. Williams, you have a way of overcoming,
that hardly all my reading affords an instance of; and it is
the more noble, as it is on this side, as I presume, the happy
ceremony, which, great as your fortune is, will lay you under
an obligation to so much virtue and beauty, when the lady
becomes yours; for you will then have a treasure that princes
might envy you.

Said my generous master (God bless him!), Mr. Williams,
it is impossible that you and I should long live at variance,
when our sentiments agree so well together, on subjects the
most material.

I was quite confounded; and my master, seeing it, took
my hand, and said, Look up, my good girl; and collect
yourself.—Don't injure Mr. Williams and me so much, as
to think we are capping compliments, as we used to do
verses at school. I dare answer for us both, that we say not
a syllable we don't think.

Oh, sir, said I, how unequal am I to all this goodness!
Every moment that passes adds to the weight of the obligations you oppress me with.

Think not too much of that, said he most generously.
Mr. Williams's compliments to you have great advantage
of mine: For, though equally sincere, I have a great deal
to say, and to do, to compensate the sufferings I have
made you undergo; and, at last, must sit down dissatisfied,
because those will never be balanced by all I can do for
you.

He saw my dear father quite unable to support these
affecting instances of his goodness; and he let go my hand,
and took his; and said, seeing his tears, I wonder not, my
dear Pamela's father, that your honest heart springs thus
to your eyes, to see all her trials at an end. I will not pretend to say, that I had formerly either power or will to act
thus: But since I began to resolve on the change you see,
I have reaped so much pleasure in it, that my own *interest*

will keep me steady: For, till within these few days, I knew not what it was to be happy.

Poor Mr. Williams, with tears of joy in his eyes, said, How happily, sir, have you been touched by the divine grace, before you have been hurried into the commission of sins, that the deepest penitence could hardly have atoned for!—God has enabled you to stop short of the evil; and you have nothing to do, but to rejoice in the good, which now will be doubly so, because you can receive it without the least inward reproach.

You do well, said he, to remind me, that I owe all this to the grace of God. I bless Him for it; and I thank this good man for his excellent lessons to his daughter; I thank her for following them: and I hope, from *her* good example, and *your* friendship, Mr. Williams, in time, to be half as good as my tutoress: and that, said he, I believe you'll own, will make me, without disparagement to any man, the best fox-hunter in England.—Mr. Williams was going to speak: And he said, You put on so grave a look, Mr. Williams, that, I believe, what I have said, with you practical good folks, is liable to exception: but I see we are become quite grave; and we must not be too serious neither.

What a happy creature, my dear mother, is your Pamela! —Oh may my thankful heart, and the good use I may be enabled to make of the blessings before me, be a means to continue this delightful prospect to a long date, for the sake of the dear good gentleman, who thus becomes the happy instrument, in the hand of Providence, to bless all he smiles upon! To be sure, I shall never enough acknowledge the value he is pleased to express for my unworthiness, in that he has prevented my wishes, and, unasked, sought the occasion of being reconciled to a good man, who, for my sake, had incurred his displeasure; and whose name he could not, a few days before, permit to pass through my lips! But see the wonderful ways of Providence! The very things that I most dreaded his seeing or knowing, the contents of my papers, have, as I hope, satisfied all his scruples, and been a means to promote my happiness.

Henceforth let not us poor short-sighted mortals pretend
to rely on our own wisdom; or vainly think, that we are
absolutely to direct for ourselves. I have abundant reason,
I am sure, to say, that, when I was most disappointed, I
was nearer my happiness: for had I made my escape, which
was so often my chief point in view, and what I had placed
my heart upon, I had escaped the blessings now before me,
and fallen, perhaps headlong, into the miseries I would have
avoided. And yet, after all, it was necessary I should take
the steps I did, to bring on this wonderful turn: oh the un-
searchable wisdom of God!—And how much ought I to
adore the divine goodness, and humble myself, who am made
a poor instrument, as I hope, not only to magnify His
graciousness to this fine gentleman and myself, but also to
dispense benefits to others! Which God of His mercy grant!

In the agreeable manner I have mentioned, did we pass
the time in our second happy tour; and I thought Mrs.
Jewkes would have sunk into the ground, when she saw Mr.
Williams brought in the coach with us, and treated so
kindly. We dined together in a most pleasant, easy, and
frank manner; and I found I need not, from my master's
generosity, to be under any restraint, as to my conduct to
this good clergyman: For he, so often as he fancied I was
reserved, moved me to be free with him, and to him; and
several times called upon me to help my father and Mr.
Williams; and seemed to take great delight in seeing me
carve, as, indeed, he does in everything I do.

After dinner, we went and looked into the chapel, which
is a very pretty one, and very decent; and, when finished
as he designs it, against his next coming down, will be a
very pretty place.

My heart, my dear mother, when I first set my foot in it,
throbbed a good deal, with awful joy, at the thoughts of the
solemnity, which, I hope, will in a few days be performed
here. And when I came up towards the little pretty altar-
piece, while they were looking at a communion-picture, and
saying it was prettily done, I gently stept into a corner, out

of sight, and poured out my soul to God on my knees, in supplication and thankfulness, that, after having been so long absent from divine service, the first time I entered into a house dedicated to His honour, should be with such blessed prospects before me; and begging of God to continue me humble, and to make me not unworthy of His mercies; and that He would be pleased to bless the *next* author of my happiness, my good master.

I heard my master say, Where's Pamela? And so I broke off sooner than I would, and went up to him.

He said, Mr. Williams, I hope I have not so offended you by my conduct past (for really it is what I ought to be ashamed of), as that you will refuse to officiate, and to give us your instructions here to-morrow. Mr. Peters was so kind, for the first time, to offer it; but I knew it would be inconvenient for him; and, besides, I was willing to make this request to you an introduction to our reconciliation.

Sir, said he, most willingly, and most gratefully, will I obey you: Though, if you expect a discourse, I am wholly unprepared for the occasion. I would not have it, replied he, pointed to any particular occasion; but if you have one upon the text—*There is more joy in Heaven over one sinner that repenteth, than over ninety-nine just persons that need no repentance;* and if it makes me not such a sad fellow as to be pointed at by mine and the ladies' servants we shall have here, I shall be well content. 'Tis a general subject, added he, makes me speak of that; but any one you please will do; for you cannot make a bad choice, I am sure.

Sir, said he, I have one upon that text; but I am ready to think, that a thanksgiving one, which I made on a great mercy to himself, if I may be permitted to make my own acknowledgments of your favour the subject of a discourse, will be suitable to my grateful sentiments. It is on the text—*Now lettest thou thy servant depart in peace; for mine eyes have seen thy salvation.*

That text, said I, will be a very suitable one for me. Not so, Pamela, said my master; because I don't let you *depart* in *peace;* but I hope you will *stay here* with *content.*

Oh but, sir, said I, I have seen *God's salvation !*—I am sure, added I, if anybody ever had reason, I have to say, with the blessed Virgin, *My soul doth magnify the Lord ; for He hath regarded the low estate of His handmaiden—and exalted one of low degree.*

Said my good father, I am sure, if there were time for it, the book of Ruth would afford a fine subject for the honour done my dear child.

Why, good Mr. Andrews, said my master, should you say so?—I know that story, and Mr. Williams will confirm what I say, that my good girl here will confer at least as much honour as she will receive.

Sir, said I, you are inexpressibly generous; but I shall never think so? Why, my Pamela, said he, that's another thing: it will be best for me to think you *will;* and it will be kind in you to think you *shan't ;* and then we shall always have an excellent rule to regulate our conduct by to one another.

Was not this finely, nobly, wisely said, my dear mother? —Oh what a blessed thing it is to be matched to a man of sense and generosity!—How edifying! How!—But what shall I say?—I am at loss for words.

Mr. Williams said, when we came out of the little chapel, he would go home, and look over his discourses, for one for the next day. My master said, I have one thing to say before you go—When my jealousy, on account of this good girl, put me upon such a vindictive conduct to you, you know I took a bond for the money I had caused you to be troubled for: I really am ashamed of the matter ; because I never intended, when I presented it to you, to have it again, you may be sure: But I knew not what might happen between you and her, nor how far matters might have gone between you; and so I was willing to have that in awe over you. And I think it is no extraordinary present, therefore, to give you up your bond again cancelled. And so he took it from his pocket, and gave it him. I think, added he, all the charges attending it, and the trouble you had, were defrayed by my attorney; I ordered that they should. They

were, sir, said he; and ten thousand thanks to you for this
goodness, and the kind manner in which you do it.—If you
will go, Mr. Williams, said he, shall my chariot carry you
home? No, sir, answered he, I thank you. My time will
be so well employed all the way, in thinking of your favours,
that I choose to meditate upon them, as I walk home.

My dear father was a little uneasy about his habit, for
appearing at chapel next day, because of Misses Darnford
and the servants, for fear, poor man, he should disgrace my
master; and he told me, when he was mentioning this, of
my master's kind present of twenty guineas for clothes, for
you both; which made my heart truly joyful. But oh! to
be sure, I can never deserve the hundredth part of his goodness!—It is almost a hard thing to lie under the weight of
such deep obligations on one side, and such a sense of one's
own unworthiness on the other.—Oh! what a Godlike power
is that of doing good!—I envy the rich and the great for
nothing else.

My master coming to us just then, I said, Oh! sir, will
your bounty know no limits? My dear father has told me
what you have given him.—A trifle, Pamela, said he, a little
earnest only of my kindness.—Say no more of it. But did
I not hear the good man expressing some sort of concern
for somewhat? Hide nothing from me, Pamela. Only,
sir, said I, he knew not how to absent himself from divine
service, and yet is afraid of disgracing you by appearing.

Fie, Mr. Andrews! said he, I thought you knew that the
outward appearance was nothing. I wish I had as good a
habit *inwardly* as you have. But I'll tell you, Pamela, your
father is not so much thinner than I am, nor much shorter;
he and I will walk up together to my wardrobe; though it
is not so well stored here, as in Bedfordshire.

And so, said he, pleasantly, don't you pretend to come
near us, till I call for you; for you must not yet see how
men dress and undress themselves. Oh, sir, said my father,
I beg to be excused. I am sorry you were told. So am
not I, said my master: Pray come along with me.

He carried him upstairs, and showed him several suits,

and would have had him take his choice. My poor father
was quite confounded: for my master saw not any he
thought too good, and my father none that he thought bad
enough. And my good master, at last (he fixed his eye
upon a fine drab, which he thought looked the plainest),
would help him to try the coat and waistcoat on himself;
and, indeed, one would not have thought it, because my
master is taller, and rather plumper, as I thought; but, as
I saw afterwards, they fitted him very well: And being
plain, and lined with the same colour, and made for travelling in a coach, pleased my poor father much. He gave
him the whole suit, and, calling up Mrs. Jewkes, said, Let
these clothes be well aired against to-morrow morning.
Mr. Andrews brought only with him his common apparel,
not thinking to stay Sunday with us. And pray see for
some of my stockings, and whether any of my shoes will fit
him: And see also for some of my linen; for we have
put the good man quite out of his course, by keeping him
Sunday over. He was then pleased to give him the silver
buckles out of his own shoes. So, my good mother, you
must expect to see my dear father a great beau. Wig,
said my master, he wants none; for his own venerable
white locks are better than all the perukes in England.—
But I am sure I have hats enough somewhere.—I'll take
care of everything, sir, said Mrs. Jewkes.—And my poor
father, when he came to me, could not refrain tears. I
know not how, said he, to comport myself under these great
favours. Oh my child, it is all owing to the divine goodness,
and your virtue.

——o——

Sunday.

THIS blessed day all the family seemed to take delight to
equip themselves for the celebration of the Sabbath in the
little chapel; and Lady Jones and Mr. Williams came in
her chariot, and the two Misses Darnford in their own.
And we breakfasted together in a most agreeable manner.
My dear father appeared quite spruce and neat, and was

greatly caressed by the three ladies. As we were at breakfast, my master told Mr. Williams, We must let the Psalms
alone, he doubted, for want of a clerk: but Mr. Williams
said, No, nothing should be wanting that he could supply.
My father said, If it might be permitted him, he would, as
well as he was able, perform that office; for it was always
what he had taken delight in. And as I knew he had learnt
psalmody formerly, in his youth, and had constantly practised it in private, at home, on Sunday evenings (as well
as endeavoured to teach it in the little school he so unsuc-
cessfully set up, at the beginning of his misfortunes, before
he took to hard labour), I was in no pain for his undertak-
ing it in this little congregation. They seemed much
pleased with this; and so we went to chapel, and made a
pretty tolerable appearance; Mrs. Jewkes, and all the servants, attending, but the cook: And I never saw divine
service performed with more solemnity, nor assisted at with
greater devotion and decency; my master, Lady Jones, and
the two misses, setting a lovely example.

My good father performed his part with great applause,
making the responses, as if he had been a practised parish-
clerk; and giving the xxiiid psalm,* which consisting of

> * The Lord is only my support,
>   And He that doth me feed:
> How can I then lack anything
>   Whereof I stand in need?
> In pastures green He feedeth me,
>   Where I do safely lie;
> And after leads me to the streams,
>   Which run most pleasantly.
>
> And when I find myself near lost,
>   Then home He doth me take;
> Conducting me in His right paths,
>   E'en for His own name's sake.
> And tho' I were e'en at death's door,
>   Yet would I fear no ill:
> For both Thy rod and shepherd's crook
>   Afford me comfort still.
>
> Thou hast my table richly spread
>   In presence of my foe:

but three staves, we had it all; and he read the line, and began the tune with a heart so entirely affected with the duty, that he went through it distinctly, calmly, and fervently at the same time; so that Lady Jones whispered me, That good man were fit for all companies, and present to every laudable occasion: and Miss Darnford said, God bless the dear good man!—You must think how I rejoiced in my mind.

I know, my dear mother, you can say most of the shortest psalms by heart; so I need not transcribe it, especially as your chief treasure is a Bible; and a worthy treasure it is. I know nobody makes more or better use of it.

Mr. Williams gave us an excellent discourse on liberality and generosity, and the blessings attending the right use of riches, from the xith chapter of Proverbs, ver. 24, 25. *There is that scattereth, and yet increaseth; and there is that withholdeth more than is meet, but it tendeth to poverty. The liberal soul shall be made fat: And he that watereth, shall be watered also himself.* And he treated the subject in so handsome a manner, that my master's delicacy, who, at first, was afraid of some personal compliments, was not offended. Mr. Williams judiciously keeping to generals; and it was an elegant and sensible discourse, as my master said.

My father was in the clerk's place, just under the desk; and Lady Jones, by her footman, whispered him to favour us with another psalm, when the sermon was ended. He thinking, as he said afterwards, that the former was rather of the longest, chose the shortest in the book, which you know is the cxviith.*

> Thou hast my head with balm refresh'd,
>   My cup doth overflow.
> And finally, while breath doth last,
>   Thy grace shall me defend:
> And in the house of God will I
>   My life for ever spend.

> * O all ye nations of the world,
>   Praise ye the Lord always:

My master thanked Mr. Williams for his excellent discourse, and so did the ladies; as also did I most heartily:
and he was pleased to take my dear father by the hand,
as did also Mr. Williams, and thanked him. The ladies,
likewise, made him their compliments; and the servants
all looked upon him with countenances of respect and
pleasure.

At dinner, do what I could, I was forced to take the
upper end of the table; and my master sat at the lower
end, between Mr. Williams and my father. And he said,
Pamela, you are so dexterous, that I think you may help
the ladies yourself; and I will help my two good friends.
I should have told you, though, that I dressed myself in a
flowered satin, that was my lady's, and looked quite fresh
and good, and which was given me, at first, by my master;
and the ladies, who had not seen me out of my homespun
before, made me abundance of fine compliments, as soon
as they saw me first.

Talking of the psalms just after dinner, my master was
very naughty, if I may so say: For he said to my father,
Mr. Andrews, I think in the afternoon, as we shall have
only prayers, we may have one longer psalm; and what
think you of the cxxxviith? Oh, good sir! said I, pray,
pray, not a word more! Say what you will, Pamela, said
he, you shall sing it to us, according to your own version,
before these good ladies go away. My father smiled, but
was half concerned for me; and said, Will it bear, and
please your honour?—Oh ay, said he, never fear it; so
long as Mrs. Jewkes is not in the hearing.

This excited all the ladies' curiosity; and Lady Jones
said, She would be loath to desire to hear anything that
would give me concern; but should be glad I would give
leave for it. Indeed, madam, said I, I must beg you

And all ye people everywhere
Set forth His noble praise.
For great His kindness is to us;
His truth doth not decay:
Wherefore praise ye the Lord our God;
Praise ye the Lord alway.

won't insist upon it. I cannot bear it.—You shall see it, indeed, ladies, said my master; and pray, Pamela, not always as *you* please, neither.—Then, pray, sir, said I, not in my hearing, I hope.—Sure, Pamela, returned he, you would not write what is not fit to be heard!—But, sir, said I, there are particular cases, times, and occasions, that may make a thing passable at one time, that would not be tolerable at another. Oh, said he, let me judge of that, as well as you, Pamela. These ladies know a good part of your story; and, let me tell you, what they know is more to your credit than mine; so that if I have no averseness to reviving the occasion, you may very well bear it. Said he, I will put you out of your pain, Pamela: here it is: and took it out of his pocket.

I stood up, and said, Indeed, sir, I can't bear it; I hope you'll allow me to leave the room a minute, if you will read it. Indeed but I won't, answered he. Lady Jones said, Pray, good sir, don't let us hear it, if Mrs. Andrews be so unwilling. Well, Pamela, said my master, I will put it to your choice, whether I shall read it now, or you will sing it by and by. That's very hard, sir, said I. It must be one, I assure you, said he. Why then, sir, replied I, you must do as you please; for I cannot sing it.

Well, then, said my master, I find I must read it; and yet, added he, after all, I had as well let it alone, for it is no great reputation to myself. Oh then, said Miss Darnford, pray let us hear it, to choose.

Why then, proceeded he, the case was this: Pamela, I find, when she was in the time of her confinement (that is, added he, when she was taken prisoner, in order to make me one; for that is the upshot of the matter), in the Journal she kept, which was intended for nobody's perusal but her parents, tells them, that she was importuned, one Sunday, by Mrs. Jewkes, to sing a psalm; but her spirits not permitting, she declined it: But after Mrs. Jewkes was gone down, she says, she recollected, that the cxxxviith psalm was applicable to her own case; Mrs. Jewkes hav-

ing often, on other days, in vain, besought her to sing a
song: That thereupon she turned it more to her own supposed case; and believing Mrs. Jewkes had a design against
her honour, and looking upon her as her gaoler, she thus
•gives her version of this psalm. But pray, Mr. Williams,
do you read one verse of the common translation, and I
will read one of Pamela's. Then Mr. Williams, pulling
out his little pocket Common Prayer-book, read the first
two stanzas:

I.

When we did sit in Babylon,
   The rivers round about ;
Then in remembrance of Sion,
   The tears for grief burst out.

II.

We hang'd our harps and instruments
   The willow trees upon :
For in that place, men, for that use,
   Had planted many a one.

My master then read:

I.

When sad I sat in B——n hall,
   All guarded round about,
And thought of ev'ry absent friend,
   The tears for grief burst out.

II.

My joys and hopes all overthrown,
   My heart-strings almost broke,
Unfit my mind for melody,
   Much more to bear a joke.

The ladies said, It was very pretty; and Miss Darnford,
That somebody else had more need to be concerned than
the versifier.

I knew, said my master, I should get no credit by
showing this. But let us read on, Mr. Williams. So
Mr. Williams read:

III. .

Then they, to whom we pris'ners were,
   Said to us tauntingly,
Now let us hear your Hebrew songs,
   And pleasant melody.

Now this, said my master, is very near ; and read :

III.

Then she, to whom I prisoner was,
   Said to me tauntingly,
Now cheer your heart, and sing a song,
   And tune your mind to joy.

Mighty sweet, said Mr. Williams. But let us see how the next verse is turned. It is this :

IV.

Alas ! said we ; who can once frame
   His heavy heart to sing
The praises of our living God,
   Thus under a strange king ?

Why, said my master, it is turned with beautiful simplicity, thus :

IV.

Alas ! said I, how can I frame
   My heavy heart to sing,
Or tune my mind, while thus enthrall'd
   By such a wicked thing ?

Very pretty, said Mr. Williams. Lady Jones said, Oh, dear madam! could you wish that we should be deprived of this new instance of your genius and accomplishments ?

Oh! said my dear father, you will make my good child proud. No, said my master very generously, Pamela can't be proud. For no one is proud to hear themselves praised, but those who are not used to it.—But proceed, Mr. Williams. He read :

V.

But yet, if I Jerusalem
   Out of my heart let slide ;

> Then let my fingers quite forget
> The warbling harp to guide.

Well, now, said my master, for Pamela's version:

V.

> But yet, if from my innocence
> I ev'n in thought should slide,
> Then let my fingers quite forget
> The sweet spinnet to guide.

Mr. Williams read:

VI.

> And let my tongue, within my mouth,
> Be ty'd for ever fast,
> If I rejoice, before I see
> Thy full deliv'rance past.

This, also, said my master, is very near:

VI.

> And let my tongue, within my mouth,
> Be lock'd for ever fast,
> If I rejoice, before I see
> My full deliv'rance past.

Now, good sir, said I, oblige me; don't read any further: pray don't! Oh pray, madam, said Mr. Williams, let me beg to have the rest read; for I long to know whom you make the Sons of Edom, and how you turn the Psalmist's execrations against the insulting Babylonians.

Well, Mr. Williams, replied I, *you* should not have said so. Oh, said my master, that is one of the best things of all. Poor Mrs. Jewkes stands for Edom's Sons; and we must not lose this, because I think it one of my Pamela's excellences, that, though thus oppressed, she prays for no harm upon the oppressor. Read, Mr. Williams, the next stanza. So he read:

VII.

> Therefore, O Lord! remember now
> The cursed noise and cry,

That Edom's sons against us made,
　When they ras'd our city.

VIII.

Remember, Lord, their cruel words,
　When, with a mighty sound,
They cried, Down, yea down with it,
　Unto the very ground !

Well, said my master, here seems, in what I am going to
read, a little bit of a curse indeed, but I think it makes no
ill figure in the comparison.

VII.

And thou, Almighty ! recompense
　The evils I endure
From those who seek my sad disgrace,
　So causeless, to procure.

And now, said he, for Edom's Sons. Though a little
severe in the imputation.

VIII.

Remember, Lord, this Mrs. Jewkes,
　When with a mighty sound,
She cries, Down with her chastity,
　Down to the very ground !

Sure, sir, said I, this might have been spared! But the
ladies and Mr. Williams said, No, by no means! And I see
the poor wicked woman has no favourers among them.

Now, said my master, read the Psalmist's heavy curses:
and Mr. Williams read :

IX.

Ev'n so shalt thou, O Babylon !
　At length to dust be brought :
And happy shall that man be call'd,
　That our revenge hath wrought.

X.

Yea, blessed shall that man be call'd
　That takes thy little ones,

> And dasheth them in pieces small
>   Against the very stones.

Thus he said, very kindly, has *my* Pamela turned these lines:

IX.

> Ev'n so shalt thou, O wicked one!
>   At length to shame be brought;
> And happy shall all those be call'd,
>   That my deliv'rance wrought.

X.

> Yea, blessed shall the man be call'd
>   That shames thee of thy evil,
> And saves me from thy vile attempts,
>   And thee, too, from the d——l.

I fancy this blessed man, said my master, smiling, was, at that time, hoped to be you, Mr. Williams, if the truth was known. Sir, said he, whoever it was intended for *then*, it can be nobody but your good self *now*.

I could hardly hold up my head for the praises the kind ladies were pleased to heap upon me. I am sure, by this, they are very partial in my favour; all because my master is so good to me, and loves to hear me praised; for I see no such excellence in these lines, as they would make me believe, besides what is borrowed from the Psalmist.

We all, as before, and the cook-maid too, attended the prayers of the church in the afternoon; and my dear father concluded with the following stanzas of the cxlvth psalm; suitably magnifying the holy name of God for all mercies; but did not observe, altogether, the method in which they stand; which was the less necessary, he thought, as he gave out the lines.

> The Lord is just in all His ways:
>   His works are holy all:
> And He is near all those that do
>   In truth upon Him call.

> He the desires of all them
>   That fear Him, will fulfil;

And He will hear them when they cry,
And save them all He will.

The eyes of all do wait on Thee;
Thou dost them all relieve:
And Thou to each sufficient food,
In season due, dost give.

Thou openest Thy plenteous hand,
And bounteously dost fill
All things whatever, that do live,
With gifts of Thy good will.

My thankful mouth shall gladly speak
The praises of the Lord:
All flesh, to praise His holy name,
For ever shall accord.

We walked in the garden till tea was ready; and as he went by the back-door, my master said to me, *Of all the flowers in the garden, the sunflower is the fairest!*—Oh, sir, said I, let that be now forgot! Mr. Williams heard him say so, and seemed a little out of countenance: Whereupon my master said, I mean not to make you serious, Mr. Williams; but we see how strangely things are brought about. I see other scenes hereabouts, that, in my Pamela's dangers, give me more cause of concern, than anything you ever did should give you. Sir, said he, you are very generous.

My master and Mr. Williams afterwards walked together for a quarter of an hour; and talked about general things, and some scholastic subjects; and joined us, very well pleased with one another's conversation.

Lady Jones said, putting herself on one side of me, as my master was on the other, But pray, sir, when is the happy time to be? We want it over, that we may have you with us as long afterwards as you can. Said my master, I would have it to-morrow, or next day at farthest, if Pamela will: for I have sent for a license, and the messenger will be here to-night, or early in the morning, I hope. But, added he, pray, Pamela, do not take beyond Thursday. She was pleased to say, Sure it will not be delayed by you, madam, more than needs!—Well, said he, now you are on my side, I will leave you with her to settle it: and, I hope, she will not let little bashful niceties be important with her; and so he joined the two misses.

Lady Jones told me, I was to blame, she would take upon her to say, if I delayed it a moment; because she understood Lady Davers was very uneasy at the prospect, that it would be so; and if anything should happen, it would be a sad thing!—Madam, said I, when he was pleased to mention it to me first, he said it should be in fourteen days; and afterwards, asked me if I would have it in the first or the second seven? I answered—for how could I do otherwise?—In the second. He desired it might not be the last day of the second seven. Now, madam, said I, as he was then pleased to speak his mind, no doubt, I would not, for anything, seem too forward.

Well, but, said she, as he now urges you in so genteel and gentlemanly a manner for a shorter day, I think, if I was in your place, I would agree to it. She saw me hesitate and blush, and said, Well, you know best; but I say only what I would do. I said, I would consider of it; and if I saw he was very earnest, to be sure I should think I ought to oblige him.

Misses Darnford were begging to be at the wedding, and to have a ball: and they said, Pray, Mrs. Andrews, second our requests, and we shall be greatly obliged to you. Indeed, ladies, said I, I cannot promise that, if I might.— Why so? said they.—Because, answered I, I know not what! But I think one may, with pleasure, celebrate an *anniversary* of one's nuptials; but the *day itself.*—Indeed, ladies, I think it is too solemn a business, for the *parties* of our sex to be very gay upon: it is a quite serious and awful affair: and I am sure, in your own cases, you would be of my mind. Why, then, said Miss Darnford, the more need one has to be as light-hearted and merry as one can.

I told you, said my master, what sort of an answer you'd have from Pamela. The younger miss said, She never heard

of such grave folks in her life, on such an occasion: Why,
sir, said she, I hope you'll sing psalms all day, and miss will
fast and pray! Such sackcloth and ashes doings, for a wedding, did I never hear of!—She spoke a little spitefully, I
thought; and I returned no answer. I shall have enough
to do, I reckon, in a while, if I am to answer every one that
will envy me!

We went in to tea; and all that the ladies could prevail
upon my master for, was a dancing match before he left this
county: But Miss Darnford said, it should then be at their
house; for, truly, if she might not be at the wedding, she
would be affronted, and come no more hither, till we had
been there.

When they were gone, my master would have had my
father stay till the affair was over; but he begged he might
set out as soon as it was light in the morning; for, he said,
my mother would be doubly uneasy at his stay; and he
burned with impatience to let her know all the happy things
that had befallen her daughter. When my master found
him so desirous to go, he called Mr. Thomas, and ordered
him to get a particular bay horse ready betimes in the
morning, for my father, and a portmanteau, to put his
things in; and to attend him a day's journey: And if,
said he, Mr. Andrews chooses it, see him safe to his own
home: And, added he, since that horse will serve you, Mr.
Andrews, to ride backwards and forwards, to see us, when
we go into Bedfordshire, I make you a present of it, with
the accoutrements. And, seeing my father going to speak,
he added, I won't be said nay. Oh how good was this!

He also said a great many kind things at supper-time,
and gave him all the papers he had of mine; but desired,
when he and my mother had read them, that he would
return them to him again. And then he said, So affectionate a father and daughter may, perhaps, be glad to be alone
together; therefore remember me to your good wife, and
tell her, it will not be long, I hope, before I see you together, on a visit to your daughter, at my other house: and
so I wish you good-night, and a good journey, if you go

before I see you. And then he shook hands, and left my
dear father almost unable to speak, through the sense of
his favours and goodness.

You may believe, my dear mother, how loath I was to
part with my good father; and he was also unwilling to
part with me; but he was so impatient to see you, and tell
you the blessed tidings, with which his heart overflowed,
that I could hardly wish to detain him.

Mrs. Jewkes brought two bottles of cherry-brandy, and
two of cinnamon-water, and some cake; and they were
put up in the portmanteau, with my father's newly presented clothes; for he said, he would not, for anything,
be seen in them in his neighbourhood, till I was actually
known, by everybody, to be married; nor would he lay
out any part of the twenty guineas till then neither, for
fear of reflections; and then he would consult me as to
what he would buy. Well, said I, as you please, my dear
father; and I hope now we shall often have the pleasure
of hearing from one another, without needing any art or
contrivances.

He said, he would go to bed betimes, that he might be
up as soon as it was light; and so he took leave of me, and
said, he would not love me, if I got up in the morning to
see him go; which would but make us both loath to part,
and grieve us both all day.

Mr. Thomas brought him a pair of boots, and told him,
he would call him up at peep of day, and put up everything over night; and so I received his blessing, and his
prayers, and his kind promises of procuring the same from
you, my dear mother; and went up to my closet with a
heavy heart, and yet a half-pleased one, if I may so say;
for that, as he must go, he was going to the best of wives,
and with the best of tidings. But I begged he would not
work so hard as he had done; for I was sure my master
would not have given him twenty guineas for clothes, if he
had not designed to do something else for him; and that he
should be the less concerned at receiving benefits from my
good master, because he, who had so many persons to employ

in his large possessions, could make him serviceable, to a
degree equivalent, without hurting anybody else.

He promised me fair; and, pray, dear mother, see he
performs. I hope my master will not see this: for I will
not send it you, at present, till I can send you the best of
news; and the rather, as my dear father can supply the
greatest part of what I have written, *since* the papers he
carries you, by his own observation. So good-night, my
dear mother: And God send my father a safe journey, and
a happy meeting to you both!

—o—

Monday.

MR. COLBRAND being returned, my master came up to me
to my closet, and brought me the license. Oh how my heart
fluttered at the sight of it! Now, Pamela, said he, tell me,
if you can oblige me with the day. Your word is all that's
wanting. I made bold to kiss his dear hand; and, though
unable to look up, said—I know not what to say, sir, to all
your goodness: I would not, for any consideration, that
you should believe me capable of receiving negligently an
honour, that all the duty of a long life, were it to be lent
me, will not be sufficient to enable me to be grateful for.
I ought to resign myself, in everything I may or can,
implicitly to your will. But—But what? said he, with a
kind impatience.—Why, sir, said I, when from last Thursday
you mentioned four days, I had reason to think that term
your choice; and my heart is so wholly yours, that I am
afraid of nothing, but that I may be forwarder than you
wish. Impossible, my dear creature! said he, and folded
me in his arms: Impossible! If this be all, it shall be set
about this moment, and this happy day shall make you
mine!—I'll send away instantly, said the dear gentleman;
and was going.

I said, No, pray, sir, pray, sir, hear me!—Indeed it cannot
be to-day!—Cannot! said he.—No, indeed, sir! said I—And
was ready to sink to see his generous impatience. Why

flattered you then my fond heart, replied he, with the hope
that it might?—Sir, said I, I will tell you what I had
thought, if you'll vouchsafe me your attention. Do then,
said he.

I have, sir, proceeded I, a great desire, that, whenever the
day is, it may be on a Thursday: On a Thursday my dear
father and mother were married; and, though poor, they
are a very happy pair.—On a Thursday your poor Pamela
was born. On a Thursday my dear good lady took me from
my parents into her protection. On a Thursday, sir, you
caused me to be carried away to this place, to which I now,
by God's goodness and your favour, owe so amazingly all
my present prospects; and on a Thursday it was, you named
to me, that fourteen days from that you would confirm my
happiness. Now, sir, if you please to indulge my superstitious folly, you will greatly oblige me. I was sorry, sir,
for this reason, when you bid me not defer till the last day
of the fourteen, that Thursday in next week was that last
day.

This, Pamela, is a little superstitious, I must needs say;
and I think you should begin now to make another day in
the week a happy one; as for example; on a Monday, may
you say, my father and mother concluded to be married on
the Thursday following. On a Monday, so many years ago,
my mother was preparing all her matters to be brought
to bed on the Thursday following. On a Monday, several
weeks ago, it was that you had but two days more to stay,
till you was carried away on Thursday. On a Monday, I
myself, said he, well remember, it was that I wrote you the
letter, that prevailed on you so kindly to return to me;
and on the same day you *did* return to my house here;
which I hope, my girl, will be as propitious an era as any
you have named: And now, lastly, will you say, which will
crown the work; And, on a Monday I was married.—Come,
come, my dear, added he, Thursday has reigned long enough
o'conscience; let us now set Monday in its place, or at least
on an equality with it, since you see it has a very good title,
and as we now stand in the week before us, claims priority:

And then, I hope, we shall make Tuesday, Wednesday, Friday, Saturday, and Sunday, as happy days as Monday and Thursday; and so, by God's blessing, move round, as the days move, in a delightful circle, till we are at a loss what day to prefer to the rest.

Oh how charmingly was this said!—And how sweetly kind!

Indeed, sir, said I, you rally my folly very agreeably; but don't let a little matter stand in the way, when you are so generously obliging in a greater: indeed I like Thursday best, if I may choose.

Well, then, said he, if you can say you have a better reason than this, I will oblige you; else I'll send away for the parson this moment.

And so, I protest, he was going!—Dear sirs, how I trembled! Stay, stay, sir, said I: we have a great deal to say first; I have a deal of silly prate to trouble you with!—Well, say then, in a minute, replied he, the most material: for all we have to say may be talked of while the parson is coming.—Oh, but indeed, and indeed, said I, it cannot be to-day!—Well, then, shall it be to-morrow? said he.—Why, sir, if it must not be on a Thursday, you have given so many pleasant distinctions for a Monday, that let it then be next Monday.—What! a week still? said he. Sir, answered I, if you please; for that will be, as you enjoined, within the second seven days. Why, girl, said he, 'twill be seven months till next Monday. Let it, said he, if not to-morrow, be on Wednesday; I protest I will stay no longer.

Then, sir, returned I, please to defer it, however, for *one* day more, and it will be my beloved Thursday! If I consent to defer it till then, may I hope, my Pamela, said he, that next Thursday shall *certainly* be the happy day?—*Yes, sir*, said I: and I am sure I looked very foolishly!

And yet, my dear father and mother, why should I, with such a fine gentleman? And whom I so dearly love? And so much to my honour too? But there is something greatly awful upon my mind, in the solemn circumstance, and a change of condition never to be recalled, though all the prospects are so desirable. And I can but wonder at the thoughtless precipitancy with which most young folks run into this important change of life!

So now, my dear parents, have I been brought to fix so near a day as next Thursday; and this is Monday. Oh dear, it makes one out of breath almost to think of it! This, though, was a great cut off; a whole week out of ten days. I hope I am not too forward! I'm sure, if it obliges my dear master, I am justified; for he deserves of me all things in my poor power.

After this, he rode out on horseback, attended by Abraham, and did not return till night. How by degrees things steal upon one! I thought even this small absence tedious; and the more, as we expected him home to dinner.—I wish I may not be too fond, and make him indifferent: But yet, my dear father and mother, you were always fond of one another, and never indifferent, let the world run as it would.

When he returned, he said, he had had a pleasant ride, and was led out to a greater distance than he intended. At supper he told me, that he had a great mind Mr. Williams should marry us; because, he said, it would show a thorough reconciliation on his part. But, said he, most generously, I am apprehensive, from what passed between you, that the poor man will take it hardly, and as a sort of insult, which I am not capable of. What says my girl?— Do you think he would? I hope not, sir, said I: As to what he *may* think, I can't answer; but as to any reason for his thoughts, I can: For indeed, sir, said I, you have been already so generous, that he cannot, I think, mistake your goodness.

He then spoke with some resentment of Lady Davers's behaviour, and I asked, if anything new had occurred? Yes, said he; I have had a letter delivered me from her impertinent husband, professedly at her instigation, that amounted to little less than a piece of insolent bravery, on supposing I was about to marry you. I was so provoked, added he, that after I had read it, I tore it in a hundred pieces, and scattered them in the air, and bid the man who brought it let his master know what I had done with his letter; and so would not permit him to speak to me, as he would fain have done.—I think the fellow talked somewhat of his lady coming hither; but she shall not set her foot within my doors; and I suppose this treatment will hinder her.

I was much concerned at this: And he said, Had I a hundred sisters, Pamela, their opposition should have no weight with me: and I did not intend you should know it; but you can't but expect a little difficulty from the pride of my sister, who have suffered so much from that of her brother; and we are too nearly allied in mind, as well as blood, I find.—But this is not *her* business: And if she would have made it so, she should have done it with more *decency.* Little occasion had *she* to boast of her birth, that knows not what belongs to good manners.

I said, I am very sorry, sir, to be the unhappy occasion of a misunderstanding between so good a brother and so worthy a sister. Don't say so, Pamela, because this is an unavoidable consequence of the happy prospect before us. Only bear it well yourself, because she is my sister; and leave it to me to make her sensible of her own rashness.

If, sir, said I, the most lowly behaviour, and humble deportment, and in everything showing a dutiful regard to good Lady Davers, will have any weight with her ladyship, assure yourself of all in my power to mollify her. No, Pamela, returned he; don't imagine, when you are my wife, I will suffer you to do anything unworthy of that character. I know the duty of a husband, and will protect your gentleness to the utmost, as much as if you were a princess by descent.

You are inexpressibly good, sir, said I; but I am far from taking a gentle disposition to show a meanness of spirit: And this is a trial I ought to expect; and well I may bear it, that have so many benefits to set against it, which all spring from the same cause.

Well, said he, all the matter shall be this: We will talk of our marriage as a thing to be done next week. I find I have spies upon me wherever I go, and whatever I do: But now, I am on *so* laudable a pursuit, that I value them not, nor those who employ them. I have already ordered my servants to have no conference with anybody for ten or twelve days to come. And Mrs. Jewkes tells me every one names Thursday come se'nnight for our nuptials. So I will get Mr. Peters, who wants to see my little chapel, to assist Mr. Williams, under the notion of breakfasting with me next Thursday morning, since you won't have it sooner; and there will nobody else be wanting; and I will beg of Mr. Peters to keep it private, even from his own family, for a few days. Has my girl any objection?

Oh, sir, answered I, you, are so generous in all your ways, I *can* have no objections!—But I hope Lady Davers and you will not proceed to irreconcileable lengths; and when her ladyship comes to see you, and to tarry with you, two or three weeks, as she used to do, I will keep close up, so as not to disgust her with the sight of me.

Well, Pamela, said he, we will talk of that afterwards. You must do then as I shall think fit: And I shall be able to judge what both you and I ought to do. But what still aggravates the matter is, that she should instigate the titled ape her husband to write to me, after she had so little succeeded herself. I wish I had kept his letter, that I might have shown you how a man, that generally *acts* like a fool, can take upon him to write like a lord. But I suppose it is of my sister's penning, and he, poor man! is the humble copier.

—— o ——

Tuesday.

Mr. Thomas is returned from you, my dear father, with the good news of your health, and your proceeding in your journey to my dear mother, where I hope to hear soon you are arrived. My master has just now been making me play upon the spinnet, and sing to it; and was pleased to commend me for both. But he does so for everything I do, so partial does his goodness make him to me.

WE are just returned from an airing in the chariot; and I have been delighted with his conversation upon English authors, poets particularly. He entertained me also with a description of some of the curiosities he had seen in Italy and France, when he made what the polite world call the grand tour. He said he wanted to be at his other seat, for he knew not well how to employ himself here, having not proposed to stay half the time: And when I get there, Pamela, said he, you will hardly be troubled with so much of my company, after we have settled; for I have a great many things to adjust: And I must go to London; for I have accounts that have run on longer than ordinary with my banker there. And I don't know, added he, but the ensuing winter I may give you a little taste of the diversions of the town for a month or so. I said, his will and pleasure should determine mine; and I never would, as near as I could, have a desire after those, or any other entertainments that were not in his own choice.

He was pleased to say, I make no doubt but that I shall be very happy in you; and hope you will be so in me: For, said he, I have no very enormous vices to gratify; though I pretend not to the greatest purity, neither, my girl. Sir, said I, if you can account to your own mind, I shall always be easy in whatever you do. But our greatest happiness here, sir, continued I, is of very short duration; and this life, at the longest, is a poor transitory one; and I hope we shall be so happy as to be enabled to look forward, with comfort, to another, where our pleasures will be everlasting.

You say well, Pamela; and I shall, by degrees, be more habituated to this way of thinking, as I more and more converse with you; but, at present, you must not be over serious with me all at once: though I charge you never forbear to mingle your sweet divinity in our conversation, whenever it can be brought in *à propos,* and with such a cheerfulness of temper, as shall not throw a gloomy cloud over our innocent enjoyments.

I was abashed at this, and silent, fearing I had offended: But he said, If you attend rightly to what I said, I need not tell you again, Pamela, not to be discouraged from suggesting to me, on every proper occasion, the pious impulses of your own amiable mind. Sir, said I, you will be always indulgent, I make no doubt, to my imperfections, so long as I mean well.

My master made me dine with him, and would eat nothing but what I helped him to; and my heart is, every hour, more and more enlarged with his goodness and condescension. But still, what ails me, I wonder! A strange sort of weight hangs upon my mind, as Thursday draws on, which makes me often sigh involuntarily, and damps, at times, the pleasures of my delightful prospects!—I hope this is not ominous; but only the foolish weakness of an over-thoughtful mind, on an occasion the most solemn and important of one's life, next to the last scene, which shuts up all.

I could be very serious: But I will commit all my ways to that blessed Providence, which hitherto has so wonderfully conducted me through real evils to this hopeful situation.

I only fear, and surely I have great reason, that I shall be too unworthy to hold the affections of so dear a gentleman!—God teach me humility, and to know my own demerit! And this will be, next to His grace, my surest guard, in the state of life to which, though most unworthy, I am going to be exalted. And don't cease your prayers for me, my dear parents; for, perhaps, this new condition may be subject to still worse hazards than those I have escaped; as would be the case, were conceitedness, vanity, and pride, to take hold of my frail heart; and if I was, for my sins, to be left to my own conduct, a frail bark in a tempestuous ocean, without ballast, or other pilot than my own inconsiderate will. But my master said, on another occasion, That those who doubted most, always erred least; and I hope I shall always doubt my own strength, my own worthiness.

I will not trouble you with twenty sweet agreeable things

that passed in conversation with my excellent benefactor;
nor with the civilities of M. Colbrand, Mrs. Jewkes, and
all the servants, who seem to be highly pleased with me,
and with my conduct to them: And as my master, hitherto,
finds no fault that I go too low, nor they that I carry it too
high, I hope I shall continue to have everybody's good-
will: But yet will I not seek to gain any one's by little
meannesses or debasements! but aim at an uniform and
regular conduct, willing to conceal *involuntary* errors, as I
would have my own forgiven; and not too industrious to
discover *real* ones, or to hide such, if any such should appear,
as might encourage bad hearts, or unclean hands, in material
cases, where my master should receive damage, or where
the morals of the transgressors should appear wilfully and
habitually corrupt. In short, I will endeavour, as much as
I can, that good servants shall find in me a kind encourager;
indifferent ones be made better, by inspiring them with a
laudable emulation; and bad ones, if not too bad in nature,
and quite irreclaimable, reformed by kindness, expostulation,
and even proper menaces, if necessary; but most by a good
example: All this if God pleases.

—————*o*· ·———

Wednesday.

Now, my dear parents, I have but this *one* day between me
and the most solemn rite that can be performed. My heart
cannot yet shake off this heavy weight. Sure I am ungrateful to the divine goodness, and the favour of the best of
benefactors!—Yet I hope I am not!—For, at times, my
mind is all exultation, with the prospect of what good to-
morrow's happy solemnity may possibly, by the leave of my
generous master, put it in my power to do. Oh how shall
I find words to express, as I ought, my thankfulness, for all
the mercies before me!——

—————*o*———

My dear master is all love and tenderness! He sees my
weakness, and generously pities and comforts me! I begged
to be excused supper; but he brought me down himself
from my closet, and placed me by him, bidding Abraham
not wait. I could not eat, and yet I tried, for fear he
should be angry. He kindly forbore to hint anything of
the dreadful, yet delightful to-morrow! and put, now and
then, a little bit on my plate, and guided it to my mouth.
I was concerned to receive his goodness with so ill a grace.
Well, said he, if you won't eat with me, drink at least with
me: I drank two glasses by his over-persuasions, and said,
I am really ashamed of myself. Why, indeed, said he, my
dear girl, I am not a very dreadful enemy, I hope! I cannot bear anything that is the least concerning to you. Oh,
sir! said I, all is owing to the sense I have of my own
unworthiness!—To be sure, it cannot be anything else.

He rung for the things to be taken away; and then
reached a chair, and sat down by me, and put his kind
arms about me, and said the most generous and affecting
things that ever dropt from the honey-flowing mouth of
love. All I have not time to repeat: some I will. And
oh! indulge your foolish daughter, who troubles you with
her weak nonsense; because what she has to say, is so
affecting to her; and because, if she went to bed, instead
of scribbling, she could not sleep.

This sweet confusion and thoughtfulness in my beloved
Pamela, said the kind man, on the near approach of our
happy union, when I hope all doubts are cleared up, and
nothing of dishonour is apprehended, show me most abundantly, what a wretch I was to attempt such purity with
a worse intention: — No wonder, that one so virtuous
should find herself deserted of life itself on a violence so
dreadful to her honour, and seek a refuge in the shadow of
death.—But now, my dearest Pamela, that you have seen
a purity on my side, as nearly imitating your own, as
our sex can show to yours; and since I have, all the day

long, suppressed even the least intimation of the coming
day, that I might not alarm your tender mind; why all
this concern, why all this affecting, yet sweet confusion?
You have a generous friend, my dear girl, in me; a protector now, not a violator of your innocence: Why then,
once more I ask, this strange perplexity, this sweet confusion?

Oh, sir, said I, and hid my face on his arm; expect not
reason from a foolish creature; you should have still indulged me in my closet: I am ready to beat myself for this
ungrateful return to your goodness. But I know not what!
—I am, to be sure, a silly creature! Oh had you but suffered
me to stay by myself above, I should have made myself
ashamed of so culpable a behaviour!—But goodness added
to goodness every moment, and the sense of my own unworthiness, quite overcome my spirits.

Now, said the generous man, will I, though reluctantly,
make a proposal to my sweet girl.—If I have been too pressing for the day: If another day will still be more obliging:
If you have fears you will not then have; you shall say but
the word, and I'll submit. Yes, my Pamela; for though I
have, these three days past, thought every tedious hour a
day, till Thursday comes, if you earnestly desire it, I will
postpone it. Say, my dear girl, *freely* say; but accept not
my proposal, without great reason, which yet I will not
ask for.

Sir, said I, I can expect nothing but superlative goodness,
I have been so long used to it from you. This is a most
generous instance of it; but I fear—yes, I fear it will be
too much the same thing, some days hence, when the
happy, yet, fool that I am! dreaded time, shall be equally
near!——

Kind, lovely charmer! said he, now do I see you are to
be trusted with power, from the generous use you make of
it!—Not one offensive word or look, from me, shall wound
your nicest thoughts; but pray try to subdue this over-
scrupulousness, and unseasonable timidity. I persuade
myself you will if you can.

Indeed, sir, I will, said I; for I am quite ashamed of myself, with all these lovely views before me!—The honours you do me, the kindness you show me!—I cannot forgive myself! For, oh! if I know the least of this idle foolish heart of mine, it has not a misgiving thought of your goodness; and I should abhor it, if it were capable of the least affectation.—But, dear good sir, leave me a little to myself, and I will take myself to a severer task than your goodness will let *you* do: and I will present my heart before you, a worthier offering to you, than at present its wayward follies will let it seem to be.—But one thing is, one has no kind friend of one's own sex, to communicate one's foolish thoughts to, and to be strengthened by their comfortings! But I am left to myself; and, oh! what a weak silly thing I am!

He kindly withdrew, to give me time to recollect myself; and in about half an hour returned: and then, that he might not begin at once upon the subject, and say, at the same time, something agreeable to me, said, Your father and mother have had a great deal of talk by this time about you, Pamela. Oh, sir, returned I, your goodness has made them quite happy! But I can't help being concerned about Lady Davers.

He said, I am vexed I did not hear the footman out; because it runs in my head he talked somewhat about her coming hither. She will meet with but an indifferent reception from me, unless she comes resolved to behave better than she writes.

Pray, sir, said I, be pleased to bear with my good lady, for two reasons. What are *they?* said he. Why, first, sir, answered I, because she is your sister; and, to be sure, may very well think, what all the world will, that you have much undervalued yourself in making me happy. And next, because, if her ladyship finds you out of temper with her, it will still aggravate her more against me; and every time that any warm words you may have between you, come into her mind, she will disdain me more.

Don't concern yourself about it, said he; for we have

more proud ladies than she in our other neighbourhood, who, perhaps, have still less reason to be punctilious about their descent, and yet will form themselves upon her example, and say, Why, his own sister will not forgive him, nor visit him! And so, if I can subdue her spirit, which is more than her husband ever could, or indeed anybody else, it is a great point gained: And, if she gives me reason, I'll try for it, I assure you.

Well, but, my dear girl, continued he, since the subject is so important, may I not say one word about to-morrow? —Sir, said I, I hope I shall be less a fool: I have talked as harshly to my heart, as Lady Davers can do; and the naughty thing suggests to me a better, and more grateful behaviour.

He smiled, and kissing me, said, I took notice, Pamela, of what you observed, that you have none of your own sex with you; I think it is a little hard upon you; and I should have liked you should have had Miss Darnford; but then her sister must have been asked; and I might as well make a public wedding: which, you know, would have required clothes and other preparations. Besides, added he, a foolish proposal was once made me of that second sister, who has two or three thousand pounds more than the other, left her by a godmother, and she can't help being a little piqued; though, said he, it was a proposal they could not expect should succeed: for there is nothing in her person nor mind; and her fortune, as that must have been the only inducement, would not do by any means; and so I discouraged it at once.

I am thinking, sir, said I, of another mortifying thing too; that were you to marry a lady of birth and fortune answerable to your own, all the eve to the day would be taken up in reading, signing, and sealing of settlements, and portion, and such like: But now the poor Pamela brings you nothing at all: And the very clothes she wears, so very low is she, are entirely the effects of your bounty, and that of your good mother: This makes me a little sad: For, alas! sir, I am so much oppressed by your favours, and the sense of the obligations I lie under, that I cannot look up with the confidence that I otherwise should on this awful occasion.

There is, my dear Pamela, said he, where the power is wanting, as much generosity in the will as in the action. To all that know your story, and your merit, it will appear that I cannot recompense you for what I have made you suffer. You have had too many hard struggles and exercises; and have nobly overcome: and who shall grudge you the reward of the hard-bought victory?—This affair is so much the act of my own will, that I glory in being capable of distinguishing so much excellence; and my fortune is the more pleasureable to me, as it gives me hope, that I may make you some part of satisfaction for what you have undergone.

This, sir, said I, is all goodness, unmerited on my side; and makes my obligations the greater. I can only wish for more worthiness.—But how poor is it to offer nothing but words for such generous deeds!—And to say, *I wish!* —For what is a wish, but the acknowledged want of power to oblige, and a demonstration of one's poverty in everything but *will?*

And that, my dear girl, said he, is everything: 'Tis all I want: 'Tis all that Heaven itself requires of us: But no more of these little doubts, though they are the natural impulses of a generous and grateful heart: I want not to be employed in settlements. Those are for such to regard, who make convenience and fortune the prime considerations. I have possessions ample enough for us both; and you deserve to share them with me; and you shall do it, with as little reserve, as if you had brought me what the world reckons an equivalent: for, as to my own opinion, you bring me what is infinitely more valuable, an experienced truth, a well-tried virtue, and a wit and behaviour more than equal to the station you will be placed in: To say nothing of this sweet person, that itself might captivate a monarch; and of the meekness of temper, and sweetness of disposition, which make you superior to all the women I ever saw.

Thus kind and soothing, and honourably affectionate, was the dear gentleman, to the unworthy, doubting, yet assured Pamela; and thus patiently did he indulge, and generously pardon, my impertinent weakness. He offered to go himself to Lady Jones in the morning, and reveal the matter to her, and desire her secrecy and presence; but I said, That would disoblige the young Ladies Darnford. No, sir, said I, I will cast myself upon your generous kindness; for why should I fear the kind protector of my weakness, and the guide and director of my future steps?

You cannot, said he, forgive Mrs. Jewkes; for *she* must know it; and suffer her to be with you? Yes, sir, said I, I can. She is very civil to me now: and her former wickedness I will forgive, for the sake of the happy fruits that have attended it; and because *you* mention her.

Well, said he, I will call her in, if you please.—As you please, sir, said I. And he rung for her; and when she came in, he said, Mrs. Jewkes, I am going to entrust you with a secret. Sir, answered she, I will be sure to keep it as such. Why, said he, we intend to-morrow, privately as possible, for our wedding-day; and Mr. Peters and Mr. Williams are to be here, as to breakfast with me, and to show Mr. Peters my little chapel. As soon as the ceremony is over, we will take a little airing in the chariot, as we have done at other times; and so it will not be wondered that we are dressed. And the two parsons have promised secrecy, and will go home. I believe you can't well avoid letting one of the maids into the secret; but that I'll leave to you.

Sir, replied she, we all concluded it would be in a few days! and I doubt it won't be long a secret. No, said he, I don't desire it should; but you know we are not provided for a public wedding, and I shall declare it when we go to Bedfordshire, which won't be long. But the men, who lie in the outhouses, need not know it; for, by some means or other, my sister Davers knows all that passes.

Do you know, sir, said she, that her ladyship intends to

be down here with you in a few days? Her servant told me so, who brought you the letter you were angry at.

I hope, said he, we shall be set out for t'other house first; and shall be pleased she loses her labour. Sir, continued she, her ladyship proposes to be here time enough to hinder your nuptials, which she takes, as we did, will be the latter end of next week. Well, said he, let her come: but yet I desire not to see her.

Mrs. Jewkes said to me, Give me leave, madam, to wish you all manner of happiness: But I am afraid I have too well obeyed his honour, to be forgiven by you. Indeed, Mrs. Jewkes, returned I, you will be more your own enemy than I will be. I will look all forward: and shall not presume, so much as by a whisper, to set my good master against any one he pleases to approve of: And as to his old servants, I shall always value them, and never offer to dictate to his choice, or influence it by my own caprices.

Mrs. Jewkes, said my master, you find you have no cause to apprehend anything. My Pamela is very placable; and as we have both been sinners together, we must both be included in one act of grace.

Such an example of condescension, as I have before me, Mrs. Jewkes, said I, may make you very easy; for I must be highly unworthy, if I did not forego all my little resentments, if I had any, for the sake of so much goodness to myself.

You are very kind, madam, said she; and you may depend upon it, I will atone for all my faults, by my future duty and respect to you, as well as to my master.

That's well said on both sides, said he: but, Mrs. Jewkes, to assure you, that my good girl here has no malice, she chooses you to attend her in the morning at the ceremony, and you must keep up her spirits.—I shall, replied she, be very proud of the honour: But I cannot, madam, but wonder to see you so very low-spirited, as you have been these two or three days past, with so much happiness before you.

Why, Mrs. Jewkes, answered I, there can be but one

reason given; and that is, that I am a sad fool!—But, indeed, I am not ungrateful neither: nor would I put on a foolish affectation: But my heart, at times, sinks within me; I know not why, except at my own unworthiness, and because the honour done me is too high for me to support myself under, as I should do. It is an honour, Mrs. Jewkes, added I, I was not born to; and no wonder, then, I behave so awkwardly. She made me a fine compliment upon it, and withdrew, repeating her promises of care, secrecy, &c.

He parted from me with very great tenderness; and I came up and set to writing, to amuse my thoughts, and wrote thus far. And Mrs. Jewkes being come up, and it being past twelve, I will go to bed; but not one wink, I fear, shall I get this night.—I could beat myself for anger. Sure there is nothing ominous in this strange folly!—But I suppose all young maidens are the same, so near so great a change of condition, though they carry it off more discreetly than I.

—— o ——

Thursday, six o'clock in the morning.

I MIGHT as well have not gone to bed last night, for what sleep I had. Mrs. Jewkes often was talking to me, and said several things that would have been well enough from anybody else of our sex; but the poor woman has so little purity of heart, that it is all *say* from her, and goes no farther than the ear.

I fancy my master has not slept much neither; for I heard him up, and walking about his chamber, ever since break of day. To be sure, good gentleman! he must have some concern, as well as I; for here he is going to marry a poor foolish unworthy girl, brought up on the charity, as one may say (at least bounty), of his worthy family! And this foolish girl must be, to all intents and purposes, after twelve o'clock this day, as much his wife as if he were to marry a duchess!—And here he must stand the shocks of common reflection! The great Mr. B—— has

done finely! he has married his poor servant *wench!* will
some say. The ridicule and rude jests of his equals, and
companions too, he must stand: And the disdain of his
relations, and indignation of Lady Davers, his lofty sister!
Dear good gentleman! he will have enough to do, to be
sure! Oh how shall I merit all these things at his hand! I
can only do the best I can; and pray to God to reward
him; and resolve to love him with a pure heart, and serve
him with a sincere obedience. I hope the dear gentleman
will continue to love me for *this;* for, alas! I have nothing
else to offer! But, as I can hardly expect so great a blessing, if I can be secure from his contempt, I shall not be
unfortunate; and must bear his indifference, if his rich
friends should inspire him with it, and proceed with doing
my duty with cheerfulness.

—— o ——

Half an hour past eight o'clock.

My good dear master, my kind friend, my generous benefactor, my worthy protector, and, oh! all the good words
in one, my affectionate husband, that is soon to be—(be
curbed in, my proud heart, know thyself, and be conscious
of thy unworthiness!)—has just left me, with the kindest,
tenderest expressions, and gentlest behaviour, that ever
blest a happy maiden. He approached me with a sort of
reined-in rapture. My Pamela! said he, may I just ask
after your employment? Don't let me chide my dear girl
this day, however. The two parsons will be here to breakfast with us at nine; and yet you are not a bit dressed!
Why this absence of mind, and sweet irresolution?

Why, indeed, sir, said I, I will set about a reformation
this instant. He saw the Common Prayer-book lying in
the window. I hope, said he, my lovely maiden has been
conning the lesson she is by and by to repeat. Have you
not, Pamela? and clasped his arms about me, and kissed
me. Indeed, sir, said I, I have been reading over the
solemn service.—And what thinks my fairest (for so he

called me) of it?—Oh, sir, 'tis very awful, and makes one shudder, to reflect upon it!—No wonder, said he, it should affect my sweet Pamela: I have been looking into it this morning, and I can't say but I think it a solemn, but very suitable service. But this I tell my dear love, continued he, and again clasped me to him, there is not a tittle in it that I cannot joyfully subscribe to: And *that*, my dear Pamela, should make you easy, and join cheerfully in it with me. I kissed his dear hand: Oh my generous, kind protector, said I, how gracious is it to confirm thus the doubting mind of your poor servant! which apprehends nothing so much as her own unworthiness of the honour and blessing that await her!—He was pleased to say, I know well, my dearest creature, that, according to the liberties we people of fortune generally give ourselves, I have promised a great deal, when I say so. But I would not have said it, if, deliberately, I could not with all my heart. So banish from your mind all doubt and uneasiness; let a generous confidence in me take place; and let me *see* it does, by your cheerfulness in this day's solemn business; and then I will love you for ever!

May God Almighty, sir, said I, reward all your goodness to me!—That is all I can say. But, oh! how kind it is in you, to supply the want of the presence and comfortings of a dear mother, of a loving sister, or of the kind companions of my own sex, which most maidens have, to soothe their anxieties on the so near approach of so awful a solemnity!—You, sir, are all these tender relations in one to me! Your condescensions and kindness shall, if possible, embolden me to look up to you without that sweet terror, that must confound poor bashful maidens, on such an occasion, when they are surrendered up to a *more* doubtful happiness, and to half-strange men, whose good faith, and good usage of them, must be *less* experienced, and is all involved in the dark bosom of futurity, and only to be proved by the event.

This, my dear Pamela, said he, is most kindly said! It shows me that you enter gratefully into my intention. For

I would, by my conduct, supply all these dear relations to
you; and I voluntarily promise, from my heart, to you,
what I think I could not, with such assured resolutions
of performance, to the highest-born lady in the kingdom.
For let me tell my sweet girl, that, after having been long
tossed by the boisterous winds of a more culpable passion,
I have now conquered it, and am not so much the victim
of your beauty, all charming as you are, as of your virtue;
and therefore may more boldly promise for myself, having
so stable a foundation for my affection; which, should this
outward beauty fail, will increase with your virtue, and
shine forth the brighter, as that is more illustriously displayed by the augmented opportunities which the condition
you are now entering into will afford you.—Oh, the dear
charming man! how nobly, how encouragingly kind, was
all this!

I could not suitably express myself: And he said, I see
my girl is at a loss for words! I doubt not your kind acceptance of my declarations. And when I have acted too
much the part of a libertine formerly, for you to look back
without some anxiety, I ought not, being now happily
convicted, to say less.—But why loses my girl her time?
I will now only add, that I hope for many happy years
to make good, by my conduct, what so willingly flows from
my lips.

He kissed me again, and said, But, whatever you do,
Pamela, be cheerful; for else, maybe, of the small company we shall have, some one, not knowing how to account
for your too nice modesty, will think there is *some other*
person in the world, whose addresses would be still *more*
agreeable to you.

This he said with an air of sweetness and pleasantry;
but it alarmed me exceedingly, and made me resolve to
appear as calm and cheerful as possible. For this was,
indeed, a most affecting expression, and enough to make
me, if anything can, behave as I ought, and to force my
idle fears to give way to hopes so much better grounded.
—And I began almost, on this occasion, to wish Mr.

Williams were not to marry me, lest I should behave like
a fool; and so be liable to an imputation, which I should
be most unworthy, if I deserved.

So I set about dressing me instantly; and he sent Mrs.
Jewkes to assist me. But I am never long a dressing, when
I set about it; and my master has now given me a hint,
that will, for half an hour more, at least, keep my spirits in
a brisk circulation. Yet it concerns me a little too, lest he
should have any the least shadow of a doubt, that I am not,
mind and person, entirely his.

And so being now ready, and not called to breakfast, I
sat down and wrote thus far.

I might have mentioned, that I dressed myself in a rich
white satin night-gown, that had been my good lady's, and
my best head-clothes, &c. I have got such a knack of
writing, that when I am by myself, I cannot sit without a
pen in my hand.—But I am now called to breakfast. I
suppose the gentlemen are come.—Now, courage, Pamela!
Remember thou art upon thy good behaviour!—Fie upon
it! my heart begins to flutter again!—Foolish heart! lie
still! Never, sure, was any maiden's perverse heart under
so little command as mine!—It gave itself away, at first,
without my leave; it has been, for weeks, pressing me with
its wishes; and yet now, when it should be happy itself,
and make me so, it is throb, throb, throb, like a little fool!
and filling me with such unseasonable misgivings, as abate
the rising comforts of all my better prospects.

—*o*—

Thursday, near three o'clock.

I THOUGHT I should have found no time nor heart to write
again this day. But here are three gentlemen come, unex-
pectedly, to dine with my master; and so I shall not
appear. He has done all he could, civilly, to send them
away; but they will stay, though I believe he had rather
they would not. And so I have nothing to do but to write

till I go to dinner myself with Mrs. Jewkes: for my master was not prepared for this company; and it will be a little latish to-day. So I will begin with my happy story where I left off.

When I came down to breakfast, Mr. Peters and Mr. Williams were both there. And as soon as my master heard me coming down, he met me at the door, and led me in with great tenderness. He had kindly spoken to them, as he told me afterwards, to mention no more of the matter to me, than needs must. I paid my respects to them, I believe a little awkwardly, and was almost out of breath: but said, I had come down a little too fast.

When Abraham came in to wait, my master said (that the servants should not mistrust), 'Tis well, gentlemen, you came as you did; for my good girl and I were going to take an airing till dinner-time. I hope you'll stay and dine with me. Sir, said Mr. Peters, we won't hinder your airing. I only came, having a little time upon my hands, to see your chapel; but must be at home at dinner; and Mr. Williams will dine with me. Well then, said my master, we will pursue our intention, and ride out for an hour or two, as soon as I have shown Mr. Peters my little chapel. Will you, Pamela, after breakfast, walk with us to it? *If, if,* said I, and had like to have stammered, foolish that I was! *if* you please, sir. I could look none of them in the face. Abraham looking at me; Why, child, said my master, you have hardly recovered your fright yet: how came your foot to slip? 'Tis well you did not hurt yourself. Said Mr. Peters, improving the hint, You ha'n't sprained your ankle, madam, I hope. No, sir, said I, I believe not; but 'tis a *little painful* to me. And so it was; for I meant my foolishness! Abraham, said my master, bid Robin put the horses to the coach, instead of the chariot; and if these gentlemen *will* go, we can set them down. No matter, sir, said Mr. Peters: I had as lieve walk, if Mr. Williams chooses it. Well then, said my master, let it be the chariot, as I told him.

I could eat nothing, though I attempted it; and my hand

shook so, I spilled some of my chocolate, and so put it down again; and they were all very good, and looked another way. My master said, when Abraham was out, I have a quite plain ring here, Mr. Peters: And I hope the ceremony will dignify the ring; and that I shall give my girl reason to think it, for that cause, the most valuable one that can be presented her. Mr. Peters said, he was sure I should value it more than the richest diamond in the world.

I had bid Mrs. Jewkes not to dress herself, lest she should give cause of mistrust; and she took my advice.

When breakfast was over, my master said, before Abraham, Well, gentlemen, we will step into the chapel; and you must give me your advice, as to the alterations I design. I am in the more haste, because the survey you are going to take of it, for the alterations, will take up a little time; and we shall have but a small space between that and dinner, for the little tour I design to make.—Pamela, you'll give us your opinion, won't you? Yes, sir, said I; I'll come after you.

So they went out, and I sat down in the chair again, and fanned myself: I am sick at heart, said I, I think, Mrs. Jewkes. Said she, Shall I fetch you a little cordial?—No, said I, I am a sad fool! I want spirits, that's all. She took her smelling-bottle, and would have given it me: but I said, Keep it in your hand; may be I shall want it: but I hope not.

She gave me very good words, and begged me to go: And I got up; but my knees beat so against one another, I was forced to sit down again. But, at last, I held by her arm, and passing by Abraham, I said, This ugly slip, coming down stairs, has made me limp, though; so I must hold by you, Mrs. Jewkes. Do you know what alterations there are to be in the chapel, that we must all give our opinions of them?

Nan, she told me, was let into the secret; and she had ordered her to stay at the chapel door, to see that nobody came in. My dear master came to me, at entering the

chapel, and took my hand, and led me up to the altar.
Remember, my dear girl, whispered he, and be cheerful. I
am, I will, sir, said I; but I hardly knew what I said; and
so you may believe, when I said to Mrs. Jewkes, Don't
leave me; pray, Mrs. Jewkes, don't leave me; as if I had
all confidence in her, and none where it was most due. So
she kept close to me. God forgive me! but I never was so
absent in my life, as at first; even till Mr. Williams had
gone on in the service, so far as to the awful words about
requiring us, as we should answer at the dreadful day of
judgment; and then the solemn words, and my master's
whispering, Mind this, my dear, made me start. Said he,
still whispering, Know *you* any impediment? I blushed,
and said softly, None, sir, but my great unworthiness.

Then followed the sweet words, *Wilt thou have this woman*
to thy wedded wife? &c., and I began to take heart a little,
when my dearest master answered, audibly, to this question.
I will. But I could only make a courtesy, when they asked
me; though, I am sure, my *heart* was readier than my
speech, and answered to every article of *obey, serve, love,*
and *honour.*

Mr. Peters gave me away; and I said, after Mr. Williams,
as well as I could, as my dear master did with a much better
grace, the words of betrothment; and the ceremony of the
ring passing next, I received the dear favour at his worthy
hands with a most grateful heart; and he was pleased to
say afterwards in the chariot, that when he had done saying,
With this ring I thee wed, &c., I made a courtesy, and said,
Thank you, sir. Maybe I did; for I am sure it was a most
grateful part of the service, and my heart was overwhelmed
with his goodness, and the tender grace wherewith he performed it. I was very glad, that the next part was the
prayer, and kneeling; for I trembled so, I could hardly
stand, betwixt fear and joy.

The joining of our hands afterwards, the declaration
of our being married to the few witnesses present; for,
reckoning Nan, whose curiosity would not let her stay at
the door, there were but Mr. Peters, Mrs. Jewkes, and she;

the blessing, the psalm, and the subsequent prayers, and the concluding exhortation ; were so many beautiful, welcome, and lovely parts of this divine office, that my heart began to be delighted with them ; and my spirits to be a little freer.

And thus, my dearest, dear parents, is your happy, happy, thrice happy Pamela, at last married ; and to whom ?—Why, to her beloved, gracious master! the lord of her wishes! And thus the dear, once naughty assailer of her innocence, by a blessed turn of Providence, is become the kind, the generous protector and rewarder of it. God be evermore blessed and praised! and make me not wholly unworthy of such a transcendent honour!—And bless and reward the dear, dear, good gentleman, who has thus exalted his unworthy servant, and given her a place, which the greatest ladies would think themselves happy in !

My master saluted me most ardently, and said, God give you, my dear love, as much joy on this occasion as I have! And he presented me to Mr. Peters, who saluted me ; and said, You may excuse *me*, dear madam, for I gave you away, and you are my daughter. And Mr. Williams modestly withdrawing a little way ; Mr. Williams, said my master, pray accept my thanks, and wish your *sister* joy. So he saluted me too ; and said, Most heartily, madam, I do. And I will say, that to see so much innocence and virtue so eminently rewarded, is one of the greatest pleasures I have ever known. This my master took very kindly.

Mrs. Jewkes would have kissed my hand at the chapel-door ; but I put my arms about her neck, for I had got a new recruit of spirits just then ; and kissed her, and said, Thank you, Mrs. Jewkes, for accompanying me. I have behaved sadly. No, madam, said she, pretty well, pretty well !

Mr. Peters walked out with me ; and Mr. Williams and my master came out after us, talking together.

Mr. Peters, when we came into the parlour, said, I once more, madam, must wish you joy on this happy occasion. I wish every day may add to your comforts; and may you very long rejoice in one another! for you are the loveliest couple I ever saw joined. I told him, I was highly obliged to his kind opinion, and good wishes; and hoped my future conduct would not make me unworthy of them.

My good benefactor came in with Mr. Williams: So, my dear life, said he, how do you do? A little more composed, I hope.——Well, you see this is not so dreadful an affair as you apprehended.

Sir, said Mr. Peters, very kindly, it is a very solemn circumstance; and I love to see it so reverently and awfully entered upon. It is a most excellent sign; for the most *thoughtful* beginnings make the most *prudent* proceedings.

Mrs. Jewkes, of her own accord, came in with a large silver tumbler, filled with sack, and a toast, and nutmeg, and sugar; and my master said, That's well thought of, Mrs. Jewkes; for we have made but sorry breakfasting. And he would make me take some of the toast; as they all did, and drank pretty heartily: and I drank a little, and it cheered my heart, I thought, for an hour after.

My master took a fine diamond ring from his finger, and presented it to Mr. Peters, who received it very kindly. And to Mr. Williams he said, My old acquaintance, I have reserved for you, against a variety of solicitations, the living I always designed for you; and I beg you'll prepare to take possession of it; and as the doing it may be attended with some expense, pray accept of this towards it; and so he gave him (as he told me afterwards it was) a bank-note of 50*l.*

So did this generous good gentleman bless us all, and me in particular; for whose sake he was as bounteous as if he had married one of the noblest fortunes.

So he took his leave of the gentlemen, recommending secrecy again, for a few days, and they left him; and none of the servants suspected anything, as Mrs. Jewkes believes. And then I threw myself at his feet, blessed God, and blessed *him* for his goodness; and he overwhelmed me with kindness, calling me his sweet bride, and twenty lovely epithets, that swell my grateful heart beyond the power of utterance.

He afterwards led me to the chariot; and we took a delightful tour round the neighbouring villages; and he did all he could to dissipate those still perverse anxieties that dwell upon my mind, and, do what I can, spread too thoughtful an air, as he tells me, over my countenance.

We came home again by half an hour after one; and he was pleasing himself with thinking, not to be an hour out of my company this blessed day, that (as he was so good as to say) he might inspire me with a familiarity that should improve my confidence in him, when he was told, that a footman of Sir Charles Hargrave had been here, to let him know, that his master, and two other gentlemen, were on the road to take a dinner with him, in their way to Nottingham.

He was heartily vexed at this, and said to me, he should have been glad of their companies at any other time; but that it was a barbarous intrusion now; and he wished they had been told he would not be at home at dinner: And besides, said he, they are horrid drinkers; and I shan't be able to get them away to-night, perhaps; for they have nothing to do, but to travel round the country, and beat up their friends' quarters all the way; and it is all one to them, whether they stay a night or a month at a place. But, added he, I'll find some way, if I can, to turn them off, after dinner.—Confound them, said he, in a violent pet, that they should come this day, of all the days in the year!

We had hardly alighted, and got in, before they came: Three mad rakes they seemed to be, as I looked through the window, setting up a hunting note, as soon as they came to the gate, that made the courtyard echo again; and smacking their whips in concert.

So I went up to my chamber, and saw (what made my heart throb) Mrs. Jewkes's officious pains to put the room in order for a guest, that, however welcome, as now my duty teaches me to say, is yet dreadful to me to think of.

So I took refuge in my closet, and had recourse to pen and ink, for my amusement, and to divert my anxiety of mind. —If one's heart is so sad, and one's apprehensions so great, where one so extremely loves, and is so extremely obliged; what must be the case of those poor maidens, who are forced, for sordid views, by their tyrannical parents or guardians, to marry the man they almost hate, and, perhaps, to the loss of the man they most love! Oh, that is a sad thing, indeed!—And what have not such cruel parents to answer for! And what do not such poor innocent victims suffer!—But, blessed be God, this lot is far from being mine!

My good master (for I cannot yet have the presumption to call him by a more tender name) came up to me, and said, Well, I just come to ask my dear bride (oh the charming, charming word!) how she does? I see you are writing, my dear, said he. These confounded rakes are half mad, I think, and will make me so! However, said he, I have ordered my chariot to be got ready, as if I was under an engagement five miles off, and will set them out of the house, if possible; and then ride round, and come back, as soon as I can get rid of them. I find, said he, Lady Davers is full of our affairs. She has taken great freedoms with me before Sir Charles; and they have all been at me, without mercy; and I was forced to be very serious with them, or else they would have come up to have seen you, since I would not call you down.—He kissed me, and said, I shall quarrel with them, if I can't get them away; for I have lost two or three precious hours with my soul's delight: And so he went down.

Mrs. Jewkes asked me to walk down to dinner in the little parlour. I went down, and she was so complaisant as to offer to wait upon me at table; and would not be persuaded, without difficulty, to sit down with me. But I insisted she should: For, said I, it would be very extraordinary, if one should so soon go into such distance, Mrs. Jewkes.—Whatever my new station may require of me, added I, I hope I shall always conduct myself in such a manner, that pride and insolence shall bear no part in my character.

You are very good, madam, said she; but I will always know my duty to my master's lady.—Why then, replied I, if I must take state upon me so early, Mrs. Jewkes, let me exact from you what you call your duty; and sit down with me when I desire you.

This prevailed upon her; and I made shift to get down a bit of apple-pie, and a little custard; but that was all.

My good master came in again, and said, Well, thank my stars! these rakes are going now; but I must set out with them, and I choose my chariot; for if I took horse, I should have difficulty to part with them; for they are like a snow-ball, and intend to gather company as they go, to make a merry tour of it for some days together.

We both got up, when he came in: Fie, Pamela! said he; why this ceremony now?—Sit still, Mrs. Jewkes.— Nay, sir, said she, I was loath to sit down; but my lady would have me.—She is very right, Mrs. Jewkes, said my master, and tapped me on the cheek; for we are but yet half married; and so she is not above half your lady yet! —Don't look so down, don't be so silent, my dearest, said he; why, you hardly spoke twenty words to me all the time we were out together. Something I will allow for your bashful sweetness; but not too much.—Mrs. Jewkes, have you no pleasant tales to tell my Pamela, to make her smile, till I return?—Yes, sir, said she, I could tell twenty pleasant stories; but my lady is too nice to hear them; and yet, I hope, I should not be shocking neither. Ah! poor woman! thought I; thy chastest stories will make a modest person blush, if I know thee! and I desire to hear none of them.

My master said, Tell her one of the shortest you have, in my hearing. Why, sir, said she, I knew a bashful young lady, as madam may be, married to—Dear Mrs. Jewkes, interrupted I, no more of your story, I beseech you; I don't like the beginning of it. Go on, Mrs. Jewkes, said my master. No, pray, sir, don't require it, said I, pray don't. Well, said he, then we'll have it another time, Mrs. Jewkes.

Abraham coming in to tell him the gentlemen were going, and that his chariot was ready; I am glad of that, said he; and went to them, and set out with them.

I took a turn in the garden with Mrs. Jewkes, after they were gone: And having walked a while, I said, I should be glad of her company down the elm-walk, to meet the chariot: For, oh! I know not how to look up at him, when he is with me; nor how to bear his absence, when I have reason to expect him: What a strange contradiction there is in this unaccountable passion.

What a different aspect everything in and about this house bears now, to my thinking, to what it once had! The garden, the pond, the alcove, the elm-walk. But, oh! my prison is become my palace; and no wonder everything wears another face!

We sat down upon the broad stile, leading towards the road; and Mrs. Jewkes was quite another person to me to what she was the last time I sat there.

At last my best beloved returned, and alighted there. What, my Pamela! (and Mrs. Jewkes then left me), What (said he, and kissed me) brings you this way? I hope to meet me.—Yes, sir, said I. That's kind, indeed, said he; but why that averted eye?—that downcast countenance, as if you was afraid of me? You must not think so, sir, said I. Revive my heart then, said he, with a more cheerful aspect; and let that over-anxious solicitude, which appears in the most charming face in the world, be chased from it. —Have you, my dear girl, any fears that I can dissipate; any doubts that I can obviate; any hopes that I can encourage; any request that I can gratify?—Speak, my dear Pamela; and if I have power, *but* speak, and to purchase one smile, it shall be done!

I cannot, sir, said I, have any fears, any doubts, but that I shall never be able to deserve all your goodness. I have no hopes, but that my future conduct may be agreeable to you, and my determined duty well accepted. Nor have

I any request to make, but that you will forgive all my
imperfections: and, among the rest, this foolish weakness,
that makes me seem to you, after all the generous things
that have passed, to want this further condescension, and
these kind assurances. But indeed, sir, I am oppressed by
your bounty; my spirits sink under the weight of it; and
the oppression is still the greater, as I see not how, possibly,
in my whole future life, by all I can do, to merit the least
of your favours.

I know your grateful heart, said he; but remember, my
dear, what the lawyers tell us, That marriage is the highest
consideration which the law knows. And this, my sweet
bride, has made you mine, and me yours; and you have
the best claim in the world to share my fortune with me.
But, set that consideration aside, what is the obligation you
have to me? Your mind is pure as that of an angel, and
as much transcends mine. Your wit, and your judgment,
to make you no compliment, are more than equal to mine:
You have all the graces that education can give a woman,
improved by a genius which makes those graces natural to
you. You have a sweetness of temper, and a noble sincerity, beyond all comparison; and in the beauty of your
person, you excel all the ladies I ever saw. Where then,
my dearest, is the obligation, if not on my side to you?—
But, to avoid these comparisons, let us talk of nothing
henceforth but equality; although, if the riches of your
mind, and your unblemished virtue, be set against *my*
fortune (which is but an accidental good, as I may call it,
and all I have to boast of), the condescension will be yours;
and I shall not think I can possibly deserve you, till, after
your sweet example, my future life shall become nearly as
blameless as yours.

Oh, sir, said I, what comfort do you give me, that, instead
of my being in danger of being ensnared by the high condition to which your goodness has exalted me, you make
me hope, that I shall be confirmed and approved by you;
and that we may have a prospect of perpetuating each
other's happiness, till time shall be no more!—But, sir, I

will not, as you once cautioned me, be too serious. I will
resolve, with these sweet encouragements, to be, in everything, what you would have me be: And I hope I shall,
more and more, show you that I have no will but yours.
He kissed me very tenderly, and thanked me for this kind
assurance, as he called it.

And so we entered the house together.

———o———

Eight o'clock at night.

Now these sweet assurances, my dear father and mother,
you will say, must be very consolatory to me; and being
voluntary on his side, were all that could be wished for on
mine; and I was resolved, if possible, to subdue my idle
fears and apprehensions.

———o———

Ten o'clock at night.

As we sat at supper, he was generously kind to me, as
well in his actions, as expressions. He took notice, in the
most delicate manner, of my endeavour to conquer my
foibles; and said, I see, with pleasure, my dear girl strives
to comport herself in a manner suitable to my wishes: I
see, even through the sweet tender struggles of your over-
nice modesty, how much I owe to your intentions of obliging me. As I have once told you, that I am the conquest
more of your virtue than your beauty; so not one alarming
word or look shall my beloved Pamela hear or see, to give
her reason to suspect the truth of what I aver. You may
the rather believe me, continued he, as you may see the
pain I have to behold anything that concerns you, even
though your concern be causeless. And yet I will indulge
my dear girl's bashful weakness so far, as to own, that so
pure a mind may suffer from apprehension, on so important
a change as this; and I can therefore be only displeased
with such part of your conduct, as may make your suffer-

ings greater than my own ; when I am resolved, through every stage of my future life, in all events, to study to make them less.

After supper, of which, with all his sweet persuasions, I could hardly taste, he made me drink two glasses of champagne, and, afterwards, a glass of sack ; which he kindly forced upon me, by naming your healths : and as the time of retiring drew on, he took notice, but in a very delicate manner, how my colour went and came, and how foolishly I trembled. Nobody, surely, in such delightful circumstances, ever behaved so silly!—And he said, My dearest girl, I fear you have had too much of my company for so many hours together ; and would better recollect yourself, if you retired for half an hour to your closet.

I wished for this, but durst not say so much, lest he should be angry ; for, as the hours grew on, I found my apprehensions increase, and my silly heart was the unquieter, every time I could lift up my eyes to his dear face ; so sweetly terrible did he appear to my apprehensions. I said, You are all goodness, dear sir ; and I boldly kissed his dear hand, and pressed it to my lips with both mine. And saluting me very fervently, he gave me his hand, seeing me hardly able to stand, and led me to my chamber-door, and then most generously withdrew.

I went to my closet ; and the first thing I did, on my knees, again thanked God for the blessing of the day ; and besought His divine goodness to conduct my future life in such a manner, as should make me a happy instrument of his glory. After this, being now left to my own recollection, I grew a little more assured and lightsome ; and the pen and paper being before me, I amused myself with writing thus far.

—— *o* ——

Eleven o'clock Thursday night.

MRS. JEWKES being come up with a message, desiring to know, whether her master may attend upon me in my *closet* ; and hinting to me, that, however, she believed he

did not expect to find me *there;* I have sent word, that I
beg he would indulge me one quarter of an hour.—So,
committing myself to the mercies of the Almighty, who
has led me through so many strange scenes of terror and
affrightment, to this happy, yet awful moment, I will wish
you, my dear parents, a good-night; and though you will
not see this in time, yet I know I have your hourly prayers,
and therefore cannot fail of them now. So, good-night,
good-night! God bless you, and God bless me! Amen,
amen, if it be His blessed will, subscribes

Your ever-dutiful DAUGHTER!

——o——

Friday evening.

OH how this dear excellent man indulges me in everything!
Every hour he makes me happier, by his sweet condescension, than the former. He pities my weakness of mind,
allows for all my little foibles, endeavours to dissipate my
fears; his words are so pure, his ideas so chaste, and his
whole behaviour so sweetly decent, that never, surely, was
so happy a creature as your Pamela! I never could have
hoped such a husband could have fallen to my lot: and
much less, that a gentleman, who had allowed himself in
attempts, that now I will endeavour to forget for ever,
should have behaved with so very delicate and unexception-
able a demeanour. No light frothy jests drop from his lips;
no alarming railleries; no offensive expressions, nor insulting airs, reproach or wound the ears of your happy, thrice
happy daughter. In short, he says everything that may
embolden me to look up, with pleasure, upon the generous
author of my happiness.

At breakfast, when I knew not how to see him, he
emboldened me by talking of *you*, my dear parents; a
subject, he generously knew, I *could* talk of: and gave me
assurances, that he would make you both happy. He said,
He would have me send you a letter to acquaint you with
my nuptials; and, as he could make business that way,

Thomas should carry it purposely, as to-morrow. Nor will
I, said he, my dear Pamela, desire to see your writings,
because I told you I would not; for now I will, in everything, religiously keep my word with my dear spouse: (oh
the dear delightful word!) and you may send all your
papers to them, from those they have, down to this happy
moment; only let me beg they will preserve them, and let
me have them when they have read them; as also those I
have not seen; which, however, I desire not to see till then;
but then shall take it for a favour, if you will grant it.

It will be my pleasure, as well as my duty, sir, said I, to
obey you in everything: and I will write up to the conclusion of this day, that they may see how happy you have
made me.

I know you will both join with me to bless God for His
wonderful mercies and goodness to you, as well as to me:
For he was pleased to ask me particularly after your circumstances, and said, he had taken notice, that I had
hinted, in some of my first letters, that you owed money in
the world; and he gave me fifty guineas, and bid me send
them to you in my packet, to pay your debts, as far as they
would go; and that you would quit your present business,
and put yourself, and my dear mother, into a creditable
appearance; and he would find a better place of abode for
you than that you had, when he returned to Bedfordshire.
Oh how shall I bear all these exceeding great and generous
favours!—I send them wrapt up, five guineas in a parcel,
in double papers.

To me he gave no less than one hundred guineas more;
and said, I would have you, my dear, give Mrs. Jewkes,
when you go away from hence, what you think fit out
of these, as from yourself.—Nay, good dear sir, said I, let
that be what you please. Give her then, said he, twenty
guineas, as a compliment on your nuptials. Give Colbrand
ten guineas: give the two coachmen five guineas each; to
the two maids at this house five guineas each; give Abraham five guineas; give Thomas five guineas; and give the
gardeners, grooms, and helpers, twenty guineas among

them. And when, said he, I return with you to the other house, I will make you a suitable present, to buy you such ornaments as are fit for my beloved wife to appear in. For now, my Pamela, continued he, you are not to mind, as you once proposed, what other ladies will say; but to appear as my wife ought to do. Else it would look as if what you thought of, as a means to avoid the envy of others of your sex, was a wilful slight in me, which, I hope, I never shall be guilty of; and I will show the world, that I value you as I ought, and as if I had married the first fortune in the kingdom: And why should it not be so, when I know none of the first quality that matches you in excellence?

He saw I was at a loss for words, and said, I see, my dearest bride! my spouse! my wife! my Pamela! your grateful confusion. And kissing me, as I was going to speak, I will stop your dear mouth, said he: You shall not so much as thank me; for when I have done ten times more than this, I shall but poorly express my love for so much beauty of mind, and loveliness of person; which thus, said he, and clasped me to his generous bosom, I can proudly now call my own!—Oh how, my dear parents, can I think of anything, but redoubled love, joy, and gratitude!

And thus generously did he banish from my mind those painful reflections, and bashful apprehensions, that made me dread to see him for the first time this day, when I was called to attend him at breakfast; and made me all ease, composure, and tranquillity.

He then, thinking I seemed somewhat thoughtful, proposed a little turn in the chariot till dinner-time: And this was another sweet relief to me; and he diverted me with twenty agreeable relations, of what observations he had made in his travels; and gave me the characters of the ladies and gentlemen in his other neighbourhood: telling me whose acquaintance he would have me most cultivate. And when I mentioned Lady Davers with apprehension, he said, To be sure I love my sister dearly, notwithstanding her violent spirit; and I know she loves me; and I can allow a little for her pride, because I know what my own

so lately was ; and because she knows not my Pamela, and
her excellences, as I do. But you must not, my dear, forget what belongs to your character, as my wife, nor meanly
stoop to her ; though I know you will choose, by softness,
to try to move her to a proper behaviour. But it shall be
my part to see, that you do not yield too much.

However, continued he, as I would not publicly declare
my marriage here, I hope she won't come near us till we are
in Bedfordshire ; and then, when she knows we are married,
she will keep away, if she is not willing to be reconciled ;
for she dares not, surely, come to quarrel with me, when
she knows it is done ; for that would have a hateful and
wicked appearance, as if she would try to make differences
between man and wife.—But we will have no more of this
subject, nor talk of anything, added he, that shall give
concern to my dearest. And so he changed the talk to a
more pleasing subject, and said the kindest and most soothing
things in the world.

When we came home, which was about dinner-time, he
was the same obliging, kind gentleman ; and, in short, is
studious to show, on every occasion, his generous affection
to me. And, after dinner, he told me, he had already
written to his draper, in town, to provide him new liveries ;
and to his late mother's mercer, to send him down patterns
of the most fashionable silks, for my choice. I told him, I
was unable to express my gratitude for his favours and
generosity: And as he knew best what befitted his own
rank and condition, I would wholly remit myself to his
good pleasure. But, by all his repeated bounties to me, of
so extraordinary a nature, I could not but look forward
with awe upon the condition to which he had exalted me ;
and now I feared I should hardly be able to act up to it
in such a manner as should justify the choice he had condescended to make: But that, I hoped, I should have not
only his generous allowance for my imperfections, which I
could only assure him should not be wilful ones, but his
kind instructions ; and that as often as he observed any part
of my conduct such as he could not entirely approve, he

would let me know it; and I would think his reproofs of beginning faults the kindest and most affectionate things in the world: because they would keep me from committing greater; and be a means to continue to me the blessing of his good opinion.

He answered me in the kindest manner; and assured me, That nothing should ever lie upon his mind which he would not reveal, and give me an opportunity either of convincing him, or being convinced myself.

He then asked me, When I should be willing to go to the Bedfordshire house? I said, whenever he pleased. We will come down hither again before the winter, said he, if you please, in order to cultivate the acquaintance you have begun with Lady Jones, and Sir Simon's family; and, if it please God to spare us to one another, in the winter I will give you, as I promised, for two or three months, the diversions of London. And I think, added he, if my dear pleases, we will set out next week, about Tuesday, for t'other house. I can have no objection, sir, said I, to anything you propose; but how will you avoid Miss Darnford's solicitation for an evening to dance? Why, said he, we can make Monday evening do for that purpose, if they won't excuse us. But, if you please, said he, I will invite Lady Jones, Mr. Peters and his family, and Sir Simon and his family, to my little chapel, on Sunday morning, and to stay dinner with me; and then I will declare my marriage to them, because my dear life shall not leave this country with the least reason for a possibility of anybody's doubting that it is so. Oh! how good was this! But, indeed, his conduct is all of a piece, noble, kind, and considerate! What a happy creature am I!—And then, maybe, said he, they will excuse us till we return into this country again, as to the ball. Is there anything, added he, that my beloved Pamela has *still* to wish? If you have, freely speak.

Hitherto, my dearest sir, replied I, you have not only prevented my wishes, but my hopes, and even my thoughts. And yet I must own, since your kind command of speaking

my mind seems to show, that you expect from me I should
say something; that I have only one or two things to wish
more, and then I shall be too happy. Say, said he, what
they are. Sir, proceeded I, I am, indeed, ashamed to ask
anything, lest it should not be agreeable to you; and lest
it should look as if I was taking advantage of your kind
condescensions to me, and knew not when to be satisfied!

I will only tell you, Pamela, said he, that you are not to
imagine, that these things, which I have done, in hopes of
obliging you, are the sudden impulses of a *new* passion for
you. But, if I can answer for my own mind, they proceed
from a regular and uniform desire of obliging you: which,
I hope, will last as long as your merit lasts; and that, 'I
make no doubt, will be as long as I live. And I can the
rather answer for this, because I really find so much delight
in myself in my present way of thinking and acting, as
infinitely overpays me; and which, for that reason, I am
likely to continue, for *both* our sakes. My beloved *wife*,
therefore, said he, for methinks I am grown fond of a name
I once despised, may venture to speak her mind; and I
will promise, that, so far as it is agreeable to me, and I
cheerfully can, I will comply; and you will not insist upon
it, if that should not be the case.

To be sure, sir, said I, I ought not, neither will I. And
now you embolden me to become an humble petitioner,
and that, as I ought, upon my knees, for the reinstating
such of your servants, as I have been the unhappy occasion
of their disobliging you. He raised me up, and said, My
beloved Pamela has too often been in this suppliant posture
to me, to permit it any more. Rise, my fairest, and let
me know whom, in particular, you would reinstate; and
he kindly held me in his arms, and pressed me to his beloved bosom. Mrs. Jervis, sir, said I, in the first place; for
she is a good woman; and the misfortunes she has had in
the world, must make your displeasure most heavy to her

Well, said he, who next? Mr. Longman, sir, said I;
and I am sure, kind as they have been to me, yet would I
not ask it, if I could not vouch for their integrity, and if I

did not think it was my dear master's interest to have such good servants.

Have you anything further? said he.—Sir, said I, your good old butler, who has so long been in your family before the day of your happy birth, I would, if I might, become an advocate for!

Well, said he, I have only to say, That had not Mr. Longman and Mrs. Jervis, and Jonathan too, joined in a body, in a bold appeal to Lady Davers, which has given her the insolent handle she has taken to intermeddle in my affairs, I could easily have forgiven all the rest of their conduct; though they have given their tongues no little license about me : But I could have forgiven them, because I desire everybody should admire you; and it is with pride that I observe not only their opinion and love, but that of everybody else that knows you, justify my own.— But yet, I will forgive even this, because my Pamela desires it; and I will send a letter myself, to tell Longman what he owes to your interposition, if the estate he has made in my family does not set him above the acceptance of it. And, as to Mrs. Jervis, do you, my dear, write a letter to her, and give her your commands, instantly, on the receipt of it, to go and take possession of her former charge; for now, my dearest girl, she will be more immediately your servant; and I know you love her so well, that you'll go thither with the more pleasure to find her there.—But don't think, added he, that all this compliance is to be for nothing. Ah, sir! said I, tell me but what I can do, poor as I am in power, but rich in will; and I will not hesitate one moment. Why then, said he, of your own accord, reward me for my cheerful compliance, with one sweet kiss. —I instantly said, Thus, then, dear sir, will I obey; and, oh! you have the sweetest and most generous way in the world, to make that a condition, which gives me double honour, and adds to my obligations. And so I clasped my arms about his neck, and was not ashamed to kiss him once and twice, and three times; once for every forgiven person.

Now, my dearest Pamela, said he, what other things

have you to ask? Mr. Williams is already taken care of; and, I hope, will be happy.—Have you nothing to say for John Arnold?

Why, dear sir, said I, you have seen the poor fellow's penitence in my letters.—Yes, my dear, so I have; but that is his penitence for his having served me against you; and, I think, when he would have betrayed me afterwards, he deserves nothing to be said or done for him by either.

But, dear sir, said I, this is a day of jubilee; and the less he deserves, poor fellow, the more will be your goodness. And let me add one word; That as he was divided in his inclinations between his duty to you and good wishes to me, and knew not how to distinguish between the one and the other, when he finds us so happily united by your great goodness to me, he will have no more puzzles in his duty; for he has not failed in any other part of it; but, I hope, will serve you faithfully for the future.

Well, then, suppose I put Mrs. Jewkes in a good way of business, in some inn, and give her John for a husband? And then your gipsy story will be made out, that she will have a husband younger than herself.

You are all goodness, sir, said I. I can freely forgive poor Mrs. Jewkes, and wish her happy. But permit me, sir, to ask, Would not this look like a very heavy punishment to poor John? and as if you could not forgive him, when you are so generous to everybody else?

He smiled, and said, Oh, my Pamela, this, for a forgiving spirit, is very severe upon poor Jewkes: But I shall never, by the grace of God, have any more such trying services, to put him or the rest upon; and if *you* can forgive him, I think *I* may: and so John shall be at your disposal. And now let me know what my Pamela has further to wish?

Oh, my dearest sir, said I, not a single wish more has your grateful Pamela! My heart is overwhelmed with your goodness! Forgive these tears of joy, added I: You have left me nothing to pray for, but that God will bless you with life, and health, and honour, and continue to me the blessing of your esteem ; and I shall then be the happiest creature in the world.

He clasped me in his arms, and said, You cannot, my dear life, be so happy in me, as I am in you. Oh how heartily I despise all my former pursuits, and headstrong appetites! What joys, what true joys, flow from virtuous love! joys which the narrow soul of the libertine cannot take in, nor his thoughts conceive! And which I myself, whilst a libertine, had not the least notion of!

But, said he, I expected my dear spouse, my Pamela, had something to ask for herself. But since all her own good is absorbed in the delight her generous heart takes in promoting that of others, it shall be my study to prevent her wishes, and to make her care for herself unnecessary, by my anticipating kindness.

In this manner, my dear parents, is your happy daughter blessed in a husband! Oh how my exulting heart leaps at the dear, dear word!—And I have nothing to do, but to be humble, and to look up with gratitude to the all-gracious dispenser of these blessings.

So, with a thousand thanks, I afterwards retired to my closet, to write you thus far. And having completed what I purpose for this packet, and put up the kind obliging present, I have nothing more to say, but that I hope soon to see you both, and receive your blessings on this happy, thrice happy occasion. And so, hoping for your prayers, that I may preserve an humble and upright mind to my gracious God, a dutiful gratitude to my dear master and husband—that I may long rejoice in the continuance of these blessings and favours, and that I may preserve, at the same time, an obliging deportment to every one else, I conclude myself,

Your ever-dutiful and most happy daughter,
PAMELA B——.

Oh think it not my pride, my dear parents, that sets me on glorying in my change of name! Yours will be always dear to me, and what I shall never be ashamed

of, I'm sure: But yet—for *such* a husband!—What
shall I say, since words are too faint to express my
gratitude and my joy!

I have taken copies of my master's letter to Mr. Longman, and mine to Mrs. Jervis, which I will send, with
the further occurrences, when I go to the other dear
house, or give you when I see you, as I now hope soon
to do.

————o————

Saturday morning, the third of my happy nuptials.

I MUST still write on, till I come to be settled in the duty
of the station to which I am so generously exalted, and to
let you participate with me the transporting pleasures that
arise from my new condition, and the favours that are
hourly heaped upon me by the best of husbands. When I
had got my packet for you finished, I then set about
writing, as he had kindly directed me, to Mrs. Jervis; and
had no difficulty till I came to sign my name; and so I
brought it down with me, when I was called to supper,
unsigned.

My good master (for I delight, and always shall, to call
him by that name) had been writing to Mr. Longman;
and he said, pleasantly, See, here, my dearest, what I have
written to your *Somebody.* I read as follows:

'MR. LONGMAN,—I have the pleasure to acquaint you,
'that last Thursday I was married to my beloved Pamela.
'I have had reason to be disobliged with you, and Mrs.
'Jervis and Jonathan, not for your kindness to, and regard
'for, my dear spouse, that now is, but for the manner in
'which you appealed to my sister Davers; which has made
'a very wide breach between her and me. But as it was
'one of her first requests, that I would overlook what had
'passed, and reinstate you in all your former charges, I
'think myself obliged, without the least hesitation, to
'comply with it. So, if you please, you may enter again

' upon an office which you have always executed with
' unquestionable integrity, and to the satisfaction of

' Yours, &c.'

   ' Friday afternoon.'

   ' I shall set out next Tuesday or Wednesday for Bed-
   ' fordshire; and desire to find Jonathan, as well as you,
   ' in your former offices; in which, I daresay, you'll
   ' have the more pleasure, as you have such an early
   ' instance of the sentiments of my dear wife, from
   ' whose goodness you may expect every agreeable thing.
   ' She writes herself to Mrs. Jervis.'

I thanked him most gratefully for his goodness; and
afterwards took the above copy of it; and showed him my
letter to Mrs. Jervis, as follows:

   ' MY DEAR MRS. JERVIS,—I have joyful tidings to com-
' municate to you. For yesterday I was happily married to
' the best of gentlemen, *yours* and *my* beloved master.
' have only now to tell you, that I am inexpressibly happy:
' that my generous benefactor denies me nothing, and even
' anticipates my wishes. You may be sure I could not
' forget my dear Mrs. Jervis; and I made it my request,
' and had it granted, as soon as asked, that you might
' return to the kind charge, which you executed with so
' much advantage to our master's interest, and so much
' pleasure to all under your direction. All the power that
' is put into my hands, by the most generous of men,
' shall be exerted to make everything easy and agreeable
' to you: And as I shall soon have the honour of attending
' my beloved to Bedfordshire, it will be a very considerable
' addition to my delight, and to my unspeakable obligations
' to the best of men, to see my dear Mrs. Jervis, and to be
' received by her with that pleasure, which I promise myself
' from her affection. For I am, my dear good friend, and
' always will be,

' Yours, very affectionately, and gratefully,
      PAMELA ——.'

He read this letter, and said, 'Tis yours, my dear, and must be good: But don't you put your name to it? Sir, said I, your goodness has given me a right to a very honourable one: but as this is the first occasion of the kind, except that to my dear father and mother, I think I ought to show it you unsigned, that I may not seem over-forward to take advantage of the honour you have done me.

However sweetly humble and requisite, said he, this may appear to my dear Pamela's niceness, it befits me to tell you, that I am every moment more and more pleased with the right you have to my name: and, my dear life, added he, I have only to wish I may be half as worthy as you are of the happy knot so lately knit. He then took a pen himself, and wrote, after Pamela, his most worthy surname; and I underwrote thus: ' Oh rejoice with me, my dear Mrs. Jervis, that ' I am enabled, by God's graciousness, and my dear master's ' goodness, thus to write myself!'

These letters, and the packet to you, were sent away by Mr. Thomas early this morning.

My dearest master is just gone to take a ride out, and intends to call upon Lady Jones, Mr. Peters, and Sir Simon Darnford, to invite them to chapel and dinner to-morrow; and says, he chooses to do it himself, because the time is so short, they will, perhaps, deny a servant.

I forgot to mention, that Mr. Williams was here yesterday, to ask leave to go to see his new living, and to provide for taking possession of it; and seemed so pleased with my master's kindness and fondness for me, as well as his generous deportment to himself, that he left us in such a disposition, as showed he was quite happy. I am very glad of it; for it would rejoice me to be an humble means of making all mankind so: And oh! what returns ought I not to make to the divine goodness! and how ought I to strive to diffuse the blessings I experience, to all in my knowledge!—For else, what is it for such a worm as I to be exalted! What is my *single* happiness, if I suffer it, niggard-like, to extend no farther that to myself?—But then, *indeed,* do God Almighty's creatures act worthy of the blessings they receive, when they make, or endeavour to make, the whole creation, so far as is in the circle of their power, happy.

Great and good God! as Thou hast enlarged my opportunities, enlarge also my will, and make me delight in dispensing to others a portion of that happiness, which I have myself so plentifully received at the hand of Thy gracious Providence! Then shall I not be useless in my generation! —Then shall I not stand a *single* mark of Thy goodness to a poor worthless creature, that in herself is of so small account in the scale of beings, a mere cipher on the wrong side of a figure; but shall be placed on the right side; and, though nothing worth in myself, shall give signification by my *place*, and multiply the blessings I owe to Thy goodness, which has distinguished me by so fair a lot!

This, as I conceive, is the indispensable duty of a high condition; and how great must be the condemnation of poor creatures, at the great day of account, when they shall be asked, What uses they have made of the opportunities put into their hands? and are able only to say, We have lived but to *ourselves:* We have circumscribed all the power Thou hast given us into one *narrow, selfish* compass: We have heaped up treasures for those who came after us, though we knew not whether they would not make a still worse use of them than we ourselves did! And how can such poor selfish pleaders expect any other sentence, than the dreadful, *Depart, ye cursed!*

But sure, my dear father and mother, such persons can have no notion of the exalted pleasures that flow from doing good, were there to be no after-account at all!

There is something so satisfactory and pleasing to reflect on the being able to administer comfort and relief to those who stand in need of it, as infinitely, of itself, rewards the beneficent mind. And how often have I experienced this in my good lady's time, though but the secondhand dispenser of her benefits to the poor and sickly, when she made me her almoner!—How have I been affected with the blessings which the miserable have heaped upon her for her goodness, and upon me for being but the humble conveyer of her bounty to them!—And how delighted have I been, when the moving report I have made of a particular distress, has augmented my good lady's first intentions in relief of it!

This I recall with pleasure, because it is now, by the divine goodness, become my part to do those good things she was won't to do : And oh! let me watch myself, that my prosperous state do not make me forget to look up, with due thankfulness, to the Providence which has entrusted me with the power, that so I may not incur a terrible woe by the abuse or neglect of it!

Forgive me these reflections, my dear parents; and let me have your prayers, that I may not find my present happiness a snare to me; but that I may consider, that more and more will be expected from me, in proportion to the power given me; and that I may not so unworthily act, as if I believed I ought to set up my rest in my *mean self* and think nothing further to be done, with the opportunities put into my hand, by the divine favour, and the best of men!

———*o*———

Saturday, seven o'clock in the evening.

My master returned home to dinner, in compliment to me, though much pressed to dine with Lady Jones, as he was, also, by Sir Simon, to dine with him. But Mr. Peters could not conveniently provide a preacher for his own church to-morrow morning, at so short a notice; Mr. Williams being gone, as I said, to his new living; but believed he could for the afternoon; and so he promised to give us his company to dinner, and to read afternoon service : and this made my master invite all the rest, as well as him, to dinner, and not to church; and he made them promise to come; and told Mr. Peters, he would send his coach for him and his family.

Miss Darnford told him pleasantly, She would not come, unless he would promise to let her be at his wedding; by which I find Mr. Peters has kept the secret, as my master desired.

He was pleased to give me an airing after dinner in the chariot, and renewed his kind assurances to me, and, if possible, is kinder than ever. This is sweetly comfortable to me, because it shows me he does not repent of his condescensions to me ; and it encourages me to look up to him with more satisfaction of mind, and less doubtfulness.

I begged leave to send a guinea to a poor body in the town, that I heard, by Mrs. Jewkes, lay very ill, and was very destitute. He said, Send two, my dear, if you please. Said I, Sir, I will never do anything of this kind without letting you know what I do. He most generously answered, I shall then, perhaps, have you do less good than you would otherwise do, from a doubt of me; though, I hope, your discretion, and my own temper, which is not avaricious, will make such doubt causeless.

Now, my dear, continued he, I'll tell you how we will order this point, to avoid even the shadow of uneasiness on one side, or doubt on the other.

As to your father and mother, in the first place, they shall be quite out of the question ; for I have already determined in my mind about them; and it is thus: They shall go down, if they and you think well of it, to my little Kentish estate; which I once mentioned to you in such a manner, as made you reject it with a nobleness of mind, that gave me pain then, but pleasure since. There is a pretty little farm, and house, untenanted, upon that estate, and tolerably well-stocked, and I will further stock it for them ; for such industrious folks won't know how to live without some employment: And it shall be theirs for both their lives, without paying any rent; and I will allow them 50*l.* per annum besides, that they may keep up the stock, and be kind to any other of their relations, without being beholden to you or me for small matters ; and for greater, where needful, you shall always have it in your power to accommodate them ; for I shall never question your prudence. And we will, so long as God spares our lives, go down, once a year, to see them ; and they shall come up, as often as they please, it cannot be too often, to see us:

for I mean not this, my dear, to send them from us.—Before
I proceed, does my Pamela like this?

Oh, sir, said I, the English tongue affords not words, or,
at least, I have them not, to express sufficiently my gratitude! Teach me, dear sir, continued I, and pressed his
dear hand to my lips, teach me some other language, if
there be any, that abounds with more grateful terms; that
I may not thus be choked with meanings, for which I can
find no utterance.

My charmer! says he, your language is all wonderful,
as your sentiments; and you most abound, when you seem
most to want!—All that I wish, is to find my proposals
agreeable to you; and if my *first* are not, my *second* shall
... if I can but know what you wish.

... id I say too much, my dearest parents, when I said, he
... if *possible*, kinder and kinder?—Oh the blessed man!
my heart is overwhelmed with his goodness!

Tell, said he, my dearest, let me desire you to mention
to *them*, to see if they approve it. But, if it be your
... ce, and theirs, to have them nearer to you, or even
... r the same roof with you, I will freely consent to it.

... h no, sir, said I (and I fear almost sinned in my grate-
flight), I am sure they would not choose that; they
... d not, perhaps, serve God so well if they were to live
... you: For, so constantly seeing the hand that blesses
... , they would, it may be, as must be my care to avoid,
... empted to look no further in their gratitude, than to
... lear dispenser of such innumerable benefits!

... xcellent creature! said he: My beloved wants no lan-
... e, nor sentiments neither; and her charming thoughts,
... weetly expressed, would grace any language; and this
... blessing almost peculiar to my fairest.—Your so kind
... ptance, my Pamela, added he, repays the benefit with
... est, and leaves me under obligation to your goodness.

... it now, my dearest, I will tell you what we will do,
... regard to points of your own private charity; for far
... from me, to put under that name the subject we have
... mentioning: because that, and more than that, is

duty to persons so worthy, and so nearly related to m
Pamela, and, as such, to myself.—Oh how the sweet ma
outdoes me, in thoughts, words, power, and everything!

And this, said he, lies in very small compass; for I wi
allow you two hundred pounds a year; which Longma
shall constantly pay you, at fifty pounds a quarter, for you
own use, and of which I expect no account; to commenc
from the day you enter into my other house: I mean, sai
he, that the first fifty pounds shall then be due; becaus
you shall have something to begin with. And, added th
dear generous man, if this be pleasing to you, let it, sinc
you say you want words, be signified by such a sweet kis
as you gave me yesterday. I hesitated not a moment t
comply with these obliging terms, and threw m
about his dear neck, though in the chariot, and ble
goodness to me. But, indeed, sir, said I, I cann
this generous treatment! He was pleased to say
be uneasy, my dear, about these trifles: God has
me with a very good estate, and all of it in a pre
condition, and generally well tenanted. I lay up
every year, and have, besides, large sums in gove
and other securities; so that you will find, what
hitherto promised, is very short of that proportion
substance, which, as my dearest wife, you have a rig

In this sweet manner did we pass our time till c
when the chariot brought us home; and then our
succeeded in the same agreeable manner. And th
rapturous circle, the time moves on; every hour b
with it something more delightful than the past
nobody was ever so blest as I!

END OF VOL. I.

PRINTED BY BALLANTYNE, HANSON AND CO.
EDINBURGH AND LONDON.